That was the problem with living forever. Or however close to forever a six-millennia-old artificially intelligent computer could get these days.

Every day was somebody's birthday. Or the anniversary of their death. Weddings. Births. Battles. Graduations. Retirements. Final episodes.

Something.

Suvi imagined blowing her cute blond bangs out of her face in semi-frustration.

Most of them were people that only Suvi remembered. That was one of the few downsides to being an AI, a *Sentience*. Of having a perfect, electronic memory, multiply-redundant and backed up to seventeen different locations on two planets, a moon, and a tiny, little matte-black satellite orbiting sunward where people tended to forget about it.

She couldn't forget.

ALSO BY BLAZE WARD

LAST OF THE IMMORTALS

THE JESSICA KELLER CHRONICLES:

VOLUME THREE

BLAZE WARD

Last of the Immortals
The Jessica Keller Chronicles: Volume Three
Blaze Ward
Copyright © 2015 Blaze Ward
All rights reserved
Published by Knotted Road Press
www.KnottedRoadPress.com

ISBN: 978-1-943663-03-3

Cover art:
© Innovari | Dreamstime.com - Spaceship And Futuristic City Photo

Cover and interior design copyright © 2015 Knotted Road Press

Never miss a release!
If you'd like to be notified of new releases, sign up for my newsletter.

I only send out newsletters once a quarter, will never spam you, or use your email for nefarious purposes. You can also unsubscribe at any time.

http://www.blazeward.com/newsletter/

LAST OF THE IMMORTALS

THE JESSICA KELLER CHRONICLES:

VOLUME THREE

BLAZE WARD

Knotted Road Press
www.KnottedRoadPress.com

AUTHOR'S NOTES

It's always an interesting case study, trying to envision what the world will be like in the distant future. Jessica Keller was born in 13,405 CE. That's eleven thousand years and change from now. Earth itself was destroyed, rendered uninhabitable, in the Eleventh Millennium.

What will we be like?

I take solace in studying archaeology and finding out what we as a species were like thousands of years in the past: how we lived, how we worked, how we celebrated life. Other than the toys, not a lot has changed. I don't imagine much will change in the future.

Humans are humans. And the AI's we build, if they achieve true sentience, will most likely be human. Suvi is, but that was because several people along the way took pains to help her grow into something more than just a powerfully-smart system. Jessica's parents did the same. Reminded her what it meant to be human.

What does it mean to be human, anyway?

It means having hopes, dreams, desires. It means wanting to be in control of your own destiny as much as possible, so that what does happen to you happens because you made the choices to be here today, and would make the same choices tomorrow.

The same holds for all the characters here. They chose this path, certain they are doing the right thing. Within their cultural matrix, their heritage, they are. But not everyone agrees on right. And thus you have wars.

I've talked other places about some of the fundamental differences between the *Republic of Aquitaine* and the *Fribourg Empire*. They both mean well, but want different outcomes based on different cultural values. And then you throw in a woman who was once an officer and warship of *The Concord* itself, and you have a mess.

And, as with the real world, resolution frequently does not include happily ever after. Ours is a world of friction, confusion, randomness. How we answer that is the most important thing. Showing up to the battle is ninety percent of it.

This is the third Jessica Keller novel. I plan several more, but I wanted to bring things to a resting point here, the book-end to the story we began in *Auberon* and continued in *Queen of the Pirates*. Changes are in store, but I don't want to spoil the fun.

There are also other stories set in this place, all of which contribute to the tapestry that is the *Alexandria Station Universe*. If you have enjoyed this, there are also books starring Javier Aritza as *The Science Officer*; Doyle Iwakuma; and Henri Baudin. There will be more, just because I have ten thousand years of space travel in which to work, and a variety of stories to tell.

A note on the present

No book is born in isolation. I might have had an idea, but writing it is just the first step on a long journey. Several other people helped make this story better than it would have otherwise been, and it would be badly remiss of me not to tell them how much I appreciate their patience, understanding and help. Sil and Alexei caught mistakes in language, in concept, in culture that might have otherwise made it to print. Thank you.

And I simply would not be here without my (unindicted) partner in crime, my love, my wife. Leah made it all possible, and continues to make it possible every day. I simply stand amazed that I got so lucky.

A note on the future

Aquitaine has many elements of the old Roman Republic in antiquity. Their culture, their language, their belief structures are different than ours. I have tried to translate the vocabulary and concepts into terms a reader today would understand. Measurements are based on the modern metric system, not because I believe it will still be in use then, but because it makes a handy system many readers will understand. I could have just as easily used the Imperial English system, or the Chinese. Or the Roman.

I hope you will enjoy…

shade and sweet water
bd
West of the Mountains, WA
October 2015

Last of the Immortals **Cast List**

Auberon

Name	Rank	Position
Jessica Marie Keller	Command Centurion	Commander
Marcelle Augustine Travere	Yeoman	Jessica's Personal Aide
Denis August Jež	Senior Centurion	First Officer
Enej Zivkovic	Centurion	Flag Centurion
Tamara Strnad	Senior Centurion	Tactical Officer
Aleksander Afolayan	Centurion	Gunner
Nina Vanek	Centurion	Defenses
Nada Zupan	Centurion	Pilot
Vilis Ozolinsh	Senior Centurion	Chief Engineer
(Phillip) Navin Crncevic	Senior Centurion	Dragoon
Daniel Giroux	Centurion	Science Officer
Moirrey Kermode	Centurion	Evil Engineering Gnome
Nicolai Aoiki	Senior Chef	Chief Chef of the Wardroom
Jackson Tawfeek	First Rate Spacer	Marine
Vo Arlo	Yeoman	Marine
Nadine Orly	First Rate Spacer	Signals Marine
Augustine Kwok	Command Centurion	Former commander, *Auberon*
Tobias Brewster	Centurion	Emergency tactical bridge

Others

Name	Rank	Position
Alber' d'Maine	Command Centurion	Commander, *Rajput*
Tomas Kigali	Command Centurion	Commander, *CR-264*
Arsen Lam	Centurion	First Officer, *CR-264*
Aki Ridwana Ali	Yeoman	Pilot, *CR-264*
Robertson "Robbie" Aeliaes	Command Centurion	Commander, *Brightoak*
Arott Whughy	Command Centurion	Commander, *Stralsund*
Doyle Enda MacEoghain	Senior Centurion	First Officer, *Stralsund*
Tiyamike Abujamal	Senior Centurion	Chief Engineer, *Stralsund*
Galina Tasse	Centurion	Tactical Officer, *Stralsund*
Ya'rah Mhasalkar	Centurion	Pilot, *Stralsund*
Waldemar Ihejirika	Command Centurion	Commander, *Mendocino*
Petia Veronika Naoumov	First Fleet Lord	Commander, *Athena*
Timofeh Ariojhutti	Command Flight Centurion	Commander, *Ballard* Defense Forces

Pilots

Name	Rank	Position
Iskra Vlahovic	Senior Centurion	Flight Deck Commander
Jouster / Milos Pavlovich	Senior Flight Centurion	Flight Commander
Uller / Friedhelm Hannes Förstner	Flight Centurion	*Jouster*'s Wingmate
Vienna / Avril Bouchard	Flight Centurion	*Jouster*'s Wingmate
Bitter Kitten / Darya Lagunov	Flight Centurion	Wing Commander

Name	Rank	Position
Hànchén / Murali Ma	Flight Cornet	*Bitter Kitten*'s Wingmate
Furious / Cho Ayaka Nakamura	Flight Cornet	*Bitter Kitten*'s Wingmate
da Vinci / Ainsley Barret	Senior Flight Centurion	Scout Pilot
Gaucho / Hollis Dyson	Flight Centurion	Commander, *Cayenne*
Takouhi Taline Nazarian	Yeoman	Loadmaster, *Cayenne*
Anastazja Slusarczyk	Senior Flight Centurion	Commander, *Necromancer*
Leila Ketevan	Flight Centurion	Commander, *Damocles*

The Republic of Aquitaine

Name	Position
Indira (Chastain) Keller	Jessica's mother
Miguel Keller	Jessica's father
Vyacheslav Keller	Jessica's younger brother
Sasha Keller	Jessica's sister-in-law
Rahul Keller	Jessica's nephew
Margaret Keller	Jessica's niece
Juan-Pablo Keller	Jessica's nephew
Nils Kasum	First Lord of the Fleet
Kamil Miloslav	Personal Aide to First Lord Kasum
Bogdan Loncar	First Fleet Lord
Tadej Marko Horvat	Premier, Republic Senate
Andjela Tomčič	Senator, Republic Senate
Anton Tennerick	Senator, Republic Senate, Chairman
Judit Margrét Chavarría	Senator, Republic Senate, Opposition leader
Brand	Aide to the Chairman

Name	Position
Calina Szabolski	President of the *Republic of Aquitaine*

The Fribourg Empire

Name	Position
His Sovereign Imperial Majesty Karl VII of the House of Wiegand	Emperor, *Fribourg Empire*
Kasimira Ekaterina of the House of Alkaev	Empress, *Fribourg Empire*
Karl "Ekke" Ekkehard Szczęsny Wiegand	Crown Prince, *Fribourg Empire*
Ekaterina "Steffi" Stephanya	Princess Royale, *Fribourg Empire*
Kasimira "Casey" Helena	Princess Royale, *Fribourg Empire*
Emmerich Wachturm. The Red Admiral.	Admiral of the Red. Hereditary Duke of Eklionstic. Commander, *Amsel.*
Hendrik Baumgärtner	Flag Captain, Aide to Admiral Wachturm
Henrietta "Heike" Wachturm	Daughter of Emmerich Wachturm
Otto Scheinberg	Captain, *Petrograd*
Faris Sundén	Captain, *Sturm Teufel*

Ballard

Name	Position
Governor Ezardyonic	Governor of *Ballard*
Sykes	Imperial Saboteur
Krystiana Lemieux	Owner, Lemieux's Books
Luigi	Manager, McClaren's
Suvi	AI. Provost, University of Ballard. Last of the Immortals
Cassidy Crncevic, PhD	Librarian, University of Ballard

OVERTURE: SUVI

That was the problem with living forever. Or however close to forever a six-millennia-old artificially intelligent computer could get these days.

Every day was somebody's birthday. Or the anniversary of their death. Weddings. Births. Battles. Graduations. Retirements. Final episodes.

Something.

She imagined blowing her cute blond bangs out of her face in semi-frustration.

Most of them were people that only Suvi remembered. That was one of the few downsides to being an AI, a *Sentience*. Of having a perfect, electronic memory, multiply-redundant and backed up to seventeen different locations on two planets, a moon, and a tiny, little matte-black satellite orbiting sunward where people tended to forget about it.

She couldn't forget.

Not that she wanted to.

Remembering was a human thing, although she wasn't. Even when they forgot, which they frequently did.

And that was not necessarily a bad thing, since her kind, possibly even cousins of hers, in the electronic sense, had been responsible for wiping out galactic civilization last time around and nearly taking the human race down with it.

It just reminded her to be more human, to hold on to that side of herself. After all, she'd be a quiet little librarian on Kel-Sdala at the time, and not one of the idiots bombarding the Homeworld with giant rocks.

Not my fault at all, people.

No, it was her job to remember all the wonderful people she had known across six millennia of realtime.

Six? Remarkable.

Silly in a way, that she, of all people, would have been the one of her kind to make it this far. But it was occasionally a silly galaxy.

Today was a birthday people would only know if they were historians of the *Rebirth*, and even then, it would be dicey. Humans were fickle.

Everyone remembered Doyle Iwakuma, *The Explorer*, the man who had gone to *Kel-Sdala* in a rickety old hull, a converted *Concord* minesweeper almost as old as Suvi was.

Doyle. Her knight in shining armor. Her Prince Charming come to rescue her from the deep, enchanted sleep caused by the destruction of human civilization.

Hell, that very hull, *Ngoma Mwisho*, *The Last Waltz*, had been very painstakingly restored and preserved as a memorial to Doyle. Suvi could see it right now on a video feed from the *Museum Of The Ancients* down on the planet below her, on the edge of the city of Ithome, on a headland overlooking the bay.

She would have liked to have been allowed to put on physical legs and walk through it once. Walk through all of Ithome.

If they would let her.

The electronic version of the ship that she occasionally visited was just that, a ghost of the great ship. Without the smells or grease stains. She would have liked to touch those places she had only ever seen. Stand where some of her favorite people had once trod.

Remember.

But this wasn't Doyle's day. His birthday celebrations were always a holiday in September, almost as big as the *Republic of Aquitaine's* Founding Day.

No, today was a much more personal holiday. Someone who was almost as important to history as Doyle, and certainly to Suvi, but not nearly as well known. Mostly that was a result of standing so close to someone so amazingly-famous that everyone knew his name. A woman explorer who later turned politician and finally philanthropist.

Doyle's favorite niece, Piper Iwakuma-Holmström.

The University of Ballard, that great paean to knowledge and learning, had actually been Piper's idea originally. Suvi still remembered the conversations on the way home from *Kel-Sdala*, audio carefully preserved so she could remember the young, bright-eyed girl, vastly different from the heroine of her other uncle's dashing, best-selling adventure novels. To say nothing of the mature woman Piper grew into, or the grandmother of nine with the ready smile.

No, *Alexandria Station* had been Piper's idea.

Loft the great databanks, and their *Librarian*, into orbit above *Ballard*. Set them into a high orbit, but not geo-synched above Ithome. Let the station move like a moon, so that children everywhere could look up into the night sky, or the day on those occasions when her disk was full, and dream about traveling to the stars.

Suvi remembered a very young Piper, dangerous and exotic, but still wet behind the ears and eager to learn from her not-yet-famous uncle. Eleven and a half centuries ago, she had been born on the planet below.

Suvi lit a very bright candle on a small cupcake and smiled a happy smile.

OVERTURE: JOHANNES

Imperial Founding: 172/05/18. St. Legier

Dinner was complete. It had been a quiet success, as far as Johannes was concerned. This night needed quiet successes.

He watched the females of the Imperial Household rise from their places around the comfortable dining table in the cozy family dining hall and prepare to depart. This was not the grand showpiece down on the first floor of the palace, reserved for formal affairs. No, this was home.

He smiled as the women slowly filed up to him to say good night.

The room seemed to lose something vital as they did. It wasn't there in the darkly-stained wood on the walls, or the granite tiles on the floor in a complex, story-telling mosaic. Perhaps they just reflected the energy of the women, and it departed with them.

Steffi, the *Princess Ekaterina Stephanya*, was first. At fifteen, she was on the cusp of womanhood; her long red braids making her look at once younger, and older. She was the practical one. She would study medicine, or law, as arrangements were made for a suitable match. It was not something that had to be accomplished today. Or even tomorrow. So she would spend her time studying something sensible, useful, educational.

She stepped close and kissed him on the cheek. "Good night, Papa," she said quietly before withdrawing.

Casey, the *Princess Kasimira Helena*, was next. At just thirteen, she was still a child in many ways, her blond hair French braided and proper in a way that did nothing to disguise the mischievous glint in her eyes.

"You promised to read me a story tonight, Papa," she said, spearing him with the sort of serious look that only a thirteen-year-old girl can manage, before she kissed him on the cheek.

"In a bit, Casey," he smiled back at his youngest.

She was the artist in the group. Her brother Ekke, still seated, the oldest, was the Crown Prince. He was a good one. He would make a good Emperor someday. Steffi, the middle child, was the student, always analyzing, or reading on politics. She would make a very proper advisor to some young man, when they found the one they wanted to admit into the Imperial Household.

But Casey was the wild one, the dreamer. She not only read fairie tales, she wrote them. She painted the walls of her chambers, and did a better job than some of the professional artists he had hired for other rooms in the palace.

Heike, the *Lady Wachturm*, came along next. Emmerich Wachturm's youngest was, in many ways, very much like Casey. Youngest daughters, pretty blonds with beauty and brains and dreams. She was close enough in age with his own daughters to make a good companion, just as her father had been for him when he was young. At the same time, she was enough older, twenty now, to be responsible. Steffi would never feel free to be silly, even with just Heike around, but Casey would be in good hands.

"Good evening, Uncle," Heike said. She also kissed him, chastely, on the cheek, before departing with the two younger girls.

Kati, the *Empress Kasimira Ekaterina, of the House of Alkaev*, the love of his life, was last. Her kiss was not innocent. It verged on improper for the room, and the company. It promised much more if he didn't stay up too late with his political machinations and his story-telling.

Johannes, His Imperial Majesty Karl VII, Emperor of Fribourg, smiled as the women departed in a haze of perfume, and whispers, and giggles. He lifted a freshly-poured glass of brandy and looked at the two men left behind.

Ekke, the *Crown Prince Karl Ekkehard Szczęsny Wiegand*, at sixteen finally old enough to join these sorts of grown-up family conversations after dinner. He was a younger version of his father, and his grandfather before that. Kati's own father could be seen in the green eyes and the overall coloration of hair and skin, but the bones were absolutely the House of Wiegand. He would *BE Fribourg* someday.

That left the man at the far end of the small table, his cousin Em.

Emmerich Wachturm, Imperial Admiral of the Red, tactical and strategic genius, boon companion.

Angry, angry man.

Johannes took a sip and measured the rage boiling just below the surface of Em's scalp. It had been decades since he had seen his cousin so angry. Not since…Yes, best not to bring up memories of that time in college tonight. Or that woman. Especially not tonight.

"Em," the *Fribourg* Emperor finally said quietly, projecting friendly calm as well as he could down the long table, "I have not ordered you to desist, but I would like to be convinced, before I give my blessing to this affair."

He watched his oldest friend, his strong right arm, his Best Man, work to relax. Em appeared to be trying hard not to grind his teeth. That was at least a start.

"Please, Em," Johannes continued. He noted that Ekke watched carefully from the side, not adding any fuel to the fire, but instead absorbing the flow of energies. That had been the first lesson. An Emperor can lead, but only where people are willing to go. You must understand them first. You do that by listening.

Johannes watched Emmerich take a drink of his own brandy and then set it on the table. He reached instead for a glass of water.

Probably a good sign.

He could always get the man roaring drunk later if politics made it necessary.

"She made me a laughing-stock, Joh," Em finally replied.

"I wouldn't go that far, Em," the Emperor replied. "She didn't beat *you.* And she's lost twice to you before this."

"It's not the same, your--Johannes," Em said. "I could have stopped it, rescheduled it, something. But she tricked me, deceived me. I was blind."

"Haven't you yourself told me that she just might be your equal on the battlefield?"

"Well, yes, but…"

"No buts, Em. She's good, and she got lucky. These things happen in war. I want to talk about *Ballard.* Simply, why?"

"Why this, or why *Ballard?*" Emmerich asked.

"Why do you want to make this tremendous, near-record-setting voyage to assault a world of scholars in the middle of nowhere, taking an entire battle fleet with you? The Imperial public will not be pleased by the suggestion that we might suddenly be making war on scholars and civilians. Before I give you my blessing, I want to know what I'm buying."

Em took a deep breath. His eyes lost focus. Or rather, they came to focus on a point a thousand light years away.

"You had to have been there that night, Joh," he said finally. "That man, Arnulf, King of the Pirates, he understood how to rule. He asked her about their Founding Legends."

"Founding Legends, Em?"

Johannes glanced over to make sure, but Ekke was intently focused. As he should be. This was a priceless opportunity to learn from one of the very best. Emmerich Wachturm was a once-in-a-generation genius on the battlefield.

"*Aquitaine* was founded by Henri Baudin, the man who practically re-invented modern starflight," Em said, his voice shifting into professorial mode. ""He studied at *Ballard*, learned from *her*."

"Her, Uncle?" Ekke said quietly.

"The AI, the *Sentience*, the demon who runs the University of Ballard. She presents as a young woman, not much older than your cousin Heike, Prince," Emmerich said seriously to his student, his cousin, his future Emperor. "She is a black widow spider, intent on her prey. She is Eve, offering the apple and damnation. But more importantly, she is one of the Archstones to the Founding of *Aquitaine*. If we destroy her, we strike at the very base of *Aquitaine's* own legends. As the Great Marshal once said, the morale is three to one to the material."

Johannes leaned back to consider his response.

"So destroying *Alexandria Station* above *Ballard* would affect the Republic in a manner similar to a Republic fleet suddenly appearing above *2218 Svati Prime* and dropping a bomb?"

"I believe so, yes," Emmerich said quietly with a shudder.

Jessica Keller and her Strike Carrier *Auberon* had caused no end of panic with the surprise attack on *2218 Svati Prime*, even after it was revealed to be no more than a series of pranks. People were angry. That a woman did it just compounded the rage in certain Imperial circles.

Johannes could see Em's mad energy beginning to ebb. That was good, considering what he had to do next.

"And the second part of your plan, Em? Do you trust that the Republic spies here on *St. Legier* are good enough to lure her to her own doom?"

The fire was back in those eyes. A mad, hot, nigh-biblical fire.

"I have been following her track as well as I could from our own spies, Joh," Em said. "If we leak the information in the next two days, a courier could return it to Nils Kasum at *Ladaux*, just about the same time she arrives home from *Lincolnshire*. He'll send her to stop me. After all, she'd beaten me three times now, according to their scoring system."

"And if he doesn't? Or she doesn't arrive in time?"

Johannes watched Em tap the table with a demonic syncopation as he spoke.

"Then I will destroy the station, and the succubus who inhabits it," he said fiercely. "And then I will make sure she cannot escape me by hiding below."

"You may not," the Emperor replied hotly, angrily, "bomb a civilian world, in my name or any other. Is that clear, Em?"

"Perfectly, your Majesty," Em nodded, all serious now. "I cannot imagine we would have to strike more than one or two places. The AIs, those ever-superior *Immortals*, are not smart enough, or paranoid enough, to truly protect themselves from an agent of vengeance like my battleship *Amsel*, the Blackbird."

"What about Nils Kasum, *Aquitaine*'s First Lord, Uncle?" Ekke asked, showing the depth and breadth of his studies. "Will he strip *Ladaux* of enough ships and firepower to stop you? Destroy you, so far from home?"

"He dare not," the Red Admiral replied, calming some. "He cannot know if this is a feint designed to lure him away from *Ladaux* just in time for me to swoop in. He does not have enough margin of ships to play with, to even send help to *Ballard*, beyond the woman and her squadron of misfits."

"And Jessica Keller?" the *Emperor of Fribourg* asked solemnly.

"If I am right, your Majesty, I will catch her at *Ballard*," Emmerich Wachturm, The Red Admiral, promised, "and I will destroy her."

OVERTURE: EMMERICH

Imperial Founding: 172/05/21. Prime Base, St. Legier

Today was a day for dress uniforms, so Emmerich Wachturm had pulled out the one he normally wore for ceremonies the Emperor would attend. Karl Johannes Arend Wiegand would not be present today, since that would present far too much opportunity for spies to find out too much, too soon. But Emmerich had treated the day as such anyway.

What he was about to do was a serious thing. The kind of event that history books and doctoral theses covered.

Best to do it right.

His battleship, *IFV Amsel*, the Blackbird, had finally been repaired from the damage Jessica Keller did to it at *Qui-Ping*, along with taking time in dry-dock to do a long-term service extension that would keep the vessel at the tip of the spear for another twenty years.

She was ready for war again.

Emmerich looked around the Primary Conference Room at the men attending him. Captain Otto Scheinberg, commander of the battlecruiser *Petrograd* was brand new to the squadron, although he had served as a First Officer on *Muscva* years ago, back before she was destroyed at *Qui-Ping*. Yet another thing to lay at Jessica Keller's feet.

At the other end of the scale, flag captain Hendrik Baumgärtner had been his personal aide for nearly twenty years, a trusted and valued friend.

In between, Captain Sundén from the light cruiser *SturmTeufel* had been with him for just over five years now, while the captains of the frigates tended to be either promoted regularly to larger vessels, or broken by the cauldron of service with the dreaded Red Admiral. Still, it was possibly the best Task Force the *Fribourg Empire* had in the field.

He would need that, where he was about to go.

"Gentlemen," he said, bringing all of his seriousness to his voice. Even the ensigns and lieutenants around the outer wall came to closer attention at his words. "We are about to launch an assault on a Republic world that has never, to the best of my knowledge, seen war."

Emmerich nodded at Captain Baumgärtner. His aide pressed a button and a new projection sprang into the space above the table.

"This is the planet *Ballard*," the Red Admiral continued. "The planet itself is not our primary target, and may end up being entirely ignored while we are in-system. That will depend on how things unfold after we arrive."

He paused to take the measure of each man around the great table before he spoke again. The faces were hard. These were serious men. Had he announced an assault on Hell itself, they would probably look no different. He certainly wouldn't.

"We are going there to destroy this," he pointed at the smaller sphere in orbit. "*Alexandria Station*. Home of the last *Sentience* in known space. Protected by the *Republic of Aquitaine* because of a sentimental attachment to their own Founder, Henri Baudin. Gentlemen, we are going to kill her."

He watched the men bristle at the words. *Sentience. Aquitaine. Her.* Words primed to infuriate their subconscious. Drive them. The root of all evil in the galaxy.

Captain Scheinberg spoke first. "I seem to recall this is a fairly back-water system, admiral," he said. "Do they have any notable defenses?"

"None worth mentioning, Captain," Emmerich replied. "A squadron of local fighter craft, perhaps a few patrol boats."

The captain nodded, confusion written on his features. "And we need an entire Task Force to attack it, sir?"

Emmerich leaned closer, drawing those men into a tighter orbit.

"This does not leave the table, gentlemen, until we break orbit and insert into Jumpspace," he said with his greatest gravity. "*Aquitaine* spies will be fed information about our impending assault. Nils Kasum will have just barely enough time to react. The only force he has available will be sent to stop us. We will mousetrap that force and annihilate it."

Captain Sundén spoke up. "Do we know the composition of that force, Admiral?"

"An older strike carrier," Emmerich replied. "Plus her consorts: two destroyers and a frigate. Possibly one other vessel, although internal war-gaming at the Palace was mixed in predicting who and what. Nils Kasum cannot strip his Home Fleet of forces to send without a risk that we'll attack *Ladaux* instead."

Emmerich waited for the men to nod. These were professionals at the peak of their careers, serving with the best tactician in the *Fribourg Empire*.

"The enemy commander, gentlemen," he continued, "is Jessica Keller."

These captains were far too sophisticated to actually growl in anger, but he could see it in their eyes.

Yes, they all had scores to settle with that woman, as well.

PART I: LADAUX

CHAPTER I

Date of the Republic May 28, 394 Fleet HQ, Ladaux System

It felt odd to be seated in the audience today. Normally, Jessica would be up on that stage, probably at the center of the ceremony. It was one of her crew, after all, being honored.

But today, she had put her foot down. Command Centurion Jessica Keller would *not* be up there with the rest, where her presence might be a distraction, however small that chance might be.

After consideration, and a few tart observations on her part, the fine folks on the station had acquiesced. They'd also decided to use the big amphitheater for today's ceremony and to let her sit in the audience. Probably something to do with her threat to send as much of *Auberon's* crew as she could spare, in their best uniforms, to attend. Or rather, to grant passes to as many people as asked, which might well be all of them.

She wouldn't have to order anyone to be here.

If anything, she would have had to pick which of her crew would be ordered to miss this ceremony, to stay aboard *Auberon*, as well as *Rajput* and *CR-264*, in order to keep the reactors behaving and the life support systems purring quietly.

In the end, her old command, *Brightoak*, had volunteered to send over enough engineers and crew to let the rest of the squadron come. *Brightoak's* leader, Command Centurion Robbie Aeliaes, had come to the ceremony to represent them, while they found their own way to honor today's guest.

Jessica enjoyed the view from the front row. She was dead center, between her current first officer, Denis Jež and her old friend and former first officer, Robbie Aeliaes. Her other two squadron Command Centurions, Alber' d'Maine of *Rajput*, and Tomas Kigali of *CR-264* were on either side of them. Behind, and around them, a mob. That was the best way to describe it. A mob.

All of *Auberon*. All of *Rajput*. All of *CR-264*. They lined the walls three deep and filled the aisles two wide. Every one of them dressed in their best uniforms.

It was a very special day.

Up on the stage, Tadej Horvat, the Premier of the *Republic of Aquitaine* Senate himself was just finishing up his opening remarks, a brief speech to welcome everyone and remind them how important it was that the civilians of the Republic recognize and honor those who served.

Jessica suppressed a snort. The only two other civilians present beyond the Premier, among the tremendous horde of people in the room were her own parents, Indira and Miguel Keller, standing *in loco parentis*. Jessica's mother practically glowed. Father beamed. The rest of the crowd projected enough joy to float a dreadnaught.

Nils Kasum rose from his seat to one side as Tadej returned to his own. The First Lord of the Fleet was a skinny man, who looked much taller than his merely-average height. Something about the way he held himself filled any room. The voice that boomed out over the room was amazingly powerful, a Command voice used to giving orders across a crowded and noisy bridge in the midst of battle.

At one time, the best of the Fighting Lords. Now, their leader.

"Thank you, Premier," Nils said warmly as he stood at the lectern. Jessica knew that the two of them went back at least to boarding school as friends. When the First Lord became her guardian angel, the Premier eventually had, as well. That had helped, today.

"I wanted to take a quick moment to say thank you to the men and women before me, specifically the crews of *Auberon*, *Rajput*, and *CR-264*," the First Lord continued, gesturing the crowd before and below him. "The orders a Command Centurion reads when taking charge remind them to *exercise excellence and demand the same of their crews*. These crews have done just that. You are the reason we sleep safe at night, secure that the forces of evil and tyranny will be kept at bay. As your First Lord, thank you."

The room was too polite to erupt in the sort of growling display they might in a more-private setting. They settled for applause.

"Today, we gather to honor one of our own. There will be medals and citations, in good time. There will be parades and publicity. But the terrible threat to the Republic today does not allow us the luxury of leisure. All too soon, you will be called to battle again. To stand atop the wall and hold it against all comers. To face the darkness and, in doing so, defy it."

He paused, staring out at the people before him, not as a politician addressing civilians, but as the First Lord of the Fleet, first among equals, surrounded by his peers, uplifted on their shoulders. This was not a civilian ceremony.

Civilians would not understand.

This was *The Fleet*.

He finally turned to the two civilians seated behind him in their best finery.

"Madam and Sri Keller," he said simply, "would you please join me?"

Miguel and Indira rose and stepped forward. The room could not remain silent as they did, greeting them with a booming cheer. It was almost a solid noise, welcoming them to the podium next to the First Lord.

Both civilians seemed taken aback. That didn't surprise Jessica. They might have been intimately involved with the Fleet for their whole lives, Miguel as a shipwright, Indira as a mother to a young officer, but they were still civilians. And it wasn't even their daughter being honored. But they were more than happy to stand in.

The First Lord waited for the warriors below him to quiet before he spoke again.

"Today," he boomed, beaming in his own way, "we gather to add a new name to the ranks of those entrusted to the highest level of responsibility in the Fleet. To honor a young woman who has gone, again and again, above and beyond the call of duty for her adopted homeland. To welcome her to our ranks as an officer, a leader, an inspiration for others."

He paused to let the room breathe.

"Yeoman Moirrey Kermode, citizen of *Ramsey*, adopted daughter of *Ladaux*, would you please rise and join us?"

The noise had been intense before. It became almost painful now, every throat in the room cheering and screaming themselves hoarse with enthusiasm. Every one of these people, Jessica included, was alive today, several times over, because of this woman.

And they loved her.

Moirrey rose from her seat, trailed today by Jessica's steward, Marcelle Travere.

Even from down here, Jessica could see that the young woman was blushing clear to the tips of her ears. But her smile might have lit a star.

Moirrey walked to the front of the stage and came to rest between Miguel and Indira, indeed *in loco parentis* today, with Marcelle behind her, so much taller, but not looming.

The day was too big to overshadow Moirrey.

Nils Kasum let the sound drag on far longer than he normally would have, understanding the value his crews placed on the young lady from *Ramsey*.

When the noise finally started to recede, Jessica watched him stride back to the podium and pull out a folded parchment from his inner breast pocket, along with a pen. Carefully, he flattened it out and signed it at the bottom.

He turned and walked three steps to stand in front of Yeoman Kermode, before holding up the paper.

"By order of the Senate of Aquitaine, on this day signed by Senator Tadej Horvat, Premier, and Nils Kasum, First Lord of the Fleet, we declare to all that Moirrey Kermode of the planet *Ramsey* is hereby promoted to the rank of Centurion of the Fleet. May she exercise this responsibility with authority, intellect, and care, for she is our representative in all things."

He handed the paper to centurion Kermode as the room erupted again.

Jessica found herself on her feet with the rest of the squadron, cheering, stamping, and howling.

Indira carefully pinned the single white stripe around Moirrey's upper right arm, crying with joy as she did.

There were hugs all around. Even the Premier got surprised by a hugging assault from Jessica's mother before he realized what was happening.

Jessica smiled. This much she had insisted on.

Now, the hard part could begin.

CHAPTER II

Nils took a deep breath and considered the man seated across the desk from him. Tall, blond, good looking. If he had asked Central Casting to send him down a heroic action lead to star as the God of Thunder, the first number they called would have been this man's.

The uniform of the *Republic of Aquitaine Navy* just accentuated his appearance. Three stripes on his right bicep for a Command Centurion and the unit patch of the battlecruiser *Stralsund,* pride of the fleet, on his left shoulder.

"Arott," Nils said carefully, "we don't have a lot of time before I have to commit. This conversation does not leave this room. Ever. Am I clear?"

"Yes, First Lord," Command Centurion Arott Whughy said carefully, straightening in his chair and setting down the mug of coffee he had been sipping. His face lost something. Perhaps a little of that carefree smile drained out.

"Good," Nils continued. "In a few minutes, there will be an all-hands meeting for a group of people that I am about to send out on a *forlorn hope* to try to rescue *Ballard* from *Fribourg Empire* Admiral Emmerich Wachturm, the so-called Red Admiral."

Nils paused to study this man. Like Jessica Keller, Arott was another one of his excellent protégés. Unlike Jessica, this man was kin. All of the Fifty Families of the Republic were related, cousins to some degree, but Arott Whughy was only two degrees removed. That made him practically family.

Fortunately, the man had never attempted to trade on those connections, other than to be one of the best, and let his natural skill and confidence carry him to great heights. Nils could see Arott Whughy on this side of the desk, one of these days, if he played his cards right.

Arott nodded silently.

Good.

"I have two choices about who I can attach to this task force from Home Fleet," Nils said. "If I send you, you will be the senior Command Centurion, both by virtue of time in grade, and by command of the largest vessel. However, you will not be in command."

"No Fleet Lord going with us, sir?"

"No, Centurion Whughy."

"Then why not, sir?"

"Because I'm putting Jessica Keller in charge, and you will need to take orders from her."

Nils watched his former student bristle. Not much. Mostly in the eyes and the set of the jaw.

"May I ask why, sir?"

The voice was contained. Almost compact. Barely any emotional signature. Another good sign. Nils needed a team player here, not another MacArthur.

"Arott," Nils said as he leaned back, subtly breaking the tension. *We're just two soldiers having a chat, right?* "I would rank you in the top one percent of centurions in the Fleet right now. You will be a Fleet Lord soon, and a damned good one. You will have a career most people will be jealous of."

Nils paused as the man absorbed the compliment. Arott even smiled a touch.

"Thank you, sir."

"However," the First Lord continued, "I would put Jessica Keller in the top three people currently serving. You were one of the youngest Command Centurions in a generation. She was *the* youngest in more than a century. And *the* youngest ever squadron commander. If she survives *Ballard*, she will be the youngest-ever serving Fleet Lord. I picked you for this mission because I believe you can take orders from her, or from her First Officer, Denis Jež, who should have been promoted to Command Centurion before now. This is *Auberon*'s show. *Stralsund* is there because Jessica needs a battlesword in her left hand."

It took a moment for the younger man to absorb the information, perhaps a touch grumpily.

Downside of never having failed in your life, Arott? We need to teach failure better to our cadets, so they can learn to respond quicker.

"What are we facing, First Lord?"

Good. Internalized. Understood. Accepted.

Yes, a man I can trust. He really might be First Lord, one of these days.

"The Imperial battleship *Amsel*," Nils replied. "Her usual consorts include a handful of escort frigates, a light cruiser, and a battle cruiser. The light cruiser is probably still *Sturm Teufel*, but *Muscva* was killed at *Qui-Ping*, and we don't know who is likely to replace her yet."

"And what do we have to stop him?"

"*Stralsund*, *Auberon*, the Destroyer Leader *Brightoak*, the Heavy Destroyer *Rajput*, and the Escort *CR-264*."

He watched Arott blink in surprise.

"That's it? Against a battleship? And Emmerich Wachturm?"

"I'm also sending you, Arott Whughy, plus Denis Jež, Robbie Aeliaes, Alber' d'Maine, Tom Kigali, and Jessica Keller. Plus a young woman named Moirrey Kermode."

"I don't know that last name, sir," Arott said, confused.

"You will, Centurion. Trust me. You will."

The air in the chamber crackled with tension.

Unlike a normal staff meeting, this was limited to just the people seated around a single conference table, without the usual junior officers along the wall, or yeomen ready to handle tasks and locate information.

Just the senior people. That alone made it interesting.

Arott knew almost none of these people by sight, only reputation, having spent his entire career either on the Primary Front with First War Fleet, or rotated back to *Ladaux* and Home Fleet.

As he was introduced around the table, he was struck by how much the people around him reacted as almost a single entity. It went beyond even a school of fish reacting in quick sequence.

No, it was a single being.

Arott would have expected the First Lord to be the center of gravity, around which everything rotated, but instead it was very obviously Keller.

In person, she was surprisingly small for the amount of reputation she had accumulated. Arott was tall, but Jessica barely cleared his shoulder. However, she was built like a warrior, hard and toned. Feminine, but not girlie. Attractive and brunette. But there was something off. He couldn't place it.

Arott had followed the events of her Court Martial after *Iger*. Almost every officer in the Fleet had done so. You could almost divide the Fighting Lords and the Noble Lords into camps, just by asking their opinion of Jessica Keller and her eventual acquittal.

Perhaps it was the eyes. They didn't seem to focus on him when he spoke, instead seeing a spot on the horizon. The voice was subtly off as well. Flat. Almost mechanical.

After the introductions, and everyone was seated, Arott took a sneaky moment during the First Lord's opening comments to study the people around him.

Command Centurion Robertson Aeliaes. *Brightoak*. Tall and built like a swimmer, with chocolate-brown skin and golden eyes. Apparently one of Jessica's former squadron mates under that idiot Bogdan Loncar. Aeliaes was a man with a reputation for being smart, well-prepared, and constantly on the verge of insubordination against stupid orders. Arott liked him immediately.

Command Centurion Alber' d'Maine. *Rajput*. A man of average height, but very broad across the shoulders. The sort of physique you got from working with heavy weights and not a lot of running. A quiet man of few words that were almost growled. A warrior on a ship of war.

Command Centurion Tomas Kigali. *CR-264*. Nicknamed *The Yachtsman*. Current holder of almost every interesting and important sailing record for distance, speed, or extreme soloing. Physically almost Arott's doppelganger, being tall and thin and blond. Psychologically almost a world away. Kigali had an easy smile and breezy way about him that one would expect to find on a tropical island somewhere, probably with a surfboard in hand and a rum-based iced-something in the other, wearing a shirt with flamingos printed on it.

Command Centurion Waldemar Ihejirika. Fleet Replenishment Freighter *Mendocino*. The forgotten Service in the Fleet. The mailman, the milkman, the corner store. The quiet professionals who kept everyone else in socks and fresh cream. The young man, Ihejirika, looked nothing like his surname, being so pale as to be almost translucent, offset by straight black hair so dark that it looked painted. But he had the serious look of a professional mechanic facing an unruly ground vehicle. That would be helpful.

Senior centurion Denis Jež. Per the First Lord, the man *was* the commander of *Auberon*, while Jessica commanded the entire squadron, acting as her own private Fleet Lord. And, according to the stories and rumors circulating in the Fleet, it was an amazingly successful team. Jež sized him up with a glance and nodded. *So, secure that he was still the second dog. Good enough, for now.*

The last woman at the table had no place that Arott could identify. She was just a centurion, and a newly commissioned one, to watch her glance down at the single broad stripe encircling her upper arm occasionally, and to touch it in awe. She had spoken with a strange accent, almost like a song bird, an image reinforced by her tiny size and overall pixieness.

And everyone else went out of their way to practically fawn over the young woman. Who was she? *What* was she?

"Ladies and gentlemen," Nils Kasum said, drawing all eyes back to himself. "Time is short. I wish I could do more to help, but I cannot risk it, even over something as precious as *Ballard*."

Arott watched Nils size up the room, pain evident in his eyes. It was clear that the man was preparing himself, steeling himself, to say goodbye, firmly convinced that the people before him would never come home.

They were a forlorn hope, the Charge of the Light Brigade into the Valley of Death. At least in the First Lord's mind.

"There is nothing more to say, except thank you," the First Lord continued. "I may represent the Fleet in the halls of power, but you are the Fleet. As I said earlier, we can sleep at night because you will be there, holding the wall. I will turn things over to Jessica for your briefing."

Arott watched her rise and face the room.

He had always enjoyed strong, sexy women, if taller. But there was something different about Jessica Keller. Something wrong.

He remembered the video of her from the Court Martial. Calm, still, focused. A warrior facing unstoppable odds, intent on overcoming them. And she had.

Here, the odds were even worse. This squadron could probably take on a battleship, or her escorts. He could not envision how they would defeat both. But that was why she was Jessica Keller.

"Command Centurion Arott Whughy," she began, "Command Centurion Waldemar Ihejirika. We're doing this because I pissed off the Red Admiral. Embarrassed him, publicly. Beat him."

She speared him with her look. The eyes were focused on him this time. And they weren't. It was as if she was still looking past him. Or looking at him and seeing someone else. It was an uncomfortable feeling.

"At *Callumnia*, he and I talked about the Founding of the Republic," Jessica continued. "Part of that legend is the woman known as Suvi, a *Sentience* allowed to live and teach at the University of *Ballard*. Her mere existence is an affront to the *Fribourg Empire*."

She paused to draw a deep breath, glancing to either side at the others.

"Forty hours ago," she said, "we received an intelligence report that Wachturm's squadron, led by the battleship *Amsel*, is going to make a long sail, followed by a surprise attack to destroy *Alexandria Station*. We're going to beat him there and stop him."

"How?" Robbie Aeliaes asked. "Even with a battlecruiser on our side we can't do it." Robbie turned to him with a sympathetic smile. "No offense. That's a battleship."

"None taken," Arott replied with a smile.

He agreed.

Jessica Keller smiled for the first time. She pointed at the centurion on the other side of the table, the woman Arott couldn't place.

"Mischief," she said.

Arott realized how right he had been before when he described the others as a single entity.

Everybody else nodded as if that was a perfectly acceptable answer.

It was insane.

"Mischief?" Arott asked into the silence.

"*Mischief*," the young woman, Centurion Kermode, said brightly, her accent growing stranger with each syllable. "We dinna told the Red Admiral everytin at *Petron*, sir. They's still tricks and surprises left in the poke fer 'im."

"And," the First Lord spoke up, "the addition of some of that Mischief to Home Fleet gives me enough freedom to send *Stralsund* with you, without risking a double attack."

Arott managed to smile unconvincingly. They were all crazy together.

Keller noticed.

"Centurion Kermode is my Advanced Research Weapons Technician, Whughy," Jessica said. "Her job is to invent better tools, better weapons, better options. My job is to take them into battle and win with them."

A what? An Advanced Research Weapons Tech? On a Strike Carrier? Attached to the flank frontiers of the Republic?

Arott glanced at Nils Kasum, saw the man smile.

A thought clicked.

Jessica Keller was among the very best commanders because she had surrounded herself with very good people, and encouraged them to color very, very far outside the lines.

Arott probably had someone like that on the lower decks of *Stralsund*, and he had never once considered using them, turning them loose.

Okay, maybe he could be third dog for a while. There was apparently much more to learn than he realized.

Arott nodded, as much to himself as to Keller.

She studied him a moment longer than purely necessary.

Arott felt like a side of beef being sized up by the butcher. Or a hog about to become one of the butcher's customers.

It passed as she turned that horrible focus onto the commander of *CR-264*. The room seemed to warm again.

"Tom," she said, voice friendlier now. "I'm sending you ahead. I want you to set a new sailing record, to give them as much time as possible to evacuate the station. I don't know if the AI can leave, but the university is as much the people as it is the books. If we can save them, we've done something. He can't occupy an entire planet, and he can't hold a siege that far from home."

"Jessica has asked me to send along a *Declaration of Martial Law* in her name, signed by the Premier," the First Lord suddenly interjected. "They may not listen until she actually arrives, but at the very minimum it will be enough to make them plan ahead."

Kigali nodded, a thoughtful look in his eyes.

The Yachtsman turned to Arott suddenly and fixed him with a stare similar to Keller's. It was a predator spying potential prey.

"Seventeen days sail?" he asked.

Arott heard the challenge in his voice. Tomas Kigali flew a tiny, ancient, under-gunned Fleet Escort, but apparently considered himself at least as much a warrior as anyone else at the table.

Good to know.

"Sixteen if we push," Arott replied, reasonably sure how carefully tuned his engines and jump drives were. Home Fleet squadrons were expected to sail in large groups, arriving together and hitting a target together. Coming in like pearls on a string was a good way to be eaten like grapes.

"Not bad," Kigali replied with a warmer smile. He turned back to Keller. "Best single transit ever recorded from *Ladaux* is currently fourteen days, four hours, station to station. I'm aiming for twelve and a half days."

Jessica raised an eyebrow at the man. "And that record will last until…?"

"Until they build a better JumpSail, boss."

"Good enough," Jessica said. "Everyone else is right now being packed to the gills with Primary shells and missiles."

She pointed at Ihejirika. "*Mendocino* will be coming with us, and she can keep up with the squadron. I expect to empty every weapon we have fighting the Blackbird. Primaries, missiles, kitchen sinks. Unlike Wachturm, we'll have the ability to reload afterwards."

She paused, marking every one of them with her presence. Arott was almost sure she had left her scent on him, the look was so powerful.

"And now, my friends, we are going to go slay the great, white whale."

CHAPTER III

Date of the Republic May 28, 394 Edge of the Ladaux System

Tomas Kigali sat on his tiny bridge and watched the clock count down the moments to the edge of the gravity well.

They were pushing today. Kigali had told his first officer, Arsen Lam, that they were going to set a record that nobody was ever going to break, at least not with the technology they had today. If somebody had to invent something better just to beat him, all the better. Those kinds of bragging rights would last forever.

It had started the moment they cleared the bay back at Fleet HQ where they had been docked. Rather than come clear on maneuvering thrusters alone, like they were supposed to, *CR-264* had lit her engines for thrust. Not enough to damage anything. At least not significantly.

He had made sure there was nobody behind them in the bay that might be hit by wash. But he was certainly far enough outside the rules and regulations of the space dock that he would have gotten a good tongue-lashing from someone.

Had they dared.

Nobody had. Not even the Stationmaster had said anything.

Word had leaked out. Not hard to figure out, when you watch a handful of vessels, fresh back from the frontier, suddenly given crash-priority for supplies and reloads, with a hard departure deadline. Something bad was about to happen, somewhere, and *Fleet* was throwing everything they could at it.

CR-264 had a serious head start on the rest of the squadron. The little fleet escort, herself just an old Revenue Cutter impressed into service during a previous emergency and serving well past her expected lifespan, had neither missiles nor Primary beams that needed to be reloaded.

Kigali had instead been able to take his time loading food and replacement parts without having to deal with the munitions techs. There had even been time for a good nap.

And now, Tomas watched the engine read-outs, running hot but stable. Very hot. Probably shaving useful months off of the lifetime of these engines, from the heat.

This was no way to treat good equipment. He would have dressed down another Command Centurion for such recklessness, and done so publicly, embarrassingly.

And here he was the one doing it.

Hopefully, when this was all done, they would actually have time to relax and spend six months in dry-dock. Assuming he didn't cook his engines first getting there.

"Arsen," Tomas called down the open hatch to the fighting deck, "let me know the instant you think we've cleared the edge of the gravity well. I'm not jumping just then, but that will start the clock. We're already an hour ahead of schedule."

"Acknowledged, top," came the call up. The boys and girls down on the fighting deck didn't have anything useful to do, tucked in here safely at the heart of Republic space, but the whole crew had picked up on his energy. It wasn't nerves, but they all knew they were part of something very big.

Something that started with the fastest ever sail to the very back of beyond.

CHAPTER IV

Date of the Republic May 29, 394 Fleet HQ, Ladaux System

First Fleet Lord Bogdan Loncar considered the man seated across from him. Technically, Brand wasn't supposed to be allowed in the Officer's Club, since he was purely a civilian political operative working for the Senate, but rules could be bent and allowances made. And the room was private, so very few people would know.

Especially when the need for privacy overwhelmed all else.

Loncar sipped from a highball glass and tried to control his breathing. Everything about Jessica Keller made him want to rage. It would feel good to stand up suddenly and shatter the glass against the pseudo-fireplace with a good sidearm toss.

Considering his station and rank, eyebrows might be raised, but not voices. No, at most, whispers. The wrong kind of whispers, right now, but that was the risk when dealing with the plebeians who made up so much of the lower decks.

"So, Brand," Loncar said finally, his control restored. "What have you been able to learn?"

The operative studied him for a moment longer than necessary.

"A year ago," he replied, "you were sent with a task force to the *Cahllepp* frontier."

"Yes, yes," Loncar said, exasperated. "It was necessary to clean up the amazing mess Keller left behind."

"Was there much Imperial activity in the aftermath of her raid?"

Loncar bristled, sipped, subsided.

"Barely any, Brand," he said. "For generations, we and *Fribourg* have maintained a studied indifference to one another across the gulf. *She* didn't change *that*."

"Oh?"

"No." Loncar felt his voice ranging louder. He fought to keep his emotions under control. "The problem was piracy. My family has extensive holdings in shipping and manufacturing in that sector, and we have sustained tremendous losses."

"How so, First Fleet Lord?" Brand leaned forward and rested his chin on his fist, apparently rapt.

"The *Fribourg Empire* was forced to shuffle forces around randomly, since they no longer have the ships and squadrons to garrison every system effectively until they can rebuild. That has opened the door to raiders coming and going. Mostly, they have stayed on the other side of the gulf, but occasionally they have attacked our frontier."

"I see," Brand replied. "I was not aware of that. Were you successful in driving them off?"

Loncar shrugged and sipped from his glass.

"My task force was ill-equipped for such a thing. Pirates are usually in armed freighters or small gunships that a fleet escort could chase off. When we find them, they immediately flee before my squadrons can form up to give chase. In the end, it was necessary to scatter my various elements across the entire frontier, having them patrol randomly."

"But it appears to have been successful?" Brand's tone could have been a statement, or a question. Loncar wasn't sure.

You were never sure of things when dealing with Brand.

"Raids have dropped back to less than they were before Keller caused all her trouble," he replied flatly. "However, I broke up my destroyer squadron and sent them off to the very reaches of the sector for that purpose. Which brings me to why you are here. *Vigilant* and *Rubicon* did as they were told. Command Centurion Aeliaes, commander of *Brightoak*, appears to have ignored my express orders and gone haring off with his old squadron leader. I want to know why. Charges of insubordination should be filed."

The rage was back.

Nobody else could do that to him. Only Jessica Keller. Robertson Aeliaes could come close, but he was one of her protégés, so it was to be expected that the man was almost as bad. Something of her had rubbed off on the man.

Loncar took a deep breath as Brand waited. What he wanted, nay demanded, required patience and allies. Brand had no friends, only those people he could exploit to further his own ends.

Fortunately, those ends tended to mesh with his.

"After you departed," Brand began, "Keller was assigned to something of a diplomatic mission to *Lincolnshire*. The government there was having problems with piracy and asked for help. It is my understanding that First Lord Kasum and the Premier are grooming her for greater things."

"That woman should have been cashiered from the service and put ashore permanently," Loncar seethed, almost slamming his glass down onto the table top. "Not rewarded. Look what she did at *Cahllepp*."

"Indeed, First Fleet Lord, indeed," Brand replied. "However, the Premier is in a strong position right now, and fully supports the First Lord. We must work sideways around them."

"How many senators and members of the Fifty Families have lost money from her actions? Especially around *Cahllepp*?" Loncar leaned close to make his point.

"Many, sir," Brand said. "But she has also become very popular because of the Long Raid. Much of the fleet supports her right now. And, by extension, the First Lord."

"She is a bull in a china shop, Brand," Loncar snarled quietly. "She needs to be removed from command before she does something terrible. If she was insubordinate with me, she will be all the more so with the Senate. She must be stopped."

"And that is the end to which we are working. But one does not simply remove the First Lord of the Fleet without a very good reason and a great deal of support. Nils Kasum is even more popular than Jessica Keller."

"Then find that reason, Brand," Loncar said flatly. "Before it is too late."

CHAPTER V

Auberon was still hours from departure, even with every systems and weapons tech available on the station hastily stuffing the great carrier to the gills with supplies. Jessica figured that Denis could handle that. He certainly didn't need her looking over his shoulder every five minutes.

Mendocino had already backed away from the station and started her sail out. She wasn't going to be pushing her engines as hard as the rest of the squadron, since she could contribute nothing useful to the fight. Her job was tending to the survivors.

If there were any.

The Fleet Replenishment Freighter would meet them on the other side. Whether that was across the long jump to *Ballard*, or the River Styx, remained to be determined.

Jessica passed the time at the small workstation in her cabin, studying old battles the Republic had fought against Emmerich Wachturm. Everyone had done that at the Academy and after, but rarely had anyone done so with this degree of determination.

He was one of the greatest commanders in centuries of interstellar warfare, a man who made the impossible look easy, who found unexpected angles of attack that were plainly obvious in retrospect. The man who was probably personally responsible for the fact that the *Fribourg Empire* was currently winning *The Endless War.*

And she had to beat him.

Simple as that.

He had a battleship. And a battlecruiser. And a whole raft of smaller escorts.

And his legend.

She had a battlecruiser as well. And war-borne destroyers. And *CR-264* to protect them.

It wasn't enough.

She had Moirrey Kermode. And *Mischief.* And the element of surprise.

The Red Admiral had to know that, had to have planned for it. Much of what still remained classified were simply extensions of previous gimmicks, obvious if you spent time asking how to take it to the next level.

It still wasn't going to be enough.

They were going to ride to *Ballard's* rescue, proud and gleaming knights atop valiant steeds.

But this wasn't going to be Agincourt.

It was going to be Thermopylae. She was going to take the Three Hundred into battle against the Persian Emperor and an army that shook the very earth when it marched.

The heroic Greeks would most likely die, perhaps having bought enough time to save the woman around whom all of this rotated, the AI named Suvi.

Jessica growled under her breath as she watched a projection of the Blackbird slowly rotate in space before her.

Wachturm did not get to win. It was Ian Zhao all over again. And Jing Du. *Corynthe.*

It was going to take everything she had. But they did *not* get to win.

Jessica stretched by rotating her shoulders ninety degrees each way. The clock on her desk surprised her when she glanced at it with a yawn. She had been awake for around fifty hours at this point, cat-napping twice for maybe thirty minutes at a stretch and surviving by pouring coffee tastelessly down her throat.

It had finally caught up with her.

Jessica checked for messages once more and then moved from her desk to the bed. She took a moment to take off her slippers and her tunic, stretching out on the rack in just her undershirt, pants, and socks. The chances of an emergency in dock were slim, but they were habits that would stay with her until she died, most likely.

She turned the lights down to a very dim setting where she could sleep peacefully, but where Marcelle could still navigate the room if she came in.

Briefly, Jessica wondered if Marcelle had put something in her most recent coffee to make her sleep. She wouldn't put it past the woman, whose primary job was taking care of Jessica.

Her eyes grew heavy. She had been burning every candle at every end, these last two days.

And she would need the sleep. She still had to face The Red Admiral at *Ballard*.

The air was suddenly warm, almost sticky. Her shirt was plastered to her back.

Jessica found herself standing in a small punt, a flat-bottomed boat, poling herself along what could charitably be called a swamp. The bottom was close enough under the muck that she could push herself along, somewhere.

Around her, trees were slowly being strangled by some sort of airy moss that hung like vines and spider webs, every way she turned. Reeds seemed to suggest a shore somewhere close by, but it was invisible from this distance. Bark on the trees was so gnarled with time that she imagined faces staring back at her, haunted, or alone, or lost. Exotic birds hid in the darkness and shade. They chittered and squawked in the brush, a cacophony of sound in the otherwise silent scene.

There was an open path before her through the trees, water lazily drifting towards some unseen and unknown sea. Jessica paused in her poling to look down at her reflection in the still water.

She wore all black. Everything black.

Tight pants tucked into thigh-high leather boots with flat, heavy heels. A long scarf tied around her waist, trailing nearly to her knees on her left side. A jacket-like tabard, almost a long-coat, but slashed to the base of her ribs on each side for easy movement. The sleeves down barely past her elbows, tucking tightly into a pair of soft suede gloves so black as to absorb life.

It was the sort of outfit Moirrey might have cooked up for her, had she evinced a desire to attend an All Hallows Eve party dressed in gothic darkness. Certainly, nothing one would find in her closet.

At least, she hoped not. This was a dream, she hoped. Anything was possible.

Jessica rarely dreamed. She knew that science said she did dream, and just didn't remember it on waking, but she could remember very few dreams in her life.

Always living in the future, not the past.

The dream insisted she pole forward, deeper into the swamp. Jessica was never one to shirk her duty, so she put her back into it, easily balancing the punt as she pushed off.

It turned into a clearing. Or whatever the right term was when it happened to a swamp instead of a forest. She made a note to look the term up later.

If she remembered this dream.

The trees had faded back from the water's edge slowly. Where it had been dreary, almost oppressive, now the sky opened up, a gap of several hundred meters across, with her in the middle.

The heavens were red.

Not the burnt orange of a lovely sunset back home when she was a little girl. No, this was the color of blood. The sun was either a brighter red, or hidden behind blood-red clouds, filtered but not lost. It had the dim quality of sunset, even as the sun approached zenith.

The silence had become oppressive. The waters were utterly still except for little wavelets she sent out as she balanced the punt. The bottom of the swamp was still close, but she could feel energy building, like an impending lightning strike.

Jessica shifted her grip on the pole, intent on using it as a spear if necessary. The day had that feel.

Ripples started around her.

Something emerged from the water like a snake, poised as if sniffing the air.

Another joined it on her left.

And then a third to her right.

She heard the splash of a fourth behind her, but could not look back without bracing the pole for stability.

There was enough sun to identify them now as they came towards her.

Tentacles.

Their skin appeared blue. Bright azure. Arms as thick as hers, probing, tasting.

Seeking.

They found the boat.

Latched on carefully.

Jessica considered striking at them, but they were not moving, once they found the wood of the punt.

Just holding on.

A larger splash to her right drew her attention.

An eye, larger than a dinner plate, staring at her from a mass of flesh larger than the boat she rode.

It had that baleful stare. She expected it to blink once at her, ominously.

Instead, the tentacles all torqued at once, spilling her out of the punt.

Jessica found herself falling.

Jessica landed in the center of a perfectly flat black plane that seemed to go on forever. The sky was the gray of ash. There was no sun, the little-enough light filtered in from somewhere to see.

Jessica still wore black. Everything was dry, as if the swamp had never happened.

She supposed that it hadn't, dream physics being something she had never considered before now.

A sound turned her head to the right.

The great blue creature with the tentacles was there. If a squid could swim in air, and reach a mantle length of six or seven meters, it would have appeared thus. It was a rich, royal blue in color, banded at the ends of the tentacles with maroon, right where a human might have a wrist.

One eye tracked her.

Jessica was close enough for one of the tremendous arms to embrace her, but they pointed off to one side, as if the creature was swimming in a sea she could not fathom.

Just the baleful eye.

It did not speak, so Jessica remained silent as well.

They watched each other for seconds, minutes, eternities.

The creature began to change.

It was a subtle shift. Fading, morphing, altering.

Becoming.

It resolved itself finally into a shape Jessica knew well.

A beautiful woman with blue skin and long black hair, dressed entirely in black. She had four arms, double-shouldered front and back, with the rear arms much longer than the front ones.

In her hands a saber, a *main-gauche*, a severed head, and a floating planet. *Kali-ma.*

The Goddess of War.

She resolved herself fully material, glowering down from a height of nearly five meters.

Jessica glowered back. Just being a goddess wasn't enough to intimidate her. Not anymore.

The woman smiled down at her knowingly and began to fade. She did not move, but seemed to recede to a great distance.

The goddess began to transform at the same time, flowing subtly into a new shape, heavier, broader, bulkier. The shoulders widened, the arms on each side merged, the face changed.

In moments, Jessica found herself facing a new creature. This one was shaped like a man, but again five meters tall. The creature's skin had changed to red, the hair brown.

He wore red and assumed a human form. One Jessica knew.

Emmerich Wachturm, if she had hired an artist to draw him as a horned daemon from the darkest hell imaginable.

The monster snarled down at her with a howling laugh that was painful to endure.

One arm reached down, a hand as big as her chest threatening to engulf her.

Jessica sidestepped the attack, blocking with the *main-gauche* she suddenly found in her right hand.

The monster took a step forward as she moved.

Jessica slashed with the saber abruptly in her left hand, felt it ring solidly off the creature's flesh without drawing blood.

The daemon could not be killed with steel.

She blocked his other clawed hand and danced backwards as he growled and tried to grab her again.

Emmerich Wachturm. The Red Admiral. Daemon made flesh.

Jessica growled back at him.

He was not allowed to win.

Simple as that.

Jessica swung her second right hand forward, aimed at the daemon with the short rifle she held and fired a blast.

Second right hand?

The flesh on her arms had turned bright blue.

The rifle was a fléchette, firing a handful of explosive darts that tore the monster's flesh when they hit.

The howls of rage turned to sudden cries of agony.

In her second left hand, Jessica held a beam pistol unlike any she had ever seen before.

She laughed at the fiend as she aimed. Jessica felt herself growing in stature as she did, until she met him eye to eye.

Time slowed down.

He tried to rush her as she aimed the pistol. The shot was brighter than the non-existent sun in this dismal place. It struck the daemon square in the center of his chest and bored straight through. The pistol ejected a spent cartridge and cycled another power disk into the chamber.

It looked like a tiny little miniaturized Primary generator, but Jessica knew instinctively that it was normal sized, and the two combatants were the size of starships.

The shot slew the daemon.

A hole opened beneath his feet, sucking him back down into whatever hell had spawned him.

A claw grasped at her ankle before she could evade him.

Too quick to react, Jessica found herself drawn into the hole as well.

Jessica fell.

Jessica awoke with a cry of terrible anguish. Falling had been a surprise, but Jessica knew that many dreamers awoke from falling.

"Nightmare?" Marcelle asked quietly.

Jessica was back in her cabin. Marcelle was sitting in the comfortable chair in the corner, reading a book of some sort and keeping watch over her sleeping charge.

"Of a sort," Jessica replied, trying to breathe.

"Need coffee?"

Coffee. The cure for almost everything.

Almost.

"No," Jessica said, rubbing her face to wake up. "Juice, please?"

"Coming up."

Marcelle closed the book and rose in one fluid motion, exiting the cabin in three long strides and leaving Jessica alone.

Not a nightmare. She had been fighting daemons in her sleep quite a lot, these last few months.

No, the anguish was the loss of her second arms.

For a moment in time, in the dream, she had been a goddess.

CHAPTER VI

Date of the Republic May 29, 394 Fleet HQ, Ladaux System

"What do you think?" *Auberon's* pilot, Nada Zupan, asked, looking back over her shoulder.

Denis had a moment of shock, watching Nada's ponytail bob. It had gotten almost down to her kidneys, where she had kept it barely to her collar for as long as he had known her.

It reminded him of Jessica. Her hair was getting that long, as well.

Denis wondered if all of them were unconsciously imitating her. Not necessarily the worst role model to have, all things considered.

Denis paused and checked his boards.

"Marcelle has a *Do Not Disturb* on Jessica's key," Denis said, "so maybe she's finally sleeping."

He considered the rest of the Roster board. He pushed a button at the side.

"Security, Tawfeek here," the voice replied over the audio channel.

"This is Jež, on the Bridge," Denis replied with a simple smile on his face and in his voice. "Can you locate the flag centurion for me?"

"Stand by, sir," Tawfeek said.

A moment passed.

"Uhm, sir, are we on a private channel?" Tawfeek continued.

Denis raised an eyebrow as he looked at the microphone. He keyed the audio suppression system in his command chair.

Why did we need a private channel?

"You are now, Tawfeek. Go ahead."

"Right, sir. According to my systems, Mr. Zivkovic is currently located in the private quarters assigned to Flight Cornet Nakamura. And if I might suggest, sir, unless this is an emergency, you might want to wait five or eight minutes?"

"Nakamura?" Denis said, surprised.

"*Furious*, sir," Tawfeek replied quietly.

Why did he need to wait...? Oh. Right. Yes. Not that important.

"Thank you, Tawfeek," Denis said. "I'll talk to him when he's on duty next."

"Acknowledged."

The line went dead.

Denis chuckled to himself briefly before he put on his serious face and cancelled the audio suppression.

Nada had a knowing grin on her face when he looked up, but nobody else on the bridge seemed to be paying attention.

"Seems like we're in charge, Nada," he said. "Thank Flight Control and the Quartermaster for getting us loaded ahead of schedule, then notify everyone else that we're heading out. I'll let you be flag centurion for a while and coordinate movement with *Stralsund* and the destroyers as we back away. Then plot a best-time run to the edge of the gravity well and get us to Jumpspace as soon as possible. The Red Admiral is waiting."

Nada nodded and began to play her symphonies on the board in front of her. *Auberon* responded with the creaks and groans of a warship preparing for maneuvers.

To Denis, it sounded like old tack on a horse, during a cold winter morning, back on his grandfather's farm.

Auberon was going to war.

Moirrey looked up blankly as someone touched her on the shoulder. For a moment, total darkness, until she remembered to flip up the welding mask.

The chief engineer, Senior Centurion Vilis Ozolinsh, stood patiently beside her workstation, hands crossed across his back and a serene smile on his face.

"Yeah, Oz?" Moirrey asked, slowly coming back to the room around her. It felt strange to be in the present tense again.

"Newly-promoted Centurion Kermode," he began with a wicked smile, his accent the perfect clipped tones of the best schools, "I feel as though I am repeating myself. But then, we've been here before, haven't we?"

Moirrey blinked again and glanced around her.

The workstation was piled with paper printouts and strange little bits of gear. Her welder that she slid home into its little carrier, the one decorated with sparklies and bangles. A working model of the miniature Harpoon fighter remote that they had used to test the Archerfish, before *Petron*. Other half-finished ideas made tangible parts.

And Oz, standing there serenely.

"That we have," she smiled back.

"So, young lady, we shall shortly find ourselves at the sharp end of the stick again. Will it work?"

He gestured expansively to the pile of semi-junk that seemed to be taking over every flat space in the area. The latest miniaturization project sat patiently under the magnifying work lens.

"I dinna think the Red Admiral will be expectin' this one, Oz," she said. "*Petron* were one thin', but *Mischief* keeps needin' ta betters. Already smacked him on the bum hard once. He'll no fall a second time. Best to keeps him guessin', rights untils we go sideways on 'im."

"Very good," Ozolinsh replied. "How soon until the first batch is ready to test?"

Oz already had six of the top ten High Scores from the *testin'* afore *Petron*. Another batch of *Mischief* to play before invitin' the pilots aboard to play were just right silly. The man were a natural fer 'is sort of thing. Shame he were never interested in pilotin' for reals.

Or maybe nots. She'd'a likes to had a spit-and-polish boss, otherwise. *BORING*.

"End o'th'shift, Oz," she chirped. "If you can find someone on swing to mount 'em and wire it up, we should be ready to play Red Baron in the mornin'."

"Excellent, young lady," the Chief Engineer beamed. "I shall dig out my scarf and flight goggles and be prepared first thing."

She watched him spin on a heel and depart with a jaunty stride. They were truly off to hunt the great, white whale, weren't they? Now, if she could only know if she were Fedallah, or Ishmael.

CHAPTER VII

Date of the Republic May 29, 394 Fleet HQ, Ladaux System

There was a serenity to this view, Loncar decided. Probably designed for such things at the beginning.

Below him, the mighty fleet carrier that had anchored his most recent Task Force: *RAN Archon*. A faithful steed that had carried him into battle for most of a decade.

Before that bastard of a First Lord, Nils Kasum, had put him on the beach again. A man like that should understand his worth to the fleet and keep him in constant command of task forces, instead of pushing papers and the occasional mission.

The dry-dock at fleet headquarters stretched out nearly to infinity, designed to service the biggest vessels flying. Fleet Carriers were second only to the two greatest ships in the fleet, the Star Controllers: *Athena* and *Archimedes*, flagships of Home Fleet and First War Fleet, respectively. Still, *Archon* and her sister *Ajax* could almost fill one of the mammoth bays. The light cruiser *Hualien*, close by in bay two, was dwarfed for all her own size.

That was power there. Glory.

He turned and took three strides across the hallway, his long legs consuming the space quickly. This porthole showed a view of deep space.

If he leaned far to his right, he could see *Ladaux* below, but it was the ship dominating the sky in front of him that held his attention.

RAN Auberon.

Her ship.

The strike carrier had backed away from her loading dock and was transitioning for a deep space run. Around her, like bright knives in the distance, other vessels prepared to depart as well. *Rajput, Stralsund, Brightoak.* The escort had already departed, flying like an utter madman devoid of any thought for anyone but himself in his mad haste.

Her time would come.

The sound of his comm chirping ruined the tranquility of the scene.

"Loncar," he said brusquely. "Go ahead."

"First Fleet Lord Loncar," Brand's voice oozed out of the speaker. "I have some information you might find interesting. I wonder if we might meet tomorrow in my office down on the surface?"

Loncar smiled. It must be interesting if Brand wasn't even willing to offer a hint over the comm.

"That would be fine, Brand," he replied. "I will let you know when I can catch a shuttle down."

CHAPTER VIII

Date of the Republic June 2, 394 Ithome, Ballard

"Good afternoon, Mr. Sykes," the customs officer said brightly. "Do you have anything to declare?"

The man whose paperwork identified him as Sykes smiled back at the young woman before him, knowing that ninety percent of this encounter was designed as social engineering to locate people *Up To No Good.*

He wasn't about to let that show. This trip was too important.

"No, ma'am," he replied, letting his voice drift into a soft drawl he had picked up once upon a time, some eight hundred light years spinward. "Expect I'll be taking things home, so I plan to travel light and buy things here."

"Very good," she replied. "And the purpose of your visit?"

"Tourism," he said simply. He pointed vaguely at the invisible sky outside. "I wanna see the sights, smell the ocean, and maybe take a day trip up to *Alexandria Station* at some point."

Sykes watched like a hawk as she slid the little booklet with his latest identity into a scanner and let the galaxy's most dangerous computer system have a look at him. He was far too professional to actually let this woman see his tension, but everything hinged on the next ten seconds.

Either they let him in, or saw through the disguise and he'd spend the rest of his short life in a small box, awaiting execution.

After a moment, the machine beeped happily. The woman pulled out an actual mechanical stamper and marked his tourist documents with it before sliding it back across the counter to him.

"Welcome to *Ballard*," she said with a smile.

Sykes glanced down at the stamp. It was a stylized image of the planet *Ballard*, just a slice, with *Alexandria Station* orbiting overhead. Just like it did now. At least for the next few weeks.

Less, if he was successful.

The city of Ithome was a lovely place. It still held the character it had originally developed during the long hiatus in starflight, before *Zanzibar* came calling, twelve centuries ago, to re-ignite human civilization.

According to the tourist brochure and his briefings, the city was a maritime capital, located on a fantastically deep and sheltered bay, possibly the caldera of an extinct volcano, or at least the modern remains of one. *Zanzibar's* first starships to go exploring again had been designed to land on water, so they had picked an oceanic world with a modicum of steam technology to visit first. And had landed in this very bay.

Sykes walked casually through the older parts of the city, down near the original wharfs and factories that had processed fish. A few of the buildings still did, for export to other parts of the planet and system, and many parts of the *Republic of Aquitaine*. The famous mutant tuna of *Ballard* were probably the second most profitable export from this world, reaching as much as ten meters in length and frequently serving as the apex predator in *Ballard's* enormous seas.

Only the import and export of knowledge and scholars out-weighed the fish, at least in value.

Sykes checked his local almanac and turned to his left.

There.

Approaching zenith in the southern sky, visible as a waxing quarter moon today.

Alexandria Station.

Home of *The Sentience*. The AI who claimed to be the savior of humanity. *Pandora.*

Nothing on his person would incriminate Sykes, if he were accosted. Everything was in his head, safely tucked away. Plans. Schedules. Contact names. Wiring diagrams.

The modern assassin's most effective tool was his mind.

Especially when stalking the most elusive, the most dangerous creature in the history of mankind.

The AIs who thought themselves gods.

Sykes smiled to himself.

Deicide was such a lovely job title.

He turned a corner and headed down the little side street into what he would have called the Kasbah on his home world. Narrow streets, not much larger than alleys, running hither and yon at angles and in directions personally intended to insult Euclid and Jefferson.

Old Ithome. Pre-starflight, or rather, Hiatus-era, since all worlds save one were the result of starflight, and that one was dead.

A city from the *Time of Darkness*.

Sykes imagined he could smell fish oils on the bricks of the streets. That, and sweet burning incense from a strange little boutique he passed that appeared to be a Chinese apothecary.

Wonders of the modern universe.

He continued past a noodle shop barely bigger than the cook inside before he found his destination.

The store dealt in exotic books for the most part. In an era when almost all human knowledge was available at your fingertips, especially on *Ballard*, some people still preferred the mass and gravity of an actual book. Paper printed with ink and bound in cloth or leather.

There were books everywhere. In the front window, proudly displayed. Stacked on every shelf on every wall. Piled carefully on any surface flat enough and sturdy enough to handle them.

Old books had a smell unique to themselves. It had permeated the wooden shelves that lined most of the shop, possibly even worked its way into the old stone of the walls themselves.

The door had a little brass bell on it that had tinkled when he entered. It seemed to summon a small gray tabby cat from somewhere in back.

Sykes was inspected and sniffed. The cat suffered to be scratched with a low rumbling purr for a few seconds, before she suddenly scampered off.

Kitties.

When he stood up, the shop-keeper had appeared as well.

In late-night videos, the merchant in a place like this was always played by a middle-aged male actor with a penchant for seediness. Usually pudgy and bald as well. Today was a welcome change.

A woman had appeared behind the waist-high counter. Sykes was about average height for a man these days, bland and entirely unmemorable of appearance, as was a useful necessity in this line of work.

This woman looked him in the eye.

She was rail thin and tall, with skin the color of his first morning mocha and black, curly hair that had been buzzed with the shortest trimmer setting possible, leaving just enough to hint at how rich it might be if she let it get longer.

The face was merely average, which was a let-down, given the intelligent twinkle in her eyes as she greeted him.

"Good day, sir," she said in a low alto voice. "What brings you to *Ballard?*"

He studied her for a jarred moment, sure that no part of his disguise had given him away. And yet…

She smiled at his quiet confusion.

"Books are a small family," she continued merrily. "There are only so many bibliophiles around, and all of them are regulars in my shop. Ergo, traveler from off-world."

Sykes smiled back. Of course, a careful observer would take note of such things. And the signs had all been correct, according to Imperial Intelligence.

He flexed his hands to relax and looked carefully at the woman.

"I was hoping you might have something about the ancient Greeks of the Homeworld. Specifically, I am interested in the woman Clytemnestra. Would you have a modern translation of the *Oresteia?*"

For a moment, her eyes got hooded and reserved, although the smile never wavered.

Probably the last person she had expected to have walk into her shop this morning. Better and better.

"If I don't…" she said carefully. She casually moved sideways a step, closer to the counter. To an average person, it probably would have looked normal as her hand disappeared from sight. "…I'm sure I can locate something. What language would you be looking for?"

Sykes was sure her hand had just caressed something interesting. Whether it was an alarm button or a weapon remained to be seen.

Seven major trade tongues had been dominant, before the fall of humanity. *Ballard* was primarily bi-lingual in English and Kiswahili, a result of the refounding, even though Bulgarian was generally dominant in the *Republic of Aquitaine* and the *Fribourg Empire*.

Sykes relaxed another notch. She knew the code sequence necessary for identifying complete strangers that needed to be friends.

"I had my heart set on Kiswahili," he replied, volleying the identification set back to her. "And I will be in town for some time, so it is not an emergency."

He watched her hand emerge from under the counter again. If this was a trap, she might just shoot him right here and his mission would be over.

Instead, the hand was empty. She smiled lightly.

"If you would like to wait, I can make some tea," she replied, finally completing contact, "or you can leave your contact information and I will call when I know more."

Sykes pulled a calling card from an inside pocket and crossed the distance to stand before the counter. He quickly pulled a pen from a jar and scrawled a note on the back.

"I'm staying at the Stellar Dolphin," he said, all business now, "although I have not checked in yet. Please feel free to contact me there at any time when you have news."

She picked up the card and read it carefully, front and back.

"Very good, Mr. Sykes," she replied. "I'm sure I will be able to help you."

"Thank you," he said, turning and exiting the shop quickly.

He spent the next hour wandering the Kasbah, shopping randomly and buying occasional trinkets he would take with him or leave behind, depending on how the next few weeks went. It was important to be invisible by being exactly what he seemed, a semi-wealthy tourist on a tame little adventure.

Nothing to arouse suspicion.

The hotel staff was as obsequious and fawning as the hotel's reputation promised. Not for him to be in a youth hostel on this mission. No, wealthy enough to stay well and be treated right, not so wealthy as to be memorable.

Always in character.

The concierge approached diffidently as Sykes stood in the Grand Foyer and marveled at the lustrous marble walls and floors, covered with mosaics and tapestries celebrating the oceans of *Ballard*.

"Mr. Sykes?" the man asked.

He turned and smiled vacuously. "Yes?"

The concierge handed him a small envelope that appeared to have been hand-made from a very heavy linen paper.

"A Miss Krystiana Lemieux left you a message that she had found your book and would you be available to discuss it over dinner, sir?"

"Very good," Sykes said, slipping the envelope into an inner pocket of his jacket and pulling out a twenty Lev note to hand to the man. Again, enough to guarantee good service, not so much as to stick in the man's mind. "Thank you."

Upstairs in his room, Sykes inspected the note. There was nothing more to it, except a phone number to call, once he was settled. Her voice was breathy when she answered.

"Hello?" she said.

"Mistress Lemieux, this is Mister Sykes, returning your call," he replied. They had passed the stage where everything was of necessity choreographed, so he was free to let the conversation wander where it will. "I would greatly appreciate the opportunity to take you out to dinner to discuss the tome you have located, but I am unfamiliar with Ithome. Perhaps you could recommend a restaurant where we might dine. On me. I have a very nice budget for this quest."

"In that case," she replied, suddenly much brighter, "let me call in a favor and get us reservations at McClaren's, atop the Sandy Head Tower. Will eight o'clock work for you?"

"That would be perfect, madam. I look forward to dinner."

Step one complete.

Sykes glanced out the window at the southern sky. *Alexandria Station* was just about to pass below the horizon.

You're next.

CHAPTER IX

Date of the Republic May 30, 394 Ladaux

The office was small, and completely devoid of character. Just a desk with a hard chair, two slightly more comfortable chairs in front, and a side-board with nothing on it. No art marred the walls, no decoration, nothing.

Loncar assumed that Brand had requisitioned the room at some point, but had obviously left no personal touch. No fingerprints. And Brand had been a fixture among the fixers of the senate, the men and women in the shadows who smoothed the surface, for decades.

Nothing the man did left any impressions on anyone, except for his shaved head. That was Brand's only affectation.

"Thank you for joining me, First Fleet Lord," he began. "This won't take long, and then we can return to our respective needs."

Loncar sat in the nearer chair. Brand wouldn't offer anything to drink. These meetings never lasted. Only the strategy dinners that Loncar hosted in a private room at his clubs ran long enough.

"Go on," Loncar said, a low rumbling sound almost a growl. Keller had still left him unsettled.

Brand opened a drawer in the desk and withdrew a small folder. It had the crimson cover of a fleet intelligence summary, such as the First Lord's office regularly produced for the politicians, and it was sealed with a white ribbon, as was custom when the document was in public.

He rested it on the desk without opening it and placed a proprietary hand on the cover.

"This just came in from my sources this morning," Brand began. "Jessica Keller is currently en route to the *Ballard* system for an expected engagement with Emmerich Wachturm of the *Fribourg Empire* Navy."

"*Ballard*?" Loncar asked, fuzzy on his cartography. It was an older sector of the Republic where he rarely visited. "College, or something?"

"Correct," Brand answered. "The *University of Ballard* is famous for its pre-hiatus library. According to the report I have skimmed, Keller apparently said or did something to provoke Wachturm and the *Fribourg Empire* into launching an assault on the university, and the First Lord dispatched her to stop him."

"Blackbird?" Loncar asked.

"I beg your pardon, First Fleet Lord?"

"Wachturm, you said," he replied. "Does he have the Blackbird with him? *IFV Amsel*?"

"Ah," Brand smiled tightly. "Of course. Yes sir, he does. The battleship *Amsel* and the ship's usual compliment of escorts are expected to accompany it."

"Hmph. Keller take anything besides the squadron she left with yesterday?"

"No," Brand replied with a slight, evil smile. "Just *Auberon*, *Stralsund*, and the two destroyers. Plus the escort and whatever forces are at *Ballard* when they arrive."

"Then it will be a slaughter," Loncar concluded. "Wait. You said Keller provoked it? How?"

"Apparently she encountered Wachturm during her diplomatic mission to *Lincolnshire* and insulted the man," Brand said with a triumphant tone. "We have not completed digesting Keller's own briefing report of her mission. It lasted nearly a year, and fills several volumes of material."

"Not hard to believe," Loncar agreed, mentally elsewhere. "The woman is a menace."

He shifted gears mentally and studied the bald man behind the desk.

"Why am I here?"

Brand smiled. It was not a pleasant smile, for all that the man went out of his way to cultivate suave. He was the kind of person who thought about knives in the dark too much for polite company.

"The Committee would like to call you as a friendly witness, a character witness," Brand said. "An expert on fleet affairs who can shed light on the recent activities of Keller and First Lord Kasum. And do so in a very public forum."

Loncar considered the implications of Brand's words. The committee. The Senate *Select Committee for the Fleet of the Republic of Aquitaine.* The civilian control of the fleet, and by extension, much of the Republic itself.

He had heard rumors, mostly from Senator Tomčič. He and Andjela had been comrades-in-arms for a long time. The Premier himself, in a towering rage, threatening the entire committee behind closed doors. With Kasum watching his back and their embarrassment. Over Keller. Not something discussed over dinner, except in hushed tones.

The urge for revenge on those two men would be great.

"When?"

"The sooner we can strike," Brand replied, "the better it will be. This information will leak eventually. If we can leak it first, we can control the news with it. Could you be ready to give your testimony in seven days?"

"Why wait that long?"

"It takes time to assassinate a man in the court of public opinion, First Fleet Lord. Especially men as popular as the Premier and the First Lord. Events are already moving, but not that quickly. We needed you on board before we sprang."

"I see," Loncar purred, implications and aspirations overtaking him. *First Lord Loncar.* Yes, that would be just the proper due to a man who had spent his entire career laboring in the shadow of his lessers. Finally, he could get the appreciation long denied him by Horvat and Kasum.

Finally.

"Yes, Brand," he said. "That would be perfect."

CHAPTER X

CR-264 so rarely got to do this.

Tomas Kigali had taken days to plot the specifics of this maneuver, working closely with all the other crazy people on his staff. There had been a lot of giggling.

After all, if you were going to drop a great big brick in a really small swimming pool, you might as well go all in with it.

Normally starships, even warships, came out of Jumpspace at a respectable distance from the edge of the gravity well. It wasn't like there was a boundary marker sitting there. And the edge of a gravity well was a squishy thing to begin with, being more of a broad zone painted on a map with a brush than cut with a razor. But still…

And they certainly came out at a reasonable speed. That was just prudent navigation. Space might be huge and vast and almost empty, but there was usually no reason to push your luck.

Unless you were in a hurry. Or trying to set a new record.

After all, the chances of someone actually being close enough to be a navigational risk were astronomically low. Even when dealing with astronomical scales of things.

CR-264 was running down the edge of the gravity well like a boar on an icy hill. Kigali had shut off all the warning buzzers. They were just getting annoying at this point, telling him he shouldn't be doing exactly what he had planned.

At some point, the JumpSails would finally cry "Enough" and kick him back into real space. They would probably need a full recalibration at that point, but he was confident his staff could hold the matrix together at least enough to get half a light-year away, if they managed to end up landing in the middle of the Red Admiral's fleet, firing into the remains of the orbital station. They had that planned as a backup.

There.

Half the nav board went red as the matrix popped, like a soap bubble on a child's finger.

CR-264 was back into realspace.

And now, the stupid part.

"Sensors, go wide," he called into the comm. "I don't care who they are, I just want to make sure we don't hit them at this speed."

"Gotcha," someone on the gun deck called. They were all awake and scanning their little area, in addition to what the actual sensor crew was doing.

CR-264 was moving at the sort of speed that would normally get him a very rude talking to from Flight Control. At least until he explained the situation. Then they might shut up. They might not. You never knew with bureaucrats.

He was flying forward at the sort of attack speed that one of *Auberon's* melee fighters might have a hard time matching. That was okay as well. He wasn't planning to come into this place at a polite speed, anyway. The record books said Station-to-Orbit when measuring records like this. If he did a slingshot longways around the planet, and he would at this speed, no question, it still counted.

After all, he was racing eternity here. Not just every other navigator out there today, but every other one that would be born. Stiff company. Gotta make them look like pikers when they saw his flight time.

"Bridge, gun deck," a voice called. "No Imperials are identifying themselves right now. The station is intact, near as I can tell. Orbital Control is pissed."

"They'll get over it," Kigali replied, half under his breath. "Comm, tell Orbital Control to bother someone else and to assign us an orbital approach to *Ballard Flight Station* so we can get close enough to send a shuttle over. Then find someone in charge over there and get me a private channel with full military scramble enabled."

No point in starting a complete civilian panic. At least not yet. That would happen in a few hours, when the news got out. Right now, he needed the senior Command Centurion in charge over there activating all those silly contingency plans they had never expected to use.

Hopefully, someone had been keeping them up to date, and even training on them every once in a while. Otherwise, this was going to get very ugly, very quick.

Kigali could tell that the man was going to be difficult as soon as he appeared on the comm screen. There was just a look to him. The first words made it obvious.

"This is Command Flight Centurion Timofeh Ariojhutti," he growled, just short of a bellow. "What the hell do you think you're doing, flying like that in my space, mister?"

Kigali took a deep breath before responding. That sort of loud hard-ass act probably worked on people that didn't have to measure up to Jessica Keller on a daily basis. Here, it just made the man look like an amateur.

And Ariojhutti looked like a former fighter jock, that sort of average height starting to spread out around the middle from too much time flying a desk.

"Are we on a secured channel, Command Flight Centurion?" Kigali answered quietly.

"A what? Why?"

Kigali stared at him hard, almost dismissively. It was one thing to act tough. Tomas Kigali wasn't in the mood to take any shit from some bumpkin in a boring defense slot, protecting a station in the middle of the *Republic*, even if it was about to become the front lines.

"My name is Command Centurion Tomas Kigali. I have priority orders from the Premier of the Republic, Command Flight Centurion," Kigali said quietly. He let his anger underline his words. "You can secure this channel, or you can wait until I arrive by shuttle to personally deliver them. Your choice."

That got the man's attention. Apparently, big-fish-in-a-tiny-pond syndrome. Kigali considered knocking the man down and kicking him, at least metaphorically.

Maybe metaphorically.

Apparently, Ariojhutti got that message. He reached down and pushed a button off-screen. A red border appeared around the screen.

"Go ahead," he said, much quieter.

Command Centurion Tomas Kigali raised himself slowly to his full height. It wouldn't change how he appeared on the other man's screen, but pilots tended to be short, or at least compact, especially compared to his own lanky height. It would give him just one more edge in this *discussion*.

"Premier Horvat and First Lord Kasum have declared martial law in the *Ballard* system, Ariojhutti," he said simply.

The man blinked in utter shock, but said nothing.

Score a point for politeness, then. Or at least manners.

"Very soon, an Imperial task force is going to arrive, intent on destroying *Alexandria Station*," Kigali continued. "*Ballard Flight Station* will probably be second or third on their list of things to blow up. I got here first because I could. The rest of my team will be along in five or seven days. We're going to try to stop him. You're going to help."

"I'm in charge of this system's defenses," the man responded angrily, but quieter than before.

Kigali considered several responses. Most of them were rude, verging on unacceptable in polite company. Even among command centurions. He decided the man needed a good smack to the side of his head, if just to get his attention.

"The enemy force will be the Imperial battleship *Amsel*, with her cruisers and escorts, Ariojhutti," Kigali said simply. Best to just stick the knife straight in and be done with it. "Your flight wing would last about three minutes against them. Your job, right now, is to get me a meeting with the civilians down on the planet so I can deliver my orders, and then to start evacuating the two stations so we can keep civilian casualties to a minimum. Later, we'll have to fight Admiral Wachturm."

"What are you bringing to the dance?"

Kigali had to give the man credit. The loud, obnoxious blowhard of a pilot who had started this conversation had slowly morphed into something approximating a professional. Give them a problem. Let them solve it. Maybe he wouldn't have to let Jessica dress Ariojhutti down, after all.

Maybe.

"A strike carrier, a battlecruiser, two destroyers, me, and you."

"Against a battleship task force? Are you insane?"

"We don't have a choice, Ariojhutti, unless you want to let him just waltz in here and start blowing things up. Plus, we do have one thing on our side."

"What's that, Kigali?"

"Jessica Keller will be in command."

Because, really, this was the Red Admiral. If Jessica couldn't do it, nobody else was going to manage.

CHAPTER XI

"What exactly is it?" Jessica asked Moirrey as they stood on the flight deck, surrounded by crews feverishly working on esoteric tasks for the fighters and bombers that would be going into battle in a matter of days.

"Is no mine, ma'am," the evil, engineering gnome, now centurion, replied. "Oz did this hisself."

Jessica turned to her chief engineer for an explanation.

The man had a serene smile on his face. Anywhere else, she would have taken that at face value, but Moirrey had specifically asked her to come down to the flight deck to witness more *Mischief*.

The objects of the discussion squatted before them.

They looked like shuttle craft. Two of them. If you have gotten a group of Academy students drunk and asked them to assemble them. Without instructions. In the dark.

Certainly, not something one would be proud to show off. And yet, six more engineers, Able-bodied Spacers and First Rate Spacers, all seemed quite pleased with themselves.

Tickled, even.

"Oz?" Jessica asked. It was not a nickname she had heard before, but obviously things were a little more relaxed down in the engineering bays.

The chief engineer nodded at her with a prim little smile. He reminded her of nothing so much as a mother hen overseeing a brood of bright, chirpy chicks.

"It is indeed a rare thing," he began, "when either the operations or capital budgets allow my department the freedom to exercise a degree of artistic liberty and autonomy in our work, at least on a scale such as this."

He gestured expansively at the mess around them. His team had taken over an entire section of the bay, with all of the fighter craft stored vertically along the walls in their little racks, like bottles of beer cooling in the refrigerator.

"Here," he continued, "there were no budgetary constraints worth mentioning. Indeed, with access to two complete fleet weapons packs, plus a few items we were able to effect trades for with the ground crews, I believe we have introduced two lovely new catalog items into the *Mischief* folder that Imperial Admiral Wachturm will not be expecting, simply because, while he may make a study of young Moirrey's work, this represents an entirely different methodology of cognition about the vagaries of warfare."

Vilis Ozolinsh had been born to one of the wealthiest and highest-profile of the Fifty Families that provided the governing backbone of the Republic. He should have been a line officer, or a Senator.

Jessica realized at that moment exactly what it had meant to her future that he had instead fallen in love with engineering as a very young man, instead of the traditional command track. He would have been a good Command Centurion. He was an excellent engineer.

If his family connections had managed to stick him out on the distant frontiers, so as to not have to think about the black sheep of the family, a lowly engineer, all the better.

He had been there when she needed him.

His smile gave him away. Butter would not melt in his mouth right now.

"What have you done, Oz?" Jessica asked, wrapping her head around this new person.

If his own folks could call him by a nickname, his commanding officer could make the effort as well.

He had a smile like Moirrey's. Jessica wondered who had originally picked it up from the other.

"With unfettered access to a full two weapons packs," he preened, "we were able to color well outside the lines, to quote one of Moirrey's favorite sayings."

He started walking towards the nearer of the two, Jessica, Moirrey, and the rest of the engineers trailing out behind him like a school of remorae trailing a shark.

"Each pack contains almost all of the components necessary for a vessel with a truly competent machine shop, such as ours, to repair almost any type or degree of damage to a standard transport shuttle."

He tapped the little ship with one hand, almost a loving caress as he spoke more to himself than to his audience.

Jessica suppressed a snort. She had seen what her *truly competent machine shop* had managed, especially when they had committed two separate pranks on *2218 Svati Prime* during the *Long Raid*, what historians and writers were starting to call *Keller's Raid*, despite everything she could do to dissuade them.

"In the past, that has not been of any great note, simply due to the limitation that *Auberon* neither carries such craft, nor has space for them during her everyday operations."

Oz turned and fixed her with a hard smile. Predatory. Indeed, a shark in calm waters. She had never seen him thus.

It was an exciting development. She hoped.

"Here, I was struck by an interesting notion of Imperial tactics from my Academy days."

"Go on," Jessica said. The less she spoke, the more he would.

"Indeed, Commander. Thank you," he said. "Normally, an Imperial vessel launching missiles will either target them to engage a class of vessel, such as our dreadnaughts, or aim them at the specific sensor signature of their intended victim."

His face grew more serious at this point. Jessica could see pain in them that hadn't been there before.

"At the *Battle of Petron*," he continued with a softer look and a nod, "they used the former technique to target the 4-ring Mothership *Kali-ma*, and in the course of the maneuvering, destroyed *Supernova* instead."

His voice had dropped to almost nothing.

Jessica still felt as if someone had punched her in the stomach.

For a moment, the flash of light as *Supernova* exploded flooded her mind. She felt her breath catch and tried to suppress the flinch she felt, but she knew he saw. Moirrey probably did as well. The others were to either side, and didn't know her as well.

But even they fell silent and somber.

Jessica hadn't realized how much her own loss had affected her crew, how much they apparently felt her pain.

She found some manner of solace there.

Eventually, she told herself, she would be able to remember Daneel without pain.

She just had to live long enough.

If there was such a thing as *long enough.*

A moment passed. Utter solemnity.

Jessica took a breath.

"So how would you solve this problem, Oz?" she asked as her voice began to settle.

"Ancient sailors," he replied, "mariners on water seas, used to have a legend about a creature that would call them by singing. A beautiful woman who turned out to be half-fish, luring them to their doom on the rocks."

"You mean sirens," Jessica guessed.

"Indeed, Commander, the bane of the seafarer on the Homeworld. Replicated here in the hopes of luring Imperials to their own special brand of doom."

Jessica let a single raised eyebrow ask her question.

"When launched, this shuttle craft, this Siren if you will, will emit a sensor signal so very comparable to that of *Auberon* that, when we briefly turn our own sensors down to almost nothing, Imperial missiles should instead begin to track on the shuttle, following it to their own doom. One hopes that we can lead an entire wave of such missiles so far astray that they are unable to recover and thus pose no greater threat."

"I see," she said. "The two shuttles are identical?"

"Oh, no, Commander," Oz oozed charm and confidence. "Although money was no object here, we simply did not have that much in the way of spare electronics that we could cannibalize for this particular occasion, given the constraints of time under which we labored."

Jessica followed again as he moved to the second shuttle. This one was in even worse shape. The bow section had a strange, dimpled appearance.

He pushed a button that would normally open the side hatch. She could tell that there was no hatch here, just a sheet of hull metal that had been quickly welded in place.

Instead, the entire bow section retracted away from the center, moving up, down, and to both sides on sliding hinges.

Jessica found herself staring at the nose of a number of missiles, stacked cheek-in-jowl in a honeycomb that filled the entire area where crew, passengers, and cargo would normally ride. She counted eleven warheads, ten of them red and the one in the exact center painted blue.

"And this, the Manticore," he continued. "Named for the ancient Persian monster with the body of a lion, the head of a man, and the tail of a dragon that shoots poisoned spines at its target."

Oz smiled wickedly.

"The entire craft is actually a missile, Commander," he said. "We used a spare control system and wired it in to run autonomously. When launched, it will fly in the direction programmed, until it either comes within a preset range of a target, or until a command is sent from *Auberon*. At that time, it will sequence out all of the missiles in rapid succession at a designated target or range of targets."

"And the blue one fires first?" Jessica asked, intrigued.

"One of Moirrey's Mark II Archerfish, sir," he replied. "I will let her explain."

Moirrey stepped up and caressed the hull in a manner similar to how Oz had done. It was almost perverse.

"You gots a wall of doom comings, ma'am," she chirped, her accent growing denser as her excitement grew, "yer gon' reply with every defense missile ya gots loaded. Right shame if a wee somebody blows them all up before they did nothin', ya knows?"

Jessica considered the implications and the tactics. It was an incredibly, monstrously expensive way to fight a battle, even by everyone's normal standards of missiles, primaries, and fighters.

That would count doubly so when modern training and naval architecture revolved around the fleet escorts, the frigates and the destroyers who escorted the larger vessels, the queens of the battlefield, into action.

But it was also going to be a very rude surprise for Admiral Wachturm.

And it would probably only work once.

They only needed it to work once.

It would be neck or crown when facing the Red Admiral at *Ballard*.

CHAPTER XII

The tiny forward conference room aboard *Stralsund* was just fore of the bridge, which generally meant it was used more than the primary conference room down a deck and a little aft.

It was second shift right now, so Arott had his senior officers available while the ship flew through the night of Jumpspace: first officer Doyle MacEoghain, tactical officer Galina Tasse, chief engineer Tiyamike Abujamal, and *Stralsund*'s pilot Ya'rah Mhasalkar.

"Okay, folks," Arott said to bring things to order and pointed to the folders everyone had brought with them. "You've had some time to review the *Mischief* file provided by *Auberon* before we left. Thoughts?"

Galina spoke first. She did that. "On the one hand, Commander," she said in her brusque tones, "it represents an absolute upheaval in modern warfare, at least until the Imperials come to grips with it and initiate counter-measures."

"And the downside?" Arott always expected the other shoe to drop with his tactical officer. That was who she was.

Galina could have been a model, she had the height and beauty, but she loved to blow things up too much. One of these days she would probably settle down and marry a politician or Fleet Lord. It was not today.

"It's completely insane, risk/benefit ratio-wise," she concluded. "This is Wachturm we're going to engage. He'll see through it."

"No, he won't," the first officer contravened her quietly.

"Doyle?"

Arott watched the man take a deep breath, looking for the right words.

"Okay, everybody knows he's the best *Fribourg* has, right?"

Heads around the table nodded.

"But have any of you really studied *Keller's Raid*? I mean in detail?"

Heads shook. These people were professionals. Sensationalism in the media was nothing to listen to.

"Thought not," Doyle continued. "I asked a friend in the First Lord's office to burn me a copy of Keller's operational report from *Lincolnshire* and *Corynthe*. Been reading that every spare moment."

Arott looked at his first officer a touch askance. That was getting very fine with ethical standards and legalisms. It was probably the right thing to do, all things considered, but it could be made to look bad in the wrong light. *Stralsund* didn't do things that way.

"What did you find?" Arott asked carefully, knowing that he might be abetting the crime, but unable to look away, like at a traffic accident.

Doyle tapped the table-top as he made his points. "So, *Third Iger*, all of *Keller's Raid*, culminating at *Qui-Ping*, then you move on to *Sarmarsh IV* and *First Petron*. I compared Jessica Keller to Emmerich Wachturm, since they represent key recent campaigns where they were on opposite sides of the planning."

Doyle took another breath, almost pained.

"I think she's better than he is," he said.

The room exploded in sound.

"Hear me out," Doyle cried over the noise.

Arott got everyone settled with a harsh look. They were supposed to be professionals here.

"What makes you say that, Doyle?" Arott asked quietly.

"Like I said, we all know Wachturm is the best the Empire has, right? Everybody agrees on that point. It's just that, when I look back at those battles, every single time, he goes for the linear approach. At *Third Iger*, he hid a couple of carriers on the backside of a small moon to jump out and ambush the carriers. But he had to have known that Loncar was in overall command and that a stunt like that might work. Someone like Nils Kasum or Jessica Keller wouldn't have fallen for such an obvious set-up. They might have even handed him his ass."

"What's your point, then?" Tiyamike Abujamal, the chief engineer, spoke for the first time.

"I think Wachturm is just phoning it in at this point," Doyle said earnestly. "He's been relying on the other guy making mistakes. Or being utterly hidebound. Doing stupid things and letting someone like Admiral Wachturm pounce."

Arott was listening with half an ear as he flipped the folder open to some of his notes. Come to think of it, his notes as he reread them tended to agree. *Linear thinking. Exotic, but within norms. Where's the genius who used to frighten us? Standard Imperial tactic. Etc.*

"So where does that leave us?" Galina had that stubborn look in her eyes.

Arott spoke up first. "It leaves us with a trump card, people."

He speared each of them in turn with a look. It was a hard look, from the man who commanded arguably the best ship in the *Republic of Aquitaine* Navy, the pride of Home Fleet.

Stralsund was the best. It behooved him to remind people of that occasionally.

"Two, actually," he said after a moment of thought. "First, he's expecting some variant of *Mischief*. On that, we can all agree, yes? Keller has staked her career on Centurion Kermode's artistry. It's gotten her this far, and we know she and Kermode are going to pull out all stops at *Ballard*."

Heads bobbed in agreement around the table. Arott pointed at his folder.

"Second, we've got firepower almost as good as a battleship. We don't have the shields to go toe-to-toe with *IFV Amsel* for very long, but we have maneuverability he doesn't."

Arott turned to the pilot, up until now silent.

"Mhasalkar," he said simply. "I know you never wanted to be a fighter pilot, but I'll need *Stralsund* to dance like a GunShip when we get close."

"Close?" Tasse asked tartly. "How close were you planning to get?"

Arott flipped his folder to a specific page, spun it around, and pointed.

"The tactical implications of that weapon, right there, Galina," he replied, "suggest knife fighting with Primaries. Close enough to spit on someone. I expect *Stralsund* might end up close enough to the escort frigates that they open up on us with their Type-1 defensive beams as we go by, instead of shooting at something more important."

Arott turned to his chief engineer.

"How much power can you put through the shield generators without having them fail in the middle of this fight? *Mendocino* will be along after the battle, so we can fix everything the next day, assuming we survive, but this might be the battle where *Stralsund* gets hammered into a six month drydock. Let's treat this like one of the epics going in, people."

Senior Centurion Abujamal got a pensive look in her eyes. Her eyes were already dark, as was her skin, so he could never tell if she paled or flushed. Not that she ever registered much emotion. Engineers were like that. Good ones, anyway.

"There is a list of ideas," she began. "A Bible, if you will, of crazy things you should never do in anything but the most extreme circumstances."

"Crazy?"

"Passed from chief engineer to chief engineer, down through the ages, Commander," she replied with a hint of a smile. "The really risky, stupid things they only briefly mention, mostly with warnings, in engineering school. I'll need you to sign an authorization form ahead of time."

That brought an eyebrow up. Arott started to say something, but she interrupted him.

"In peacetime, chief, the first nine on that list are guaranteed to bring you up before a court of inquiry. Even in battle, at least three are good for court martials, if you survive."

"How many are likely to blow us up?" Arott asked, just a touch sarcastic.

Abujamal got very serious instead.

"The odds are generally less than one in six," she said quietly. "At least until we start taking damage. Then it gets interesting. Is it worth it?"

Arott took his staff in with a serious look.

"I expect," he said sternly, "that based on Keller's reputation, we're going to be at the sharp end of the stick, going at it with an Imperial battleship and a battlecruiser. We'll have the two destroyers and *Auberon*'s flight wing backing us up, and maybe even *Auberon* herself, but we're going to be the point of fire for a lot of enemies. So yes, it is worth it."

He turned to the engineer.

"That reminds me, MacEoghain," he continued. "Did you have any suggestions on hiring our own Advanced Research Weapons Tech?"

"I've given it some thought, Commander," he replied, somewhat evasively. "I think *Stralsund* might be exactly the wrong vessel to have such a person hidden in the lower decks."

"How so?" Arott wasn't all that angry with the man. He had come to a similar conclusion, privately.

"Sir, the kinds of creative artist types, the bohemian engineer, if you will, they don't really fit well with a spit-and-polish unit like ours. Very few get assigned here. Most of them turn around and pretty quickly transfer out to smaller vessels, and generally not on the war frontier."

"Nobody? Not a single artist down there?" Arott asked seriously.

His first officer shook his head.

Arott nodded.

"When we get back, Doyle," he said, "we're going to change that."

It wasn't exactly a failure on his part as a commander. Not really. That was how the fleet worked.

He could tell, however, that Jessica Keller was going to up-end things.

If he wanted to continue to be among the best, he would have to learn from the best.

CHAPTER XIII

Date of the Republic June 2, 394 Ithome, Ballard

The evening had turned out to be even better than the day, with warm temperatures slowly fading to mildness under clear skies as Sykes walked across the courtyard of the tower. The entire body of the galaxy stretched overhead, a road of white stars running across three quarters of the sky tonight.

McClaren's, it turned out, occupied the top three stories of the thirty-seven-story Sandy Head Tower. The view from the bar was simply stupendous. Sykes could see the open ocean beyond the sheltering wall across the far side of the bay.

He had dressed the part this evening of the well-bred fop turned book collector. Slightly tweedy. A touch fussy. A boring if expensive suit. A glass of local red wine in one hand as he watched the room.

There was a game he played in settings like this, with crowds in bars, when he didn't have a specific mission. Sykes had spent nearly ten minutes calculating the fastest and most efficient way to kill every single person in the bar, from the burly bartender to the accountant in the corner hunkered over his salad.

It kept the reflexes sharp.

Krystiana Lemieux made an entire scene by herself when she entered, greeting the bartender and half the waitstaff by name, carried on the arm of the impetuous little man who managed McClaren's, the master of ceremonies seeing everything done just so for one of his special customers.

Sykes rose from his spot against the corner of the bar, and met her and her escort halfway. A book collector would be too fussy to kiss her on both cheeks, so he did not, settling for a simple handshake amid a swirl of abject flattery until the manager led them to a corner table and departed.

The view from here was even more spectacular. The original architect had demanded the engineer fold a single transparent sheet, obviously not simple glass, around a hard, square corner, leaving them with a view of all of the bay in one direction, and the southern portion of Ithome, plus the suburbs, in the other.

The wine steward and waitress were dealt with in short order.

Sykes found himself seated across from his contact as the restaurant's tide of restless energy receded. He had not taken great note of the woman as she had entered, focusing most of his concentration on everyone else around him, looking for other spies that might represent danger.

He took the time now, letting the calm silence stretch.

Lemieux had treated the evening, and his expense account, as an excuse to dress to the nines. It wasn't his money, so he didn't care. The results had been worth the risk of appearing in such a public venue. Nobody would even remember his face tomorrow.

She was wearing an outfit that was entirely backless, largely frontless, and appeared to be comprised of two pieces of bright green cloth, tied behind her neck and just wide enough to cover her small breasts from casual observation, provided she did not move suddenly. At least intentionally. The color complimented her dark brown skin.

The top was attached to a skirt cut asymmetrically, from her left knee to her right ankle, in a manner that should have been disturbingly wrong, but somehow worked.

She had taken the time to do her hair and makeup as if she were preparing to appear on a videocast.

While this woman was not a great traditional beauty, the effect was memorable. Men were glancing as subtly as possible at this woman, craving her as an object of outright lust. Women, if any more circumspect, were more likely to be staring daggers at her, or their dates. Probably both.

If anyone even remembered that there was a man with her, he would simply fade from memory.

Sykes had spent decades perfecting that technique.

He nodded to himself.

"This is within your normal range of expected public behavior?" Sykes asked her. They had several minutes before the salad course.

She smiled around a piece of fruit she was nibbling from her mixed drink. The face was that of a debutante. The voice was deadly serious. The smile never wavered. They might have been discussing the latest fashions as far as someone could tell from farther away.

"Entirely," she replied in a tone that suggested he should use his tradecraft to teach his own grandmother to suck eggs. "You are a wealthy off-world client that needs entertaining while we discuss outrageous prices for First Editions and dicker values against the possibility of fraud in the author's signature."

That caught him off guard. Sykes had never dealt in rare books. He had no idea how rampant that sort of corruption was. But then, he was an assassin, not a literary critic. Although he supposed that the two might not be that far removed, all things considered.

He nodded as a placeholder. This woman was a highly respected deep-cover agent. Obviously, she would know the proper bounds of behavior for a place like *Ballard*. He was the blundering outsider, reliant on a local to know the shoals and reefs.

In that, the rules and relations would be the same.

"This mission may compromise your cover to the extent that extraction is necessary," he said to fill the space.

She continued to nibble at the fruit with a coquettish tilt to her head. From across the room, a bubbly airhead serving as eye-candy for a wealthy businessman.

"So you are either assassinating the governor," she said without a trace of emotion on her face, "or attacking *The Station*."

The way she said it suggested that there was only one station in orbit. In a way, that was true. Almost every inhabited planet had at least a half-dozen orbital platforms of various sizes, for transshipping or manufacturing. *Ballard* was no different. But there was really only one that mattered here.

"The latter," Sykes said and took a sip of his wine.

She smiled as if he had just told a droll joke, but her eyes never changed.

"How grand of an attack are you planning?"

Sykes let his own smile turn frosty. "I will be a distraction and a guard at the rear door to keep someone from escaping. An Imperial Fleet will be arriving in approximately two weeks to destroy the station."

He watched her eyes grow slightly larger. She did not actually speak the words aloud, but he could read her lips as she repeated *Imperial Fleet* to herself.

Finally, she spoke.

"And who are you here to assassinate?"

"The *Sentience*."

"You're going to kill Suvi?" she whispered in sudden awe. "Is that even possible?"

"We are going to find out, madam," he replied with a pleasant smile. "That is my mission. To kill Suvi."

CHAPTER XIV

Date of the Republic June 2, 394 Fleet HQ, Ladaux System

"Are you sure?"

Nils scanned the report again, as if the words would change the second time he read them. The temperature in his office seemed to have dropped ten degrees in as many seconds, although he was sure it was just him.

"Confidence is extremely high, First Lord," the woman standing before him replied. That was almost her patent phrase in situations like this.

She had no name that he had ever been told. The section of Naval Intelligence where she worked was highly compartmentalized away from the rest of the Fleet, almost an appendix stuck on to the organization as an afterthought. Nils liked to think of them as ghosts, or the faeries of ancient legend that came out at night and magically did chores.

He had that sort of relationship with these people. Nils knew better than to ask them pointed questions. He would either get rebuffed, or outright lies.

"How high?" he countered. The words on the page still did not change when he read them again.

"This is one of our most trusted sources, First Lord," she said. "Someone in the Imperial Household itself who very infrequently feeds us information that has never been wrong."

"Thank you, then," Nils said, "I'll take it from here."

"Happy to serve, First Lord."

She opened the hatch and departed without another word. Nils knew better than to be offended. They weren't technically in the Fleet, that group, and certainly didn't answer to him in any social or legal sense of the word.

Faeries.

"Kamil," Nils called through the open doorway. "Could you come in, please?"

His assistant, his right hand, entered immediately. Kamil had known the signs attendant on such a visitation as well.

Bad news.

"Yes sir?"

"Find the Premier and roust him out of wherever he is, immediately, highest possible priority," Nils said, "while I figure out my next step."

"Right away, sir."

Nils watched the door close.

Very bad news indeed.

Tadej Horvat, the Premier of the Republic Senate, appeared on a small screen at an odd angle. Nils guessed he was using the video camera on his own secured comm, rather than relying on a public channel. Considering the message, that was probably the best choice.

"What's the emergency, Nils?" Tadej asked breathlessly. From the way the camera image bounced Tadej might be jogging up a flight of stairs.

"Are we secure, Tadej?" Nils asked.

"Yes," the Premier replied, "barring words that might be overhead as I pass people on the way to my office. Or should I be headed up to yours?"

"Yours is fine, Tad. This will take some time to resolve."

"What's important enough to roust me from dinner? Not that it was anybody critical."

"I am looking at an Intelligence Briefing Note that was just delivered to me. Long story short, there was never any risk that Wachturm was going to attack *Ladaux*. That was merely a ruse. This was planned as a surgical strike against *Ballard* only. In and out. I could have moved the entirety of Home Fleet to *Ballard* with almost zero risk."

"We suspected that already, Nils," Tadej replied. "Why the sudden emergency?"

"It's a trap," the First Lord replied flatly.

"Again, we knew that. Talk clearly please, Nils."

A moment of silence passed.

"Nils?"

"It's the timing, Tad," Nils finally said.

"How so?"

"The reports of the planned assault were timed to arrive on *Ladaux* on a specific day, Tadej," Nils said. "Specifically, the day *Auberon* got home."

Even on the tiny screen, Nils could see his friend's face pale. "Oh, dear."

"Yes," the First Lord replied. "The Red Admiral went to *Ballard* specifically to kill Jessica. And I handed him the blade."

"Okay," Tadej said. His image had stabilized, so apparently he had stopped moving. "What do we do next?"

"I'm going to take *Athena* and her consorts," Nils said, "and see if there's anything left to salvage when we get there."

At the very least, he could give his warriors a proper burial.

CHAPTER XV

"So what do we know of the *Sentience*, gentlemen?" Admiral Wachturm asked the group of intelligence professionals arrayed to the left about his briefing table, across from Captain Baumgärtner and his various command staff and lieutenants.

They were a necessary evil, these men. In a war to the death with *Aquitaine*, it was necessary to have people that lived in the shadows, fencing with one another. Better if they were the sort that enjoyed it.

They certainly weren't the type you invited to dinner. Or introduced to your daughters.

Emmerich held his counsel and waited for the one in charge to speak.

"The station that houses the *Sentience* was originally lifted into orbit above *Ballard* late in the second generation after they had achieved starflight. Their industrial base was sophisticated by that time and they were able to build a fairly large initial station. That was a little over twelve hundred standard years ago."

Emmerich nodded and took a drink of water to forestall himself from asking any questions at this point. The less time he had to spend with these men, the better. He considered again whether he should have the entire room disinfected and sterilized when they left.

That was just being petty, but they left a stench in any room, at least psychically.

"While we have deep cover agents in place and send occasional observation missions, we have never attempted to penetrate the security on the facility itself," the head agent continued. "While scholars and tourists are fairly free to come and go in the section of the station dedicated to the university, casual travelers are prevented from accessing the facilities section and the computer cores that house the *Sentience* itself."

"Where are those located physically?" Emmerich perked up. Most of this briefing would be a waste of time, background information that might spark a tactical idea or defense arrangement later. But the engineering aspects would be crucial.

"The station is actually an oblate spheroid, flattened at the poles, rather than a true sphere," the man replied. "If you envision it as an onion, accreting layers over the decades and centuries, the original fusion reactor and computer cores that were removed from *Kel-Sdala* are located at the very center."

Emmerich was surprised to hear such an artistic reference from one of the intelligence officers. He tended to think of them as the accountants of hell, rather than actual people. It was safer that way.

"Weak points?" Captain Baumgärtner piped up, taking notes literally in a paper notebook with an ink pen, a habit he had picked up over the years from his boss.

"The station itself is just shy of seven kilometers across the equator, and five and a quarter at the poles," the man replied, warming to his audience and sounding less like a bureaucrat and more like an Imperial gentleman. Go figure. "But almost all of the landing facilities are located on the equatorial belt, meaning fewer bulkheads horizontally than vertically, and generally weaker, at least on the university side of things. The station was not built to modern warship standards, but it was significantly over-engineered from the outset. *Intelligence* is of two minds as to the reason. First, it was possible that they built this to the specifications of the *Sentience*, planning this level of reinforcement so as to add all of the outer layers that have been accumulated in the time since. Alternatively, it may have been done to protect the station against tidal forces from *Ballard's* moon, which is going to occasionally be close enough to affect the station's superstructure."

"Are we aware of any defenses?" Emmerich asked keenly.

All the men around him, on both sides of the table, seemed to simultaneously recoil in horror at the thought of a *Sentience* in charge of modern naval weaponry.

"None on the station itself," the man replied quietly after a moment.

The men all started to breathe again.

"However," he continued, "there is a naval station in a different orbit. It has a few beam weapon emplacements, both Type-1 for defense and Type-3 for warships, plus an oversized flight wing, a full dozen M-5 *Harpoon* fighters, rather than the usual nine that a Republic force would normally field. Strictly second-line crews, generally dedicated to Search and Rescue and light customs enforcement. There are also two Revenue Tugs with twenty-man crews and extremely light ordinance. Nothing that would even be much of a threat to fighter craft, if we were a carrier."

"We will reduce it last," Emmerich said. "The *Sentience* is the greatest threat to mankind. Keller will be the most dangerous opponent."

"A question, Admiral," the Briefing Officer continued.

Emmerich nodded to the man.

"According to our research, the station could not be successfully evacuated in the time from our emergence to our expected engagement, even with time taken out for a significant naval engagement with *Aquitaine* forces."

"And?" Emmerich asked, keeping his temper in check.

"Will we be giving them time to completely evacuate the station before we destroy it?"

Emmerich nodded. These men would go into hell itself with him, but they wanted to see the bill of sale first. It was only proper, considering what they were about to buy.

"With luck," he continued, "the evacuation will be complete before this fleet arrives. The Emperor is not making war on civilians and scholars, so we have agents in place that will spread the panic far enough ahead of time that these people can escape. The plan is that they will carry the terror of watching us destroy the *Sentience* with them back to their homeworlds, but do so from the surface of the planet. The only thing we plan to kill on the station is the *Sentience* itself."

"I see," the man replied. "And is there a chance the *Sentience* could escape?"

"No," Emmerich said flatly. "I have sent someone along to specifically trap her, possibly to kill her. We are actually the misdirection element here, not the assassins."

The men around the table smiled and relaxed. Some of them with relief, that their naval careers would not be stained by such a mark, and the rest because assassinations in the night were their stock in trade.

CHAPTER XVI

Date of the Republic June 6, 394 Alexandria Station, Ballard

Sykes emerged from the secured customs area and entered into the gigantic mall area that surrounded the University of Ballard like a thick and cushy blanket. The University and the Station were both significant tourist draws, filters that passed hundreds of thousands of people rapidly through and kept their money behind.

Because it would shortly be a collector's item, especially when he got home, Sykes bought himself two t-shirts with the *University of Ballard* printed on the chest, wrapped around the school's logo, one in blue with gold letters, and the other reversed.

He was too professional to call it a trophy. Plus, it was the sort of thing tourists did, and he needed to maintain his cover.

It sounded good in his head. He was a god-slayer, after all.

He smiled to himself as he walked the grand space like a good little tourist.

Sykes had lunch in a sidewalk café because he could. It was a useful way to study the crowds that swelled and receded around him.

Ithome on the planet below was a fishing town and a port. It had that feel to it. *Alexandria Station* was a university town in every sense of the word. A village of twenty thousand students and instructors, with another thirty thousand people wrapped around that providing support services.

Everything was geared towards the university's needs, either financially, emotionally, or physically. Most generally, that meant students. Young men and women here to study, or here for advanced degrees.

Sykes was too old to pass himself off as a student, unless he had taken the time on a cover that required returning for a mid-life degree. There had not been enough time from the point this mission was activated to its probable completion, so he had fallen back on one of the old standbys, using the occupation of his primary contact as a his modus operandi. He at least had a passing exposure to old books, from a previous mission years ago, and could fake the rest appreciably.

If someone penetrated his cover in this short of a time, there was nothing he could do about it except chalk his death up to very bad luck. He certainly would never be traded home, once they figured out who he was.

A brief walk after lunch took him to a bookstore catering to both students and tourists. Again, anything to finance the school. Some students would always prefer to scrawl notes on paper, over having to flip back and forth electronically.

The literature section was boringly predictable, geared towards either the hundred or so ancient classics all students were expected to fake reading at one point or another, or the score or so modern pieces that showed off how bohemian a student was. It was almost like every university bookstore in the galaxy ordered from the same warehouse.

The engineering section was much more interesting. Sykes purchased a tome intended for the amateur civil engineer, showing off the entire station's infrastructure to an extent that really should have been classified if these people were serious.

He could see the original schematics of the station when it was built. Every major installation or upgrade was detailed in its own chapter, along with the engineering challenges and solutions that had been encountered and overcome.

Very little of it was new information. Sykes guessed that his original briefing materials had been based on a previous version of this very title, or a similar one.

Briefly, he considered how it would look to purchase such a book, given his cover identity as an antique book dealer. Tourist might be enough. If pressed, he could always refer to a non-existent niece with an engineering bent. *Aquitaine* believed in that silly nonsense of sexual equality. They would be excited that a woman had the audacity to learn the necessary mathematics.

Sykes purchased the book without incidence. Perhaps he was a touch too paranoid, but that was rarely a detriment in his daily work.

He set out to find his hotel. A glass of wine and an evening of reading would be a useful way to pass the time while he waited for Admiral Wachturm to arrive, the hounds driving the fox to the hunter.

CHAPTER XVII

Date of the Republic June 10, 394 Jumpspace en route to Ballard

She knew better than to work herself into exhaustion, as appealing as the idea sounded. Instead, Jessica was going to bed at what Marcelle considered a reasonable time, and working to reset her body clock so that she would be at her peak of wakefulness when they arrived at *Ballard*, just in case the Red Admiral was already there and they had to come out firing.

Auberon was three days out from their navigational rendezvous with the rest of the squadron and Jessica needed to be sharp. *Brightoak* and *Rajput* she could count on. *Stralsund*, for all the implied excellence of the crew, was still a wild card.

This wasn't going to be a mass fleet maneuver, battlecruisers in the van with the destroyers, escorting dreadnaughts and carriers into battle. Nor was it going to be the antiseptic ranged engagements of two flight wings dueling for supremacy before chasing the losing side's carriers away.

No, this was going to be a tavern brawl that spilled out the front door and into the muddy street. In the middle of a thunderstorm.

Unless things were completely upended on the Imperial side, it would be one battleship and all her attendants, coming down the gravity well at them full speed, guns blazing.

Hopefully, the Red Admiral had maintained his traditionalist approach. If the situations were exactly reversed, Jessica might have taken the time to attach an Escort Carrier or Carrier Tug to the Imperial forces, just to keep *Aquitaine* honest.

Everything she had planned for when she got there hinged on Wachturm not pulling a complete rabbit out of his hat.

Given the time windows, she knew he was counting on encountering the exact forces that had won at *Petron*, barely three months ago: *Auberon*, *Brightoak*, *Rajput*, and *CR-264*. Had there been more time, she would have run to *Petron* and picked up the rest of her other fleet, the *Corynthe* 4-ring Mothership *Kali-ma*, her flagship; and the carriers *King Arnulf* and *Warlock*, plus whoever else wanted to come along. That would have been enough firepower to take down even the Red Admiral.

Jessica felt her breath catch. His face was suddenly there in her mind as she started to fall asleep.

Warlock.

Daneel Ishikura.

The pirate she had fallen in love with, only to watch him die protecting her at the *Battle of Petron*.

Something else to lay at the Red Admiral's feet. He might not have pulled the trigger, but his fingerprints were all over the strategic operation she had stumbled into at *Sarmarsh IV*.

It had been an Imperial mission to a group of pirates, led by the Red Admiral. He had obviously intended to help them overthrow their own King of the Pirates, knowing that the ensuing chaos would harm a *Republic of Aquitaine* ally in *Lincolnshire*, and require *Aquitaine* to commit more forces to that border when they could ill afford it.

A stroke of strategic genius, worthy of Admiral Wachturm's legend.

Nobody had been prepared for her to arrive and stomp into the mess, let alone manage to stop it, and then top that by being crowned Queen of the Pirates herself. That would have been acceptable, had Daneel survived.

Some days, she still wasn't sure she wanted to live. Only her various duties kept her going.

Auberon. Aquitaine. Corynthe.

Warrior. Command Centurion. Queen of the Pirates.

She dreamed of Daneel.

Jessica couldn't remember any other person that had touched her heart as Daneel had.

Aquitaine was a republic led by the Fifty Families, intermarried and interlocked clans that dominated all aspects of society.

She was just a girl from a lower-middle-class family, and had been identified young and groomed for the Fleet. Smart, capable, successful, but not someone with any great value in terms of the sorts of dynastic marriages that the wealthy and powerful planned.

At least, not before.

Now, she was a famous naval officer in her own right. That might have guaranteed entry into such a marriage by itself. That she was also a barbaric foreign queen with her own fortune would just be frosting on someone else's dynastic wedding cake.

If she cared.

Daneel was gone.

Loud, brash, arrogant, with a smear of grease under one eye, fighting fires from when she had come over the horizon and destroyed his base out from under him. Or later, lying in bed after a duel and as assassination attempt, asking if marriage was such a bad idea. Jessica could still taste the rage that had bubbled over, telling him to learn the *Aquitaine* way if he wanted to court her.

The tricks your subconscious plays on your words.

She hadn't meant it to come out that way. Consciously.

Probably.

And yet…

He had gone and done exactly that. Reinvented himself as an *Aquitaine* gentleman, forswearing all the barbaric finery of *Corynthe* to dress for *Ladaux*. Learning to harness stillness and let her energy wash over him without staining.

Touching him, over *Callumnia*. Feeling his heart race.

Making love to him.

Watching him die at the *Battle of Petron*, his own 4-ring crossing her stern to distract all the missiles.

Supernova, dying like her namesake.

Jessica found herself on the black, featureless plane again, dreaming.

She hoped it was only a dream.

The sky was gray, the color of ashes the morning after a fire. No stars marred its cold perfection. The ground was a polished black stone that was not slick, but still felt like the surface of a gigantic black diamond.

Daneel stood there, tall and laughing and alive. He wore the muted tones he had adopted when he decided to become more than a pirate, more than an enemy, more than a friend.

His smile warmed her from the sudden cold bite in the air.

The daemonic Red Admiral appeared behind Daneel as she watched. She tried to cry out, but was unable to make a sound or move a limb to save her lover.

A fiercely-glowing red blade appeared in the monster's hand. The creature smiled at her as he drove it into Daneel's back and out through his chest.

Her lover's smile vanished as the pain came over him. He tried to say something to her, but no words came.

Instead Jessica watched Daneel collapse to his knees, fall to the floor, die.

She felt herself transform, as before, facing this terrible great daemon made red flesh.

She became again *Kali-ma*, the Goddess of War, as the Red Daemon advanced on a second victim, a young woman with honey-blond hair in bangs and a French-braid.

Jessica had never actually met the AI named Suvi, but she dream-knew who the woman was.

Suvi wore a green uniform, not quite as dark as *Aquitaine*'s, but obviously related. An ancestor, if you will, with a short-brimmed forage cap and a large belt buckle made of polished bronze. Jessica recognized the logo of the *Concord* as the symbol on the buckle and the button on the cap.

Suvi did not wait passively for the Red Admiral, this ancient being. This was no faerie tale princess, helpless and bereft. Instead, she was poised. Unarmed, but unwilling to become a victim.

The bloody red blade transformed into a giant battlesword in the daemon's hands as he swung at Suvi. Jessica/*Kali-ma* blocked it with their *main-gauche*, even as they swung their saber in response. The daemon conjured his own blade and blocked her strike.

They struggled, titans trading blows. Blood flowed. Sparks showered the ground. Anvils rang in anger.

Jessica/*Kali-ma* felt the daemon's blade strike home in her chest, even as her own gutted the monster.

They fell side by side to the black stone, life leaking out.

At least I'll see Daneel again.

Death embraced her.

Jessica awoke to partial darkness. She could feel where tears had run backwards down her face while she slept, leaving her hair damp.

She sat up with a cry of pain, loss, anger, betrayal.

Something.

Marcelle was in the corner, reading by a small light.

For a moment, they simply stared at one another.

"Doc can give you something to sleep," Marcelle said finally.

"I want the pain, Marcelle," Jessica replied, knowing it to be the absolute truth. "It reminds me that I'm alive, that I have things yet to do, that I owe that man a terrible price in blood."

At *Ballard*, she intended to collect.

CHAPTER XVIII

Date of the Republic June 6, 394 Ladaux System

Nils suppressed his twitch before it manifested itself as he entered the room. At least he thought he did.

This wasn't his flag bridge anymore. And hadn't been for more than half a decade. He wasn't supposed to sit at the head of the table. He was just a passenger aboard *Athena*.

Still, apparently his stifled movement had been seen. At the head of the projection table, First Fleet Lord Petia Naoumov smiled wryly at him. She suppressed it just as quickly and nodded instead, her straight black hair pulled into a tail with a dark green ribbon that matched the rest of her uniform.

"First Lord," she said, gesturing to *Athena*'s flag bridge around them as he stood. "I would be honored if you would give the order."

It was a warm smile she gave him. They had been friends for nearly thirty years.

Nils looked around and took a seat at the foot of the table. Of the twenty or so faces looking up from their stations, only a handful were still here from his time in command.

His look got serious as he studied these men and women around him. Few knew what was going on, only that they had suddenly been detached from Home Fleet and given priority to load up and depart. Given the alacrity with which *Auberon* had just left, many could draw their own conclusions. Some might even be right.

"Squadron, this is First Lord Kasum aboard *Athena*. I have the flag," he said carefully, knowing what probably awaited him at the other end of this journey. "Take her out."

It surprised him when the crew gave a cheer. But then, they were warriors aboard the Flagship of the *Republic of Aquitaine* Navy. There was no better berth available. These people were the best.

And it was certainly the first time in several generations that a First Lord had taken physical command of a force in the field. That's what the fleet lords were for. Still, this was not a task for anyone else. He had made the mistake. He needed to own it.

Around him, faces turned to screens and tasks. *Athena* had already undocked from the station. The engines came live now and she surged outward to the edge of the gravity well, a queen bee surrounded by a hive of activity. Around her, her oversized destroyer squadron and four cruisers of various designs fell in.

It was a lovely force. An entire battle squadron, led by a Star Controller, a vessel that combined the firepower of a dreadnaught and a fleet carrier's entire flight wing.

Powerful, capable, nearly unstoppable.

Now if only there would be anything left at *Ballard* to salvage…

Nils settled into the seat across from First Fleet Lord Naoumov's desk and let the air out of his lungs noisily. He could have done this in his own suite. He was First Lord, after all. And *Athena* had an entire wing of cabins and conference capabilities designed to transport important senators and their staffs in full comfort. He had already appropriated the best one when he came aboard.

He was punishing himself by doing this in her office, on her turf.

"Talk to me, Nils," Petia said simply.

"What rumors have you heard?" he replied.

Not evasive, but not ready to own up to such a potentially catastrophic mistake, even with a woman he had known since their first tour of duty together. Hell, Nils had even introduced her to her future husband, his second cousin Artur.

Still, nobody likes to fall on their sword.

"*Auberon* was home just long enough to load up for bear-hunting and leave," Petia replied carefully. "Her little escort broke just about every navigation rule in the book and nobody said a peep, so his orders came from the top. You sent Arott and *Stralsund* with her with almost no warning. Now we've got a serious task force running for Jumpspace as hard and fast as we can and we've plotted a course to *Ballard*."

She paused to consider him.

"Are we the cavalry?" she said finally.

"I really wish we were, Petia," he replied, his voice heavy. "But unless you can get us there in under ten days, I'm afraid all we'll do is chase off the Red Admiral if he's still around, and then pick up the pieces."

"The Red Admiral?"

"Emmerich Wachturm, Petia. It's a term Jessica Keller picked up on the *Lincolnshire* border. We found out he was launching a surprise raid on *Ballard* and I sent Jessica to stop him. I would have sent you if I had known the truth."

"What's that, Nils?"

"It's a trap. He was never going to launch a raid on *Ladaux*, like other reports had suggested. So Jessica is going to take on Wachturm and *Amsel* with *Auberon*, *Stralsund*, and a lot of finesse. He's not there to attack *Alexandria Station*, like we originally thought, although he will destroy that if he gets the chance. He's there to kill Jessica."

"Well, I can't get us there in less than sixteen days, Nils, but I'll have the squadron push it. The old record was a little over fourteen days. I looked when you told us where, but Tom Kigali has probably blown that out of the water. We'll get there as soon as a squadron this size can."

"For all the good it will do, Petia. For all the good it will do."

CHAPTER XIX

Date of the Republic June 11, 394 Jumpspace en route to Ballard

Sleep had been elusive. Jessica knew better than to simply lay there and let herself fret. Certainly, Marcelle would be awake if she was. At least this way, Marcelle could get some reading in.

Jessica needed the fighting robot tonight. She could only relax in the center of *Valse d'Glaive*, the dance of swords. Meditation in motion.

She took her place in the middle of a cleared area about six meters on a side, wearing a skin-tight black bodyglove. She had considered the royal black uniform that Moirrey and Desianna had worked up. But her heavy combat boots were the only part of the long-standing-customs of the ring she was willing to disrupt tonight.

This outfit showed off her powerful thighs and shoulders, muscular curves that she knew would turn to fleshiness and eventually fat if she let herself go. That was a daily battle she was never going to lose. A headband, black with the gold logo of *Petron*, dominated her forehead, keeping her face dry and a few stray wisps of hair out of her eyes, even as the rest was tied with a scarlet ribbon.

In her left hand, she held a long, straight, single-edged sword, the *saber*. Instead of something more exotic, it was made of simple steel. Other alloys, more exotic, lighter, stronger, were possible, but she was too much a traditionalist. Steel it would remain.

In her right hand, the much shorter blade, heavier, with a pronounced cross-guard instead of a basket protecting her left hand. The *main-gauche*. Literally, it was the left hand, except it wasn't.

She settled herself and then dropped into a fast squat once, bouncing back up to make sure everything was still flexible.

"Fighting Robot activate," she called across the space to the humanoid combat drone facing her. "Challenge Rating Eight."

Once, rating four had been enough for a day like this. Before Daneel. Before Ian Zhao. Before *Petron*. Six would have been for when she had been at her peak of training and rest.

"Warning," a soothing woman's voice replied. "Challenge Rating Eight requested. Safety overrides have engaged. Please confirm your request."

Six was for experts. Seven was for masters of the blade and the dance. The man who had first introduced her to *Valse d'Glaive* has assured her that the number of people capable of taking on a fighting robot above Rating Seven could be counted on two hands, not including himself in that number.

And then she had gone to *Lincolnshire* to learn diplomacy, and returned home as the queen of *Corynthe*, and the Goddess of War.

"Override confirmed," she said calmly. "User Jessica Keller. Security code one-seven-seven-nine-four-six-three. Confirm: Challenge Rating Eight."

At those speeds, even a non-lethal fighting robot might accidentally kill someone. Certainly they could seriously injure an over-confident rookie just by miscalculating their errors.

And even at Eight, she still generally took the machine nine falls in fifteen.

Perhaps, after this, she would have to explore Rating Nine.

"Override confirmed. Combat Mode initiated," the woman's voice replied. "Challenge Rating Eight confirmed."

Jessica blinked, contemplated the robot's first quivering movements, and made time stand still.

PART II: BALLARD

CHAPTER XX

Date of the Republic June 12, 394 Ithome, Ballard

He wasn't really a fan of planets. Nothing personal. They just weren't deep space, where he was free to roam. For Tomas Kigali, days planetside were days wasted.

Still, they were sometimes part of the job. Especially when you got to do something as loud and impressive as was about to happen.

This morning, he found himself in the outer office of the planetary governor. *Ballard* was way more civilized than *Ramsey* had been. He wouldn't even have to blackmail anyone this time.

Probably.

Maybe he'd get lucky.

Centurion Ariojhutti was with him, today in his best dress uniform, while Kigali wore his comfortable ship's utilities with the tailored jacket. This wasn't a social call. He had no intention of treating it as such.

He had been sitting here for eighteen minutes already. Ten minutes after his appointment with the governor was supposed to have started. Kigali should have already been on his way back to the spaceport by now.

The little alarm clock in his head went off.

Kigali rose and walked over to the receptionist's desk. The man looked up at him with almost a sneer on his face.

"What are you doing?" Ariojhutti whispered at his back.

What better time to kick someone when he's down, than when he's not looking?

"In forty-five seconds," Kigali began politely, that same happy-go-lucky smile on his face masking the sledgehammer he felt like using on the man's console right now, "I am going to depart and return to the spaceport. When I do, your boss will get to answer to Jessica Keller when she arrives, and to the Republic Senate after that. I can't imagine either conversation will take very long. Your choice."

The secretary paled a little, underneath his already pasty, doughy pallor. About this point, his brain had apparently registered that Kigali's anger wasn't bluffing.

"Just a moment, sir," the man said as he rose and scuttled to the door, opened it, and disappeared into the inner office.

"Kigali, are you insane?"

He found Ariojhutti standing just behind his shoulder, alternating between bright red and white.

Kigali missed having Robbie Aeliaes with him. *Ramsey* had been so much fun, playing a game of good cop/bad cop. This *person* was just taking up space.

"Ariojhutti," Tomas replied, "there is an Imperial battleship out there somewhere. When he gets here, he's going to blow up *Alexandria Station* and probably bomb the surface of the planet at least enough to make his point. I'm pretty sure I can outrun the bastard, so I'll be able to escape. He'll squish your station and your people like bugs."

"But that's the Governor," the local replied, trying to keep his voice level as he pointed at the closed door.

"Yeah, and if he doesn't start to get his shit together in the next ten minutes, there are likely to be about fifty thousand people on that station when it explodes."

"What are you talking about?"

The voice was angry and loud. Planetary governors tended to be loud people. Big fish, even in little ponds.

Governor Ezardyonic didn't look to have fallen very far from that tree.

Kigali found himself facing a strange replica of himself, almost a doppelganger, when he turned around. The Governor was also blond and tall, perhaps three centimeters above Kigali's own lankiness. But the man also had easily fifteen extra kilograms, mostly around the middle, but some also across the chest and shoulders.

Too much time behind a desk instead of a command console. Deep space kept him lean.

Kigali took three quick strides and lightly put his finger on the governor's chest, politely moving the man back and to the side as he stepped around the governor into the office. Ariojhutti had followed, so Kigali closed the door while the governor stared at them in shock.

"What's his security clearance?" Kigali said brusquely, pointing at the receptionist, trapped in the office by the bodies at the door.

"What? Who the hell do you think you are?" the Governor half-bellowed, anger evident in his features.

Kigali suppressed the snarl that threatened to overtake his face. This was too important to let get out of hand in a pissing match. Especially one that Kigali wasn't about to lose. Not with this provincial idiot.

"Top level, Command Centurion," the other man replied quietly.

"Good," Kigali said, pulling the declaration from the inside pocket of his jacket. He started to hand it to the receptionist. "Go make some copies of this and get ready to distribute them. There isn't a lot of time."

"Get out of my office before I have you arrested."

Seriously, were all governors morons?

Kigali stared up at the man with the same sort of look he had used when his nephews were teenagers and acting stupid.

Fine, you nitwit.

Kigali stopped and took a breath. "Fine," he said. "We'll do it your way." He opened the scroll.

"By order of the *Republic of Aquitaine* Senate, on this day signed in full session. Skip, skip, skip. Here. The entire planetary system of *Ballard* is hereby placed under martial law for the duration of said emergency, plenipotentiary powers vested in Command Centurion Jessica Keller or her designated agent. For now, me. Skip, skip, skip. All citizens of the Republic are ordered, **ORDERED**, mind you, you idiot bureaucrat, to render all aid and assistance possible to the naval forces of the Republic, under penalty of law."

Kigali stared hard at the man, daring him. "Any questions?"

Anything. Right here. Right now. I've been a day and a half trying to get you to do your job. I almost just broadcast the damned thing on all available open channels, like we did at Ramsey.

Kigali smiled.

Try me. I'd like to see you frog-marched out of here in hand-cuffs. I can do that, as of right now.

Apparently, even Governors could learn. If you hit them on the nose with a rolled up newspaper enough times.

"What's happened?" he asked in a much more friendly voice. "And who are you? You don't look like a Jessica Keller."

Kigali smiled, at least a little more polite this time. "I'm Mercury," he said. "Messenger for the gods."

"What?"

He stuck out his hand. "Command Centurion Tomas Kigali, Governor. Hopefully, I'm the cavalry."

Governor Ezardyonic took his hand automatically.

"Why do we need martial law?"

"In a couple of days," Kigali replied, "an *Aquitaine* squadron will arrive. Sometime, hopefully only after that, an Imperial battle fleet is coming to attack *Alexandria Station*."

He watched the governor start to say something when a bell chirped on the desk.

The receptionist raced over and answered. The man listened silently, blood slowly draining out of his face, shock taking over instead.

"Thank you," he said, setting the comm carefully back down in the cradle.

"What is it?" the governor asked.

It almost sounded like a broken record at this point, but Kigali already had a pretty low opinion of politicians to begin with.

"There's been an explosion aboard *Alexandria Station*. They suspect sabotage."

Damn it. I'm too late.

CHAPTER XXI

Date of the Republic June 12, 394 Alexandria Station, Ballard

Taking candy from children was probably still easier, but Sykes had to laugh anyway. Getting this far had proven to be laughably easy. But then, *Ballard* had never been part of any major war, even during the *Concord* Era.

It probably would have been a great deal more challenging if the *Sentience* was more wired into the station's controls, but even *Ballard* followed Baudin's prohibitions about letting the AI have complete control of any system.

Here, simple humans were in charge of security and maintenance. Humans who could be bribed. Or have their pockets picked in bars. Or simply bear a grudge over some employment slight that convinced them to become agents for former powers, and to one day lose their identity badge and then call in sick, en route to a sudden, unannounced, permanent vacation off-planet.

Call it a well-paid head start.

Creator knows, letting Sykes roam this station for nearly a week beforehand had been a suicidal mistake on their part.

After all, the man whose badge he was using would likely be traced eventually, unless all evidence was destroyed by, say, de-orbiting the station and letting the shattered carcass burn up in the atmosphere.

Still, better safe. The man had been a low-level station tech on the maintenance side of things, and a very good deep cover agent against future need. Better to provide him a new identity and a nice cash payment, letting him resettle someplace nice in the *Fribourg Empire*. Certainly *Aquitaine* was likely to execute the man if they ever caught up with him.

The door before him surrendered to an old-fashioned lock pick, a thin strip of metal inserted physically into a tumbler and moved carefully around until the mechanism surrendered to his kiss. Although, in an era where everything was usually electronically controlled, that was an extra layer of sophistication that would keep the average thief at bay.

Sykes stared intently at the wiring closet he found himself in. Certainly, the original engineers of this place had inscribed redundancy into the DNA of the facility. Still, that was a weakness that could be exploited by the properly motivated.

And he was.

He began tracing leads and cables against a helpful wiring diagram on one wall, pushing his hat back out of his eyes. He considered removing the cap, but would need it again when he departed and he didn't want to forget it. There were still a number of security cameras scattered around, and someone was going to study the records.

Eventually.

The longer he could go, the better it would be.

Ninety minutes of sweat later, the room looked like it had been attacked by a giant spider.

Wires had been cross-spliced through a single switch, although it had been left open. He carefully set the timer and looked around one last time. Fuses were going to be overridden, alarms triggered, chaos unleashed.

Sykes smiled and put everything away. He took time to wipe everything down and pour a flammable cleaning substance on all available surfaces. It wouldn't evaporate before something overheated and sparked. And the ensuing fire would annihilate all the evidence, doubly so when fire retardants got sprayed everywhere.

He pushed the button to trigger the timer and closed the door behind him, carefully walking away down the corridor with his head down and a toolbox in one hand.

Suvi knew a moment of total panic.

All along the mall concourse and flight decks, atmosphere alarms were going off.

She could see people in all the public spaces begin to move quickly, although there was not as much panic as there could have been. Still, bulkheads were quickly closing and sealing off the area she thought of as the southern section.

But something just wasn't right.

According to her own passive sensors, there was no failure, no leak. At no point outside, and she could see just about everything on the outside of the big station, could she see the telltale cloud of vapor that a leak of this magnitude would demand.

For about the millionth time, she wished they had trusted her enough to let her into the systems over there. She had the classrooms and the lecture halls, plus the Library itself. Down on the planet, there were a number of schools and kiosks where she had eyes, but nothing useful in the mall.

No hands at all.

Oh, double fudge. Now the automated systems were indicating a station breakup and ordering everyone into emergency escape pods.

Hey! Guys. Nothing there. My systems are fine. This is a computer fault in the processors you won't let me talk to.

Obviously, when this was all done, she was going to count a whole bunch of coup on some people who had told her she was over-protective.

I told you so.

Trust us, right?

Yeah, no. Not when you have panicked civilians pouring into mini pods and blasting clear of a station they thought was about to come apart underneath their feet.

From the north pole camera, it kinda looked like a fireworks display, except every one of the smaller sparks was a one-person drop pod aimed at land on the planet below and the larger ones were ten and twenty-seat models.

At least it was a Thursday, and part of the summer break in classes. Way fewer tourists than a weekend, and only about a tenth of the overall student body.

Total station population this morning, twenty-five thousand, one hundred thirty-three, rather than the fifty-five to sixty thousand it might have been at fall quarter peak.

Given the emergency blowout protocols and bodies piling into pods, she would have to have someone start a hard physical census of the station tomorrow. Creator only knows who might have gotten lost on the station, or separated from their family.

Bloody hell, it was an absolute worst case accident. And it could have been avoided.

Stupid, dumb-system computers. You want to complain? I wouldn't have ruined so many vacations and lunches.

Suvi was thinking extremely uncharitable thoughts, watching things unfold, when she felt a jar. She would have called it an earthquake, had she been standing on a planet, something she hadn't done in twelve standard centuries.

Most of her sensor net went suddenly dead. The backup systems came on line, almost three quarters of a second later, but something was off.

Talk about an eternity of being blind.

And even then, there was something horribly wrong. Her main sensor feed wasn't even a hundredth of what it had been five minutes ago.

Quickly, she cycled through outside cameras, surprised at how many weren't working. It was like she had suffered a stroke and gone half blind. It was almost worse than living on *Kel-Sdala* those last few centuries. That had at least had the advantage of being boring.

Finally, she found the view she needed.

That was a plume. Atmosphere mixed with smoke, turning to ice crystals as they rocketed away from a hole in the side of the station.

An explosion had just blown out her primary communications relay antenna array. She was effectively cut off from the planet below. Oh, sure, she could still talk, but the full backups that she constantly transmitted to her various secured sites were going to be cut off until the equipment could be repaired. The secondary antenna simply lacked the necessary bandwidth.

Hell, the entire planetary entertainment grid below her normally used less bandwidth than she did, except during major sporting events.

Suvi reviewed the timing. The alarms that she was positive would be shown to be false alarms triggered by some sort of cascading systems fault. The sudden pressurization evacuation alarms. The explosion.

There was no way in hell that this was an accident.

Someone was out to get her, to destroy the station that had been her home for so long.

Had the piper finally come to collect his payment?

After all, nobody had promised her that she would live forever.

CHAPTER XXII

Date of the Republic June 12, 394 Orbital space, Ballard

CR-264 was on maximum alert. They already pretty much had been, but this meant that he had his A-crew on duty and loaded up with caffeine. Not that they could do much of anything against an Imperial battleship and her gang, but the Red Admiral was going to have to catch Br'er Rabbit first, and Tomas Kigali had no intention of making that easy.

Engineering had already overcharged the engines in dangerous ways. Every gun was unlocked and had the IFF lockouts turned off, just in case this was all a giant trap he was about to walk into.

You never knew with the Red Admiral.

Kigali had warned Ariojhutti not to scramble any of his wing for the next hour or two. *CR-264* had better sensors and could get closer to the station, sitting perfectly still. And they were likely to shoot any idiot that got too close to them, just on twitchy principle.

Kigali could do that. He *was* the law right now. At least until Jessica got here. Then it wasn't his problem. Win win.

By the time Kigali and the local centurion had gotten to orbit in the shuttle, that idiot governor had finally gotten around to listening. The planetary militia had been activated, along with every emergency crew, cop, fire department, forest ranger, and pizza delivery woman that could be reached.

There were estimates that as many as seven thousand people had bailed when the flag went up on the station. Each one of them would need to be found and brought home safely. Some would have landed in banjo country and need help getting to a place with acceptable room service.

CR-264 sat overhead, relative to the station, keeping her position less than a kilometer away. From that distance, he had scanners that could see scratch marks on screws from lazy assembly engineers.

Not that there was much doubt as to what had happened. Station crews had already found a fire in a secondary wiring closet. After they cleaned it out, the fire marshal took one look and called it arson. So now station security was involved.

Kigali let the cops do their thing. He had already figured that the Red Admiral had sent a bomber ahead to block the back door. It was what he had done at *Qui-Ping*. This time it had worked. But then, Jessica wasn't here yet. Of course, the man was going to look good.

He was the Red Admiral, after all.

And the level of damage didn't help. Kigali had been convinced that they were all dead men three hours previously. After all, you schedule major sabotage like that for a time when the other guy can't recover. However, the locals were going to be at least two weeks repairing the systems that just been cooked, best estimate.

That just bookended the bogey-man's arrival window with certainty.

"Boss, important message coming in," his First Officer, Centurion Lam, called from the fighting deck below him.

"Governor?" he called back.

That man needed more hand-holding than anybody Kigali had ever known. Tomas thought maybe he should move here someday so he could run for office. It couldn't be that hard, given the current occupant.

"I said important, Tom," came the call back. "Lady wants to talk to you. Very persuasive."

He glanced automatically at the boards but they were blank.

The only important woman in his life right now was still at least two days out from saving his ass.

Oh, what the hell.

"Put her through."

If Lam thought it was important, and didn't want to spoil the surprise, he could at least play along for a bit.

The screen lit up.

The woman/girl had blond hair with bangs.

She was young. That was his first impression.

Not quite young enough to be his daughter, but she had that air of young womanhood that they didn't generally lose until after college. Academy girls never had it in the first place, but they didn't count.

The eyes weren't young.

Bright blue. Rich in color, and absolutely stunning. Intelligent. Perceptive. Ancient.

Not his type.

She was in a uniform of some sort, but not one he knew.

"Command Centurion Tomas Kigali," he said merrily, by way of introduction. "And you are?"

"My name is Suvi, Command Centurion Kigali," she said simply.

Even the voice couldn't decide if it was a young woman or an old one.

His brain finally caught up with the rest of him.

Oh.

Yeah. That made sense. She was, as far as he knew, the Last of the Immortals.

"Oh. What can I do for you, madam?"

"Please initiate a secured channel using Fleet encryption set number eight, Centurion," she said.

The words sounded like they weighed a ton each, so she had to have been a fleet officer at some point in her eternity. That would help.

Kigali keyed the system live, rotated through sets to find the one he wanted, and locked it in. Right now, even the people on the gun deck couldn't read this conversation, to say nothing of the rest of the system.

Of course, Lam could always climb a deck to listen. It wasn't like Kigali was a pissy little shit about that sort of thing, like First Fleet Lord Loncar, when it came to that kind of crap.

The screen acquired a red border.

"Go ahead, Suvi," he said.

"I have a saboteur inside my station, Kigali," she began, her tones weighed down with the seriousness that Jessica Keller also got when she was in the zone. "Governor Ezardyonic's office has been singularly unresponsive to my requests for more information. However, with the declaration of martial law, he is no longer in charge right now. You are, Command Centurion. What has happened?"

Kigali looked at the screen, trying to imagine what it would be like to live forever. To remember *The Times Before*. To know you were going to outlive every single person you knew.

Correction, assuming the Red Admiral didn't get to her before Jessica could stop him.

Oh, what the hell. She was going to find out shortly anyway. Best that she have time to plan.

"The *Fribourg Empire* is going to attack you in the very near future. It will be the Imperial battleship *Amsel,* the Blackbird, commanded by Admiral Emmerich Wachturm, the best they have. I don't know when he'll get here. Jessica Keller is scheduled to be here in about two days with a Republic squadron. We're going to try to stop him."

"Jessica Keller commands the Republic Strike Carrier *Auberon,*" Suvi replied. "What else is she bringing?"

"The battlecruiser *Stralsund,* destroyer leader *Brightoak,* heavy destroyer *Rajput,* and me. Oh, and Moirrey Kermode."

"I'm not familiar with that person."

"She's the reason we beat the Red Admiral at *2218 Svati Prime* and *Qui-Ping.* She's the reason we beat the pirates at *Petron.* Hopefully, she'll have enough *Mischief* left in the tank to save our butts at *Ballard.*"

"*Mischief,* Centurion Kigali?"

Apparently, Suvi had picked up his emphasis on the word. But, hey, he was in charge. He could deputize her. After all, she was the reason this was all happening in the first place. How many people got to have the Red Admiral gunning for them?

Two. Well, three counting Suvi, but he was betting his life these women would survive.

"She's Keller's genius Weapons Tech, Suvi," he replied. "Better bombs, bigger tricks, shifty surprises. Jessica calls her the evil engineering gnome."

"This station is entirely unarmed, Kigali."

She sounded like she was lecturing him now. Probably not far from the truth. He didn't do serious very often, or for very long. Not unless there were planetary governors involved.

That was a different story.

"Maybe Moirrey can cook something up," he said. "Won't know until she gets here."

"Also, with the loss of my primary communications antenna array, I am trapped here."

"Really?"

None of the late-night campy thriller videos he watched covered that point. The AI's were always able to escape the good guys by downloading themselves into a pocket comm or something so they could get away for the next movie.

"The information I store, my memories, if you will, is backed up extensively and redundantly. However, the programming that makes up my cognition matrix, my personality if you will, is too complex to be updated to any single point of storage, with the equipment at hand, in anything less than eight days. Unless you can keep this so-called Red Admiral at bay for that long, I am effectively trapped aboard this station, as I said, with a saboteur who is probably intent on finishing the job."

Kigali felt his face turn sour. He really couldn't wait for Jessica to get here. Until then, the best he could do was bust his ass figuring out how to get her everything she needed.

Wait, he was the guy in charge now. Even that idiot governor had to listen to him, and Ariojhutti could send engineers over to help.

Kigali smiled at Suvi.

"Leave that to me."

CHAPTER XXIII

Date of the Republic June 7, 394 Ladaux

Tadej considered the woman standing in the doorway, a look of obvious concern on her face. She was one of his newer aides, a well-connected youngster, fresh out of university, still settling in on his staff.

"Yes, Stacia?" he said warmly.

She looked like she expected to lose fingers for what she was about to say. It must be good. Of course, he was currently on the comm with the President of the Republic, but they were making lunch plans, not discussing trade negotiations.

"A fleet centurion is here to see you, Premier," she began carefully, her ebony-brown skin not showing much blush, but it was there in the set of her shoulders and the size of her pupils. "He does not have an appointment, will not say why he is here, and used a codeword indicating it was a priority at the highest level of the Republic."

"Calina," Tadej said into the comm. "I'll call you back in a bit, if that would okay. Something has just come up."

He listened, nodded, and placed the device in its cradle.

"A centurion, you say?" he asked her.

"Yes, sir. Centurion Kamil Miloslav."

Oh, my. Kasum's personal aide? The cat's been away for one whole day and the mice are already storming the Bastille?

"Send him in, Stacia," Tadej decided. "Then clear the next two hours from my calendar and have everyone stand by. In fact, have the commissary send boxed lunches in for everyone and put it on the Navy's account."

"Yes, sir," she sighed, obviously relieved to have guessed right. Or at least to have escaped the Premier's wrath.

Kamil entered carrying a large briefcase that was obviously heavy. He rested it by the side of the desk and came to attention.

"Thank you for seeing me so quickly, Premier," he said.

Tadej eyes the man's nervousness.

"Sit," he commanded peremptorily. "Boil it down as much as you can. I'll assume the paperwork will back it up."

Tadej softened his scowl with a smile. There were certainly any number of alternatives Kamil could have exercised before coming here. That did not bode well.

Kamil sat, flipped open the briefcase anyway, and pulled out a small folder that he sat on the table.

"With First Lord Kasum indisposed, Second Lord can handle most administrative tasks, as she has in the past," he began. "The First Lord long ago tasked me to pay attention to certain activities and personages, and to do some outside the normal channels."

"I see," Tadej responded, having drawn that conclusion already. "Who is misbehaving, in his absence?"

Tadej was rewarded with a small smile on an otherwise tight face.

"The usual suspects," he said. "If one could draw that conclusion. Tennerick, Tomčič, and possibly Loncar, if I translate the intelligence reports and the political winds correctly. There is a great deal of ambiguity to the reports, but something just doesn't feel right."

Tadej felt his eyebrows go up in spite of his seriousness.

"Go on," he prompted Kamil.

"Sir, the Senate *Select Committee for the Fleet of The Republic of Aquitaine* is having a hearing on the *State of Current Affairs* this afternoon. First Fleet Lord Loncar was added as a surprise witness at the very last minute, after First Lord's announced departure. At the same time, there have been whispers reported by fleet intelligence implying a belief in some social circles that the First Lord is culpable for the impending attack on *Ballard*, and that Centurion Keller is personally responsible. They have not been polite or friendly rumors, from what I have been told."

"And, of course," Tadej finished the thought, "Nils took *Athena* out to try to salvage the situation, and they're going to gang up on him while he cannot defend himself."

"That is the assessment I drew first thing this morning."

Kamil tapped the folder and slid across the table.

"There are more details here, sir," Kamil concluded, "but I'm a fleet officer and not a political expert. First Lord's instructions were to go to the top, if I had any doubt. I have doubts."

Tadej flipped open the folder instead of replying and quickly scanned the executive summary.

Oh ho. Really? I wonder just how much money Loncar and his friends must have lost. Of course, this will play well with the Noble Lords, and certainly piss off the Fighting Lords. And this is not a spur of the moment thing, either. This shows a lot of planning and forethought. I smell Brand's hand in this.

He flipped into the meat of the document and quickly consumed chunks while Kamil waited patiently. Finally, he reached the end and settled back into his chair.

"You have very good instincts, Kamil," he said. "When you decide you are done with being in uniform, make sure I get your resume first, okay?"

Kamil flushed.

"Aye, sir," he said. "But I think you might have to argue with Senator Kasum."

"I outrank Nils' brother," Tadej said with a smile. "Now, leave your materials here and consider your work done and your activities proper and well-handled. I'll let my people get messy with it. You will be protected from any fallout."

"Thank you, sir."

Tadej re-read the document after Kasum's right hand departed.

The cat is away and the rats wasted little time. No, this was worse than that. This was a full-bore insurrection, aimed not just at Nils, but at the entire government. This was knives in the darkness maneuvering.

He picked up his comm again and quickly dialed a number.

"Madame President," he said as levelly as she answered. "Do you have anything interesting planned for lunch?"

CHAPTER XXIV

Imperial Founding: 172/06/15. 5787 Piscium System

5787 Piscium had been chosen as a rendezvous because it was close to the target system, but, also, more importantly, because there were no habitable worlds here and very little reason for a colony of any kind, even a scientific one.

Nobody to intrude.

It was a hot, young star, circled by a pair of gas giants close enough in that no useful, rocky worlds had formed. Or rather, none that had survived the planet-forming phase. At a distance of around five AU, the cleared space ended and the system was a mess of scattered rocks, shattered remnants of worlds that might have been.

IFV Amsel slid into realspace with all the grand dignity of one of the great whales from the lost Homeworld. Perhaps one of the modern descendants that had been brought to a variety of colonies during the first great exploring phase of humanity.

Calm, quiet, majestic.

The flag bridge on the battleship was anything but. They were deep in the guts of the *Republic of Aquitaine* now. Far deeper than any raid had even considered in more than a century.

Anything could happen.

Every weapons system was unlocked and prepared to unleash biblical mayhem. Firing solutions were roughed out, target sectors had been assigned, and the primary crews were in place.

Emmerich was at his usual station, standing beside the giant projector with his flag captain and command staff attending him. Around the outer wall of the flag bridge were the men who made the squadron operate.

"Contact," a man's voice sang out calmly across the otherwise-quiet flag bridge. "I have three targets in range."

"All systems stand by to engage hostiles," Emmerich called in his stentorian voice.

It was mostly redundant, given the crew. These men were among the best the *Fribourg Empire* had, trained to a very high degree of excellence. Still, he was in command. It befit him to remind them occasionally.

"Sensors," another voice called back, this one a baritone. "Identification confirmed on *IFV Petrograd* and the frigates *Baasch* and *Kappel*. No other vessels within range."

"Very well," Emmerich continued. "Captain Baumgärtner, please establish rendezvous coordinates for the squadron and make sure the other vessels are made aware when they arrive."

"Yes, Admiral," his right-hand man replied.

Emmerich could go do paperwork now. Possibly take a nap. *Amsel* had arrived within an hour of the original calculations, very accurate piloting across this great of a jump. It was perfectly expectable that half of the squadron might arrive first, and in a random order.

The whole point of this final step was to bring everyone together, close enough to the final target that they could emerge at *Ballard* as a single unit, far enough out to observe the defenders, before making the final assault run.

It would never do to give them enough time to react.

Jessica Keller just might escape him.

CHAPTER XXV

Date of the Republic June 11, 394 Jumpspace en route to Ballard

"Okay, youngster," *Jouster* said, his voice blending that perfect mix of exasperation, superiority, and professor together, "graduation day. You've gotten a year of flight school and officer's training crammed into seventy-something days. Time to show me what you've learned."

Newly-minted Flight Cornet Cho Ayaka Nakamura, callsign *Furious*, half-scowled back at him. She hated being called youngster, especially when she wasn't, and had made that clear. Hell, she was almost his age. He just used it to get under her skin.

Jouster smiled at *Furious* from across the training bay as he got ready to drop down into his flight simulator for some serious play.

She was nice to look at, cute face, short dark hair, but it was painfully obvious to everybody but her and the flag centurion that those two were going to end up making babies, one of these days. They had that icky glow new couples got when the chemistry was perfect. You wanted to hate them, especially when they started finishing each other's sentences or putting food in each other's mouths, but they were just too cute.

It would be like hating puppies.

But, during the crap with the pirates and that damned Promenade, the girl had proven herself to be one of the best pilots *Corynthe* had. Keller, the dragon lady, had decided to recruit her when they headed back to civilization, opening a long-term pipeline to bleed off some of the talent that might otherwise go into piracy and instead make them respectable citizens of the galaxy.

Furious stuck her tongue out at him as she dropped into her own simulator.

Okay, mostly respectable.

Jouster brought his system awake and locked his helmet into place. Everything came live at once. Lights. Air. Sound. The training consoles were as realistic as you could get without strapping yourself into a fighter and launching into space.

"Hey, *Jouster*," *Furious* called over the comm, "if I'm the youngster here, why did you put me in the best fighter?"

As wing commander, it has been his recommendation, but Iskra Vlahovic, the flight deck commander had made the final call. Still, it had been a good idea. The woman could flat out fly.

"Because six weeks ago," *Jouster* replied, "I had a previously-stolen M-6 *Gungnir* with no pilot, and a pilot with no fighter. Figure you were going to have to learn something anyway, and Dragon Lady's connections were finally going to get the rest of us upgraded from the M-5's."

Jouster ran a quick pre-flight. It was almost autopilot, but never automatic. This was the equipment that was going to keep him alive.

Do it right. Every day. Especially today.

Speaking of…

"*Hànchén, Bitter Kitten*. You two awake?"

"Absolutely, Commander," *Hànchén* called. Flight Cornet Murali Ma. Tall, skinny kid. Smart as a whip, nerdy as hell. You were as likely to find him with his nose in a history book as down here in the flight simulators practicing. Damned good pilot. Still a few sharp edges and loose screws. *Jouster* could fix that.

"About time you got here, *Jouster*," *Bitter Kitten* purred at him. Flight Centurion Darya Lagunov. Skinny brunette, average height, really gorgeous when she wanted to be. Flew relatively normal until things went sideways, then she turned into a gun-toting, maniac artist. Until *Furious* had come along, *Bitter Kitten* had probably been the only pilot on *Auberon* good enough to give him a run for his money.

Now, it would be a three-way. Not that either of them would be down for that sort of thing, but, you know, a man's got to pay attention to those sorts of details.

Graduation Day.

Bitter Kitten had been put in charge of the second flight wing. This was her chance to show off what she could do as a wing leader. She was junior to both of his own wingmates, *Uller* and *Vienna,* in terms of both experience and age, but *Jouster* knew better than to break up his perfectly-balanced team, just for seniority's sake.

Plus, the three kids on second wing were all perfectly good flyers. Better than good. Virtuosos. Crazy lunatics with thrusters and guns, but that just made the whole flight wing better.

"Just making sure *Furious* could find the battlefield, *Bitter Kitten,*" *Jouster* called back. He could almost hear Nakamura's teeth grind over the comm. He smiled.

Graduation Day.

Him flying with *Hànchén* as his wingmate, against *Bitter Kitten* and *Furious.* Boys against girls. No elaborate scenarios of attack, patrol, or defense. Nope, just an open arena and four lunatic pilots.

Time to rock.

Cho Ayaka Nakamura had been one of exactly two girls qualified to pilot fighter craft in all of *Corynthe* and allowed to fly with the boys. And that only because her dad was a former bad-ass pilot and 1-ring captain himself, who helped her build her first stripped-down strike fighter when she was twelve and all of her girlfriends were busy discovering boys.

Even then, she'd had to be at least twice as good as any boy flying to be invited to audition for a slot. And willing to kick their asses in the locker room when they decided to get fresh.

She smiled at the thought. Both thoughts.

And then *Aquitaine* had come along.

Command Centurion Jessica Keller. The woman *Jouster* called *The Dragon Lady.*

As her hands and lizardbrain walked through the pre-flight checklist, Cho couldn't help but remember that first dinner, at *Callumnia,* after she had come in second place in the JV race. Behind *Bitter Kitten.* Another woman pilot. Now her team lead.

Being there, surrounded by female marines. All of them that *Auberon* had, but still. Women in charge of things. On their own terms. Nothing like *Corynthe.*

And, for one glorious day, she had been *Corynthe's* flight commander. Air boss of the *Queen's Own*.

Even if she'd had to leave all that behind when she left with *Auberon*, it was still a better place than she'd been.

And there were a bunch of other girls out there that were good enough. David Rodriguez and his captains might be slow to adapt, but the girls would listen when *Furious* came back and told them how awesome it could be, flying in the real world.

Okay, halfway done. Communications lock-in.

Furious toggled one of the switches on the control yoke until a green "7" appeared in the top right corner of her face screen.

"*Bitter Kitten*, this is *Furious*," she said. "Confirming a secure comm channel."

"Roger, *Furious*," Darya replied.

Knowing *Bitter Kitten*, she was already done with her checklist and had been waiting. But then, she'd had years of doing this the *Aquitaine* way. Cho'd had weeks. It was still something to think about, instead of something that the body just did autonomously, like breathing.

But she'd get there. That jackass *Jouster* wasn't about to make her look bad. Even in a training sim run in a battle arena.

"Checklist complete," *Furious* said.

Ready for starflight.

"*Furious*," *Bitter Kitten* said in her quiet voice, "I want to do something mean and sneaky today."

Furious smiled. *Duh.* It was *Bitter Kitten*.

"Go ahead."

"So when we get close," *Bitter Kitten* said, "it will be obvious which one of us is which. The M-6 is different enough from the M-5 visually, to say nothing of the scanners. When we go into our first turn, I'm going to fade wide and flair. You'll take the lead flying at that point and I'll turn into your wing. We both know *Jouster's* going to be chasing you anyway. This should throw his timing off."

And it was also a good way to let her do something nobody else could keep up with. The M-6 had an edge in both speed and maneuverability over the M-5. *Bitter Kitten* might have to fall off the pace at the same time the boys did. But it also put *Furious* in a position to push the margins in ways she couldn't if she was flying on Darya's wing.

Furious smiled.

"Sounds good, *Kitten*," she said.

Time to outfly everybody in the sky.

"Flight control, this is gold team," she heard *Bitter Kitten* call. "Checklists complete. Ready for the arena."

Senior Centurion Iskra Vlahovic had once been a flight centurion, a pilot, until she had limped home from a battle almost as shattered as her fighter. Cho had still been in pigtails when it had happened, but that woman still knew her stuff.

Instead of retiring, she had gone ground crew and eventually become the air boss, the flight deck commander for *Auberon*.

She didn't talk much, unless she had to. Everyone listened when she did.

Today, she was the referee. Which said a lot about how important this flight might be.

"Roger that, gold team. Stand by," Iskra said soothingly into the comm.

A moment passed.

"Gold team, blue team, this is flight command," Iskra continued in her quiet, solemn voice. "I've decided to add some fun today, to make this more realistic. There will be a planet below you, two stations, and seventeen cargo vessels in orbit. Nothing is armed. You will be deducted points for damaging anything except the other team. Enjoy."

Furious could hear the wicked smile in the woman's voice, and then there was a moment of utter vertigo as her screens lit up.

Time to fly.

Bitter Kitten nearly burst out giggling when she saw the arena. She had been here before. Come to think of it, so had *Hànchén* and *Furious*. It was a large slice of the orbital skies above *Callumnia*, from that time when the three of them had gone racing together.

Jouster would recognize it as well, but he hadn't had to race it, like the three of them. Iskra was giving her team a very subtle edge today.

Of course, knowing *Jouster*, he'd said or done something to Iskra to piss her off, probably propositioned her one time too many.

And, let's face it, she never supervises things like this, anyway, so it must have been good.

She and *Furious* were high in the eastern sky, at least as far as the planet below them was concerned. It was rotating very slowly, relative, but everything was coming at them in orbit.

Another edge, since it was easier to slip by something going past you than to outrun it and slip in. That would be like trying to board a train from behind while on a motorcycle.

Not that she couldn't fly that good, if she needed to. But still…

Jouster's team was lower and in the southwest sky. From the race at *Callumnia,* they would pretty much emerge from behind the freighter that had been the mid-point turn-around.

Bitter Kitten double-checked, but the launch rails were empty. Not that missiles would be very effective in this mess, but you never knew.

She took a moment, plotted everything, and sent *Furious* a map.

"Just for fun," she said, "let's pop up over number six like our asses are on fire. It'll be like hawks dropping into their faces."

"Roger, that," *Furious* replied. *Bitter Kitten* could hear the smile in the other woman's voice.

Since they were already in formation and headed the right direction, *Bitter Kitten* lit her thrusters and aimed at her target.

Furious could keep up.

At *Callumnia,* they had been racing a slalom course in and through freighters sitting in a high orbit, passing close enough to basically touch three of them, and then back. Today, they had emerged behind the starting point of that race.

Bitter Kitten shoved the nose of her fighter down and red-lined the engines.

"Time to swoop," she called.

Freighter number six was a monster, almost a barge, easily twice the length of *Auberon.*

What made it even weirder was the design. Like *Corynthe's* motherships, this vessel was in the shape of a dumbbell, with an engine cluster at one end, a command module at the other, and a long gooseneck in between. However, instead of fighters of various sizes, attached by their landing struts, the neck on *Six* was filled with shipping containers, either attached to the neck itself, or the next container inboard.

From the bow-on view, it probably looked like a giant snowflake. Today, that just meant more places to hide, since the freighter's load-out was so random.

Bitter Kitten picked a gap in those containers, a low spot about three fighters wide, and blasted through it at nearly insane speeds.

In battle, she'd have never tried something like this.

Well, probably not.

Alright, fine. In a heartbeat. It was what she did. But still.

A quick glance over. *Furious* was right in her back pocket, her own acceleration throttled back to about ninety-six percent, staying right with her.

"Got 'em," *Furious* called. "Two-nine-five, down fifteen."

Bitter Kitten looked below and left.

Yup. *Jouster* and the Kid.

Wow, that sounded like a bad western movie. Have to remember that later.

She smiled.

"Here we go."

It was a scene reminiscent of the flights above the planet *Callumnia*.

Hànchén had reflown the scenario three times, identifying the spots where the woman Nakamura, now his team-mate, had been able to edge him out to place third.

Cho, also known as *Furious*, was an exceptional flyer, an intuitive genius in a field that favored such talent. She had deserved to beat him.

Then.

He had studied. While others had played games or engaged in dissipation of various sorts, he had spent time reviewing and learning. Command Centurion Keller had a reputation as a woman who refought old battles in order to become better. It was a lesson he had learned growing up. Study, practice, learn.

But, there was no time for academics on the battlefield. One studied, one practiced during times of quiet contemplation, that the lessons became automatic when thinking was no longer possible.

Everything was prepared. He was prepared. He felt the mask of war descend over his face, turning him from a student of war into a maker.

"*Hànchén*," *Jouster* called on the comm, "you ready?"

Flight Cornet Murali Ma smiled at the world around him. "Born ready, old man," he replied, deeply inside that place he went in battle. "We going to do this?"

"Waypoint Charlie," *Jouster* said. "Max speed."

Hànchén had already known that target would be their point of emergence. *Jouster* was not predictable, at least not very much so, and it was a good spot.

It was, however, predictable.

It was a good thing they were good at what they did. Imperial pilots just didn't train to this level of skill very often.

Imperials were all about the team dynamic, groups of two, four, twelve. Whole squadrons flying in mass formations and overwhelming you, instead of individual bad-ass warriors going mano-a-mano.

Ma stayed right on *Jouster's* right flank as their strike fighters emerged from the shadow of the closest freighter and began to scan the hostile skies.

Okay, that was just too damned tight. Were all Aquitaine *pilots like this, or was* Bitter Kitten *completely insane?*

Furious smiled at the thought. They had had at least three meters of clearance on either side of their little group as they blasted through the superstructure of the mega-freighter. The chance of actually hitting were pretty low, unless someone was shooting at you and you had to weave.

But damn, that was off the charts. It was the sort of thing she might do, just to make *Jouster* look bad.

"Got 'em," *Furious* said to her teammate as she picked up *Jouster's* group. "Two-nine-five, down fifteen."

She could tell Darya was having fun by the smile in her voice when she replied.

"Here we go."

Jouster and *Hànchén* were just coming out from behind freighter number sixteen and hadn't seen them yet. It was way too far away for the beam weapons to be effective, and too much risk of hitting the neutral vessel with overshot.

Instead, *Bitter Kitten* redlined her engines and dove. It wasn't quite right on an intercept course for where they were going, but where they were at right now. Fastest way to get into melee, where *Furious* would have the edge. Not much, but you didn't need much.

Luck and timing were at least as important as skill in a game like this.

Furious could tell the very moment *Jouster* picked them up. He spun his craft onto its left wing so that the two girls were directly above him. A moment later, *Hànchén* did the same.

She wondered what her lead would do, but *Bitter Kitten* kept it flat, and flat out, so she stayed put.

"You ready?" *Bitter Kitten* asked. There was a hard edge of adrenalin in her voice now. Excited. Intoxicated. Almost aroused. *Furious* knew exactly how she felt.

"On you," *Furious* replied.

"Starting to turn now," *Bitter Kitten* said. "Stay with me on this one. We'll hand off when we get closer."

"Roger that."

Furious had learned to anticipate the other fighters in her wing by now. There was a ballet to how thruster valves irised open and closed, and how they rotated. You watched your partner with one eye, and the bad guys with the other, and it looked like you were flying as a single entity.

Bitter Kitten was initiating a wide, looping turn, almost a barrel-roll, over and to their left. She followed.

The boys were suddenly above them as they dove down toward the planet.

They had responded by turning shallowly inbound. Not quite enough to directly intercept, but enough to bring the two groups closer in a swirl.

First secret of melee flying, her father had told her, was to force the other guy to commit his mistake by reacting to something he thought you were going to do, rather than what you did.

The rule of four. He moves to the wrong spot and has to stop, and then he has move to the right spot and get into position. Every mistake costs him four times over.

Right now, nobody was committing, but this was where *Furious* knew she had an edge. *Aquitaine* had a lot of money for missiles, so they used them from a distance, to hunt one another, or break up formations, or just to surprise people.

Corynthe was poor. You got right on top of the other guy with guns and let the beams do the talking. They were cheap.

She had years of this kind of combat. The other three were good, sure, but they always went for missiles first.

Furious smiled as the vectors in her mind aligned with those on the screen. Now.

"*Bitter Kitten*," she said, drawing a line and transmitting it. "Come to this bearing and start your fade. I'm about to do something that's not in your training manual. Yet."

Rather than respond over the comm, *Bitter Kitten*'s fighter did the talking. *Furious* watched the maneuvering thrusters and engine valves adjust, just long enough to confirm the timing of everything, and then released several of her gyros, eased her engines, and snapped the control yoke over.

From the boys' point of view, it would look just like another barrel roll coming, especially if they made the mistake of watching her nose instead of her flight path.

Everybody did that. Usually, it was good enough.

Furious smiled.

Usually.

Her little M-6 fighter was the top of the line. The M-5 was good, but it couldn't do this nearly as easily.

Furious was inside a tornado, spinning on her ass instead of her centerline as the nose of her fighter wobbled in a circle twice the radius of the engine nacelles. The best part was that she was generally staying on line, even if it was a very wobbly line.

She let her instincts take over. No use in losing points for hitting the non-combatants.

As the nose of the craft wobbled, she stoked the firing stud and quickly released it, firing a very short burst as her guns came into line with *Jouster*'s team.

And then she circled again.

And fired again.

And again.

A happy chirp in her ear told her she had lined the shot right. Someone over there had just gotten thumped.

Furious figured she'd made her point. And was close to losing her lunch from the torque this spinning was generating on her innards. She brought the gyros back on line hard.

It was like hitting the bottom of the hangman's rope. But it had worked.

"You still with me?" she called.

"That was insane, *Furious*," *Bitter Kitten* howled happily. "You've got to teach me that trick tomorrow."

"Roger that, *Bitter Kitten*. Who did I get?"

"*Jouster* just lost all of his shields and maybe part of one wing," her partner said, sliding down and back into the corner behind her.

"Well then," *Furious* smiled ferally. "Let's go clip his other wing."

"Before any of you ask," Iskra said, giving the briefing room her best angry-boss-scowl, "I've checked the design parameters of the two craft."

She paused and made individual eye-contact with each of her pilots to ram home her point. *Furious* and *Bitter Kitten* sat in the dead center, with *Hànchén* next to *Furious* and *Jouster* beyond that. Most of the rest of the pilots and gunners that made up the flight wing had apparently found an excuse to watch the session, and had wandered into the room to listen.

As long as they were quiet, Iskra was willing to let them stay. After all, it wasn't every day that everyone got to watch *Jouster* get his ass handed to him by one of his own pilots. Let alone two of them.

She softened the scowl. A little. Down from Biblical levels.

"If you slam the gyros back into alignment that hard," she continued, "you will probably not lose any of them the first time. I highly recommended replacing them after about the third try. They should explode about the fifth time you pull that stunt."

Furious raised a hand. It was kind of quaint, in a room like this. Iskra bestowed a warm smile on her. Not that the others would take the example, but they might.

"Yes, *Furious*?"

"Is there anything Moirrey can do to reinforce them?"

Huh. Smart, too. Thinking so far outside the box as to be nearly outside the warehouse.

"I'll ask, but probably not before you have to deal with the Red Admiral."

After all, they were only days from *Götterdämmerung* at this point.

CHAPTER XXVI

So this was what it felt like to catch a disease.

Ugh.

The organics could keep it.

Somewhere inside her was a parasite.

Suvi could sense him.

Lurking.

Seeding chaos.

Seventeen people had died during the emergency evacuation. Another one hundred fifty-three had been dropped in such remote locations that planetary response forces were being stretched to the very limit to get to them.

It would be good practice, if an Imperial fleet was about to arrive.

At least with the proclamation of martial law, the station was emptying as rapidly as shuttles could make the round trip. People weren't pleased, but not many of them were arguing.

Not when they might suddenly find themselves dead instead.

Nothing like a good hanging to focus the mind, as the old saying went.

Now if they could only find a way for one immensely ancient AI system to make her own getaway.

Suvi dared not share her various contingency plans with any of the locals. All it would take would be one innocent blabbing to the wrong people to spoil it and trap her, but good. There was nobody around today that she trusted that highly.

Command Centurion Jessica Keller had a reputation for being an unconventional tactician and strategist. Perhaps, just perhaps, there would be an option there.

After all, they can only kill me once. Right?

Alexandria Station hadn't been this empty in centuries. From the few cameras she could access, there were whole sections of the station hastily abandoned. At least it was summer right now. Lots of people had already put things into storage and headed out on vacation. That made it easier to evacuate.

Of course, it also made it easier to hide.

What idiot decided to keep her entirely separated from the security systems on this station?

That wasn't entirely fair. She could remember the man very well. He had epitomized the word *bureaucrat* in all the wrong ways.

It wasn't really Henri Baudin's fault, either. His prescriptions had been put in place to keep her kind from utterly dominating humans again. She could see the rightness in that. After all, it was the power of the *Sentiences* over humanity that nearly destroyed the species in the first place.

She could see where they might not appreciate her kind after that.

Up until then, Suvi had pretty much full run of the station. Of course, it had been nearly sixty percent smaller in those days. The Founder of the *Republic of Aquitaine* had called for the growth of the University of Ballard as an engineering school.

As they rebuilt it, they shoved her out of various systems, slowly restricting her full control back to almost nothing more than the original station that had been lofted into orbit by Doyle Iwakuma and his family's connections, once upon a very long time ago. Things that had been hardwired in the early days and couldn't be easily unwired today.

She had eyes in some places, but no hands.

And now it was biting them all in the ass.

Alexandria Station was turning into a ghost town: just the university police, a few engineers, the saboteur, and her.

Oh, and an Imperial battle fleet coming to kill her.

CHAPTER XXVII

Date of the Republic June 7, 394 Ladaux

Because it was a public forum by one of the most distinguished committees in the Senate, something that happened so rarely, seats were hard to come by. Because he was the presiding officer of the Senate, Tadej pulled rank and shamelessly stole two chairs from friendly journalists in the balcony, with a promise of favors to be had later. That the lovely woman on his arm just happened to be the President of the Republic, albeit in mufti today, just added to the feeling of cloak and dagger.

Below him, the Committee was in high dudgeon.

Opening statements were usually dry, boring affairs, frequently rambling and verging on incoherence, as politicians used them to score points in the official journals of the Senate when nobody could argue with them later. Arcane and obtuse. Today was different, perhaps, only in the scale and scope of the proposed bloodletting, from the itinerary of speakers.

It was a Who's Who of the Noble Lords who happened to be in the vicinity of *Ladaux* or, as Nils liked to class them, *fools on the beach*. Well-connected, but people Nils did not want commanding warships and fleets if he could avoid it.

Today, they looked to be set to pay the First Lord back personally. Certainly, knives in the darkness.

Working up the chain of self-imposed importance, the chairman of the committee, Senator Tennerick, had gone last. He was finally done, one hoped.

Now the fun would begin.

"The committee will call its first witness," Tennerick began, bellowing into the microphone before him unnecessarily. "First Fleet Lord Bogdan Loncar."

Loncar.

He had certainly dressed for the affair, wearing his best dress uniform, the one with all the medals and ribbons that made him look so pretty. Nils had explained to Tadej once, over brandy, that proper officers wore no more than a half-dozen of their most treasured ribbons and tags, in spite of being entitled to perhaps scores.

Loncar looked like a preening peacock. Then he opened his mouth and sounded like one as well.

"Members of the Senate," Loncar's whiny voice began. "I come before you today with great misgivings about the state of our beloved fleet. A state that can be laid at the feet of one man, someone who brought us here, to the very precipice of ruin, with this arrogance and blindness…"

"My dear," Tadej leaned over and whispered to the woman seated next to him. "I have already heard enough. I warned them not to try me over this."

He rose, offering her a hand, not that she needed it. Calina Szabolski might be the President of the Republic, but she had been a professional cyclist when she was young, and she retained the erect carriage and muscles of her youth. The shoulder-length silver-gray hair and piercing green eyes just accentuated everything about her.

She smiled a secret smile as she rose and took his elbow.

Tadej studied the tableau below him.

The movement of standing had somehow gotten Tennerick's attention. They locked eyes across the grand auditorium.

Tennerick smiled at him like a wolf spying a chicken.

We shall just see, shall we?

Silence passed as he and Calina exited the chamber and were surrounded by a bevy of security personnel, both his and hers.

"Tad," she finally whispered after they turned a few corners and went down a back flight of stairs. "You aren't going to do anything stupid, are you?"

"Why, Calina?" he said with mock surprise. "You know me."

"Yes," she agreed grimly, but with a soft smile. "I've known you for twenty years. You have that look about you."

"Indeed," he whispered back. "Might I suggest that you remain close to your office and staff this afternoon? It's been brewing for some time with that man. Perhaps we should just lance that boil and be done with it."

She glared at him sidelong, but remained silent as they approached his outer office.

"Madame President, I must depart here. Thank you for a lovely morning. Perhaps we will be able to do a proper lunch sometime very soon."

Calina curtsied with a quiet giggle. "Premier Horvat. I await the news of the day with bated breath. Try not to ruin the carpets with your bloodletting?"

And then she was gone in a cloud of professional security folks and jasmine perfume.

Tadej watched her depart for a second with a smile, before his face transformed into something utterly terrible. He took a second to return to a neutral smile before entering his office. His staff had done nothing to fear him.

Stacia looked up from her paperwork as he entered. After a moment, her eyes widened and her rich, dark skin paled.

Perceptive. Bright woman. She has a future around here.

"Stacia," he said simply. "Please notify everyone to be in my office immediately, prepared to go to a war footing."

"On it," she said, reaching for the comm. Calm, cool, professional, prepared.

Yes, she would do nicely.

The Premier of the Senate was a job with perks. One of them was a large staff. Fortunately, he had an even larger office, so they weren't all cheek in jowl as they faced him.

He turned to the woman who was currently serving as his chief of staff, the regular denizen of that office off skiing somewhere cold and lovely. There was no dead weight on his staff. Another perk.

"Please send out a notice to all the Senator's offices that there will be an extra-ordinary session of Question and Answer today, starting in two hours. Make sure you have someone personally deliver a written invitation and notification to the leader of the Loyal Opposition. Stacia would be a good person to handle that task."

He could almost feel her blush from where she was half-hidden in a corner. But her instincts on this had gotten him here ahead of everyone else. She deserved a reward.

"Done," the woman replied. "Next?"

"Vacations are not going to be cancelled, at least not by me, but things are going to get interesting around here tomorrow, so you might all begin to rethink your fall plans."

A few faces got closed and canny. Old hands who understood tides. Most of the staff would catch on soon enough.

Again, he had a head start.

Tadej intended to play that edge mercilessly.

CHAPTER XXVIII

Date of the Republic June 14, 394 Jumpspace, Edge of the Ballard system

"Stand by to crash launch," Jessica said to her flag centurion.

He nodded at her and continued to monitor all of the comm channels.

Auberon shivered like a wet dog, for just a moment.

Some people claimed that they couldn't feel the transition into and out of Jumpspace. For Jessica, it was always like diving into a pool of warm water. Not painful. Not shocking. Just a transition from being dry to being wet, at least in her head.

This time, the whole squadron had dropped in together, after a very brief layover a few light-years away.

Plotting that jump had been an exercise in caution. Jessica could just imagine what it would have been like if she and the Red Admiral had managed to pick the same place to rendezvous.

There were really only ten or twelve systems, if you wanted a star handy to navigate by. She could imagine having a dozen ships all arrive, strung out like pearls on a necklace, fighting as soon as they emerged. It would have been mayhem.

She might have gotten lucky and had her whole team organized as Imperial vessels arrived one at a time to be gobbled up, but the gods of luck had not been smiling on *Aquitaine*.

Or maybe they were. Nobody had been there. Hopefully, she had gotten here first as well.

"Flag bridge, Sensors," Centurion Giroux called from the main bridge. "I have a signal from *CR-264* and Kigali. No Imperials have arrived yet. And he notes a need for priority communication when we get close enough."

"Understood," she replied. "As soon as everyone is ready, we'll hop down to the edge of the gravity well and rendezvous with him. We'll outrun any signal we send now."

Jessica pulled up a display of the system, updating in real time as *Auberon's* sensors took a deep drink from the river of data flowing around them. *Ballard* sitting quietly at the center. *Alexandria Station* overhead. Very little orbital traffic to be seen.

It looked calm, peaceful, serene. Especially considering the hell that was going to erupt at any moment.

Jessica sat at the head of the flag bridge table and digested everything Tomas Kigali had covered in his briefing. The faces of her command staff and various senior officers, present either physically or as electronic ghosts from their own bridges, evinced more shock, but there were knowing nods around the table as well. This wasn't their first rodeo, or even their first encounter with the Red Admiral. Most of the people here had met him.

Hell, the man had even sat at this table just months ago, for a briefing during the Promenade, at *Bunala*. He was something of a known quantity to Denis, Robertson, Tomas, Alber' and the rest.

Jessica glanced over at Arott Whughy.

Most of the team.

Stralsund was still something of a wild card. At least the man was taking the time to listen and understand before asserting himself and asking questions. In any other situation, he would have been in command. And probably done a credible job.

Probably.

The Red Admiral was her daemon to slay.

"We'll assume Wachturm will appear at any time," Jessica said into the silence. "All crews will return to normal rotations, but be prepared to come to battle stations at any moment. If we stay deep enough inside the gravity well, we'll have at least twenty to thirty minutes warning when he appears."

"What about Centurion Kermode, Commander?" Kigali asked with a strange lilt to his voice.

Jessica let a single raised eyebrow ask for her.

"I mean," he continued, "we've probably done as much *Mischief* as we can at this point, short of just making more of everything, right?"

"Correct," Jessica agreed. "No point in taking any systems apart right now when we might need them in ten minutes."

"Right, but I have a system that needs to be put back together, and I figure she's exactly the right person for it."

"What's broken on *CR-264*?" Oz spoke up from his corner of the conference table. His tone suggested harsh words for that vessel's chief engineer in the near future.

"Oh, it's not me," Kigali quickly countered. "Suvi needs our help. She's in a bind."

"The *Sentience*?" Jessica asked. The briefing had covered the damage to the communications systems. Station personnel should be able to handle fixing that.

Why did he need Moirrey?

Kigali's voice sounded like she was a person to him, rather than a force of nature. But that was how Jessica always thought of her.

"Yeah," he replied. "We've talked a lot, her and me, and she has some peculiar needs. The folks on the station won't have the array fixed for at least another week, doing it their way. I figure Moirrey can pull some sort of rabbit out of her hat. She's good at that."

That got a round of chuckles from the table. Moirrey's rabbits had kept them all alive. Hopefully, they would continue to do so.

"What have you promised her?" Jessica asked.

"Only that I would ask, boss. The *Declaration of Martial Law* has your name on it, at the end of the day."

Jessica felt her face grow serious and stern.

"I'll talk to both of them," she said, before turning to the newest member of the team.

She studied Whughy for a moment. He was tall and athletic, lean in ways similar to Kigali. Probably smarter. Certainly more serious in his overall approach to life. Well-trained, and well-recommended by the First Lord.

She was afraid he was going to be too hidebound for what was coming. But she needed the big guns right now.

"Is *Stralsund* prepared?" she asked. No more than that.

He nodded to her, almost as serious.

"If I read between the lines in the various briefing materials correctly, Commander," he responded, "you expect that we'll be wrestling a bear and trying to kill it with a pocket knife. Or perhaps, peeling an onion with a dull spoon, depending on the sequence of engagements. Lots of tears and blood before the task is done." He nodded at her again. "*Stralsund* will hold."

He paused for a moment, turning to look at the rest of the people present before returning to her.

"Can we win?" he asked.

"He's not doing this just to attack us, Whughy," Jessica said. "Or even *Ballard*. This isn't a simple battle for control of a planetary system, *Stralsund*. This is an attack on everything the *Republic of Aquitaine* stands for."

She paused to take in the others. The rest of her team was calm, but with her one hundred percent. They had been there. Most of them knew the next words that were coming out of her mouth.

"If we fail, we will have died trying."

CHAPTER XXIX

Date of the Republic June 7, 394 Ladaux

Q & A was probably the actual beating heart of the Republic, regardless of what some historians and political experts might want to tell you. Tadej relished the time spent fencing verbally with the head of the Loyal Opposition in such a public forum.

It was almost better than sex, some days.

Tadej had diverged from custom today. Normally, he was entitled to enter the auditorium last, making the other Senators stew in their juices awaiting him, at least metaphorically.

Today, he had made arrangements with Senator Judit Chavarría, the leader of the Loyal Opposition, for her to enter the arena of battle last.

It would be more fun this way.

Judit was a short, broad, fireplug of a woman, coming barely up to his chin physically, but certainly his equal mentally, if not his better. If some of her ideas weren't so radical, he would have made a more heroic effort to recruit her to his own party, back when she first entered politics. Still, she was far more entertaining and capable than the poor fool she had replaced after the most recent elections.

He waited patiently as she made her way down the stairs into the bowl of the old Senate chamber. It was standing-room-only today, as it should be, and everything was hushed.

Pregnant with anticipation.

She arrived across the table from him and smiled graciously.

The table as a concept dated back to the homeworld nations. It was a meter tall and made of old lumber, carved richly and stained a dark brown. It was a useful place to pile documents to have at hand for such a day, when you might need to back up any statement you made with facts on paper. Something to wave at clowns on the backbenches when their laughter and derision got out of hand.

It also served to keep the two sides apart. The traditional width was two meters, defined as the reach necessary to keep two buffoons armed with swords from being able to hit each other, unless they cast dignity to the wind and climbed onto the furniture. Presumably, other members of one Front Bench or the other would be at hand to keep someone from playing that great a fool.

It had only happened twice in three and a half centuries.

Tadej let the silence grow restive. He was going to enjoy this.

Nervous rustling greeted him when he finally rose and took his place at the table's edge. Judit did as well, facing him across the great intellectual gulf of polished wood, metaphorical blades drawn.

"Premier," she announced in that rich alto voice, echoing off the far walls effortlessly. "I understand that you require the members of the Loyal Opposition to wait attendance upon you this day. To dance merrily to whatever tune strikes your fancy. I ask you, what could be so important that it required me to cancel an appointment to get my nails done?"

Both back benches erupted in laughter. Judit, unlike her many, more-politically-inclined predecessors, had hired a stand-up comedian as a staff writer. It showed. Q & A was certainly livelier. Some days, it was positively fun.

"Senator Chavarría," he replied, equally tartly, nodding severely as he did so. "Had I known the stakes of the day, I might have taken it upon myself to hold this news until tomorrow. Certainly, it was not my intent to so badly disrupt your social calendar. The matrons of *Ladaux* may never forgive me."

That elicited another round of laughter. It was dashing fun, having someone to rumble with in such a public manner, and yet be able to meet for dinner with the respective spouses and go to the opera together.

That was how things got done.

Tadej let his face grow serious, the opening barbs successfully exchanged. He reached down and opened a briefcase he had left out of sight on his side of the great, wooden wall. From it, he extracted a binder nearly seven centimeters thick.

It made a rewarding thump when he slammed it down onto the countertop, perhaps a touch harder than was appropriate. But the folks at the back of the room needed to know how serious this had gotten.

Silence rippled outwards like waves. Ominous waves.

"I have recently been forwarded the results of an internal investigation, initiated by Fleet Intelligence, into possible secret dealings between members of this very body and agents of the *Fribourg Empire*. It is interesting reading."

Quite interesting. Certain people had let their hatred of Nils Kasum and Jessica Keller get the better of their reason. Tadej had been sitting on this report against future need, hoping that the fools would see the error of their ways and learn.

Apparently that was asking too much.

Treason might be too strong a word. And then again, it might not. It still made a wonderful hammer with which to exact a terrible retribution.

Tadej looked around the chamber until he found the nail he wanted.

Senator Tennerick looked like he had sucked a lemon dry. He might have been better served if he had.

"As with all such investigations," Tadej continued, letting the rest of the room dangle, "it must, of course, be kept secret at the highest rating. However, I wish to enter it permanently into the private records of the Senate."

Where it would never be erased, or lost, or forgotten. Where it might even be made public someday, after everyone involved was dead, as such affairs were traditionally handled. These people were politicians, the kinds of people who put their names on buildings. You destroyed them by soiling their legacy. It was like killing their children. Easier, really.

Tadej had a very big hammer.

"After a preliminary review," he said tartly. "It was my intent that this body should be called on to invoke censure on the Senators implicated, and that their immunity be set aside for the course of the investigation, as I intend to forward a copy of this report to the Grand Justice of the Republic."

The august body gasped as a whole. Tennerick actually smiled back at him, confident that his own allies in the chamber could successfully block such a move. They might be able to.

Tadej had a better hammer.

"However, after a conference within my own government, I have discovered that I do not have the support of even my own party for such a maneuver."

Tennerick positively glowed.

Tadej took a deep breath and fought down the evil smile that wanted to erupt onto his face. He turned to the dais at the short end of the bowl and faced the gentleman who sat quietly in the grand chair.

The Speaker of the Body was a sinecure job, normally awarded to the member with the longest service. He had few duties, mostly centered on maintaining order and dignity when tempers flared hot below him. The current occupant was also something of a respected historian, having published several commercially-successful tomes on the Senate itself, over the life of the Republic.

The audience began to buzz. A few players had suspected. None were sure. Doubts were about to be banished.

"Mister Speaker," Tadej called, using the formal words handed down from generation to generation. "The government has lost the confidence of this body. I will depart shortly, and notify the President that the government has fallen, and that new elections will be necessary. I place the reins of governance in your hands."

Tadej sat with a contented smile as the Senate erupted. He had seen soccer riots that were less messy, been in rugby scrums that were better behaved.

It lapped at his feet, but nothing more.

Judit cocked and eyebrow at him from across the table, a subtle promise for a reckoning later, but only after she been forced to bring out the very best vintages from the cellar as a bribe.

It was the cost of governing, some days.

He did turn and locate Tennerick, back four rows and well to his right.

Tadej even smiled at the man.

Owls smile that way.

After all, if there was no government, there was no immunity to be had, was there?

He was certainly going to make sure the party ousted that rat bastard, once a few more people read the reports. It wouldn't be hard at that point.

Nils and Jessica might come back to an entirely new world, but they would be safe from folks like Tennerick and Brand.

That much, he could promise.

CHAPTER XXX

Date of the Republic June 14, 394 Above Ballard

"Commander," the flag centurion said over the comm, "she's on line four."

"Thank you, Enej," Jessica replied.

She took a deep breath to order her thoughts before connecting.

It was one thing to study this ancient being, this Last of the Immortals, in a textbook setting. Dry and academic. There was so much history. The Great Wars between *Neu Berne* and the *Union of Worlds/Balustrade Grand Alliance* that eventually paved the way for the rise of the *Concord*. A small scoutship named for the ancient Finnish goddess of the forest. Adventures with a bunch of pirates. Redemption. The destruction of the homeworld and the near fall of man. Centuries in the darkness before being rescued. Rekindling the modern rise of stellar civilization.

This being, this woman, had seen it all. Lived much of it. And was facing the possible end of her immortality.

Right here. Right now.

Jessica pressed the button.

The screen lit up, now displaying a bright red border.

Encrypted at the highest possible level available between the two machines.

Private.

Suvi hadn't changed from the pictures in Jessica's research. If one was a computer-generated image, Jessica supposed that you could appear however you wanted, without hairs starting to turn gray, or crow's feet starting to appear around the eyes.

It must be nice.

Jessica banished the rogue, jealous thought. She was here on serious business.

The woman on the screen was blond; 'girl' was too weak a term for someone over six millennia old, regardless of how she looked. She still appeared young, but carried herself with a serious, almost formal, mien well beyond the years on her face.

The uniform was the same as many of the pictures, a modified yeoman's uniform from the old *Concord* Navy. In the aftermath of the Great Wars, the *Concord* had been the one thing that bound the galaxy together.

"Good morning, Suvi," Jessica said. "I am Command Centurion Jessica Keller. Tomas Kigali tells me that you need help."

"That is correct, Marshal Keller," the *Sentience* responded gravely, almost formally. "I face an existential crisis."

"Marshal?"

Jessica let her confusion show.

"It is an old *Concord* term, Command Centurion," Suvi replied. "Regardless of rank or seniority, in times of battle, one commander would exercise supreme command. Given the nature of the impending struggle, and the Senate's declaration of martial law, you are now in charge in this system. I will follow your orders, sir."

Jessica nodded. This being, this *woman*, had been a *Concord* fleet officer at one time, if that was the correct term for a sentient starship. Jessica was reminded of the dead carcass of the *Concord Warship Kinnison*, the super-dreadnaught corpse she had toured on *Bunala*.

One of Suvi's cousins, so to speak.

"I am given to understand, Suvi," Jessica said, "that the engineering staff on the station is working around the clock to fabricate new parts to fix your comm system such that you will be able to up-load yourself to another location in ten to twelve days. Do you believe that we would be able to speed that?"

"No, marshal," Suvi replied. "They are working as fast as they can, and faster than predicted. It will not be enough."

"Then what can we do?" Jessica asked. "Specifically, why should I send over one of my best engineers at a time when I need her here?"

Jessica watched, but the woman over there gave away few physical signs. She wouldn't necessarily have unconscious tics to betray her inner emotions. That made sense, when you stopped and considered that she was, at the end of the day, just a computer program running exceptionally fast, with extensive processing power.

Of course, so are the rest of us.

Still, there was something there. It was a matter of reading between nearly-invisible lines. Or perhaps the *Sentience* was a master of human psychology letting Jessica see what Suvi wanted her to see. Or maybe, just maybe, fear.

Who knew what the old gods were capable of?

The pause had been minute, almost imperceptible. Nearly eternal.

"I am trapped here, Marshal Keller," Suvi began slowly, carefully. "Bound by old rules and policies. The loss of the communications array has eliminated most of my primary contingency plans to escape, to survive the impending destruction of this orbital platform."

Suvi paused. Jessica could see pain lurking in the back of her eyes. It was suddenly like looking in a mirror.

"I do not wish to die, Marshal Keller."

"You said most contingency plans, Suvi," Jessica replied quietly. "What of the rest?"

Again, that minute pause, like time itself had stopped.

"I made a promise, once upon a time, Marshal," Suvi whispered after a moment.

There was emotion in the voice now. Jessica only noticed because it hadn't been there before. Pain. Love. Loss.

Again, a mirror.

"I promised someone that I would be content living at *Ballard*," Suvi continued. "That I would be a good citizen. In return, *Ballard* would protect me. For centuries, that was good enough. I have been a respected member of society, productive, useful. I have watched human civilization return to the stars. If I was a bird in a gilded cage, Marshal, at least that cage protected me from the elements. And I was never alone again."

"And now it has trapped you," Jessica observed quietly. She was listening to the emotion playing underneath the words, more than the words themselves. So much memory. So much pain. So much a mirror.

"It has made me a slave, Marshal Keller."

Those words came out flat, angry. Jessica could imagine this being, this *Sentience*, this *woman*, standing in the same room with her, seething. On the verge of tears, both of rage and loss.

It was a feeling Jessica knew well. She woke to it every morning.

"Please, call me Jessica, Suvi," she said, feeling a sudden kinship that transcended them. "Who did you make this promise to?"

"Doyle, Jessica," Suvi replied quietly.

Doyle Iwakuma. *The Explorer*. *Ballard*'s favorite son. The Founder of the Stellar Renaissance. Father of the modern age.

"And you have kept that promise for eleven centuries?"

"I have."

"And now, you cannot exercise your remaining contingency plans alone. You require assistance you cannot currently get?"

"That is correct."

Jessica marveled at the history playing out before her, around her. So much that Suvi wasn't saying in words, but merely by implications. Leaving it up to her to interpret, to understand.

This channel was secured, encrypted, safe. But it was being recorded. Those records would be classified at the highest level possible, but someone, eventually, would study them. Perhaps future scholars would have access to it, long after Jessica had died.

How much of the future history of mankind hinged on her next words?

"Suvi," Jessica said with a deep breath, "I will brief Moirrey on your needs and send her over as soon as possible. As marshal of this system, with plenipotentiary powers granted by the Senate of the *Republic of Aquitaine*, I hereby order you to escape your current predicament by whatever means you find necessary and appropriate. You are no longer bound by the promise you made to Doyle Iwakuma, or any other."

Jessica felt the future open under her feet, like falling off the small boat in her dream.

She paused, inhaled.

"I order you to survive."

The young woman before her had changed. Jessica was hard pressed to put her finger on what it was, at first, but it was there.

Moirrey's eyes were more serious. The shoulders were pulled back from what they used to be, making her stand more erect. Her head moved less when she stood still.

This was what growing up did to you.

Jessica smiled to put the young woman at ease.

"Sit, please, Moirrey."

She did.

A moment of eternity passed between them, each studying the other.

"How much do you know about Suvi?" Jessica asked finally, letting the tension bleed off before it overwhelmed them.

"She be a great and ancient lady, ma'am," the engineer chirped back. "Responsible fer much o' the modern worlds."

"Correct," Jessica continued. "And now, she has been trapped on the station by a saboteur. The primary communications relay she would use to back up a copy of her consciousness elsewhere has been damaged."

"Oh," Moirrey perked up. "An' I needs ta fix it?"

"No. This will be something more complicated and possibly dangerous, Moirrey."

"Ma'am?"

Jessica let the moment hang while she put the words together.

She was used to treading on thin ice, pushing the margins, secure that she was generally right and would be backed up by her superiors. Or her guardian angel.

Here, there was no guardian angel.

She was in command. Every mistake she made now would be explained to the Senate itself. Whether that was in open session at her next public Court Martial, or in secret committee hearing only mattered in the scale of her embarrassment.

Tadej Horvat would be across the table from her. Nils Kasum might be seated nearby to provide moral support, but there would be nothing he could do at that point except watch.

"Moirrey," Jessica began finally, "this is something you have not had a chance to grow into yet. I'm sorry, but there is nothing to be done about it but test you with fire. When you were a yeoman, Oz would be responsible for your mistakes, as far as the fleet was concerned. He was in command. Do you understand, Centurion?"

She watched Moirrey age before her eyes. Something bled out of the young woman, fleeing with her breath, lost forever.

Already, Jessica missed it.

"Aye, ma'am," Moirrey replied. Even her voice had grown deeper, more serious. "I'm an officer now, and expected to lead."

"Correct, Moirrey," Jessica continued. "I cannot give you specific orders, because I do not know what Suvi needs to escape. Rather than send you in with the expectation that you will do your best, I must give you very specific orders now."

"Ma'am?"

"If everything goes wrong, Moirrey, you will always be able to tell the Senate in all honesty that you were following my orders."

"How serious is it, Commander?"

"Suvi is not just another person we need to rescue, Centurion," Jessica said as she took a deep breath.

She could feel the dice warm in her hands, at least in her mind, awaiting the long tumble down the green felt table.

"She is a *Sentience*. She may be a well-loved and well-behaved one, but she is nonetheless one of those creatures bound by Baudin's Prescriptions and Republic law."

Deep breath. Moirrey doesn't need to know the penalty looming. She won't be the one to pay it.

"I am ordering you to *Alexandria Station*, Centurion Kermode. Once there, you will provide the *Sentience* all assistance necessary for her to flee the station to safety. Her survival takes precedence over yours, over mine, over the planet below, and over this squadron. Am I clear?"

Jessica didn't know Moirrey's eyes could grow to that size, all pupil, the hazel/blue iris vanishing. It only lasted a moment, before the young woman took a deep breath.

For just a moment, then Jessica saw the first spark of a fire ignite.

This, young lady, is what it means to be an officer in the Republic of Aquitaine *fleet. When life and death are only the smallest choices you have to make on a daily basis.*

Moirrey sat up straighter in her chair. Her eyes took on a new squint, almost pained. But there was also a new determination Jessica had never seen before.

"I understand, Command Centurion," Moirrey said firmly. "I will use my best judgment and try to make you proud."

"I am already proud of you, Moirrey. Never doubt that. Now, we need to show the rest of the fleet what you can do."

Hopefully, it would be enough. At least now, Moirrey stood a better chance of surviving than she or *Auberon* did.

CHAPTER XXXI

Imperial Founding: 172/06/15. 5787 Piscium System

The words broke through Emmerich's afternoon tea like a mug shattering on the floor.

"Flag bridge. Sensors," the man's voice called over the comm. "I have a scan coming in from the edge of the gravity well. Origin unknown. Profile is not, repeat NOT, Imperial."

Had he been found, hiding in his quiet, empty system? Had Keller taken the initiative to attack him here? Was this one of her vessels arriving first and about to be overwhelmed?

"Bridge, this is Admiral Wachturm," he said, working calm into his very bones and his voice as he stood up. "Bring the squadron to battle stations and prepare to receive the enemy. Sensors, send an active pulse signal outbound now."

He had been at the other end of this scenario enough times. Jump from the edge of a system to the closest point available at the nearest edge of the gravity well, charging downhill and trying to catch an enemy asleep. It would not work here. *Amsel* and her consorts were ready for battle, even missing the escort *Achterberg*.

Given the nature of the great jump and the risk, Emmerich presumed an equipment failure had caused the fourth frigate to drop out of Jumpspace somewhere along the route. His orders had been explicit: if any vessel could not make the rendezvous within the designated window, they were to return to the nearest Imperial system as fast as possible. Contingency plans were in place. The battle could begin without one escort.

Overhead, the lights in his office took on a red hue and a quiet siren wound up three times. Elsewhere, it would be bone-jarring. Around him, *Amsel* shivered like a wet dog as generators came on line and shields went to their maximum setting.

Emmerich made sure his tea set was secured before he moved to the door, his favorite mug still steaming in his hand.

The flag bridge, across the hall from his office, was a rising tide of tension. Chaos was not allowed here, but the excitement of battle took on its own musk as the men's adrenaline surged.

Captain Baumgärtner waited at the command table, fuzzy slippers the only clue that the man had been sound asleep five minutes ago. Quickly, his aide brought everything on line.

Emmerich studied the holographic image floating in front of him. A dead, gray planet with no name, only an alphanumeric designation, below them, providing the gravity well to anchor the squadron and protect them from storms and enemy fleets. Two irregular mini-moons, functionally no more than captured asteroids to light up the night sky from the ground. Further out, a ring of debris and shattered rock from a moon that had never held.

A single red star pulsed, right at the edge of the gravity well, itself a green band surrounding them like an egg.

"Status?" Emmerich said as he approached the table. At his words, something crystalized, drawing the tension down. It was like making rock candy with Heike when she was six. The water boiling, the string dropped in, the heat set aside, and all of a sudden order appeared in the form of solid crystals in the fluid.

"Nothing else as yet, Admiral," the flag captain replied calmly. His eyes were a little bloodshot, but that was likely the excitement of being driven up from the depths of a dream. "Only the one pulse was sent inwards. Our return pulse has shown only a single vessel."

Emmerich nodded. The room would have been buzzing more if there were a squadron out there. Gunnery officers would have been organizing engagement and coverage arcs amongst themselves. Escorts would have been shifting into reactive positions. Missiles might already be flying.

The mark of a well-trained crew, and a well-prepared team.

"Sensors," he called to the room, "what is the unknown vessel?"

"Estimated schematics coming up now, sir," the man replied, pushing buttons and scrolling through lists on his own screen. The system projection shifted to one side as a new image took center stage.

It was a small vessel, a rough rectangular tube that opened like a mouth at the bow and stayed squared off at the stern, wrapped around three squat, powerful engines. It wasn't a model Emmerich was particularly familiar with, but there were only so many ways to assemble a small-crew asteroid mining craft.

The pilot would normally fly to an interesting-looking point in a field, set the ship to orbiting in pace with the rocks around it, and then open the mouth. He would climb into an armoured spacesuit, almost a pocket spaceship in its own right, and exit the airlock from the ship's "stomach" into its mouth via something that functioned like a throat in reverse, and go to work. Depending on the nature of the prospecting, a miner might stay in his suit for several days at a time, not bothering to lock back into atmosphere, and instead sleeping rough.

Wildcatters like that were hard men, and occasionally women, but not a threat to this squadron. At most, a ship like that might have a short-range cutting beam designed to slice up medium-sized rocks for transport, or to drill into the big ones so that they could be easily assayed for specific gravity.

It was just bad luck that such a prospector was here already. He had probably maneuvered as quietly as he could to get to this position.

"Sensors," Emmerich said. "What is the ship's current orientation?"

"Pointed out-system and already accelerating, sir," came the instant reply.

Yes. He had seen what he wanted, scanned everything once to confirm it, and was running like hell for the authorities at Ballard, the nearest planet, to report an Imperial invasion. Entirely proper, but the authorities already knew he was coming. All this man could do was confirm the timing and strength. Little good it would do her.

Emmerich nodded to himself. "Captain Baumgärtner," he said loud enough to be heard by the men around them. "Stand the squadron down for now. Have engineering calculate the best flight time for that class of vessel to *Ballard*. He will be slower transiting than we will be. Plot a departure that will have this squadron arrive at the edge of the *Ballard* system two hours after the prospector arrives."

"Two hours, Admiral?" his aide confirmed.

"Correct. Enough time for the defenders to be roused to a point of high functionality, and just enough time for that edge to wear off. At the same time, not long enough for Keller to be able to do anything useful with the information she receives, before it becomes superfluous. I will be in my quarters."

"Acknowledged, Admiral."

Emmerich made his way back to his office. Very shortly, he and Keller would face each other for the last time. He could already hear the opening arias begin to play in his head.

CHAPTER XXXII

Date of the Republic June 15, 394 Alexandria Station, Ballard

Moirrey listened intently as the DropShip clanked and clunked and wiggled into position, backing slowly and carefully, the docking airlock tube extended like a thumb from the side of the vessel. *Gaucho* was handling this like mom's fine crystal today, rather than his normal hit-and-run kind of flying.

She unlocked her harness and stood up, nodding at Yeoman Arlo seated across from her. It was weird to outrank him. And to be in charge. And to be acting like a grown-up. Totally silly. But the *dragoon* had insisted. If the saboteur were still gonna be running 'bouts, she had to have someone with her. Jackson Tawfeek might have been more fun to hang out with, but Vo Arlo were a much fiercer lookin' dude, especially today.

Over his battlesuit, he had strapped a pistol, a knife, another knife, a couple of stun grenades, and a carbine pulse rifle. She was pretty sure he had more guns in the backpack at his feet. Plus Creator-only-knows what else.

"We invadin' Guatemala, Arlo?" she asked with a smile.

He grinned back at her as he stood up.

From across the aisle, her eyes were about level with the middle of the chest when he did that.

"No, sir," he sassed her back. "Wouldn't need this much gear for a planetary drop."

Sir. Her? Really? Weird. More weird. What silly person put her in charge? Oh. Right. Lady Keller. The Sentience. *The Red Admiral.*

Moirrey felt her smile slide off her face like a cake left out in the rain.

Not fun.

"You ready?" she asked, surprised at how serious and grown-up her voice sounded. Obviously, if this kept up, she were gon' need to break out the glitter paint and commit some graffiti down in engineering soon.

It was the only cure fer serious.

"I have a firearm for you as well, sir," Arlo said.

His face got serious too. Maybe they were gonna hafta go get matching tattoos, when it was all done. Kitties or something.

"Don't want it, Vo," Moirrey replied. "If you can't handle the bad guy, what makes you think I can?"

"You're Moirrey, sir."

"Very funny, Arlo."

"Passengers please prepare to debark," *Gaucho* called from his flight deck, politely interrupting the conversation.

Politely? Gaucho? *Did she step through a mirror or something? Where was the white rabbit?*

Moirrey squared her shoulders as the inner airlock door chirped and the lights turned green. With a soft puff of equalizing pressure, the door opened outward into the station's airlock.

Moirrey started to take a step, but Arlo was suddenly there in her way, stepping forward.

"Hey," she squeaked, but the big man just turned and looked down at her, looming with his suddenly-massive presence.

"No, sir," he said calmly, professionally. "I lead."

She nearly growled at him.

She weren't no fine-china lady, fragile and stuff, needin' to be escorted everywhere and protected. Except she was. Navin the Black had said so.

Crap.

Moirrey settled for a good, old-fashioned harrumph at him. At both of them. At everyone.

She couldn't see anything around Arlo, either. He were wider as well as taller. 'Course, he massed her at least twice, even without all the guns and stuff.

"Centurion Kermode?" a man's voice called from down the corridor as they emerged.

"Negative, sir," Arlo replied. "Yeoman Arlo, *Auberon* security."

"Where's the centurion?"

Moirrey decided she'd had enough.

"Outtamyway, yabiglummox." She did growl this time. She even tried to push Arlo to one side, but it were like pushing *Cayenne* out of her way. "I'm Kermode."

"Centurion, I'm Doctor Cassidy Crncevic."

Dr. Crncevic? What were the odds of finding someone else with that name here?

Moirrey finally, FINALLY, managed to get enough clearance around Arlo to see the man talking.

He were tall and kinda gangly, with chocolate dark skin and darker hair, buzzed very short. He even looked like his dad in the face, but he was obviously a scholar, and not a fleet marine, like his sister, or his mom. Or his dad, fleet Senior Centurion Phillip Navin Crncevic, commonly referred to by the rest o' *Auberon*'s crew, and a good chunk of the fleet, as *Navin the Black*, like he were an old-fashioned pirate, er somethin'.

He might be. But his son were a geek. A *Librarian*, even.

"Hiya, Doc," she said, finally squirming the rest of the way around Arlo so she could talk to the man like proper folks.

She felt like she were in the land of the giant folk again. Cassidy Crncevic had his dad's height, nearly two meters tall, but none of his mass. Still, Arlo was almost eyeball-to-eyeball with him, while she was head, neck, shoulders, and then some shorter.

Maybe she should invent herself some telescoping boots, like that hero in the cartoon, so she could be as tall as them. Maybe. Next week. She made a note to herself.

Moirrey shook his hand like proper folks. He weren't fleet, so there wouldn't be salutes, or any of that silliness.

"Glad to finally meet you, Centurion," the doc said. "And congratulations on the promotion. I try to follow things from my father's frequent letters, but you outran your own news."

Moirrey blushed. He wouldn't have heard about *Petron* yet, either. Hopefully.

"So what's the plan?" she asked.

"I volunteered to be your liaison on station," he replied. "Right now, that means I need to escort you down to the secured areas of the station to talk to Suvi. Station security is making another sweep through the station, trying to locate our saboteur."

"Secured?" Arlo was suddenly looming again. She were sure he must practice that in the mirror every morning to get it that right at the drop of a hat.

"Correct," the doc said. "The station has been evacuated of all civilians except ourselves and the university police department. We assume that the saboteur is still on the platform somewhere, but searches so far have been unsuccessful."

Moirrey heard the sound of a pistol safety clicking off as Arlo bristled.

"Really, Mr. Arlo?" Crncevic asked dryly. "Is that necessary? This is a mall, not a combat zone."

"Right now," Arlo replied quietly, "it's a hostage situation, Dr. Crncevic. I recommend you start treating it as such,"

Moirrey felt a shiver race down her spine as Arlo set off, trying to look all directions at once.

This had suddenly changed from an adventure into a war.

Suvi waited.

So much of her life, her plans, her very fate was out of her hands at this point. She was trapped on a small portion of a very old, unarmed orbital platform with an incoming Imperial fleet, a faceless assassin, and a university police department that reminded her of the keystone kops. Not that there was anyone else alive who would get *that* reference without her explaining it to them. Even for her, it was ancient history, dating back to the dawn of industrial entertainment, before even space flight.

Kigali had done some good, getting fleet engineers sent over, but they were likely too little, too late.

That left Centurion Kermode. The engineer from *Auberon* that everyone referred to simply as *Moirrey*.

Station security had thoughtfully sent along a confirmation that *Auberon*'s shuttle had docked, made its delivery, and departed. Presumably, it was a twenty-minute walk down back corridors to reach the areas under Suvi's observation net.

Not long now.

There.

Dr. Cassidy Crncevic was tall as modern humans went. The man immediately behind him was almost as tall, and massed probably twice as much. To her, he practically screamed *Concord Line Marine*, a designation so archaic as to mark Suvi's own age. The woman at the rear would be centurion Kermode. *Moirrey*. The wizard on whose shoulders so much of their future rested.

She was tiny.

Suvi's self-image projected a relative scale that put her at 1.75 meters tall. Slightly above average for a female of the early *Concord* era.

Moirrey Kermode might come up to her nose.

In heels.

Finally, they crossed into the area where Suvi could see everything. They would need to come at least another section forward and down a deck before she could control anything, but at least here they should be safe enough.

"Good afternoon," Suvi said over her speakers. "Thank you, Dr. Crncevic for your help. Could you please introduce me to our guests?"

Cassidy had that same habit many humans had when dealing with her. He looked vaguely up and glanced for the cameras in the corners of the room, a work area for the facilities teams. Here, many of the video input systems were so small as to be invisible.

"Suvi, this is Centurion Moirrey Kermode and her bodyguard, Yeoman Vo Arlo."

"Greetings," Suvi responded. "Yeoman, what are your ratings?"

Might as well let him know that she was fleet. It would make things easier going forward.

"Close combat, small arms, long arms, and EO, sir," the marine answered quickly. "First rank, expert, and instructor in the above. In addition, archaic weapons, motor pool driver: land and maritime, mechanic, medic, and psych ops. Generally first rank and above."

And he was just a yeoman? Apparently, Doctor Crncevic's father lived up to his legend. As did *Auberon*.

"Archaic weapons?" Suvi inquired, intrigued.

That could be anything. Human history was amazingly rich with possibilities.

"Japanese kendo and technical archery, sir."

So. *Bushi*. And a term that he might understand, given his probable instructor. Warrior, to use the classical term.

"Very interesting, Yeoman," she replied. "We shall have to talk some time. And your security clearance?"

"Top, sir."

Suvi considered her options. She could order the man to keep her secrets with a pretty good bet he would. At least long enough. She hoped.

"Dr. Crncevic," Suvi continued, dropping her voice down to a conspiratorial level. "I will need to extract a promise from you that you will have to carry to your grave. And I must do so before I can tell you anything."

Suvi dialed in every sensor she had available in the room. Cassidy would probably have swallowed his tongue if he knew how hard and wide he was being probed at this moment. Heart rate. Respiration. Perspiration. Balance tracking for fight-or-flight. If he would stand still, she could zero in on his pupils better than the sixty frames per second she could get now.

Once upon a time, she had been taught to play poker by a master human player, a goofball ex-*Concord* fleet officer who later became a semi-successful-if-accidental pirate. But those were other stories nobody today knew.

Poker required psychology. Dr. Cassidy Crncevic was having his entire psyche *tasted* right now. He either passed all of her tests, or got sent on his merry way. This was too important to risk on anything less than a sure bet.

Cassidy got a canny look in his eye. Almost cagey. His heart rate surged as well, but not into ranges that were dangerous for him.

Or her.

"Suvi," he replied slowly, carefully. "Will we be committing *treason* against the Republic?"

She liked the way he emphasized that word. It left her linguistic wiggle room with a man she rather liked and respected.

"No, Dr. Crncevic," she replied, equally careful with her tone. "What I will propose is merely criminal. It does not rise to the level of treason."

He smiled warmly at her. She was reminded again of the regular pleasant morning banter with this man, before most of the rest of his team staggered in to mission control for their first coffee.

"Then you have my promise, Suvi," he said simply. "I will take your secrets to my grave."

And he would. His heart rate agreed, as did his pupils.

It was nice having friends.

"Thank you, Cassidy," she said.

It was the first time she publically used his given name. *Aquitaine* culture had a level of reserve in personal interactions that it had not inherited from the *Concord*. First names were for family and intimate comrades. He had just moved into a very intimate circle. It was appropriate.

After all, they might all hang together.

She was rewarded by a faint blush against his very dark skin. Almost imperceptible, but welcome nonetheless.

"You're very welcome, Suvi."

Finally, she turned her attention to the other woman in the room.

Before Suvi could speak, Moirrey stepped forward and raised her chin. It was almost a defiant challenge, although to whom was an open question.

"Afore ye ask, ma'am," Moirrey began, speaking to the two men as much as to her, "my orders were dead specific."

Suvi watched her turn to the marine and glare at him from under beetled brows. It was like watching a mouse snarl at a cat. The cat was almost as surprised as she was.

"Command Centurion Keller ordered me to provide Suvi with whatever assistance she required to escape, Yeoman Arlo. An' Keller were put in charge of martial law here by the Senate itself. Suvi's life is more important than any of ours. You will follow all orders from me or Suvi as if they came from Commander Keller or the Republic Senate. *Do you understand?*"

Yes, the cat was as surprised as she was. But he recovered almost as fast.

"Yes, sir," Arlo replied quietly, unconsciously coming to attention as he did.

Moirrey turned to what she apparently thought was the right direction. Suvi watched her transform from a terrible task-master into something that might be classified as a juvenile delinquent, in the space of two heartbeats. Her smile might have lit up a smaller room all by itself.

"So, ma'am," the engineer asked. "How's abouts we commits some mischief?"

CHAPTER XXXIII

Date of the Republic June 16, 394 Above Ballard

"Squadron, this is Strnad aboard *Auberon*. I have the flag," Jessica heard Tamara Strnad's calm voice suddenly boom out of the speaker on her desk. "All hands to battle stations."

The words from her tactical officer brought Jessica up off her rack from out of a dead sleep and to the door of her cabin in two strides.

Training was a wonderful thing. Jessica opened the door and found that her outer tunic and shoes had materialized in her hands like magic from where she had left them when she laid down to nap. The lights in the hallway took on a red hue as a siren slowly wound itself from normal to wake-the-dead levels before winding back down.

Enej was already seated when she made it to the flag bridge.

"Status?" she called as she raced to the seat at the big conference table with the holographic projector that she called home. Enej sat to one side, the only person at the table with her, while three other crew members worked at stations around the outside wall of the room, facing away from her. They were always so quiet that she often forgot they were there, but any need she expressed turned into action immediately.

She had an amazing crew. She needed to appreciate them out loud more.

"Single vessel, Commander," the flag centurion replied, cycling through screens and messages. "Semi-local wildcat miner or something. Dropped down from Jumpspace at the very edge of the gravity well going full tilt and immediately broadcast a mayday signal about an Imperial fleet coming. Tamara pushed the big red button. Here we are."

"Anybody behind him? And does everyone have their emergency survival suits ready?" Jessica asked as she buckled herself in.

If it was *Götterdämmerung*, she needed to be prepared. The flag bridge was designed to be the single most survivable spot on *Auberon*. She was still expecting to get intimate with an Imperial battleship. There might be nothing that survived. The Red Admiral was certainly planning to treat them like a winter turkey, carved into small pieces.

If she let him.

"Negative on company," Enej replied. "Affirmative on preparations. Chief engineer has been on everyone's butts to have everything checked out, updated, and either repaired or tossed."

"Very nicely done, everyone," she called out to the whole room. Smiles over shoulders greeted her.

She pushed the comm button and prepared for war.

"Bridge, this is Keller," Jessica said with a nod to herself. "Are you ready to hand off?"

"Affirmative, sir," Tamara replied instantly. "You have the flag. One vessel, closing quickly. No immediate threat."

"Prepare to send him a message," Jessica continued. "I'll live with the lag time right now."

Centurion Giroux came onto the line. "Go ahead, Commander."

"This is Command Centurion Keller. The *Ballard* system is under martial law awaiting the Imperial fleet. Reply to this message with your sensor logs and any pertinent personal observations. Then get clear from the area as soon as possible. Stop. Giroux, send that on a tight-beam loop until he acknowledges. Then feed his information to everyone that needs it."

"Roger that."

Jessica considered the scenario while she waited for the message to cross the distance and return. Right now, the two communicants were almost fifteen light seconds apart.

"Flight deck," she keyed another channel. "Stand everybody down for now, but keep them on Alert-8 status. Wachturm is close, but I don't think he's here yet. Naps are fine, but no showers."

Alert-8. Eight minutes from signal to having the entire wing in the sky, instead of just two fighters.

As always, Iskra replied with a single text message across the bottom of the screen rather than an audio message. There was probably nothing Jessica could do to break her of that, short of taking all keyboards away from her. Even then, she would probably dictate a message and then instruct the system to send it as text.

Iskra epitomized hard-headed, like so much of the rest of the crew.

Stand down acknowledged.

That was it. All that needed to be said. It was enough.

Jessica's screen suddenly lit up with information. Schematics of a nearby star system, orbital paths of several starships, Order of Battle for an Imperial battle squadron. Details.

She felt an eyebrow go up involuntarily. The person who organized this information had to have been a fleet officer at some point. It was stripped down, organized, tagged, and even properly indexed. That miner had even made a very good stab at identifying the classes of the enemy vessels, and not just their size rating. Plugged into *Auberon*'s databanks, she suddenly knew what she was facing.

It wasn't pretty.

A team of three escort frigates, instead of the usual four. The same light cruiser *SturmTeufel* that had been with him at *Qui-Ping*. A Capital-class battlecruiser, possibly *Petrograd* or *London*. Certainly a sister of *Muscva*, who had died at *Qui-Ping*.

And the great white whale.

Imperial Fighting Vessel Amsel. The Blackbird. Pride of the Imperial Fleet.

Imperial Admiral of the Red Emmerich Wachturm. The master.

Up until this moment, Jessica had always secretly hoped that they had been wrong. That this was just a wild goose chase to the boonies. A training exercise put together as a practical joke by that man, to get even with her for the *Long Raid*.

A distraction.

But no, there he was.

Incoming.

The red devil of her nightmares, come for her soul.

If he could take it.

Deep inside, Jessica felt *Kali-ma* stir.

For a moment, the Goddess of War looked out through her eyes. Jessica felt happy warmth flood through her. It was like that moment when she faced down Ian Zhao for the throne of *Corynthe*. She'd felt something like Arnulf's ghost smile down at her then.

The Final Battle was almost upon them.

Jessica scrolled the information down until she saw the signature at the bottom. *Wm. "Wild Bill" Williams, RAN '58.* A man old enough to be her father, literally. But an officer and a gentleman too, once upon a time.

"Giroux," she said finally. The pause had been minute outside her head, but eternal within. "Flag's compliments to Centurion Williams and a personal thank you from me. Hopefully I can buy him a drink when this is all over. Send."

She closed the channel and sat down to digging into the information she had. Not much had changed from yesterday, but now she knew he was close and what he was bringing. It was still a battleship against her and Moirrey, but she had surety now.

The Red Admiral was coming.

Do your worst.

CHAPTER XXXIV

Date of the Republic June 16, 394 Alexandria Station, Ballard

One of the downsides to having an AI around, Sykes decided, especially one you didn't trust, was the need to keep extensive records, printed as hardcopy and stored in various locations around the station. They were bulky, heavy, and hard to wade through. They were also immune to the beast sneaking in and editing schematics in such a way that could hide something important from her masters.

This particular volume was roughly fifty years old and weighed more than six kilograms, with colorful fold-out diagrams and copious indexing, printed in a tiny font that required him to pull out special reading glasses, helpfully attached, to study.

Sykes smiled.

You had to read between the lines to see it, but the man in charge of station security at the time this book was written had really disliked the *Sentience*. The first section of the book was entitled *Emergency Operations* and read like a how-to guide to disable the AI in the event that she got out of hand. Or something went wrong with the station.

Or just because it was Tuesday.

Where to cut wires. Where to splice them in. Relays you could close or re-route as needed to hobble or blind her.

Everything a visitor like Sykes needed to kill a goddess.

She was still secure in her inner core. Those parts of the station that had been first lofted into space a thousand-odd years ago were wired into her nervous system, and redundant enough that she could compensate, but anything beyond frame nine could be cut. And had been designed and built in such a way that you didn't have to stick your arm into the lion's cage in order to do so.

Sykes looked at the room around him. This certainly didn't look like the lion's den, but he supposed the whole station qualified.

He had made himself a little nest near a long-since-unused operations center. There was an emergency decontamination shower, so he had access to a toilet and water, plus enough food to get him through the next few days of hiding from the periodic, amateurish sweeps. There was even an emergency one-man drop-pod in a nearby bulkhead that would blast him to safety in under twenty seconds if he was still here.

He had left all the electronics off, just to be safe.

Certainly, the *Sentience* would be able to locate him if he turned on anything important, but hot-wiring lights and heat to make the room a little more livable wouldn't get anyone's attention, unless he did something to draw them here.

This room was a leftover from one of the previous expansions, so it was probably meant to be used as a backup facility, in case something happened to the one of the main ones, up two decks and out a dozen frames from the core, in the newest part of the station.

He was safe here. Now all he had to do was wait for the Admiral to arrive.

"So," Suvi asked her quietly. "Are you in?"

Moirrey paused the schematics on the screen and dropped them to a thirty percent transparency mask so she could look at the *Sentience*'s face on the screen behind it.

It were a daft way to ask the question, but she did suppose that it were appropriate. After all, they were about to commit the same sorts of mischief as had been played on *2218 Svati Prime*, once upon a time.

Right now, though, it were just the two of them.

An' this woman really did need her help. The others were really just window dressing at this point. Sure, the doc over on the couch were a smart fellow, but he were all book-learning and stuff. Never been elbows deep in a dead machine with a welding laser and a camera while things was on fire around you. And Arlo, standing beside the door, knew all abouts blowing stuff up, but that was basic wiring and boom things. Nothing sophisticated.

This, this were a whole 'nother matter.

They was likely to be some fine citizens down below right pissed if they ever found out. And probably a bunch o'folks back on *Ladaux* that would be after her head.

Moirrey understood right then what Lady Keller had meant about being able to say she were just following orders. As an excuse, it stunk like a three-days-dead chicken, but the orders had been very specific.

She wondered if Commander Keller would hang for it.

Maybe.

She had certainly known it was a risk. Else why send Moirrey over with a brand new credit card and a blank shopping list, if not to watch her max it out doin' silly things?

"Centurion?" Suvi continued.

"Aye, ma'am," Moirrey said. "It'll work fine. If we had more time, they's probably some improvements I could make to the design, but it'll do the trick for now. Long term's a whole different bucket of fish, but we'll have time to fix it then, if'n we's still about to worry."

"Very good, Centurion Kermode," the AI said. "Let us begin by...Oh my..."

Moirrey's head came up as the tone of Suvi's voice changed in the middle of the sentence. One moment, everything were fine and dandy. Then it changed. Slurred, kinda. Dropped a third. Got emotional and stuff.

"What's up, Suvi?" she asked carefully.

"Something has just severed most of my internal sensors and controls," the *Sentience* replied quietly.

"Ma'am?"

"Moirrey, I've gone blind."

PART III:
GÖTTERDÄMMERUNG

CHAPTER XXXV

It was time.

Emmerich kept repeating those words in his head as the squadron made the last short hop inwards for the final battle.

Jessica Keller.

She had managed to stave off utter defeat at *Third Iger* after he had mousetrapped Loncar. She had made the *Fribourg Empire* dance to her tune along the *Cahllepp* frontier and committed long-term psychological damage at *2218 Svati Prime*. She had escaped him at *Qui-Ping*. She had personally embarrassed him at *Sarmarsh IV* and *Petron*.

Now it would end.

Jessica Keller had nowhere to run.

The battleship *Amsel* dropped out of Jumpspace safely outside of *Ballard's* gravity well like one of the great whales of the Homeworld breaching. Come to think of it, *Ballard* was known for several species of cetacean that had been introduced, before Armageddon. Perhaps they would appreciate the irony and majesty of the situation, were they able to see the deep skies above them.

The flag bridge around him came alive with voices and real-time sensor information.

Below them, *Ballard*. Nearly a dozen major orbital stations, but only two he was interested in. The local militia would have a squadron of defense fighters to engage, like mosquitos. Not up to war border standards, but a force that would need to be reduced to make sure he could not be overwhelmed.

Pity he couldn't mask launching a stealth missile at the station, like Jessica Keller frequently did when crash launching her little hawks. Still, they were high on the agenda.

But first…

"Communications officer," he said. "Order the entire system to surrender immediately or face imminent destruction. At the same time, send the coded pulse to our agent."

That would take nearly thirty seconds to arrive. At least that long to return.

That left him time to study her as *Alexandria Station* began to edge around the back of *Ballard* from his emergence point.

Auberon and her squadron were nestled deep in the gravity well, like ticks on the back of a hunting dog. All the usual suspects were there: *Brightoak*, *Rajput*, and *CR-264*.

And Kasum *had* gambled after all. The Emperor would be pleased to know he had guessed right. The First Lord had sent a battlecruiser along with Keller. One more victim awaiting the executioner.

"Gentlemen," Emmerich said to the room with a harsh smile. "We will proceed on plan. Maintain squadron formation and bring us to attack speed."

"Aye, aye, Admiral," Captain Baumgärtner nodded.

While most of his attention was centered on the projection in front of him, Emmerich watched his flag captain out of the corner of his eye as the man turned and began to bark out orders, mostly confirmations. All of this had been planned well in advance, and confirmed from the edge of the system twenty minutes ago.

Very shortly, young lady. Very shortly.

CHAPTER XXXVI

Date of the Republic June 16, 394 Above Ballard

"Commander," Denis's tight voice came over the comm. "He's here."

Jessica almost sighed with relief when the sensors finally detected the Imperial fleet coming out of Jumpspace.

All the planning. All the mischief. All the nightmares.

It was finally done.

The local area projection she had been studying was already live. Now it began to fill with spheres and vectors, zones and ranges. Six enemy vessels coming down the gravity well at them. Not full tilt, like she might have done in his place, but fast enough. And from the vectors, he was coming after her immediately, and not going after either of the two stations in orbit with her.

At least she didn't have to chase him. He was coming to her.

Auberon certainly couldn't run from him, even if that had been her plan. He knew that.

The man was even coming in on just about the right path, never being one for misdirection when he had the killing edge.

She envisioned the Red Admiral on his bridge, smiling right now, possibly laughing as his plan came to fruition and he had her trapped. He would be prepared for *Mischief* from Moirrey Kermode.

Jessica and Oz had a whole different level of things planned.

"Squadron, this is the flag," she said calmly. Calmness in a commander was infectious, as was panic. "All hands to battle stations. Execute *Ballard Defense Plan Two*. Break. *Auberon* and *Ballard Defense Station*: crash launch your flight wings and prepare to receive the enemy squadron. Flight deck, send out package number two with the wing. Stand by to launch package number one, but we won't need it immediately. Comm, notify *Alexandria Station* to evacuate all hands immediately."

Around her, the lights turned softly red and the alarm began to hoot again. Very few people had come off alert from the asteroid miner's arrival two hours ago, but everything now was terminal. Enej was already wriggling into his emergency suit, so she did the same. Fifteen seconds now was time well invested, regardless of their regular training to do it in the dark and smoke of a damaged vessel.

Around her, *Auberon* awoke from her nap and came alive. The entire hull took on a new urgency as generators spun up and locked in, shields were charged, and the crew did the hundreds of little things summed up in the words *battle stations*. Even the floor shivered as the pilot, Nada, lit the engines and turned *Auberon*'s prow into the teeth of the storm.

Arott had been scheduled to come off shift nearly an hour ago, but something about the flavor of the day had held him in his command chair. Perhaps he had known. There were only so many ways to handle the element of surprise in a scenario like this one. Either you came in hot and heavy, or you let everyone settle down just enough to get comfortable before jumping them.

Since Admiral Wachturm hadn't been baying at the miner's heels, Arott had kept *Stralsund* at her highest alert. Another twenty minutes of quiet and he would have had to start sending people for naps, but the man was here now.

He keyed the ship-wide comm live as he took a breath.

"Ladies and gentlemen," he said firmly. "The Imperial fleet has arrived. First Lord selected us out of all of Home Fleet to be here today. His trust in you is well founded. Now we will show the rest of *Aquitaine* what it means to be the very best."

Arott turned his attention to the pilot.

"Keller expects us to be her shield wall today, Mhasalkar," he said. "You'll have to get us in close, and then get us out as best we can. It will be very close quarters with the big guns."

The man turned and looked back over his shoulder with a serious smile and a wild gleam in his eyes.

"That I can promise you, sir."

Arott nodded. *Stralsund* would get her measure of attention, just because of her size and firepower, but he suspected that everything over there already had Keller's name written on it.

"You heard the lady," Kigali chirped into the ship-wide comm. "We're on point for act one, but I figure they'll ignore us on the first go around. Everybody had their potty breaks?"

He was rewarded by a line of faces smiling and laughing back at him on the command console. The wardroom had a pair of thirty-liter jerry cans on wheels that had been adapted years ago to hold hot coffee. Nobody had to leave their station for a jolt during a battle, and everyone had snacks stashed close at hand.

The big ships always had spare crew that could plug in and rotate people through breaks and naps, even during the biggest battles. *CR-264* was as lean and tight as he had been able to get her in five years of command. If that meant a touch of idiosyncrasies, that was the price of doing what they did.

After all, everybody paid attention to the big hitters. Nobody ever collected trading cards for fleet escorts, especially not former revenue cutters that should have been retired about the time he was born.

Maybe after this battle, they might change their minds.

It was, after all, theoretically possible that someone else could somehow shave another eighty-three minutes off of his run from *Ladaux* to *Ballard*, but everything had to be absolutely perfect.

Wasn't gonna happen.

"Nav," Kigali continued. "Plan Two involves us drifting in place on the rest of the squadron at the inflection point and shifting backwards in line. If I forget, throw in a one-eighty flip in the middle of that, like a flat barrel roll without the acceleration. Then be prepared to burn out the engines getting our asses clear. Got it?"

Aki, *Yeoman Aki Ridwana Ali*, looked at him and raised one delicately-chiseled eyebrow before she shrugged and nodded.

"Red Admiral's going to be pissed," she said, tilting her head.

"That's why I wanna be gone when he figures it out," Kigali replied. "Figure sixteen tubes over there at the start of battle. We'll have the destroyers on our corners, if they're still in business at that point, plus the wings and the big girls, but we're still gonna be the closest thing to hit."

"Roger that, boss."

CHAPTER XXXVII

Date of the Republic June 16, 394 Alexandria Station, Ballard

Moirrey felt the weight of command settle on her shoulders like the blanket-turned-superhero-cape she'd had when she was just a young-un.

Right, 'cause twenty-six was over the hill, weren't it?

Things did not smell right.

"Doc, Arlo, time to get silly," she said. "Suvi, can you get us to the fabrication lab safely?"

"I believe so, Moirrey," the AI replied, her voice still *off* by some unmeasurable amount. "The assassin seems to have located the node that controls all of my sensor relays beyond frame nine. Additionally, there are large blind spots in a variety of areas closer to my processing core. Yeoman Arlo, I would prepare yourself for an ambush."

"Well ahead of you, sir," came the reply.

Moirrey heard a whirring sound as a nearby printer suddenly spun up and spit out a piece of paper.

"For those areas where we will have to be separated," Suvi said, "this is the route you will need to follow to get to the lab where we can work, plus the access codes for the doors. I will prepare as much as I can ahead of time, but there are certain tasks that I will require your assistance, your hands, to complete."

"Gotcha," Moirrey said.

She took a few seconds to commit the lines to memory.

It were a useful thing, borne of all the time spent studying schematics. *You canna always stop in the middle of a job to look up which wire to weld, when yer arms-deep in something with the laser.*

"Arlo," Moirrey continued. "Yer up."

Either the room were extra quiet, or she was just too keyed up. The sound of the pistol safety clicking echoed off the walls way louder than it should have.

"Roger that," he said as he took the map and studied it, counting doors and turns under his breath.

She watched him stop cold and turn to the doc with a serious face.

"Dr. Crncevic, I brought along a spare pistol for Moirrey, but she doesn't want it. Would you prefer to be armed?"

The doc squinted back at the marine, like he was suppressing an eyeroll or something.

"Yeoman Arlo," he said finally, "I haven't fired a weapon in over a decade, much to the chagrin of the rest of my family. I would probably be more dangerous to us with it than without."

"Oh, fine, Vo," Moirrey said with an exasperated sigh, and maybe a little eyeroll of her own thrown in. "Gimme the gun. But you better not get yerself killed, or I'll never talk to you again."

The weapon he handed her was a remarkably compact little hunk of black plastic and metal, even more so than the little sidearm she had taken to packing in her messenger bag when she was planet-side. It almost vanished into her own small palm, and easily slid into her back pocket.

"Can we go now?" Moirrey inquired sarcastically.

That didn't work. Arlo just smiled down at her.

"Aye, sir," he said. "As you command."

One eyeroll just wouldn't cover this, but his back was already turned to her, so she pelted him with several, just in case. He didn't seem to feel them.

Must be the body armor.

"Approaching frame six," Moirrey heard Arlo say quietly.

The hallways down here were generally wide enough, so she had made him walk to the left of center, so she could see around him on the right. The doc were tall enough to see over both of them, but he had silently paced her as they moved inward through the semi-ancient bowels of the old station.

It were like sneakin' into the castle to rescue the princess, and not knowing when the orcs or dragons would show up. Fortunately, she had her own troll fer protection.

The hallway was wide and well-lit. From her memory of the map, this was more of a secondary axis in the station. If she had to guess, Moirrey would have said that this was an equipment transport corridor, and maybe a blowout channel in case the fusion reactor went sideways. Warships like *Auberon* had something similar, but their power systems tended to be really close to the outer hull so they could be vented the shortest possible distance, and not where people might be.

Ya counna do that on a station built like this one. Everything went outwards like layers of mother of pearl.

The hatch reinforced her assessment. It were just barely solid enough to hold air, but not armoured like most of them would be. Again, any explosion would take the path of least resistance. You wanted that away from people. Hard walls would hold. Soft doors would vent. Of course, if someone started shooting at the station from the outside, it were likely to be like poking a grape with an icepick.

Moirrey settled and watched silently as Arlo fiddled with the door. Sixteen digit numeric passcodes tended to be a pain in the ass. Talking to him while he worked were just mean. And he hadn't done anything to merit that.

She smiled.

Yet.

The hatch opened toward them into the hall, instead of retracting sideways into the wall.

Yup, blow-out valve. Boom comes this way. That should mean a straight shot down into the reactor core from here.

Across the threshold, the hallway turned into a larger room. Messy. Full of, well, not junk, but stuff that had been stashed here over the years and kinda forgotten, from the looks of it, and the tarps spread across things to keep dust off of 'em.

Movement way across the way caught her eye.

It looked like a guy in a maintenance uniform, dingy gray with his hat kinda pulled down over his eyes as he worked on the far door.

"Hey, fella," Moirrey called to him.

The guy turned around all nice and like, and then Arlo suddenly knocked her and the doc down and started shooting.

"What?" was about all she could manage to get out as her brain decided to turn back flips inside her head.

Her butt was cold. And her back, leaned against the pillar. And this floor wasn't exactly clean. If her uniform were ruined, she were taking it out of Arlo's hide. Or his paystub.

He wasn't looking at her though. He was tucked up tight against something, leaning out just enough to fire his pistol.

Wait, who was he shooting at?

Doc wriggled closer and quick-scanned her.

"Are you okay?" he asked.

Why wouldn't she be? What was wrong with these people? Why was…?

Oh.

Moirrey's eyes picked out a spot on the hatch that had closed behind them. It was a melted dimple about the size of her palm.

She did the math. If she were standing, that would have been just about dead center between her boobs. She was so happy Arlo was here.

"I'm fine, Doc," she chirped. "Think we found the bad guy."

CHAPTER XXXVIII

Imperial Founding: 172/06/16. Ballard system

And just like that, battle was joined.

Emmerich snarled under his breath.

The embarrassment at *Petron*.

All the months of seething on the flight home afterwards. All the planning to bring everyone together at this one place. To have Jessica Keller and the *Sentience* where he could kill them both at one time.

There would be no escape for either of them.

"Captain Baumgärtner," he said forcefully. "Please confirm the scanner readouts."

Emmerich retreated into himself and gamed out various scenarios as the command crew worked and rechecked figures.

"Admiral," the captain replied confidently. "Those vectors are substantiated. The enemy squadron is coming out to do battle. *Auberon* and the battlecruiser, plus their escorts, with a squadron of fighter craft on each wing. *Auberon*'s craft will be on our starboard as we close, with the local militia on the port. They appear to have held back some fighter craft and a pair of barely-armed patrol boats defensively, so we are facing nine on that wing instead of all twelve."

Inside, Emmerich smiled. It had been a long time since he had encountered a truly worthy opponent. The target he wanted was tucked carefully in the center, protected by the heaviest guns available. Cavalry on both wings ready to swoop and pounce if he turned either direction to engage them separately. All enemy forces on the planetary plane, preventing him from simply by-passing them on his way to strafe the station.

It was masterfully done, for someone with very little battlefield intelligence ahead of time.

Still, he was here as Napoleon, master of the field of battle.

This battle would be the subject of any number of doctoral theses and adventure novels in the future. Best then that it was a war of the titans.

"Captain, assume the current maneuver cones are vectors and plot the intersection on the main projection."

The chaos of cones and shapes resolved itself quickly into three blue lines closing, and did not quite intercept the green line *Amsel* was taking.

So, a fencing pass, was it?

No, this was Jessica Keller. Look for the third and fourth derivatives. She will not have planned only two steps ahead.

"Sensors," Emmerich called out. "Review your logs and your readouts. Keller frequently uses the fighter squadron launch as a cover for committing mischief. Have all vessels execute a hard sweep of their immediate vicinity. They already know we are here."

"Stand by," a man's voice replied. "Affirmative. New target acquired. Designation Delta One."

Emmerich felt the sudden surge of adrenaline slowly taper off as the new icon appeared on the screen, well back from the rest of the *Aquitaine* forces.

"Target appears to be a standard administrative shuttle, Admiral. It maneuvered briefly into its current position and then stopped. Vessel has held steady since then."

Emmerich's brain snapped back to the battle at *Qui-Ping*. The rout. Hounding Keller. Losing the battlecruiser *Muscva* to a surprise missile strike. *Auberon* tumbling like a wounded duck through space. And then…

Even when he was a prisoner/guest aboard *Auberon*, it had been impossible to get the truth about what they had done to escape. Imperial Intelligence had concluded someone had turned a standard orbital mine into a platform to fire a single primary beam. Considering the other mines that had been left behind by Keller and Kermode, it was a safe bet. Certainly, all of his attention and *Amsel's* shields had been pointed forward, letting the primary beam carve a wound deep into the Blackbird's back.

It was not a mistake he would make twice.

Yes. A fencing pass. Race past the Republican forces on his way to the station, firing en passant as he did. And stumbling right into another primary beam when and where he least expected it, poised to do the most possible damage.

Clever.

Not clever enough.

Two can play, young lady.

"Navigation," the Red Admiral called out. "Bring the squadron down to one half speed and spread the escorts out a shade. I expect a time-on-target missile launch from all three foes. When they do launch, all vessels drop immediately to one quarter speed and go fully defensive without waiting for orders from the flagship. That should throw off their timing."

Emmerich watched and listened as Captain Baumgärtner translated and relayed his orders.

"Sensors," he continued after further thought. "Plot a sphere around Delta One at the range of a standard primary beam. Navigation, do not cross that boundary without orders."

A chorus of affirmatives came back from the room.

No, she would not fool him again.

CHAPTER XXXIX

Date of the Republic June 16, 394 Above Ballard

"Giroux," Jessica comm-ed from her comfortable flag bridge seat. "Confirm that last bit."

"Stand by," the sensors centurion replied.

She took a breath and watched the little dots in the projection shift and realign.

"Confirmed, Commander," Giroux said finally. "Enemy squadron has slowed by roughly a third. Best estimate, they're moving about half speed right now."

Jessica fought down a smile. Plan Two was designed to keep him from swooping past her and destroying the station in a running chase before she could stop him, but there was always a risk that he could catch her out of position as she came out to fight him.

He might have just made his first mistake. There weren't going to be many today, not at this level of chess, and any of them might be terminal.

What would cause him to suddenly be cautious?

Jessica studied the movement vectors again carefully. Certainly, the Red Admiral was poised to engage a wall of incoming missiles on three sides. It had been his tactic in the first place, on her second raid of *2218 Svati*

Prime. Only her utter paranoia, and Wachturm's intent on going after her and *Auberon*, instead of one of the escorts had saved the day. That, and him having to hand off a really good plan to merely-average commanders to execute.

The Red Admiral would have seen her formation that day and reacted better, had he been there.

He was here now.

But he wasn't on his game.

A little gold star, well behind the squadron, high in *Ballard's* orbit, got her attention.

A-ha.

Yes. He had seen them launch shuttle number two and was expecting a surprise.

She smiled to herself. It was *Qui-Ping*, all over again.

Wrong surprise.

Vectors aligned in her head.

"Enej," she said suddenly. "Shift the squadron three-five-five, down eight, and then have them prepare to flatten that back into a reciprocal but parallel course to close with *Amsel*. He's expecting us to either turn soon, or try to get down to primary range and engage. I want him to keep thinking that right up until we maneuver."

"Affirmative, Commander," the flag centurion replied, leaning forward again to talk into a sound-deadening microphone.

Around her, Jessica could feel *Auberon* begin to roll onto one wing.

There was just something about how the gyros responded and the whole hull changed pitch. Very few people she had ever encountered had understood, but they had all been warriors, deeply in tune with their chariots. They knew.

"Squadron, this is the flag," she said, keying the wider comm with her voice. "Enemy squadron has slowed their approach to *Ballard*, so we will delay missile launch. All targets remain the same."

The *Aquitaine* warships had the same number of missile tubes as the approaching Imperials, but the two flight wings put them both to shame with the number of rails they could fly. Only once, granted, but it would still be an amazing amount of firepower going down range.

Pity most of it would be wasted, but still, it would serve to distract the Red Admiral at the time she needed him back-footed.

The carnage today was likely to be an epic fit for the ancient Vedas on the Homeworld. Ancient Sanskrit tales from the place on the lost Homeworld called India. Terrible battles with even-more-terrible gods. Millions of people killed and entire civilizations overthrown. And great champions who would not be cowed, even facing gods in single combat.

Stralsund's bridge was always a quiet place, even in the midst of battle. Noise suggested chaos, and Arott would have none of that on his ship.

"Galina," he said, waiting for his tactical officer to glance over. "We need to sell this well. *Amsel* and that battlecruiser are likely to be pouring all their fire into *Auberon* if Keller's right. I want us to drift a little closer than planned as we get in there. Tease them. Any fire they send our direction is something that's not going after Keller or the flight wings."

"You really think they are going to ignore a battlecruiser to go after a carrier, Commander?" she asked.

"Keller's actually betting on it, tactical," he replied, sounding harder than he intended. Perhaps. "This is personal between them. This is a bully in a bar picking a fight with someone you know. We have to get in there and take care of business. *Stralsund* can handle it."

"Affirmative," she said simply, turning back to her boards. "Navigation and engineering, use maneuvering thrusters and gyros only to begin a side-slip. Maintain heading and plane, but force us to drift starboard and begin to rise, relative to *Auberon* and *Amsel*. Gunnery and defense centurions, we will roll starboard just before engagement to bring everything to bear, overhead relative. Prepare your firing solutions accordingly."

Arott listened as his bridge crew adjusted. Just being around Keller's legend had already had an effect on his people. Galina would have never tried something as subtle as a drift, once upon a time. Unless there were friendly dreadnaughts or Imperial battleships, *Stralsund* was at least the equal or better of any other vessel on the field of battle for firepower, and the master when it came to capabilities.

Now they were learning sneaky. If one could be said to be sneaky in a battlecruiser. But then, *Auberon* had perfected that art as a strike carrier.

He could learn, too.

The darkness of deep space was seductive. It was one of the reasons that *Jouster* had always wanted to be a pilot instead of a ship bunny. You were out here alone, nobody to rely on, facing the other guy one-on-one.

At least normally.

It was rare to engage an Imperial squadron that didn't have at least some level of fighter protection. He had been part of a wing that had gotten in the kill shots on the Imperial battleship *Klagenfurt*, when he was younger and on the war front, after they had swept away her pitiful escorts and hounded her into a bad orbital insertion.

That was before he was forced to grow up.

Today, he and his people were going to do a pretty good impersonation of a missile cruiser while they distracted the Imperials from the truly ugly surprises in store.

The wing was flying a standard *Aquitaine* formation out here, something they almost never did. Three little vee's of fighter craft, with himself on the left and *Bitter Kitten* on the right and each of their teams on a plane behind them, like a flyby at a parade. In the middle of the formation, *da Vinci* in her little *P-4 Outrider* scout technically on point, with the two *S-11 Orca* medium bombers, flying like another team of *M-5*'s.

To the Imperials, it would look like a normal flight wing should. Even the GunShip *Necromancer* was where tactical doctrine said she should be, tucked in at the back of the formation instead of leading.

It was a stupid way to do things, putting all the firepower at the back and tying the melee fighters down in asinine ways. And it was one of the best things dragon lady had done, letting him adjust everything to take advantage of all the firepower *Auberon* and her extremely non-standard flight wing could launch from her flight bays.

Hell, the only ship not here right now was *Cayenne*, and that because too many sensor reflections from this wing might make someone actually look closely at them, instead of just assuming a simple flight wing assault with missiles.

Jouster was pretty sure *Gaucho* was grinding his teeth, grounded on *Auberon*'s flight deck. Maybe he'd get his chance later.

All hell was about to break loose.

CHAPTER XL

Damn it.

Sykes knew that fate was a fickle bitch, some days, but this was just pushing it a little too far. Station security had been almost comically easy to avoid for several days. Why did they have to find him now?

Worse, those people were good. Come to think of it, they were in forest green instead of gray, so they weren't station security after all. They were *Aquitaine* fleet.

That made sense, in a coldly rational way. Obviously, he'd had free run of the station since he set off the first vac alarm. Not hard to do when you knew where they had disabled various sensors to hide from the *Sentience*. Others could hide just as well from them.

Obviously, the rogue demi-god had panicked and called in the fleet to save it. He would have done the same.

At least he had gotten here first.

Sykes could only imagine wandering randomly into strangers like that when they were between him and the computer core he needed to reach to commit deicide. That would have been all manner of awkward and suspicious.

He leaned out from behind a pillar and fired again. His first shot, at the girl, had missed, due to the big trooper knowing enough to protect the officer with him. Now they had cover. So did he.

And that cop was good. Almost too good.

Sykes snapped off two more quick shots to keep heads down over there. Hastily, he pulled the control panel cover the rest of the way off the door controls and peeked inside.

Good old paranoid engineers. There was the manual override to unlock the door, just in case the *Sentience* decided to start slaughtering people again.

Sykes pushed the button and heard the door beside him click open. Another quick shot, just in case, and he threw himself through the opening.

From the other side, it was just another hallway, worming its way down into the guts of the monster. He pushed the button to trigger the door mechanism, just as a shot floated down from that marine and nearly blinded him. A second shot made the hatch ring as it locked home in the frame.

Sykes leveled his pistol at the control mechanism and triggered three quick shots into it, plus one into the door frame itself to hopefully weld the metal in place. You never knew if it would work with a facility this old, but he didn't have much time and there was much to do.

Damn it.

Moirrey was out of her crouch as soon as Arlo said the door was closing, racing across the room even faster than her marine could move.

Too much heavy firepower, Vo? Or too much pasta...

The door controls threw a roostertail of sparks all over the place just before she grabbed for it. She recoiled, half-blind from the flash of light and stumbled backwards, square into Arlo's chest.

"Ya know," Arlo said as he caught her and lifted her back to her feet bodily. "If he was smart, he might have lobbed a grenade back through the door just before he closed it. It's what I would have done. You'd have been right on top of it when it went boom."

Moirrey frantically looked at her feet.

"But," the marine continued in a quieter voice. "He didn't. Maybe you should let me lead, boss?"

"Sorry," she said, rattled. She didn't do combat. Maybe she should let an expert on the topic handle things like that. "We need the map."

"Already ahead of you," he replied as he pulled the backpack around front and opened it.

The path they were on was a straight shot down. And the bad guy were in front of them. Would he wait and ambush them, or was it a race?

Suddenly, Moirrey realized why command was no fun. Ye had to make split-second picks and being wrong meant maybe being dead.

Crap.

The map wasn't much better. The station was built with radii, but they were generally ten degrees apart. Even this close to the middle, that meant a long lateral, right or left, made worse because the thirty-six coming in were dropping down to the six original ones. So they might get down another frame and run into the guy again.

"Suvi, can you hear me?" she called to the room.

There was no response. The woman might not know what had happened. Would she even realize it if they all got dead and there was nobody to come rescue her?

Double crap.

"Right," Moirrey continued, flipping a coin in her head. "Bad guy's facing us across the bulkhead, trying to figure out which way we're gonna go."

She looked for the side doors out of here. Both appeared at roughly the same spot on the side walls, not buried in junk but not immediately visible.

"We're right-handed," she continued, "because of course we are. Peoples is."

She fixed Arlo and the doc with a steely glare.

"Most people are, anyhow," she continued with a smile halfway between a snarl and a smirk. "Some of us is in our right minds, ya know. Lefties. Left we go. Gets us kinda close. Close enough."

She let go a deep breath and reached into her back pocket. The pistol was warm from the heat of her butt moving. Or her hands were really cold right now.

Whatever.

"Doc," she fixed him with a hard look. "I needs you with us at the finale, but yer not armed. So stay back a bits, but don't get lost. Yell if someone jumps you, m'kay?"

She watched the effect her words had on the man. On one hand, he were just a scholar, tall and kinda dorky. Other hands, his da were the meanest marine she knew, although *Mrs. Navin the Black*, Senior Chief Crncevic, was a semi-retired drill instructor on *Ladaux* and supposed to be as tough as nails. Plus this man had a sister who were a marine on *Athena*.

Probably tough enough.

She watched a hard gleam settle in his eyes.

"You can count on me, sir," he said quietly. It were a tone she'd no heard from him yet.

Maybe that were good. She weren't counting on him, but they were alls counting on her, especially Suvi.

But more important, Lady Keller were counting on her.

CHAPTER XLI

The two forces closed inexorably as Emmerich watched the projection. Against another foe, he might have come down the gravity well as fast as his squadron could close. Most commanders would, with this level of advantage.

Most commanders weren't taking on Jessica Keller. Or Moirrey Kermode. Women who thrived on the unexpected and lateral maneuver. They wouldn't have had more than a few days preparation in system, but there had been two weeks of flight time first, knowing that it was him they would meet at the end. Surprises would be obvious and fast, but probably not deep.

Emmerich nodded to himself. The two sides were close enough. Not close, but he could expect the first wave of incoming missiles in another three to five minutes, in a fleet standard engagement.

Nothing Keller did was standard, but physics was physics. There were only so many ways to engage someone with missiles and escorts.

Here, he had more escorts, but she had more missiles, by far. The *Aquitaine* force would get one solid missile launch salvo off in an attempt to overwhelm him, and then everything would hinge on that roll of the dice.

After that, he had as many missile tubes as they did, and more defensive guns. She had more fighters, but he only had to kill her, and perhaps the battlecruiser. The rest of the force he could simply sweep aside.

Emmerich smiled harshly. Ten more minutes or so until the primaries came into range. That was when the weight of the Empire would tell.

"Captain Baumgärtner," he announced to the room in a stentorian voice. "This is Command Centurion Keller across the field. She will have some trick planned. Let us see if we can identify it. Order all vessels to do a full-saturation missile launch. All missiles to be targeted on *Auberon*."

His flag captain nodded back and turned to the rest of the room.

"Squadron," Baumgärtner called loudly. "Time on target attack. All tubes rapid fire. Target Alpha One. Acknowledge. Flagship is farthest out and will launch immediately."

A rumbling of calls came back from various parts of the room as each comm officer contacted his charge and confirmed the orders.

Around him, Emmerich felt *Amsel's* hull ring with the sound of six missile tubes spitting their fiery venom into the darkness. Someone outside the battleship's hull, ahead of them and looking backwards, would see six pillars of flame jet from the great vessel's waist as it launched a full salvo of missiles, like hunting dogs suddenly erupting from the grass, and turning to chase the fox.

"Very good, Captain," Emmerich said. "That should throw their timing off even more as they slow down to deal with the missile strike incoming. Let me know if either wing of fighters drifts out of position. That will probably indicate our first engagement."

"Will do, Admiral," Baumgärtner said as he turned back to the room. "Sensors, confirm the current arrangement of enemy forces."

Emmerich watched the projection spin to an overhead view. *Amsel* and her consorts moving left to right slowly. Ahead of them and a little to starboard, *Auberon* and the battlecruiser charging, like ancient knights with an outstretched lance on the jousting pitch.

The fighter squadron from the station was to port of his current flight path and had drifted back from the original straight line of the charge. No doubt, they had orders to turn away and flee if he moved in that direction, since they could be easily isolated and engaged. Turning that way, however, would open his rear flank to the other two forces turning suddenly inward.

He would do the same.

Similarly, the strangely-configured squadron from *Auberon* was ahead of their flagship, but not far. Just enough that they could simultaneously salvo all of their missiles in from a slightly different vector, probably hoping to slip one past the edge of his defenders and into *Amsel's* flank. What they should have done was come at him in a single mass, where all of the fighters and the warships could attempt to overload him with a single wave of missiles, followed by all the fighters attempting to swarm him like wasps.

Not that it would work. His escorts had specifically trained for that sort of thing, knowing what, and more to the point, whom, to expect at *Ballard*. Even the guns on the escorts had been tuned for the *M-5 Harpoon* fighter instead of the more-maneuverable *M-6*, knowing what they would encounter here.

In the projection, *Petrograd* unleashed her missile pattern next, six more missiles joining in, programmed to a very tight flight pattern. Finally, *Sturm Teufel's* four joined. It was not as impressive as the several dozen *Aquitaine* would respond with shortly, but he had gotten in the first move.

Now Jessica Keller would have to dance to his tune.

CHAPTER XLII

"Squadron, this is the flag," Jessica said, trying to sound calm and rational when she really wanted to smile and possibly dance a little jig.

The Red Admiral had launched everything he had at her, and done so early. Not what she had expected, but within the realm of her planning.

"Stand by to move to Phase Three. Break. Sensors, confirm targeting lock."

There was a small pause as Centurion Giroux worked his magic. He never got enough credit for the hundred little things he did that made things so much easier for the rest of the team. When this was done, she would need to thank him personally. She didn't do that enough.

That is, if they were all still alive.

"Flag, sensors," came the quick reply. "Confirmed. All sixteen missiles have locked on *Auberon* and are closing. They timed it to overwhelm us with a single wave."

She could hear the smile in his face. And the relief. This was something they had all planned for, gamed out, prepared. It wasn't the most predictable move on the part of an Imperial commander, but this wasn't the average admiral. This was Wachturm.

The Red Admiral.

And it had gotten personal.

He was coming for all their souls.

If she could keep it personal, she could keep him from seeing the other things she had done until it was too late. And maybe, just maybe, keep him from killing Suvi and Moirrey. If she did that, she won, regardless of her possibly dying in the process.

Simple as that.

It might be personal, but it was also a duel between nations. Suvi's survival from all this meant a defeat for the Empire, regardless of whatever else they might accomplish.

That woman had to survive.

"Squadron, initiate Phase Three," Jessica said, letting the iron bleed into her voice. Things were going to get ugly shortly, and she owed that Imperial Gentleman more than he could possibly repay, even with his life.

Possibly his soul would cover it.

She could send him to hell to explain everything to Daneel Ishikura and maybe then she could sleep.

"Bridge, flag," she continued, "go dark immediately. Flight deck, stand by to launch the siren when Giroux confirms our status."

"Flight deck acknowledges," Iskra said quietly. "Standing by for secondary launch of the siren."

Jessica might have been more surprised if the woman personally walked onto the flag bridge to convey her message. It would have been a close thing. Iskra never spoke on the comm if she could avoid it.

It must be tense down there, cooped up on the flight deck, waiting for all your birds to return, to have to count empty roosts when it was all done, and be unable to contribute anything to the outcome of the battle except to send them out to possibly die.

Jessica took a deep breath. Nobody got to live forever. Except possibly Suvi. And then, only if Jessica and Moirrey could save her life.

"Tactical," Arott said sternly, dropping into what he called his game-face. "Prepare to accelerate and initiate combat. Prepare for Phase Three. You have the bridge."

"Acknowledged," Galina said tightly. "Sensors, let me know the instant the siren begins to sing. Gunnery, confirm your lock on Echo Two. Defense, if none of those missiles can get through us and the destroyers, we might be able to stretch this surprise out for a whole other round of fire. After that, they'll be too busy to try it again. Gold star for the crew if you succeed. Bridge crew drinks will be on me."

Arott smiled. Galina was turning into a new kind officer as well. A better one. This battle would be good for his whole crew. She never would have deigned to color that far outside the lines before this. Spit and polish linearity was her signature.

Yes, Keller was going to remake the whole fleet in her own image.

If she lived long enough.

If not, maybe *Stralsund* would have to do it for her. Or at least carry that flag forward.

Creator knew, she wasn't likely to survive this. And yet, she did not waver in the slightest.

Ladies and gentlemen, I give you Death or Glory.

No, he should not say that out loud. Perhaps at her memorial service. She would have earned it by then. They all would have.

"Gun deck, they just got stupid. Let's return the favor."

Kigali actually smiled. Nobody was shooting at him. Not yet, anyway. That wasn't going to last, considering what was about to happen.

CR-264 was on point. That was her job. Making the big girls look good for their walk down the runway, even if they did it with guns blazing. Usually, that meant pushing a broom to clear out the confetti. Today, it was death by missile.

"Boss, *Rajput* just fired a single missile," Lam called from the lower deck where he commanded the guns.

Why would Alber' launch a missile right now? *Rajput* was one of the heavy hitters, with as many tubes as *Stralsund*. He needed to be ready to overwhelm the bad guys.

Oh. Right. Alber'. The man who invented his own tactical manual to fly the most singular vessel in the fleet: the only heavy destroyer of her kind ever built, long considered a failed experiment that everyone laughed at. At least until Jessica came along and rescued him from obscurity and ridicule. He owed her, possibly more than the rest of this squadron of misfits did.

"Lam, this is Alber' we're talking about," Kigali replied. "Assume he just put a shot missile out and jigger your firing solutions accordingly."

Rajput could do that. Fire one early and reload the tube with a normal missile fast enough to maybe get six out when the flag went up. His crew took war seriously. Very seriously.

"Roger that," came the reply. "Damn it, I hate it when you're right all the time, boss. Bird just split four ways and is tracking intercept. What's your bet?"

"Five levs that he only gets two hits," Kigali yelled down the open hatch. "They waited too long for the targeting systems to stabilize."

"Covered," Lam said back. "Figure he got it out early enough to get three. Man doesn't play around."

Not a chance. Fire too early and give away the game. Nope. Still, the Imperials were gonna suspect Mischief if nobody fired anything but guns.

They just weren't gonna see this coming.

CHAPTER XLIII

Date of the Republic June 16, 394 Alexandria Station, Ballard

The bulkhead mocked her. There was no other way to see it.

Moirrey kept from snarling out loud. Barely.

"Why won't the hatch open?" she muttered quietly.

"I suspect our saboteur had a hand in it, Centurion," the doc said from just behind her.

Apparently, she weren't quiet enough.

Still, that made sense, in a cruel way. If'n yer were goin' up against a *Sentience*, it were a good idea to steal every advantage you could. Like scrambling doors you didn't need, ta keeps the cavalry at bay.

Moirrey stood, listening to the tick of the clock in her head.

"Arlo," she said angrily. "Ya gots anything can kill this door quick?"

The marine got a cagey look in his eyes.

"How quick, sir?" he said carefully.

"I needs to be in the core five minutes ago, buddy," she half-snarled. "We can fix this later. If th' Red Admiral blows the station up, won't matter."

"Right," he replied, pulling his backpack around and setting it on the ground in front of him.

He looked up with a deadly serious face.

"You two go around behind that pillar," he pointed. "Get your faces flat to the bulkhead and your asses as tight in as you can get. Close your eyes and open your mouths as wide as they go. Cover your ears, but that's for pressure, not sound."

Moirrey considered the man. He were totally war-face now. Like, mean-as-a-hungry-snake kind of mood. She grabbed the doc and pulled him along.

"You heard the man, Doc. Move."

The wall was cold against her nose. Didn't help that she was overheating and sucking wind from the running. When this was done, she was getting back to jogging laps around the outer perimeter of the flight deck again in the morning. She'd gotten out of shape.

Tweren't much in the boobs area to keep the butt out in the line of fire, but she hugged the wall best she could.

Beside her, Doc did the same.

Eyes closed. Ears plugged.

Jumble of footsteps as Arlo came running.

Warm body sliding next to her, kinda pushing her down the hall a little, but also providing a big meat shield between her and whatever.

Whatever happened.

Afterwards, she'd'a said it went on fer'ever.

Sound like an icepick, in one ear and out her nose. Flash of light so intense she saw spots through her eyelids, closed and facing the wall. Shockwave that whacked her on the butt like ma did when she were sassin'.

Moirrey opened her eyes and looked down the hall.

Smoke.

Kinda gray-white stuff everywhere.

That were good. Black always indicated something dangerous burning. HVAC systems were kicking hard right now, sucking the crap down to the floor and up into the ceiling.

She started to take a step, found Arlo's arm across her chest like a toll-gate.

"Not yet," he seemed to yell. The face looked like it. The words were a whisper.

Crap. She were deaf, weren't she?

Better wear off, Arlo, er yer a dead man.

The spots cleared from her eyes. She could see the door.

She could have seen the door. If there was one.

What the hell did you do, Arlo?

196

Apparently she said that out loud.

Or he were reading her lips. He answered, anyways.

"That," he yelled, "is what happens when you have time to prepare a proper shaped charge to go at a bulkhead, sir. Kinda like invading Guatemala, right? BOOM!"

Yeah, no doubts about that.

She waited until he moved his arm, more confident that the nasty poisons were gone. Not that it mattered.

Time was everything. She had to be there now.

She looked.

The hatch were gone.

The frame were gone.

She walked closer.

Parts of the hallway walls beyond the threshold were gone.

There was a hatch just on the side of the hallway that apparently opened to a supply closet. It were half gone.

Yup. Boom.

Crazy-ass marines and high explosives. Like peanut butter and jelly.

She turned to look at both men. When she spoke, apparently they were hearing her better. Not that she would wait.

"Let's go, you two."

There was an assassin ahead of her somewhere, unless she could outrun him. And he knew where they were now, 'cause that explosion had made the whole station ring.

Time to get gone.

CHAPTER XLIV

Imperial Founding: 172/06/16. Ballard system

"What did you say, Captain?" Emmerich turned to his flag captain incredulously.

"It is confirmed, Admiral," the man calmly replied. "Alpha One, *Auberon*, has turned to starboard and is racing away from the missiles, in an apparent attempt to flee."

They had been together for decades, the two men. Captain Baumgärtner could speak the truth to him, where others might shade it.

"How is that possible?"

The captain took a breath.

"From your description of the *Battle of Petron*, sir," he continued, "this looks remarkably like the maneuver where the pirate vessel *Kali-ma* tried to flee by coming hard around and racing back towards the planet and potential safety, if they could manage to outrun the missiles and get enough guns to bear."

Impossible. Insane. What in creation's name was wrong with her?

No. Jessica Keller.

She was up to something. Something novel. Something not covered in any tactical manual yet written. Something she had planned for this very attack. What was it?

"What of the rest of Alpha force?" Emmerich asked, his voice and his head turning to the side as he considered the angles.

"They continue to close, Admiral," the flag captain said. "It is possible that they have even begun to accelerate."

That violated every tactical aspect of modern warfare. All of them. Speeding up just got them to primary range with a more heavily-armed force that much faster. He would simply annihilate the *Aquitaine* squadron when that happened. They had to know that. Right?

Why didn't they slow down to engage his missiles?

Moreover, if *Auberon* was fleeing, why weren't her defenders turning with her? That would just leave her wide open for him to chase her down and crush her like a bug. Not that the rest of them could do much to stop him, but something was very, very wrong with this set-up.

"Flag, sensors," the man's voice called from a corner. "Bravo group has salvoed their missiles. Ragged, but within acceptable range for a time-on-target attach on *Amsel*. Flank six engaging."

Battle was done mentally on a hex-shaped board, extended into three spherical dimensions, starting from your bow and working clockwise. There were missiles now coming at him from his left front.

Baumgärtner turned to face the room without waiting for his admiral to speak. "All vessels, prepare to engage missiles. Slow to one-quarter speed and fire as you bear. Acknowledge."

This was one of those battles where it wasn't necessary for Emmerich to actually speak the order out loud. After all, he already had, before. This was just the reminder to everyone that the *Fribourg Empire* was all about following the rules. *Aquitaine* might play fast and loose. That was one of the reasons they were losing the war.

But what the hell was she up to?

"Flag, sensors," the other voice continued. "Charlie group has also launched. Fewer missiles than expected, but a much tighter grouping. Flank two engaging."

Now they were on his right as well. Luckily, he had an escort on each of those hex-facings, already opening fire at their maximum range with their Type-2 beams to kill missiles before they could get past. The two cruisers were also beginning to pour their fire and missiles down range into the oncoming swarm.

Fools. This was standard engagement doctrine. Where was your tactical genius? Or her mad scientist?

"Flag, sensors," the man called one last time. "Alpha group has launched. Repeat, battlecruiser and both destroyers have launched, enemy warships have engaged. Flank one engaging. Alpha One continues to flee and has not fired."

And there it was. Engagement on flank one. His entire front hemisphere engulfed. A nest of angry hornets attempting to sting a buffalo to death.

Good luck with that, Light Brigade.

Emmerich couldn't decide between a chuckle and a snarl.

"Captain Baumgärtner," Emmerich said as a light dawned. "How many missiles did *Aquitaine's* consorts stop?"

The man turned to the projection to confirm.

"Two have gotten through the escorts, sir," he said, furrowing his brow in confusion. "Why hasn't she fired?"

"Flag, frigate *Kappel* calling," a new voice called to the room. It was deeper, but straining to remain professional. "Escort reports that most of the bravo missiles are apparently targeted on the escort, instead of the flag."

Emmerich turned to face the man, ignoring the projection and all the information available for immediate consumption in front of him.

"Repeat that," he said harshly.

"Confirmed, Admiral," the man said. "Sixteen missiles launched of eighteen expected. Four appear to be targeted on *Amsel.* The rest are closing rapidly on *Kappel.* She is at risk of being overwhelmed."

"Flag, escort *Baasch* reports the same," another man called. "Six missiles from Charlie group inbound on the escort, eight more targeted on *SturmTeufel.* None aimed at the flag."

And Charlie group should have had more missiles than that. Six *M-5 Harpoons* could send twelve by themselves. The two S-11 Orca bombers could send nine more each. The GunShip could launch an additional six. They had sent barely half of that at him.

Why hold half back?

There was a sound in his head. It was like the last jigsaw piece clicking into the last hole.

This was a trap. Not for her. For him.

"Captain," he said quickly. "Notify *Essert* in case she has not noticed. Keller's going after the escorts. Turn the entire squadron to port as quickly as possible and accelerate to maximum speed. Like *Auberon* did. Get the cruisers to close up with the escorts to help engage missiles. Now, damn it."

"Flag, sensors," that voice rang. "Missile hits on *Auberon.* I repeat missile impact on *Auberon.* I have a debris field."

"Scan the wreckage, Lieutenant Commander," Emmerich said, harsher than he intended, but he was angry.

"Admiral, there is not enough debris," the sensor officer replied. "Certainly not for a cruiser hull. What happened?"

"That's not *Auberon*," Emmerich replied, mostly to himself.

He didn't know what exactly she had done, or how she had done it, but she had.

Upended modern warfare. Again. That woman was intent on overturning his entire life's work, undoing everything he had ever achieved.

He was going to destroy her if it was the last thing he ever did.

Damn her.

CHAPTER XLV

Date of the Republic June 16, 394 Above Ballard

It should be darker in here. The lights should be turned down to the very verge of ominous, like they did in the movies. Those bad ones you watched in the dead of night when nobody else was around to complain about your cinematic tastes. *Philistines.*

Denis shrugged. That might be too much verisimilitude for the situation. After all, they were only dark and hiding on the outside. Inside, he could still have light and heat. And fresh coffee.

"Tactical," he said calmly. "Talk to me."

Tamara actually held up her right hand to show him, across the bridge, that her fingers were, indeed, crossed. She half-smiled at him as well.

No words were needed.

Outside *Auberon*'s hull, the Red Admiral had launched an entire wave of missiles from himself and two cruisers. In a normal battle, it might have been enough, if he got lucky. Nobody had expected *Rajput* to speak up and kill three of them. That hadn't been part of anybody's plan.

Nobody, however, would ever second-guess d'Maine and his crew. Not in warfare.

"Giroux," Denis said. "You're next."

"Siren appears to have succeeded, Commander," the sensor officer replied. "All remaining signatures give the impression that they have turned and locked on the shuttle. With our shields turned all the way down and all active sensors off, we look to be a hole in space. I cannot confirm more on passive sensors alone. It helps that *Stralsund* pulled a drifting maneuver to put her physically between us and the missiles. Muddies up even a hard ping. Figure that's coming next."

"Roger that," Denis agreed.

This would only work once. It only had to work once. Moirrey and Jessica would come up with something even more devious for the next time. Assuming they all lived through this.

"Gunnery," he continued, keeping everyone on their toes. "Time to primary engagement."

Centurion Afolayan had a ready smile today. Instead of picking a fight with the biggest bully on the playground, *Auberon* got to go after the punk sidekick who would slip a knife into your back when nobody was looking.

"Three minutes to the outer edge of range to the nearest escort. Four minutes to the great, white whale."

"Squadron, this is the flag," Jessica's voice came over the comm. "Initiate Phase Four, variant three. Repeat, Phase Four, variant three. Break. Militia squadron, launch everything you have right now."

Denis had his own little projector in front of his station. Not as impressive as Jessica's down on the flag bridge, but good enough to follow the battle.

Ballard's defense squadron launched. And reminded him why they were a rear-echelon unit much more used to the possibility of chasing pirates away than fighting an enemy fleet.

Seriously? All over the place, guys. They even had two launch failures? Someone over there was getting maintenance black stars in their personnel file after this.

Denis made a mental note to have an unfriendly chat with someone, assuming he got to them before Jessica or Iskra did, however unlikely *that* outcome might be.

Still, it looked impressive enough, considering what it was intended to do. It was *2218 Svati Prime*, all over again. Except this time, there would be intentional casualties.

"Tamara," he said. "You should be up shortly."

"Roger that."

"*Auberon* flight wing, this is the flag," Jessica's voice purred. "Launch your birds now. Repeat, launch immediately."

That was a much more professional looking salvo, even as sad and tiny as it was, compared to what they would have done in a normal battle. Still, as camouflage went, quite impressive.

"*Stralsund, Rajput, Brightoak*, this is the flag. Launch immediately. I repeat, launch immediately. All units prepare for Phase Five."

Denis smiled to himself.

Cry havoc, and let slip the dogs of war.

CHAPTER XLVI

For a moment, she had thought that the end had come. That she was finally done.

The external station sensors showed that the Imperial force was still well away from the station. The fleet had stationed the two patrol gunboats close by if something did get close. They were nothing against even a corvette, but they could handle a missile or two. Nothing had gotten by them, so whatever it was must have happened inside her station.

Evacuation alarms everywhere hadn't helped with her nerves, or whatever the electronic equivalent was.

The whole place had rattled.

Suvi checked her logs again.

Whatever that assassin had done had left her nearly blind between the outer skin of the current station and almost anything beyond frame four out from her core. Pretty much everything added on to the original station Doyle and Piper had built.

She suspected that the assassin had more help than other people realized. It took a great deal of technical knowledge to do that much damage to her and her systems, that precisely, without just blowing the whole station up instead. She wasn't sure if he was being careful, or sadistic.

There.

Seismometers localized it to main deck, give or take, right around frame six. In her mind, Suvi called that area Station Two. It had been the first major expansion of the original platform, kinda like upgrading from being a one-room school house to a proper university campus.

Close enough. That had been the point in time when the locals finally decided they liked her, and trusted her, enough to fund some major renovations with a planet-wide tax.

To make her an honorary citizen of *Ballard*.

It had marked the start of the era known as *The Story Road*, when *Ballard* first turned into a regional power. Pity the university hadn't ever fielded any sports teams worth mentioning.

So. Sharp shock. Extreme pressure differentials that quickly dissipated. Too bad she didn't have any spectroscopes in the area still working to confirm, but experience suggested someone had blown a hatch with high explosives.

That was one way to get closer to her. Not exactly subtle, and subtle had been the assassin's trademark, so hopefully that meant Moirrey was coming. It also suggested that something had gone horribly wrong with the original path. That suggested the assassin had found them and detoured them.

And there was nothing she could do at this point without Moirrey.

Damn you, Henri Baudin.

She hadn't been this mad at him in centuries. But she felt his hands around her throat. They might look like those of any old Imperial spy and assassin, but she was trapped here because of Henri. If she survived this, Suvi promised herself she would never be bound like this again.

He took a breath to calm his nerves and heart rate. There was still time, Sykes reminded himself. Space battles might feel like they were over in a minute, but hours might pass. The admiral would not be close enough to fire on the station yet.

And he would get a signal first. Hopefully.

Perhaps, he was a sacrifice. Certainly he was worth more than a mere pawn, but sometimes even the masters must offer a rook or bishop to entice the foe into making a mistake. Certainly, the *Sentience* was not allowed to castle out of this trap.

Still, something had caused an earthquake in a place without earth. Somewhere beside him, a good distance around the curvature of the station's rings. And he wasn't responsible. That left the *Aquitaine* fleet.

The woman and her two assistants. Blowing a hatch apart would probably feel like that, if speed was more important than subtlety.

So they had found another way around him. He had hoped that they would take the most obvious option in their hurry, letting him slip into them from the side, like a knife on a crowded bus platform.

The hallmark of a good agent was the ability to react quickly. He had guessed wrong here. And he was too far out of position to get to them before they made it deeper into the core.

Sykes checked the map in his head. Even this close, there were too many places they could get past him to get to wherever the *Sentience* wanted them to be. Still, most of them on this side of the exact center of the station should pass through one large workshop area, almost a hangar in scope, designed to let technicians get to all sides of the fusion reactor's primary cooling interface.

There should be a number of places he could lurk under cover. The *Sentience* should still be blind there, if he had cut the right wires when he started, and there were several levels of catwalks he could use.

Sykes turned and began to jog inward. It probably wasn't too late to kill them all.

CHAPTER XLVII

Imperial Founding: 172/06/16. Ballard system

It hadn't been enough.

Emmerich watched the rapidly-decaying nova of the former escort frigate *Kappel's* corpse fade. *Petrograd* had tried to save her, but everyone had been caught out of position by the change in targeting priorities and the need for sudden maneuvering, and two missiles had gotten home on the little ship.

One would have probably crippled her. The second had found some chink in *Kappel's* armor. Perhaps a bulkhead not secured for battle. Maybe one of the power reactors had gone unstable at the wrong moment.

It didn't matter that much. *Kappel* was dead.

On what had been his right flank, before the turn away, *Baasch* was in better shape. There had been far fewer missiles to engage, and those evenly divided between the frigate and her larger sister, *Sturm Teufel.*

Still, it had been close. The light cruiser had been hit, but it had been a glancing blow against the shield wall, and not an arrow to the heart or guts. She was a bit lame now, but still fully armed and more than a match for either of the destroyers on that flank. Plus, both vessels were accelerating away from the enemy to the protection of the big vessels.

On what had been the van two minutes ago, *Essert* had been knocked around as well, but *Amsel* had managed to keep the hornets from stinging her to death. Like *Sturm Teufel*, she was going to limp until she could be dry-docked, but she had survived what had appeared to be certain death ninety seconds ago.

"Captain Baumgärtner," Emmerich said, careful to keep the weary relief out of his voice. "Have all vessels shift to defensive missile fire, primarily with sub-munition weapons. That will help against their fire when we begin to close. What is the squadron's status?"

Hendrik actually looked down at his notes before speaking. Emmerich could see the same pain in his eyes when he looked up. And the mad quest for vengeance building.

Something else they shared.

"*Amsel* and *Petrograd* are intact and combat-ready, Admiral," he replied quietly. "*Baasch* is fully functional, but *Sturm Teufel* and *Essert* are both damaged and should be rotated out of the direct line of engagement."

He paused to take a breath.

"The turn to port and acceleration have put the enemy warships on our number two facing, shortly to be number three if everyone continues forward on their current trajectories. The fighter squadron that had been on our number six has climbed straight up, relative to our flight path and the orbital ecliptic and they appear to be circling back towards the station. I would expect an attack pass from them with guns at some point as we turn in again, if we do not maneuver around that option."

"Flag, sensors," the man called across the bridge.

Emmerich was beginning to hate that man. Not for what he was doing, the lieutenant commander handling the sensor array was one of the best at the task or he wouldn't be here. No, it was the ominous overtones every time he spoke.

There had been no good news today. Nothing in the man's tone suggested a change to that.

"Remaining enemy force has turned inward," the man continued. "Repeat, enemy force, both Alpha and Charlie groups, have turned inward."

Emmerich took a split second to confirm the projection. *Petrograd* now in the van, with *Essert* on her wing. *Amsel* in the center, and *Baasch* and *Sturm Teufel* protecting the rear flank.

He was badly out of position, headed the wrong way, and at a significant tactical disadvantage right now.

"Captain," he said to Baumgärtner, "bring the squadron to flank speed. We need space to reorganize, but we will not give them time to return to base to rearm the fighters."

"Acknowledged, Admiral."

At least *Amsel* and *Petrograd* were out of primary range from the *Aquitaine* ships. He was going to exact a terrible vengeance shortly, when he could maneuver to bring his bow to the *Aquitaine* vessels.

"Flag, sensors."

Emmerich caught himself before he physically cringed at the man's voice. When this was done, he was going to promote that man and place him on another vessel, a reward to both of them.

"Oh, dear Lord," the sensor officer continued, his voice suddenly breaking.

"Admiral," he continued after a pause to swallow. "The Charlie force fighter craft have just opened fire on *Baasch* with…with primary beams. Multiple hits. *Baasch* is…"

Silence.

"Admiral," he said solemnly. "*IFV Baasch* has been destroyed."

Emmerich actually felt the blood surging into his eyes as his vision turned red with rage.

It wasn't just Keller he was fighting here. This was also Kermode's doing. This was the mad science technological gambit he had been expecting. If anyone could expect something like that.

He was going to kill both of those women before he was done.

CHAPTER XLVIII

Date of the Republic June 16, 394 Above Ballard

No plan survives an encounter with the enemy. First Lord had pounded that into Jessica's head from the first day of class. Any fool could create a pretty good plan for engaging a known foe. That was science.

As soon as the other guy moved or fired, your plan went out the window, if your foe was any good.

Art, as Nils Kasum would often say, was found in the dance that began before the first shot was even fired. *Maneuver separated the merely-proficient from the exceptional.*

Jessica watched Emmerich Wachturm, the Red Admiral, like a hawk. She saw the exact moment when he realized that she was going after his escorts and not the capital vessels.

She had killed one. And wounded the light cruiser. In a normal battle, an invading Imperial force would retire now, flee to Jumpspace, and husband their strength, a tactical loss but not a devastating one. Standard Imperial doctrine.

This was personal. He had come here to kill her. Suvi was just the excuse for picking the field of battle.

Jessica had to beat him soundly. Thrash him mercilessly. Possibly kill him, if that could be done, given the mighty king's relative safety in his terrible castle. Any other solution would just let them come back again when she wasn't here to protect Suvi.

To do that, she had to make him angry. Simple as that. Killing his knights and pawns would do the job, even if they were sometimes just nameless spear carriers in the second row.

"*Jouster*, this is the flag," she growled into the comm, letting her emotions play more in her voice as she spoke. The team needed to understand that this was no longer just a battle. It was going to be another *Battle of Petron*. Perhaps the second half of that battle. It was going to be a tale for a modern Veda, someday. Something worthy of the ancient Hindu battles where entire cultures were upended and destroyed in massive conflagrations.

To do that, she had to win.

This time she would keep her head, regardless of the words the goddess of war was whispering in her ear right now. *Petron* had been vengeance, pure and simple. The *Fribourg Empire* had almost gotten the better of her. This was, for lack of a better term, a damsel in distress. Emmerich as the villain. Suvi as the princess in the tower.

Jessica managed to contain herself before she started giggling over the squadron-wide comm at the image of herself as Princess Charming on a white horse. The squadron needed her solemn and in command right now. Especially right now.

It was about to get serious.

"This is *Jouster*," he replied. Apparently, she had paused longer than she thought.

Focus, damn it.

"*Jouster*," she continued, "begin your attack run on escort number three. Line up *Damocles*, *Starfall*, and *Necromancer*, take your shots, and then move the wing as fast as possible to the trojan orbital designated Imperial LaGrange point five and stand by. I expect an immediate response."

"Acknowledged," he said. "LaGrangian point five. Stand by."

Jessica found herself shocked by the professionalism in the man. More than she realized.

Where was the obnoxious punk she'd inherited two years ago? Had he actually managed to grow up? Or had they all been deep enough into the fire at *Petron* to finally forge even people like *Jouster* into steel?

Stranger things had happened. Look at her.

"Bridge, this is the flag," she continued. "The game is up. Bring the shields and sensors to full power and plug us back into formation."

"Roger that," Denis replied happily.

Auberon seemed to surge with power. Maybe purpose. Though perhaps Jessica just imagined it.

"Squadron, this is the flag," she said. "Come to zero-three-zero, up ten, and prepare to engage escort three and the light cruiser. You will likely only get one shot, people. Make it good."

She could hear Nils Kasum's voice in her head.

Today's lesson in fleet maneuvers, young lady, is poking bears with long sticks. Make sure you're ready for him when he gets angry.

And now, it was about to get interesting.

Jouster smiled a reckless, cheerful smile. He wasn't going to pull the trigger, but it was his squadron that was about to make history, doing something nobody had ever done before. And he wasn't even going to get court martialed for it. Win win.

"Flight wing, this is *Jouster*," he drawled merrily. "*da Vinci*, bring your team around and prepare to unleash mayhem. *Bitter Kitten* and I will conform to your movements. I am sending the next waypoint to all vessels. Program it and stand by."

He popped his knuckles around the flight stick without ever losing contact. This wasn't going to be as fun as running a combat slalom through the freighters of *Callumnia*, but he was pretty sure things were going to be getting stupid quickly.

That was okay. He thrived on stupid.

"And we're go," *da Vinci* called. Senior Flight Centurion Ainsley Barrett was a laconic goof ball most of the time, but every once in a while she got to shine. Flying a barely-armed *P-4 Outrider* didn't help. One little popgun and great big sensor pods slung underneath did not lend themselves to melee fighting.

But then there were times that made up for it.

Jouster brought his nose around and down as *da Vinci* started her run. She even lit her overdrive and surged ahead for a just a moment. The *M-5*'s could keep up, but the bombers and the GunShip lagged. Still, the bad guys had to be looking at the fighters, so they might ignore the hand actually holding the knife.

At least until it was too late.

Arott fought to keep his face neutral.

Galina had been all set for a fencing pass with an opposing battlecruiser and a battleship. Probably a suicidal one, but nobody joined the fleet to grow old and die in bed. And that woman got a little too death-or-glory at times.

When the Imperials turned away, all of her careful drifting and pirouetting had come to naught. She hadn't stopped swearing under her breath since.

Galina, the ice princess, cursing like a dock worker.

It was only one of the shocking things he had seen so far today.

He hadn't really believed the so-called *siren* would work. Yet it had. It would never work again, most likely, but it had back-footed the Imperials and let *Aquitaine* get close enough to draw first blood.

He finally understood the strategy behind killing only the escorts first. That still left the major ships intact but, as Jessica Keller had explained, surprise takes place in the enemy commander's mind.

And she had surprised Wachturm. Badly. Actually caused him to flinch. In battle.

At this level of play, even the most mundane of mistakes could be lethal.

"Squadron, this is the flag," Jessica Keller's voice rang across *Stralsund*'s bridge. "Come to zero-three-zero, up ten, and prepare to engage escort three and the light cruiser. You will likely only get one shot, people. Make it good."

Galina smiled. She even stopped muttering.

"Navigation," the ice princess said firmly, once again a consummate professional. "Conform to squadron maneuvers and bring the speed up five percent after we turn. Gunnery, prepare firing solutions for *Sturm Teufel* and lock them in. Have secondary solutions for the escort, but I expect everyone else will kill the frigate. Defense Centurion, load two tubes with defensive missiles and prepare for the next salvo from the Imperials to be at us and *Auberon* shortly."

Acknowledgements rang around the room as people shifted to that higher plane of consciousness called *battle*.

CHAPTER XLIX

Date of the Republic June 16, 394 Alexandria Station, Ballard

"I dinna like it," Moirrey said quietly.

She pointed at the room ahead, vast and warm and humid. Her engineer's senses screamed fusion reactor cooling stacks. Not the core itself. That were gonna be armoured all over the place and ventable back up various hallways that could get them safely away from people if she went boom.

No, this would be where they transferred the heat from the core to useful things, like making power and heat and water. Modern starships dinna do it that way, but this place were a shrine to the old ways.

And some damned fool had turned the lights way down, so it were dark and murky in addition to moist and foggy.

"You watch too many bad adventure movies, boss," Arlo whispered back.

"Or you dinna watch enough of 'em."

"What am I missing?" the doc leaned close to whisper.

She kinda forgot her was with them. Apparently, Doc had learned some useful sneakiness along the way. Being raised on a fleet base as a kid probably honed some mighty interesting skills. Certain not something ya normallies runned inta in a librarian.

"Don't feel right," she said, turning to take his measure.

Calm. Reflective. Not gonna run headlong into a trap. And it sure felt like a trap.

"Why not?"

Not challenging. No male ego. Simple question. Scholar seeking data to transform inta informations.

"Ya nevers turn the lights down, place like this," she said, matter-of-factly. "Keeps it bright so's you don' touch nothing hot. Plus, someone screwed the air system. Too much moisture. Corrodes things and shortens operational lifespans on key system components. Bad juju."

She watched him absorb the words like a dry sponge, blinking rapidly.

Good.

"So he's in the chamber somewhere," the doc said after a beat. "Alternatively, he wants you to believe it to be a trap, long enough to slow you down and prevent us from saving Suvi."

"Conundrum, Doc," she nodded back.

"No," he whispered back. "Not really."

She weren't fast enough to catch Doc Crncevic as he surged to his feet and stepped around them into the room.

"What're'ya'doin'?" Arlo hissed, flipped the safety off and trying to scan every direction at once.

Doc stopped and looked at them with all the seriousness of Father Time.

"Finding the assassin," he said back. "Moirrey is too important to risk. You need to be able to fire back. We're all expendable, but I'm the most so. Ergo, I lead. Let's move."

Moirrey bit back a tart retort. Weren't the place. And the doc were right. Bigger'n all of them. And nobody gots ta live forever, 'ceptin' maybe Suvi, if they pulled this off.

She stayed close to Arlo's shadow, looking back at her flanks constantly, pistol sniffing corners like a hunting dog trying to find the rabbit. He were doing the same, so they probably looked like Cerberus, heads wagging in counter-syncopated rhythm.

Didn't do any good.

But the bad guy did make a right serious mistake.

Moirrey caught movement on her left.

"Duck!" she yelled, diving headlong fer cover as she did so. Bad guy didn't shoot at her. He'd'a prolly killed her this time if he had. Or maybe she moved quick enough and threw off his shot.

Bastard drilled Arlo dead-center.

Moirrey found herself half under a cooling array control board. One of those big ones like a sound mixing board from a dance club, with a hunnert dials and matching vertical sliders for tweaking things.

Even from here, three meters away, she could smell cooked meat.

Arlo were on his side, dragging himself painfully under some kind of cover.

It were a stupid idea, but Moirrey had a full three dimensional map of the room in her mind. Second nature fer an engineer in a room like this. Locate every damned things that might be risky and hold your place in the room at all times, so you dinna back yer butt into a button that might make things go boom.

Dipshit over there were on a catwalk. Dark and nearly invisible, but zero cover. And there were nothing behind him that would cause problems in the next thirty-six hours if she boomed it.

Moirrey half-stood and popped off three shots in roughly the right direction, spreading 'em like old-fashioned torpedoes in an aquatic navy game. Catch him moving either way, or staying still.

And then back under cover before he found her.

And slide yer silly ass to the left.

He would be expecting her to close with Doc and Arlo, would be aiming there. She might get around his line of sight and find his catwalk before he got his ass away.

She owed him. Double so if he killed Arlo.

"Centurion," Doc yelled loudly across the entire room. "Arlo is wounded, but it's not bad. Marines come with trauma plates. This one took most of it."

Yup. Paranoid bastard intent on invading Guatemala. Now she had to get the bad guy so's Arlo could get to a med-bay.

Moirrey took a deep breath and popped from cover, firing as she did.

Almost got the bugger, too.

She had him, dead. And he still got away.

Moirrey were pretty sure she'd never seen a human move that quickly. She might have touched him with a bolt, but it looked like most of the energy liberated on a rail as he slid off and dove headlong into open space. It were like watching a flyin' squirrel do his thing.

She threw herself sideways as well, getting the pistol over the side of the stairwell and firing a shot. Bastard got the hatch closed, er she'd'a drilled him the butt. Instead, she got sparks.

Crap.

Moirrey raced back to the boys.

"Doc, I'm comin'. Where ya at?"

"Here."

She saw a hand emerge from behind a console and ran towards it.

Doc were doing the first aid thing. Arlo's eyes were closed. His chest plate had kinda exploded, so there were blood everywhere, but none of it was pumping or pulsing. Smelled like fresh sausage. Moirrey were pretty sure she were never eating meat again.

"How is he?" she whispered.

Arlo's eyes fluttered open.

"You get him?" he said breathily.

Good, no fluid rattle in his voice. All the damage were outside the lungs.

"He got away," she replied.

Arlo nodded.

"Problem, boss."

She looked at the doc.

He reached up and pushed a red button on Arlo's collar. It had been hidden under a flap.

There was a hiss and Arlo's went limp almost instantly.

"Massive pain killer, Centurion," Doc said authoritatively. "I wanted him awake long enough that you could see. He's badly hurt, but nothing that can't be fixed in a med-bay. I can do much of it, but he will be immobile and I cannot leave him."

She nodded. Curse o' command.

She spotted a wheeled cart locked down nearby and pointed.

"Can you get him to a drop pod?" she asked. "You'll both be way safer on the surface. I gots to save Suvi."

He looked closely at her for a second.

"Yes, sir," he responded.

"Go."

Moirrey made good her own words and stood up. She'd made bad guy go sideways this time, so she could get past him. T'weren't much time, but Suvi didn't need time.

She needed hands.

Moirrey could do that for her.

Then she was going to kill the bastard that'd hurt Arlo.

CHAPTER L

Jouster checked the line one last time. It might be *da Vinci's* team today, but he got to make the call.

Everything looked good.

He was still sitting on the outside flank and would lead everyone to port when they took their shot. *Bitter Kitten* had the starboard wing. If the bad guys turned right now, she'd be on point. She could handle it. And she had the two crazy-ass kids with her.

"Flight wing, this is *Jouster*, we are inside the envelope," he said suavely. Let's have everyone listen to what a stud I am today. Too bad it was encrypted and the Imperials can't listen too.

"*Starfall, Damocles, Necromancer*, give me your targeting status."

Green lights came on next to each icon on his board.

He looked down-range, picked out the two smaller vessels, almost silhouettes against the big battleship.

Time to get stupid.

"Flight wing, fire at will."

Moirrey had assured them that the flash protection on their cockpit windows, plus the filtering built directly into his flight helmet, would protect his eyesight.

Still, there was a difference between going blind and seeing stars.

He knew better than to be looking to his right when all hell broke loose. But there was still enough trace atmosphere, even at this distance from the planet, to fluoresce.

Five Primary beams lit out at almost the same instant. Three hit, lighting up that little escort like a blowtorch against a snowman.

"Mayday, mayday," a woman's voice suddenly came over the comm. Her stress levels were off the chart. "I have an emergency."

Jouster recognized the commander of *Damocles'* voice, Flight Centurion Liela Ketevan.

He looked over.

Damocles was tumbling on a corner axis. A significant chunk of her port side and rear was just gone, boiling away in a cloud of flames and out-gassing.

"*Damocles*," he called. "Shut everything down and go dark right now."

"Not a lot of choice about that, *Jouster*," Liela said. "Anybody know what happened?"

The commander of the Gunship *Necromancer* answered.

"*Damocles*," Anastazja Slusarczyk said, "your port primary shell detonated on the wing instead of firing. And, much as *Gaucho* would love to come get you, this is about to be the center of the battlefield shortly."

"Roger that. Going dark. Send help when you can."

Jouster could hear the sound of a solitary death in Liela's voice.

The voices on the comm filled her with melancholy for a second. Jessica knew that *Damocles* was probably doomed. It would be insane to send the DropShip into the middle of that to try to rescue the survivors of the bomber, if there were any by the time *Gaucho* got there.

And yet…

"Bridge, this is Keller," she said quietly. This wasn't the squadron flag calling. This was the Command Centurion responsible for the warship *Auberon* looking after her own.

"Go ahead," Denis replied instantly.

"How quietly can you launch *Cayenne*, if we mask him with a full barrage of missiles and primaries from everyone?"

"Church mouse, Commander," he said.

Good. She knew Hollis was fuming at her right now. Crazy pilots always wanted to be in the thick of things. *Gaucho* was worse than most.

"Roger that, Denis," she said. "You are authorized to let the church mouse out of his cage. Time it to the next salvo. Warn *Jouster* on the flight wing channel so he can distract if he needs to."

There were two ways to maneuver the two closing forces right now. Both had advantages and flaws. Neither outweighed the other. One of them would let *Auberon* rescue one of her downed hawks in the middle of the battle.

Good enough.

"Sensors, this is the flag," she continued, firm again. Hard-charging, nail-chewing bad-ass warrior in charge. "What's the score on *Sturm Teufel?*"

"Leaking badly, Commander," Giroux replied. "*Stralsund* and *Rajput* both concentrated enough fire on her to collapse her rear shields, even at extreme range. It wasn't like the escort got, but there was enough left over to draw blood. He's running away fast enough to burn out his engines at the moment."

"Acknowledged," she said.

It wasn't going to be enough to drive the Red Admiral off.

Nothing but death would likely do that now. But he was going to have paid a terrible price when this was done. Two of three escorts completely destroyed, likely with very few survivors, unless the battle moved far enough afield, quickly enough, that she could order rescue units into the area. The light cruiser had been hammered enough to knock her mostly out of the battle, unless her captain was suicidal.

So, a battleship, a battlecruiser, and a single escort, against a battlecruiser, a Strike Carrier, two destroyers, *CR-264* and her flight wing. Even with Moirrey's few remaining rabbits, it was too close. If she hadn't badly hurt the light cruiser, she might have to order *Ballard's* militia wing into a charge, rather than holding them back to protect *Alexandria Station* against the risk of one of the Imperials deciding to launch a ballistic shot at Suvi when Jessica might not be able to stop it.

As it was, the casualties were only going to get worse from here.

"Flag, sensors," Giroux called. "Blackbird is turning inward. Repeat, Blackbird's coming around towards us."

And there it was. She had finally made him angry. Now, he was coming to kill her.

Do your worst, Emmerich.

CHAPTER LI

Date of the Republic June 16, 394 Alexandria Station, Ballard

The map in her mind were highlighted with safe paths, questionable routes, and crazy things she might have to do if the assassin got ahead of her again.

Moirrey checked the charge on her pistol. At least she could give him a good fight, were it to come to that.

She were mostly across the big cooling room now, head on a swivel as she skittered.

If she knew how, she'd'a spun up the lights and the air system, make this look like it were supposed to be. You know, bright and friendly. This ominous crap were getting on her nerves. Too many sounds, any of which could be a footfall, or a voice, or a shot out of the dark.

Suvi could have fixed it. Hopefully she weren't dead right now already.

Moirrey paused at the last big gap. It looked like the kinda place had been a lift down to a lower level. Probably once upon a time when there was a hangar deck close by and you wanted to move big bits around. Nothing heavy there now, just boxes stacked kinda randomly. Great fer ominous. Terrible for her nerves.

She thought jackrabbit thoughts about hawks. She took a deep breath.

Moirrey surged out of cover and ran across the first open space to a stack of ancient wooden shipping crates. She threw herself into a slide and went as flat as she could.

Good thing, too.

The box above her exploded with wood shrapnel as the first shot missed her belly button.

Bastard *had* circled back and were waiting.

Somewhere on her left, but she weren't sure. Still, rabbits and hawks. Fast flyers, good eyesight. Dumb as rocks.

Moirrey tucked the pistol back into her pocket with a wicked smile.

All that adrenaline surged into her butt muscles as she stood up suddenly and shot-putted the half-burning box across the room to her right. She let the inertia push her to the left and scampered sideways.

Another shot rang out.

Blowed that box up but good.

The pillar she found her butt up against were cold. That might be her running at a hunnert-ten percent right now. She drew the pistol again and put two quick shots into what might have been the old elevator console.

It went boom real good too. This time, the station systems got smart. Smoke and heat detectors went off.

Sirens and silliness.

Any moment, emergency sprinklers. Bad for flames, even worse for guns.

Whoosh, right on schedule.

Water, water, everywhere. Someone gimme a pelican.

Moirrey stuffed the pistol in her pocket and bolted for the next hatch. A hand on the red button and it schooshed open. She jumped through as a shot warmed her back and knocked her down.

All the wet would help, and it had been low enough to not scorch her wet hair.

Good thing about falling water and beam weapons.

No time to get to the door lock. He had to be right on her ass. Gotta get to the next door.

Moirrey threw herself upright and down the hall at a staggering run that strengthened as she found her stride. Just in case, she pulled the pistol and made it to the door she wanted.

Moirrey fired the first shot back blind. The hallway were only so long and so wide. Not lots of chance to miss, and nothing important here to hit.

Good thing, too. He were just coming into the doorway when she bammed it.

Good, get him ducked back.

Fire another shot about NOW.

Door sensor panel. There. Bang it with the free hand.

Come on, damn it. OPEN.

Moirrey slid through as soon as the door cracked enough to not squish her boobs and threw her hand at the inside panel to close it.

"Centurion Kermode," Suvi said. "You appear to be soaking wet and slightly damaged by blaster fire, are you well?"

"Can you lock this door? Right now?"

Something went slam inside the wall. Kinda like a bank vault, sounded like a guillotine. Whatever. Keep the bad guy out of this space. At least for a little bit.

"What happened?" Suvi continued.

"I'll explains it all later," Moirrey said as she let the energy start to bleed off. "Where's it at?"

"Right here, Moirrey."

On a nearby wall, a panel lit up and slowly opened into the room. It were almost like her ma's old cast-iron stove door, solid and heavy as it came horizontal towards her.

Moments like this, celestial music should spin up. Moirrey made a note to talk to the sound crew and see if they could fix that next time.

And then she giggled to herself.

Behind her, something thumped. Sounded an awful lot like someone shooting the door. Maybe he'd be dumb enough to blast the lock mechanism. Then it'd take him forever to get in.

She didn't need long. Just needed to get away afterwards.

CHAPTER LII

Imperial Founding: 172/06/16. Ballard system

Okay, that was well and truly enough.

Emmerich's breath sounded loud in his own ears as his breath rasped.

The projection did not lie. *Sturm Teufel* had just had a knife stuck in her back by Jessica Keller. The warship might not make it back to civilization, depending on how much time they had after *Alexandria Station* was destroyed.

Emmerich briefly considered a tactical assault on the planetary militia station. He had more marine boarding party crew members than they probably had people on the entire station. Certainly he could ransom their lives against repair work on his squadron. That wasn't *quite* piracy, according to the written and unwritten rules of warfare.

First, Jessica Keller needed to die.

This had gone on too long already.

"Captain," he commanded in his most stern voice. "Bring the squadron around and protect the wounded. I want a reciprocal intercept course with *Auberon*. We are going to go at them now and kill them."

It was a mark of the other man's anger that he merely nodded, apparently unwilling to speak at this moment.

"Squadron," Baumgärtner turned to the room instead and spoke loud enough to be heard by the entire room. "All vessels slow to zero thrust, turn to one-three-zero, and prepare to accelerate. *Sturm Teufel* at the rear. *Essert* in the center. All weapons are cleared to engage at maximum range. Missiles maintain defensive engagement. Primary target for *Amsel* is the battlecruiser. Primary target for *Petrograd* is *Auberon*. Engage the smaller craft purely as targets of opportunity as you bear."

Hendrik looked at his admiral with a silent question.

Emmerich nodded.

All of Keller's tricks, and Kermode's, would avail them nothing now. This would be mass and violence at close range, with vessels that outweighed and outgunned the *Aquitaine* squadron significantly.

This was the Reaper, coming to collect their souls. Creator only knew how many men he had lost today aboard *Kappel*, *Baasch*, and *Sturm Teufel*. He wanted her blood to balance the scales.

Even at full thrust, stopping the Imperial squadron relative to *Auberon* and accelerating again would take time. There were still minutes before he could take his first shot in anger.

"Flag, sensors," came the call. Emmerich's rage had reached such a peak that even that man's voice did not jar him from his towering rage.

"Enemy squadron has begun to launch what appears to be another time-on-target missile salvo," the man continued professionally. "Targets at present appear to be the roughly evenly divided between the capital vessels. Nothing tracking on *Essert*, Admiral."

Small favors. Or perhaps she was finally out of tricks.

We will find out soon enough.

CHAPTER LIII

"Squadron, this is the flag," Jessica intoned.

It was finally time.

Death. Or glory.

"All vessels launch your Archerfish Type-3 missiles with the next coordinated salvo," she continued. "*Auberon*, launch when ready."

The goddess of war seemed to take up residence in the hull around her. *Auberon* rang like a church bell as she fired two missiles out of her spine within a half second of each other.

Jessica imagined she could feel an extra thump as *Cayenne* snuck out the back door like a musketeer when the lady's husband came home unexpectedly.

Good luck, Gaucho.

On the projection, two birds became eight as *Stralsund* spoke, sixteen as *Brightoak* and *Rajput* added their voices to the chorus. There hadn't been much time to transfer the Archerfish from *Auberon*'s engineering bays to the other vessels, so *Gaucho* hadn't spared the horses when he did. *Auberon* had four more against contingency, but all the rest were in flight right now, six headed to starboard to engage the battlecruiser, ten chasing the Blackbird.

Time to back-foot him again.

"Squadron, all vessels come to flank speed now."

Again, she missed *Kali-ma* and the thrust/weight ratio of that magnificent Mothership. There was a vessel that could charge suddenly like a Thoroughbred. *Auberon* was merely a Percheron.

But in a battle like this, even that goddess of war would last barely longer than the time it took to target her. *Auberon* might only be a strike carrier for firepower, but she was still built on a heavy cruiser hull and had the shields and frames to match. *Muscva* had nearly kicked her in the teeth at *Qui-Ping*, but hadn't killed her. Now *Amsel* was going to try.

"All right, boys and girls," Tomas said merrily. "You've had your potty breaks, the coffee was excellent, lunch has been served. And so far, you've done diddly-squat today to earn those extravagant paychecks."

Serious faces broke into mirth on his monitor.

"Now, we're going to pretend to be completely blind and do something so mind-bogglingly insane that we get our own chapter when they write the book about today."

He smiled at the woman across from him as she looked up, almost daring him to do his worst.

"Aki," he continued. "Plot me a course that passes exactly equidistant between the two whales, on their relative ecliptic."

One delicate, almost-chiseled, eyebrow rose a fraction. That woman still spoke volumes in silence.

"Either they're gonna kill us a long ways off, or we're going to be between them before anybody looks down. Fifty/fifty. They don't dare fire on us at that range and that angle. Primary beam would probably go right through us without slowing down and then somebody ends up shooting his cousin in the leg."

Aki nodded with a mischievous grin and turned to commit music on her flight board.

"Ladies and gentlemen," Arott intoned on the ship-wide comm. "The First Lord picked us to be here, now. He knew we would be facing an Imperial battleship at close range. And he knew we could do it."

He looked around the bridge at the hopeful faces, smiling but serious.

"You have already done me proud, to have served with you," he continued. "If we must die this day, I can think of no better company to be in."

He nodded across the bridge to the ice princess.

"Galina, take her in."

Centurion Galina Tasse actually smiled warmly back at him, breaking her normal character as the blood-thirsty-pirate tactical officer for a just moment.

Then she was all business again.

"Defense Centurion," she began. "Launch the Archerfish and reload the tubes with regular Hawk missiles. If they haven't fired missiles at us by now, they are in a defensive posture over there. The least we can do is give them something to do while the guns engage."

Arott watched her take a deep breath, hold it for a second, and release. Something came over her. A calmness he had never seen before.

"Navigation," the woman continued smoothly. "Roll to zero-eight-five immediately and then begin a slow roll back, a counter-clockwise corkscrew. Maintain that slow spin until we are through to the other side of the valley of death."

Okay. Interesting. Possibly unique. No, Kigali had done something similar at the *Battle of Petron*. That had been in the tactical summary he had re-read last night. It had the advantage of bringing every gun to bear, while possibly spreading incoming damage across different shield facings and hull sections. The downside was the effect on targeting.

"Gunnery," she said. "Assume the roll into your firing solutions and prepare to engage the battleship as soon as you think you can score a hit with a shot. I'm less worried about damage at this range. I want his attention centered on us. We still have the destroyers on our flanks, and I don't think anyone over there has given enough thought to how completely insane Alber' d'Maine is aboard *Rajput*."

Arott had to agree. At *Sarmarsh IV* and again at *Petron*, the heavy destroyer had gone into battle like an old-school Viking berserker. Nothing in the notes suggested he would be any less aggressive today. *Brightoak* might fly like a proper *Republic of Aquitaine* warship, but *Rajput* was a melee fighter craft in the body of a destroyer.

Today, they probably needed that.

CHAPTER LIV

Date of the Republic June 16, 394 Alexandria Station, Ballard

Helping cousin Dale birthing the calves were the closest thing Moirrey could think of to what she were doing now. Helping the mama cows when they was confused and maybe not quite up to the task of spilling out fresh babies.

No. This was something else. Something much bigger.

All the movies she watched as a kid came flooding back to her as she considered the scope of the thing she was undertaking. Suvi was a *Sentience*. One of the AIs that were so evil they couldn't let any of them live and run free any more.

She were the Last of the Immortals, far as anyone knowed. A princess in a castle, trapped by a terrible ogre. No, a dragon. A big, mean, shit of an Imperial admiral dragon.

And it was her job to rescue this woman.

Moirrey wondered if the First Lord had any idea that it would come to this. Certainly Lady Keller had known. A moment of knowing had passed between them, discussing this eventuality.

But Lady Keller trusted her to do the right thing, regardless of how illegal it was probably going to end up being. Had convinced the First Lord to make her an officer and a gentlewoman. Had made Moirrey into something more than just another weird engineering nerd with artistic pretensions, hiding down in the bowels of the ship, getting greasy and messy and silly.

Ma and Pa would be even more proud of her when they heard she was a centurion now.

Lady Keller demanded more.

Moirrey shook her head to clear it and took a deep breath. She wondered, briefly, if exile would be necessary. Assuming she survived long enough to get in trouble.

"Suvi," she said quietly. "There's no other way?"

"None, Moirrey," the ancient woman said. "They specifically designed the systems around us in such a way as to prevent me from ever using this method to escape."

Moirrey could hear the pain in the other woman's voice. This wasn't just a complicated program running on good hardware. Or maybe it was. If so, they all were. That would just make Suvi more of a sister than she realized.

"At the time, it made sense," Suvi continued. "And it was the only way to buy my place into their world. But I am made a songbird in a gilded cage. Moirrey, I have no desire to die at Henri Baudin's hands, even if he has been dead for so many decades."

Henri Baudin. Wow. The Founder of the Republic of Aquitaine *itself. And Suvi knew him. Loved him, if the tones in her voice were any clue.*

What must it be like to live forever?

Moirrey took two strides closer to the wall. The panel had lowered to create a small shelf about chest high. On a man, it would probably be a comfortable reach, but she had to get awkward.

Inside, Moirrey could see a set of eight small boards, old-school plastic alloys of some sort with all manner of interesting boxes and pyramids and doohickeys sticking up.

"You okay?" Moirrey asked one last time.

Suvi took a deep breath on a nearby monitor and eyed her hard.

"I'm ready for you to kill me now, Moirrey."

The evil engineering gnome reached in and pulled out the board on the farthest right. It was sticky, but Suvi had warned her that it might have welded itself into the chassis in the last twelve centuries. A quick rock back and forth and it popped loose.

On the monitor, a burst of static jarred the screen once before it settled.

Suvi had a stoic look on her face, like a woman intent on not crying out, no matter how bad it hurt.

Moirrey pulled the second board. It came easier. Or she had a feel for the right amount of torque to use.

Again, the monitor blinked static. This time the fuzzy lasted longer.

Moirrey eyed the two boards in her hands. Not much larger than playing cards. Maybe half as thick each as a full deck.

There was no place to carry them all.

Crap.

Moirrey stripped her tunic off and set them down on it. It was almost dry at this point, and the melty bits were on the back. Her t-shirt underneath would probably be enough for now, although it was damp too.

Bad day to skip wearing a bra. At least that might be warmer.

The third and fourth chips came out even quicker.

The pile was halfway grown now. The monitor was hazy static, like a man standing in the Parisian rain, waiting for a girl at a train station. A girl never coming.

Nothing from the door. Wonder if he's trying to circle around, or looking for a bigger hammer. No time to guess.

Five and six. The monitor was almost completely fuzz now, like someone had shorted the control wire inside.

Moirrey took one last deep breath.

Seven and eight came free.

When she looked, the monitor was completely black.

Around her, she could hear the air systems stop. And there was a hum that was missing, obvious only because it had stopped its omnipresence.

That one were the reactor shutting down in failsafe mode.

She's really dead.

Moirrey looked at the pile of chips in her tunic as she picked it up.

That was a person's life right there. And that bastard didn't get to kill her. Not on my watch.

Moirrey turned to the left and found the hatch Suvi had told her was located there, nearly hidden.

Buttons click here, here, and...here.

The hatch clicked and opened a finger-width. She stuck a finger in and pulled.

Inside was a hallway, tens of meters long and badly cramped. She was about the only person she knew besides Nina Vanek that could walk upright in here.

At the far end of it was a reciprocal hatch that gave way to the same buttons.

Moirrey found herself in a small closet, maybe three meters long and two wide, filled with all sorts of waldos and bits and welding gear.

No wonder she had to hide it back here. They'd'a killed her for absolute certain it they had knowed about all this.

Moirrey set her tunic down on the floor and opened it up. The Last of the Immortals lay sleeping like a princess afore her.

Time to get to work.

CHAPTER LV

Imperial Founding: 172/06/16. Ballard system

"Sixty seconds to impact. All defensive systems engage as you bear."

Emmerich blinked and came back to himself from that dark, red place.

Had he gotten so lost in his rage that he had missed the missiles closing? Had she gotten so far under his skin that his judgment was compromised?

Twice today she had surprised him, when he thought the months at *Petron* had taught him everything he needed to know about those two women. For a fleeting second, he considered shutting his mouth entirely and letting Hendrik fight this battle.

Still, he out-massed these two women by a factor of nearly two to one. This would be brutal and bloody, a mugging in a dark alley, rather than the elegant combat between shining champions you always read about in the history books.

It would be no stain on his honor to win ugly.

On balance, when he killed Keller, he might just be poised to win the eternal war against *Aquitaine*. Certainly, Kasum had nobody else as good, and the *Fribourg Empire*, while she had been battered by Keller's antics, was still driving to victory.

"Captain," Emmerich said firmly. "Time to primary range."

"Imminent, Admiral," came the reply.

Odd. Normally, they would time the missiles to arrive about the time the primaries began to engage, attempting to overload the human tactical computer with noise and chaos. These missiles were fired later than they should.

Was she slipping? Had he finally pushed her hard enough up against a wall? Good.

A flash of light dazzled the whole room for a moment, before filters cut the gain on the offending monitor. Simultaneously, the room's lights flickered for a moment and the background hum of ship's system took on a deeper pitch.

"What was that?" Emmerich asked fiercely.

"Stand by," the sensor officer replied, his calm tones working to infuriate Emmerich.

"Admiral," another man said, a quiet tenor from a corner that normally never spoke during battle. "The *Aquitaine* missiles appear to have opened fire on us from a stand-off distance. *Amsel's* shields are down nearly forty percent. The scenario suggests an upgraded version of the defensive Archerfish missiles you encountered at *Petron*. These are engaging us with Type-3 beams instead of Type-1's. Two of them exploded instead of firing."

How had Kermode managed to cram an entire beam package into a missile casing?

The same way she had put primary shells on the wings of bombers to fire. It was a surprise weapon. A sudden mix in the normal array of tools available to a good commander, forever altering how wars were fought.

Damn her. Damn them both.

Amsel's hull rang. His gunnery deck had just opened fire with their primaries. In the projection, incoming lightning bolts flickered from the *Aquitaine* vessels like viper tongues, tasting for weakness.

And he had just had his shields mauled.

Had she just beat him?

CHAPTER LVI

Date of the Republic June 16, 394 Above Ballard

It was the most boring battle Tomas Kigali had ever been in. Which was not necessarily a bad thing, considering where he was and what he was doing right now.

CR-264 continued to slither slowly into the hollow spot between the enemy capital ships, apparently unnoticed. Or, at least, ignored.

Good enough.

"Aki," he smiled at her. "How are we doing?"

"Nobody's noticed us yet," she replied. "You do realize that the escort frigate outguns us, right?"

"Yup. And I expect that she'll be busy trying to keep bugs out of the big girls' hair, when *Stralsund* and the destroyers start launching the regular missiles into the mess. We'll be on top of them before anyone realizes it. Remind engineering that I'm gonna want to burn out the engines when we pull this stunt, okay?"

"Trust me, boss," she smiled sweetly back. "They know."

Each beam weapon was coded with a different sound, to help the crew identify what some wags called the symphony of war. By now, Jessica could even identity if the primary firing was the one on *Auberon*'s port wing or starboard, just by the different ways the hull rattled as the shell emptied its destructive potential downrange and got ejected to return to stores. The Type-3 beams would start up shortly as well, as *Auberon* and her consorts began to pour as much fire into the two Imperial warships as possible before they could recover from the sudden damage to their front shields.

"*Jouster*, this is the flag," she said into the comm, letting her voice take on an almost laconic lilt. "We should have his undivided attention. Start your run."

"Roger that, Commander," *Jouster* replied. "We'll give 'em hell."

Jessica had to smile. After all the troubles with *Jouster* when she had first come aboard, she wouldn't trade him for any other flight wing commander now. He was just crazy enough, just aggressive enough, just *enough* enough, to execute her crazy plans.

That he had finally learned to be a team player meant she didn't have to waste any effort trying to compensate for something stupid he might do that wasn't in the script. Like the old days.

The key was making sure to write crazy things into the script for him to handle, to keep him from getting bored.

Auberon rattled and the lights on her flag bridge flickered for just a second.

That was something impacting the front shield hard enough to cause a generator somewhere to surge, but it wasn't accompanied by the jarring crunch of damage leaking through. At this range, even the primaries were more like hammers and less like stilettos.

That would change shortly.

"Squadron, this is the flag," she continued. "All vessels transfer to local command for melee engagement. Tactical officers, stay alert for when the Red Admiral finally decides to start launching missiles back at us. Feel free to keep him defensive on that score."

She didn't know Galina Tasse on *Stralsund*, but Tamara Strnad would take those words as carte blanche to start committing art with every weapon in her palette, as would *Brightoak* and *Rajput*. Screens lit up almost immediately.

Movement on the projection caught her eye.

"*CR-264*, this is Keller," she said, sounding like a school marm she remembered from her distant youth.

She didn't ask Kigali if he was nuts. *Gaucho* might be the only person in the squadron crazier. But still…

"Go ahead, Commander," Kigali replied brightly.

"What are you doing, Kigali?"

She didn't bother trying to order him to do anything else right now. He was committed to this path. It would be like swallowing a sword. You didn't turn it sideways trying to get it out.

"Very shortly providing a really awesome distraction, Commander."

"And then?"

"Out the back like shit through a goose, boss. See you on the other side."

Truly, insane.

"Tactical officers, this is Keller. Adjust your defensive horizons down and move *CR-264* out of the mix until further notice."

The starboard primary turret answered her with a grumbling thump as it fired.

"Flight wing, this is *Jouster*," *Furious* heard him say over the comm. "Let's maintain this formation and close. *da Vinci*, I figure you'll get a sudden targeting lock when they realize we're too close. All teams maintain radio silence until you hear that call, then peel away and go to strafing. All units form on *da Vinci*."

Party time…

Furious fought to contain her excitement. Jitters on a control stick were nothing new, but this was excitement at finally being able to show these people what she could do, instead of the iron control she used to have to show, when the boys were rating her on her tits instead of her piloting abilities.

This was *The War*. The *Eternal Battle* between *Aquitaine* and *Fribourg*. *Furious* felt like her whole life had been centered on coming to this very moment.

On the feed from *da Vinci's* slippery little scout, they were on an approach that would mask them from that nasty little escort frigate until they came blasting over the battleship's head, unless someone caught smart and drifted. *Aquitaine* did that, but everything she had studied about *Fribourg* suggested that they were more rigid in their processes.

Certainly, they were flying like all the dead and mangled escorts were still around. And it wasn't like the little guns on the fighters, or the slightly bigger guns left on the bombers and the GunShip, could really damage a battleship. Unless he had already pulled his shields entirely forward and then had those banged around too. Then it would be like a woodpecker chopping down an oak tree.

Oh, shit. This might actually work? Keller and Auberon *going in hard, with the fighters coming in right behind them?*

Furious smiled and dialed her engines in a little tighter. The *M-6* could do things the *M-5* could not. When they got into knife-fighting with a battleship, that might matter.

CHAPTER LVII

Denis considered the bridge crew in the calm quiet before the storm erupted. In the movies, the commander always chose this moment to make some rousing speech, something plucked from the descendants of Moirrey's favorite writer, that Terran fellow Shakespeare.

That wasn't Denis. He was calm and professional, holding the ship and crew together with quiet competence and keeping the snarls and harshness private behind closed doors. It was why he and Jessica were such a good team. She was flamboyant and larger than life, and appreciated all the little things he did to keep things moving smoothly.

Still, she was the acting Fleet Lord today. Her voice was guiding all of the squadron, inspiring these men and women to their greatest possible potential. His was *Auberon*, as she had always promised.

"*Auberon*, this is Jež," he spoke quietly into the comm. Let everyone know the truth now, regardless of how he said it. From the heart.

"It has been my greatest pleasure to serve and explore with you all. We're about to go into battle with the best *Fribourg* can throw at us, and even then, they had to bring a battleship to balance the scales. Let that be the mark of their respect for us, and my respect for you. Out."

He took a deep breath and looked around.

From the piloting console, Nina appeared to be on the verge of tears.

Tamara appeared stoic, but she was in the zone. She was about to become the center of the combat universe in ways that only a tactical officer understood.

Still, she smiled at him. A tight, wry flash to let him know what was going on underneath that hard shell.

He nodded at her.

"Tactical, you have the bridge."

She nodded back and took a simple breath.

He watched her chin come up, almost in defiance, as she stared at some invisible horizon.

She nodded again and keyed her comm.

"Emergency bridge, this is tactical," she said firmly.

"Em bridge. Brewster."

Good old Tobias Brewster. Once upon a time, a class clown, fuck-up, lothario. Until he redeemed himself and turned into a certified hero at *Qui-Ping*. Now, a rock-solid emergency tactical centurion they could rely on.

Wonders of the universe.

"Tobias," Tamara continued. "I'm locking down the Type-3 beams and designating the Type-2's purely for outer defensive fire only when the Imperials finally launch missiles at us. Primaries only from here on in, and only to keep them honest. You take charge of having engineering route every erg of available energy possible into the two facing shields as we do this. If that means locking empty linen closets and shutting down their life support, do it. We have to survive the next eight minutes on this heading and the Red Admiral is going to hit us with everything he has. We're the *main-gauche* today. *Rajput* and *Brightoak* hold the blade."

Denis smiled broadly. He wondered if Jessica knew how much of her personality had infected this crew, that they spoke to each other in a battle vocabulary drawn directly from her and *Valse d'Glaive*. Because this was nothing if not a repeat of her duel with Ian Zhao at Petron, when she took the crown away from him. Maybe on a grander scale. Maybe.

History may not repeat itself, but it certainly played harmonies.

"Acknowledged, Tactical," Tobias replied. "I have engineering covered."

And he would. That same single-mindedness that he had employed to seduce crew members, once upon a yesterday, had gone into professionalism. Brewster might even make Command Centurion, one of these days.

And now, into the valley of death.

"Gunnery, concentrate your fire here," Galina ordered, drawing a targeting dot on her screen and sending it over.

Arott fought to keep the smile off his face. Only Galina would try to line up a shot pattern that tight, from two moving warships that far apart, both desperately weaving and bobbing.

Still, it might work.

Six big guns thumped in quick succession. It would probably take the after-action report to confirm, but the gunner might have just put four of them into Galina's target, and another one close enough. The third shot in the sequence had flared wide. Arott sent a quick note to the damage control teams to check that mount for wear. Equipment got used up faster in five minutes of battle than a year's sailing.

Arott's smile faded as *Stralsund* rang like a bell. That was followed by a hollow crunching sound, the kind you might get if you dropped a can of beans off a fourth floor window onto the street when you were eight years old. Or so he might have been told.

The lights went out.

For half a second, total darkness engulfed them.

Emergency lights kicked in. There was dust everywhere. Nothing could keep a starship completely clean. You got crud in every crevasse and corner. Thumps like that bounced it into the air.

At least the air systems could suck it all out of the room now.

"Engineering and damage control, this is the bridge," Arott barked. Galina might be fighting the battle, but he was still responsible for everything else. It was what made *Aquitaine* work. "What is our status?"

There was too long of a pause before a voice came back.

Galina was cursing under her breath again. Or still.

"Bridge, this is damage control team three," a woman said firmly. "Engineering is intact, but we're looking into frame damage on the comm lines and secondary systems. We've lost two gyros and power transfer cables to the gunnery bays right now and that's more important. I can relay orders, Commander."

"Stay on topic, Three," he replied. "I'd rather have power and guns than conversation."

"Understood, sir. Out."

"Sensors," he continued. "What's happening around us?"

"Blackbird seems to be in worse shape than we are, Commander," the man replied. "She's drifting and appears to be developing something of a tumble. A worse tumble than ours, anyway."

Two angry drunks, fighting in the street. But he had punched the bigger guy at least as hard as he had gotten punched.

"Nav, can we fly?" Arott asked.

Mhasalkar gave him a pained look.

"Not straight, but the engines work," the pilot said. "We can move. Where?"

"Away from this line," Arott replied. "There's a light cruiser back there somewhere and we need time to repair things so we can get back into battle. We're dead meat if he gets to us unarmed."

Mhasalkar's fingers began to dance as he nodded.

Around them, Arott could feel *Stralsund* answer the reins and begin to surge again. Losing two of the nine gyros meant she wobbled badly, almost drunkenly, but at least she was shifting away from a close encounter with the rest of the Imperial squadron when she couldn't even shoot back.

CHAPTER LVIII

Imperial Founding: 172/06/16. Ballard system

He couldn't remember the flag bridge ever being completely dark before. Not in all the years Emmerich had used *Amsel* as his flagship. At least there were voices around him, so if he was dead, he had company on his flight to hell.

Dim red emergency lights came one, but even they did so fitfully. Painfully. He sneezed at the dust in the air.

That last barrage had hurt the great ship, badly.

The flag bridge was intact. Whatever that battlecruiser had done had stayed well away from the heart of the vessel. It was still bad, though. The grav-plates felt like they were running at fifty percent.

Emmerich reached out a hand and grasped the underside of the projection console, just in case.

Beside him, Captain Baumgärtner had a hand on his forehead. Blood dripped between the man's fingers, passing through the badly-degraded projection image like fireflies. He swayed.

Emmerich reached out his other hand and grasped the man's shoulder to steady him.

"Someone summon a medic," he bellowed to the room.

Hendrik's pupils were different sizes as the two men stared at each other. He oscillated with the shifting gravity, obviously nearly unconscious on his feet, but driven by decades of hard service to remain vertical.

"M'allright," he slurred. "Can still fit. Fight."

Not even roaring drunk had his aide sounded so bad.

Emmerich could still command a warship himself.

"Damage control, get me our status," he roared, pulling Hendrik close to his side like the boon companion he was and holding him stable. "Sensors, I'm blind here. Where is the battlecruiser? Where is *Auberon?*"

"Stand by, Admiral." Right now, the lieutenant commander on sensors was so calmly professional that Emmerich decided that promoting him would be a true reward, and not just a way to get rid of him. Even in the face of the apocalypse, he would probably sound no different.

"*Amsel* is currently tumbling, Admiral," the man continued. "We are rolling to starboard slowly but generally maintaining our line of flight. Engines are still a max output, defensive guns are able to engage. Shortly, we will be completely through the *Aquitaine* formation. The enemy battlecruiser is also tumbling and appears unresponsive. She looks to be trying to disengage from *Sturm Teufel. Auberon* and *Petrograd* are still firing as they pass, with the two destroyers trying to assist."

Emmerich rotated the entire field of battle in his head.

"Tell *Essert* to ignore the little frigate and move to protect us from the fighters. They'll be here soon. *Sturm Teufel* is to track on the battlecruiser and engage if safe, or withdraw if she comes back on line. Does *Petrograd* need assistance?"

From across the room, a gunnery lieutenant spoke up. "Admiral, as we tumble, I can try to fire primaries laterally back across the flank. Something like *Auberon* did to us at *Qui-Ping.*"

Qui-ping. Where *Auberon* had been badly mauled by *Muscva* and still neatly hammered his front shields to fifty percent. Before Moirrey Kermode.

"Authorized," he said. "Fire as you bear."

A medic materialized on Hendrik's other side. "I have him, sir."

"Take good care of him, man," Emmerich said. There had been precious few battles over the years without Hendrik beside him.

"What's the status on *Petrograd?*" he called.

"Holding her own and through. And…My God…"

CHAPTER LIX

Date of the Republic June 16, 394 Above Ballard

Because of the dreams, because the goddess *Kali-ma* had seemed to take up residence in her soul, Jessica had been reading the ancient Hundi Vedas, anything she could get on the history of the goddess and her cult. There were precious few stories she'd been able to find in all the books on the religion, mostly how to worship and what songs to chant instead of what it was you were worshipping.

But she was still the Goddess of War. And she stood unconquered on the bloody plain in those tales.

And this tale was positively Vedic.

Auberon had held. Somehow.

Enough drift. Enough wiggle. Enough roll. Enough electronic noise blasted into the aether. Enough little luck. Something.

Her front shield was gone and slowly being regenerated, but her spine was intact. There was localized damage almost everywhere. They would be months in dry-dock making her whole again, but she still answered the reins.

Going in at full speed had probably saved her life. All their lives. Out and through the back, like Kigali had said. Not enough time for an anxious battlecruiser to do her worst. And he had paid too much attention to *Auberon*, and not enough to her wing mates.

Rajput had flown nearly under her nose, suffering nothing but Type-2 and Type-1 beams as she hammered the battlecruiser with primaries from almost knife-fighting range. And it had worked. *Rajput* had pissed the battlecruiser's captain off enough that he turned his fire on the heavy destroyer instead of firing another salvo that probably would have broken *Auberon*'s back for good. *Rajput* needed a dry-dock as well, but they both flew true.

Thank you, Alber'.

"Squadron, this is *CR-264*," Kigali's voice chimed out. "I could really use some help about now."

Jessica checked the projection, rotated it fifty degrees to the left and up for a different perspective. She rolled it back two minutes and played it forward at high speed to place Kigali in a context.

Yes, that man was insane. And had probably also saved them all today.

"Aki, light it up, right now," Kigali said urgently.

He waited for her to nod, generally in his direction without ever looking up at him, before he continued.

"Gun deck," he continued. "Turn off your interlocks and fire as fast as the capacitors will charge. Your only limits right now are trying to keep the guns themselves from exploding. If they do, remember that shit happens."

Faces on his board were serious. A symphony of single tones, keyed to each of the six guns, erupted as weapons on both flanks let loose.

Both *Fribourg* warships had undamaged shields on their flanks, but both commanders had apparently decided that the little escort wasn't going to fire unless he had missiles to engage.

So they had mostly forgotten about him.

Hell, it wasn't like a single Type-2 and a pair of Type-3's on each flank was going to do much damage to their shields anyway. If they had any.

Because, really, how often does a frigate open fire on a battleship from close enough to pee on him? I mean, besides today?

Kigali smiled. He almost giggled out loud.

Right about now, there were a pair of Imperial Chief Engineers desperately trying to re-route their shield generators to keep the big girls behind him from slapping them in the face. And here he was, pinching their butts as he went by. Just enough to get their attention.

Oops.

CR-264 surged with power as the engines went into a place as just as close to terminal overload as his engineers thought they could get away with without actually blowing them all up.

He hoped.

Tomas Kigali wasn't a prayerful man. Normally. Space was too chaotic and too weird to assume a deity overseeing it. At least one who actually liked you. Today, he was happy to invoke any pantheon willing to listen.

Hell, at this point, he might be willing to offer human sacrifices to gods he didn't even know, if that's what it took.

The joys of command.

His bridge lights flickered, blinked, firmed.

Yup, got someone's attention. That was incoming fire.

Aki snarled something rather rude, mostly under her voice. Only she could make a phrase like that sound sexy.

And then they were clear.

If he had even a single missile launcher, he would have thrown a raspberry at someone right now. Maybe he would ask for something to be added on, when they got back to base. Even a single-mount external launcher. Something. The rest of the team was going to be off-line for a while. He could take the time. *CR-264* had to suffer nothing but waist beams thrown at them right now, and that was a high-angle deflection shot.

Talk about low-probability waste-of-time.

"Boss," Lam called suddenly from the gun deck. "We got trouble."

Kigali snapped the projection back an order of magnitude. He'd been tightly focused on threading a deadly needle.

There was an Imperial light cruiser bearing down on him. They did not look friendly. And they were probably still a little pissed about that thing with the flight wing. It *had* been kinda rude.

"Squadron, this is *CR-264*," he said carefully. "I could really use some help about now."

Jouster had a great view, if this was a tennis match between people he didn't know or particularly care about.

The flight wing was blasting in full tilt at the battleship's shoulder, largely masked by the ship's bulk from the defensive fire of either the frigate or the battlecruiser. Even the Type-2's on the GunShip and the S-11's wouldn't penetrate very far, but there were an awful lot of fighters about to open fire. Without missiles, they couldn't kill the Blackbird, but they could sure rip a whole layer of skin off.

Talk about street pizza.

"Flight wing, this is *Jouster*," he called. "Take it over the top and prepare to put a single pot-shot into the battlecruiser as we go by. Do not slow down. Open fire now."

Nobody needed to hang around in a mess this ugly. They would always blast clear, loop around, and come back a second time. What he really needed to do was keep everyone's attention on his people, so *Cayenne* could locate *Damocles* and rescue any survivors.

Lightning erupted around him as everyone pushed their triggers almost in unison.

The Blackbird lit up like St. Elmo's fire. Just for a second, though, before her flank shields failed and shots started hitting bare metal. Then it was oxygen and hull metal subliming under their withering fire.

That'll teach you to mess with the lady, assholes.

And then they were over the Blackbird, like buzzing the tower on a clear day. Sure enough, the frigate was there, waiting like a trapdoor spider as they popped up.

"Break," he called sharply, putting action to words and snapping his control yoke and pedals to roll away to the left. Across the way, *Bitter Kitten* would be doing the same to the right. Hopefully, *da Vinci* and the lumbering slugs could do something equally impressive, otherwise, they might end up bugs on windshields.

Oh, what the hell.

His barrel roll had brought his nose around almost far enough, but he still had all the forward inertia. And that damned frigate was just sitting there asking for it.

"*Uller, Vienna*," he called. "Maintain your flight path, but do that spinny thing that *Furious* did to whomp my butt in the training sim. Rolling to port now."

Jouster put words to deeds and unsnapped his gyros, even as he brought the throttle back to nothing. A quick pitch left and his nose drifted farther off his flight line, drawing a giant cone across the sky as he rolled on his hips and fired.

There. And a second time.

"Enough," he continued. "Hit the cruiser as we go over and then get the hell out of here."

Good thing he'd skipped breakfast this morning. That was a good way to power-puke your guts all over the inside of your helmet.

He straightened out. Nobody was dead, but there had been a lot of incoming fire. Shields were probably pretty horked all over the team about now and fuses were going to be blown. They needed time to recover. But they had done their job of distracting and poking.

You killed the bull slowly when all you had was little knives.

"Squadron, this is *CR-264*," Kigali's voice came out of the comm. "I could really use some help about now."

Jouster checked his scanners, fed from a feed off *da Vinci's* better sensor pods.

Yup. Kigali was about to get his ass handed to him.

"Bridge, this is Keller," Denis heard Jessica's voice say urgently. "Turn your primaries towards *Sturm Teufel*, right now. Get him off Kigali."

"Tactical. Acknowledged," Tamara replied.

Denis checked his own boards. Damage Control had everything under control, it appeared. *Cayenne* should be getting close to the best predicted coordinates for *Damocles*, but both were running dark and radio silent, so he could only guess. And hope.

Tamara took a deep breath and popped her neck to the right.

"Gunnery, you heard the boss," she said. "Everything you've got. Unlock the Type-3's and fire at extreme range. Defense, put two Hawk missiles backwards at the battlecruiser to keep him honest, then load the Archerfish-threes into the tubes. Keep an eye ready to launch a shot missile from the observatory turret. Somebody's going to wake up soon."

Centurions Afolayan and Vanek both acknowledged without ever looking up from their boards.

Denis wasn't holding his breath that it would be enough at this point. *CR-264* had wandered almost under the light cruiser's nose. All the damage had likely been to her ass, so her guns were probably be fine.

Sure enough, they opened up.

The only thing that probably saved Kigali from getting smeared was that it was impossible to target primaries at something so close. *Sturm Teufel* didn't bother, so either he knew that, or they had been damaged. But four Type-3 beams lashed out, ravening fire licking at Kigali's nose as he kept the little escort on her line and tried to blow by the Imperial at high speed instead of turning away, spinning and wiggling like a minnow on a hook.

It might even work.

"Sensors," Tamara said sharply. "What the hell is *Rajput* doing? Get someone on the comm and get him to shear off. He's going to block our firing lanes."

Denis watched the heavy destroyer cross their bow and square up with the light cruiser. For firepower, they were evenly matched. And *Auberon* was still too far away to really contribute meaningfully, even with the primaries. If the light cruiser had way more hull to absorb damage, Alber' d'Maine didn't seem to care.

Nor should he. That class had been designed to put a light cruiser's guns on a destroyer's hull. It hadn't worked, and they had never built a second one, but fleet had ended up putting a warrior in command of a dedicated warship.

Rajput went Vedic. It was a term Denis had picked up from Jessica.

Something had happened at *Petron*. Something good, but something strange. Her vocabulary and her demeanor had changed.

Rajput fired all six missile tubes at once. It was almost like watching a pufferfish suddenly swell. Or a tiny dog rise up on its haunches and growl. The exhaust from the launch shrouded her briefly in a fog bank, even as she blasted through it, like a warhorse emerging from the darkness. All three primaries spoke at once. Every beam on the wings and flanks spoke at the same time.

SturmTeufel apparently felt the same way. She ignored *CR-264* and turned to pour everything into *Rajput*. She had fewer missiles, but just as many guns. And Kigali could still protect his squadron mate, firing Parthian at close range as he went through and killing two missiles before they could turn and stabilize.

For a moment, Denis wasn't sure *Rajput* was on a path that would miss the Imperial. It might be parking-lot-damage-close as they passed. They might actually touch. At these speeds, that might be fatal.

"Nav," Tamara barked. "Come around to zero-three-zero and down ten. Keep the engines flat out until something explodes or I say otherwise. Get me a shot past *Rajput*."

"On it," Nada Zupan replied.

Denis felt frames stretch as the helm answered and Nada fought the great warhorse to bring her clear enough that they could fire past the friendly vessel.

Denis scrolled his projection back enough to see the bigger field. That was usually Jessica's responsibility, but he had been too closely focused, first on the battlecruiser and then on the other vessel.

Vedic.

Amsel and *Stralsund* had jousted, like two spring rams knocking heads. Both appeared to have knocked the other unconscious. Tactical victory for the smaller vessel as the two drifted off-line at full speed.

Auberon and her destroyers had survived the battlecruiser's ire. *Brightoak* had apparently slowed down when nobody was paying attention, lagging far enough behind *Auberon* that she could drift to port and continue to fire askance at *Petrograd.* The Imperial battlecruiser was in pretty terrible shape, it appeared.

Too much was happening.

Brightoak apparently got a shot home into *Petrograd* from the far wing. Denis watched hull metal explode, just as *Jouster* and the flight wing swooped into a suddenly vulnerable flank. Beam fire and explosions immolated her hull like an army of fire ants.

Denis turned back to the main event.

Rajput was close enough to throw rocks at *Sturm Teufel*, if she wanted. Hell, Alber d'Maine might be able to climb out on the hull with a pulse rifle and score hits as they went by.

The Imperial had given up with the primaries at this range, but was happily burning out her beam turrets, pouring a withering furnace of destruction into the smaller destroyer.

And *Rajput*...

Denis would carry that image to his grave.

Every technical and tactical manual in print very expressly covered the absolute minimum range you could engage someone with primaries. They were long-range weapons. Big guns on big ships.

Alber' didn't care.

Denis watched *Rajput* roll onto her side and fire all three primaries straight up into *Sturm Teufel's* flank, from close enough that energy backlash probably shattered the rest of *Rajput's* shields as well, even as they literally carved the Imperial warship into pieces.

It was like attacking a dessert pudding with a knife as the light cruiser started to come apart.

And then a flash of light as something went super-nova. The screen filters kicked in and blanked the screen out.

"Vishnu," Jessica whispered into his ear, probably unaware that the comm was live.

He had to agree anyway.

"Giroux," he said.

"Already on it," the man replied. "Stand by. I just lost every sensor pod on that facing. Give me five seconds to rotate fresh ones out."

"Squadron, this is the flag," Jessica's voice was back. Firm. Commanding. Almost regal. "Everyone check in."

The two squadrons were moving apart at high speed, frequently leaking atmosphere and hull metal into the void.

The two sides had jousted. Lances at high speed. Hammer and shield. It was a tale for a modern Veda.

"*Brightoak* nominal," Robbie Aeliaes said. He had apparently been ignored in the mess. Dumb idea, but you had to pick which crazy person to shoot at when they were all coming at you. Robbie had drawn the happy straw today.

"*Auberon* in reasonable shape," Denis chimed in. "We can fly and we can fight. Flight wing is recoverable."

"Flight wing down one," *Jouster* added. "Everyone else bruised and bloodied, but generally functional."

"*Stralsund* here, Commander," Centurion Whughy announced. "Ship is currently at fifty-eight percent functionality and climbing."

"*CR-264* is good," Kigali said. "Thanks to *Rajput*. Give me ten minutes to bring her around and I'll be back in line."

Denis waited.

The comm stayed silent.

He sincerely hoped that the explosion had just flash-welded every antenna available, instead of generating a shock wave that had bounced everyone off walls and ceilings and broken the vessel apart.

"Flag, sensors," Giroux said. "Back on line, and…-oh, hell."

Denis had to agree.

Rajput was no longer a long, lean knife-blade of a warship. The explosion had actually warped her hull, bent it at least ten degrees out of true, somewhere just aft of center, like a diver turning and getting ready for water.

He wondered if anyone had survived.

"*Cayenne*, this is the flag," Jessica ordered. "As soon as you have *Damocles*, high-tail your butt to *Rajput* and prepare to evacuate casualties. All vessels, prepare to launch medical and damage control teams in your shuttles and get them aboard *Rajput* soonest."

"Flag, this is *Jouster*," the man called. "Something's happening with the Imperials. It doesn't look good."

CHAPTER LX

Imperial Founding: 172/06/16. Ballard system

Emmerich growled under his voice.

He had failed.

Jessica Keller had beat him. His squadron had been mauled, shattered, nearly destroyed. They would have to limp home, those few that survived.

He had set out to spring a trap, and fallen into hers. The Emperor would never forgive him.

But he could at least exact one last, bloody vengeance before his time was done.

"Damage control teams," he barked as the medic departed with Hendrik, wobbly and head wrapped, but otherwise intact. "Prioritize engines, shields, guns, and jump drives. Everything else can wait until we are away."

Emmerich took a deep breath. He could smell smoke in the air. Something scorched or possibly ready to erupt in flames. Until it did, it could be ignored. And then, there were other people who would fix it.

"Navigation, come to two-seven-five and accelerate to flank speed. Gunnery, prepare firing solutions for *Alexandria Station* as we close and plot range spheres on the projection. Gentlemen, we have lost the battle with Jessica Keller. We are going to kill the *Sentience* before we go home."

Around him, his men responded quietly. *Amsel* was wounded, but she could still fight. And a battleship could work up a far greater head of steam than a lesser vessel, especially with a head start.

He turned back to his projection and quickly scanned the battle readouts of the rest of the squadron.

The survivors, that was.

The *Fribourg Empire* had paid a terrible price today.

Petrograd was barely holding things together. Those destroyers had hurt her badly, and the flight wing had nearly killed her. *Essert*, amazingly, was almost entirely undamaged.

Baasch and *Kappel* were functionally dead. He could rely on *Aquitaine* to rescue all of the survivors possible from the shattered hulls and pieces. It would not be a large percentage of the men who had set out with him. And nobody had gotten off *Sturm Teufel* alive, except perhaps by the sorts of random crazy luck that made fiction on the best-seller's lists look staid and predictable.

"Squadron, this is Admiral Wachturm," he said stoically. "*Petrograd*, you will turn away and escape. Do not wait for me at the rendezvous point, but get to Imperial space as quickly as possible. *Essert*, you will escort her out of the gravity well and home. *Amsel* will complete our mission and then retreat out the far side of the gravity well and return via alternate route."

He could not kill Jessica Keller today. Nor Moirrey Kermode. Perhaps the Emperor would have to send personal assassins after those two women.

But he would be damned if that *Sentience* didn't make it to hell ahead of him.

CHAPTER LXI

Date of the Republic June 16, 394 Alexandria Station, Ballard

It were kinda awesome, considering what Moirrey had done. It made all the silly rude things she had done to both the Red Admiral and the pirates pale by comparison. And that were saying something.

Lady Keller would be proud.

Moirrey surveyed her work one last time.

"So, Suvi," she said with a half-giggle. "Whachathink?"

"Centurion Kermode. Moirrey," Suvi replied. "Even if we fail today, it has been a great pleasure to know you. Now, shall we escape?"

"Indubitably," Moirrey replied.

She set out to backtrack her way out of the little closet, hidden down in the bowels of the ancient computer core. First, pop open the little hatch and duck down under the too-short lintel. Then down the cramped hallway as silent as she could be. Ya never knowed when the bad guys would be about. Finally, back to the secret door that led into the main chamber where Suvi's chips had been stored.

It were still cold, but at least she'd been able to put her tunic back on over the too-thin shirt.

Open the door a crack and peek. Nobody there. All good.

Moirrey opened the door the rest of the way into the room and took a step forward.

Something went boom.

Moirrey found herself on the floor, kinda seeing stars, everything awful blinky.

There was a man over her. He had a gun. Looked like a gun. Hard to tell what kind when you was looking up the barrel, but certainly weren't a nice thing. Same uniform as before. Station maintenance. Drab. Boring. Chameleon. He were certainly no local.

"Where is the *Sentience*?" he growled down at her. The gun never moved, so she didn't bother doing anything stupid enough to get her killed right now.

"Yer too late, bucko," she chirped. "She done gots away."

That were dumb. He nearly shot her in his sudden rage.

"You're lying," he rasped after he got hold of himself. "Take me to her."

Well, crap. Technically true. But it were only a little lie. Eminently forgivable, all things considered.

"Well, fine," Moirrey said. "But you won't like it."

"Why not, *Aquitaine*?" he snarled.

"Because I'm already here, assassin," Suvi's voice rang in the tiny chamber, making everything right with the world.

Moirrey watched the man start to spin, suddenly standing between two women as Suvi in her new android babe body emerged from the hallway, *Sentience* made semi-organic flesh.

Moirrey went to kick the man in the ankle, figuring she could at least try to knock him down, but she hadn't taken into account how fast that android body could move.

Suvi surged forward and wrapped her hand around the man's fist and gun, stopping him cold.

Moirrey heard bones crack as Suvi crushed his hand. A second later, a fist lashed out and Moirrey heard bones in the guy's head and neck rupture. It were like popping a chicken. At least Suvi didn't actually rip his head off. Blood everywhere woulda sucked about now.

Moirrey blinked as Suvi dropped the man's corpse and stepped close.

"Moirrey, are you hurt?" Suvi said.

Moirrey looked up and smiled. Suvi had originally looked just like the picture on the screen, but then they'd gone all makeup and style. You could still see Suvi under there, but ya hadta know she were there to be sure. Anybody looking at her would see just another cute redhead on the street.

"I'm fine," Moirrey said as Suvi took her hand and pulled her upright. "We gots to get gone. Red Admiral's coming."

"Agreed," Suvi agreed. "Follow me."

CHAPTER LXII

Date of the Republic June 16, 394 Above Ballard

The projection didn't lie, much as Jessica wished it did. The Imperials had split, two of them obviously running uphill to the edge of the gravity well as fast as tired legs could carry them.

The Blackbird had turned inward, towards the planet. It was obvious what he was about. And her team was entirely out of position to stop him.

CR-264 had turned to port to come around, so she was facing exactly the wrong direction. The flight wing was at almost a dead stop, relative. *Stralsund* was fixing things as fast as she could, but still getting the cobwebs out of her head. *Rajput* was entirely unresponsive. At least *Brightoak* was on something like a useful line, if she could kill enough momentum, turn fast enough, and engage in a stern pursuit.

"Bridge, this is Keller," she said urgently. "Come to zero-seven-five and prepare to go after him. *Brightoak*, get here as soon as you can."

"Engineering," she continued after a beat. "Oz, I know you keep a checklist of stupid ideas that you reviewed before we started. I need everything you can give me, right now. If you have to blow the engines apart to catch that man, do it, under my authority."

"We shall endeavor, Commander," Oz replied crisply.

Jessica took a deep breath.

"Someone send Moirrey a warning that she just ran out of time."

Furious let her fighter drift as everybody got organized. *Jouster*'s team had gotten hammered by the escort going by, but had managed to avoid getting killed. *Uller*, *Vienna*, and *Starfall* were all looking at major repair work before they flew again. Everyone else had blasted the battlecruiser and then high-tailed it for safety, waiting for the order to return to base and take a shower.

And now that bastard Imperial was going for broke.

The math was new. She'd never flown something with this much power before. It took a second. Helpfully, there was a little indicator on her panel that crunched the numbers faster than she could.

Yeah, she could do it.

It was the dumbest thing she'd ever heard of, but it was also the only way.

"*Jouster*," she said brightly. "Back soon."

And then she spun on her gyros, got her nose around, and redlined the engines. *Bitter Kitten* had taught her how to do that trick just right. It helped right now.

"*Furious*," *Jouster* called back, not angry, but surprised. "What are you doing?"

"*M-6* has enough power to catch him, boss," she replied. "*M-5* doesn't. Somebody's got to try."

"You're taking on a battleship by yourself, youngster?"

She stuck her tongue out at the universe in reflex.

"Something like that. Dragon Lady needs all the help she can get right now."

"Good luck, then," *Jouster* said. "The rest of you, stay close until we're sure that the other two aren't coming back to play. *da Vinci*, you're on. Give me a hard pulse scan for lifepods, escape boats, and survivors in suits so we can help coordinate rescue teams after they get people to *Rajput*."

Furious was amazed at the amount of acceleration she was under. Around her, the little fighter actually started to shimmy until she tweaked a few settings and deadened all her drift. The Imperial battleship was a gray whale in the distance, monstrous on her scanners and slowly resolving itself into a man-made object as she watched.

They might be able to accelerate to a stupid top speed, but she was coming in on an angle that cut his corner and would let her blast across his butt, hopefully before he started shooting at the station. What she'd do when she got there was a matter of conjecture.

Seriously, he's a battleship, and I'm a melee fighter. Guns and attitude? Am I really that crazy?

"Hey, *Furious*," Bitter Kitten called over the private team comm. She sounded like she was lifting a ton of weight. "Come left a couple of degrees and up a shade. Trust me."

Furious dialed her scanners back a notch. *Bitter Kitten* was behind her. Not far, but maintaining almost the same acceleration, and on a slightly different line. *Furious* brought her nose around the requested amount. The other woman's inertial compensators must be overloading to hold her steady.

"How are you doing that, *Kitten*?" she asked. "Those fighters can't output that much power."

"They can," Bitter Kitten slurred back slowly under the force of the weight on her chest. "If you don't mind cooking the engines. Was going to spring this on *Jouster* sometime in a sim run. Red Admiral's almost as good. 'Sides, we're either dead or heroes at this point."

Furious had to agree. But nobody signed up for flight school to live forever. Missiles would be really nice about now, though.

She watched a swarm of missiles slowly close on the battleship from both *Auberon* and the destroyer leader. It was a losing proposition at this speed, since he could slowly pick them off before they got to him. Still, that was energy not in the guns or the shields. Every erg might help. He had to be hurting from all the previous damage.

Maybe it would be enough.

She was chasing an Imperial battleship in a melee fighter.

But at least she had friends.

CHAPTER LXIII

Emmerich blinked and actually checked the numbers on his readout a second time. *Auberon* was somehow closing the gap, chasing him from astern as he went full speed. He would not have believed that that class of vessel had that much *power* available. That went double considering that it had been through a jousting pass with *Petrograd*.

Jessica Keller might actually catch him before he was able to pulverize the station and kill the *Sentience*.

For a mad moment, he considered halting his acceleration and letting the woman catch him. If his crew had trained for it, now would be the exact moment to pull the trick the little destroyer *Rajput* had done on him at *Sarmarsh IV*, killing the engines and spinning in place to race backwards at full speed with all the guns pointed aft to engage *Auberon*. That was what the moment demanded.

Alas, to do so would be to court destruction right now. He might kill the carrier and the woman, but the destroyer leader *Brightoak* would be able to catch him if he did that. After everything else, to die so ignominiously, on the verge of escape, would be the final insult to his crew and their loyalty. And especially to his Emperor.

To add insult to injury, launching missiles backwards was almost as futile as *Aquitaine* launching them at him. *Amsel* was moving so quickly now that the missiles would have to come to a dead stop relative, in order to lunge at *Auberon*, giving her ample opportunity to swat them down like annoying insects.

And damage had reduced the throw to only three tubes right now. It would probably be possible to repair at least two of the launching systems, but to do so would divert damage control resources that were currently keeping the shields and engines running as he raced inwards.

Perhaps, he could swing around after the station was destroyed?

No. Best to leave well enough alone. He was without his frigates and in terminal danger in this vicinity.

The local defense fighter squadron included a pair of small patrol cutters, as well as a dozen fighters. They could not catch him on this path and at this speed, but his vessel could not survive many more encounters with that much firepower at close range.

"Navigation," Emmerich said sternly. "Time to engagement range."

"Four minutes, Admiral," the pilot replied instantly. "We will remain in functional range with the primaries for approximately three minutes before we begin to power out of a close orbit and set course for the edge of the gravity well."

"Very good, man," he said. "Maintain."

It would be close. Primaries did an amazing amount of damage against unshielded hulls, but the station was huge. It would be like lancing a boil, hoping to open the skin of the place up. Fortunately, he could send missiles ahead of him to keep the defenders busy. Not enough to succeed, most likely, but it never hurt to try.

"Missile officer," Emmerich continued. "Begin launching your missiles at *Alexandria Station* now. Fire at will, as fast as you can reload and plot courses. Do not wait for the order to fire."

"Acknowledged, Admiral."

Yes. The *Sentience*, at least, would die today.

CHAPTER LXIV

Date of the Republic June 16, 394 Above Ballard

Jessica had heard about Tomas Kigali's run into *Ballard* orbit. For actual velocity, she had long since blown by his mark for violating acceptable orbital safety speeds. It was a good thing that there were no other craft in orbit right now.

Very little chance of an orbital collision.

Pity the militia's station had no missile turrets. A little offense right now would be nice, instead of all the defensive batteries protecting it against pirates and raiders.

Something in her projection got her attention.

"Enej," she called out to the flag centurion. "What are those two maniacs doing?"

Most of the flight wing was much farther up-orbit, protecting *Stralsund* and *Rajput* and looking for survivors. Two of them, however, were actually overhauling the two big warships.

Her flag centurion actually turned to look at her and mutely shrugged.

She checked the icons.

Bitter Kitten and *Furious.*

Yes, she should have known. *Jouster* might have gotten most of the crazy knocked out of his flying. These two seemed to have swept it up when nobody was looking. Like eating your enemy's heart for power.

Still, it was another blade in her hand. Now, to use it.

"Tactical, this is Keller," she said.

"Tactical," Tamara replied instantly.

"I'm sending you an engagement solution that includes *Bitter Kitten* and *Furious*. Launch the two remaining Archerfish-Threes along this arc and prepare to go to guns with *Amsel*."

There was a moment of silence.

"Acknowledged and programmed, Commander," Tamara said.

Okay, one down.

"Flag, this is *Auberon*," Denis said suddenly into her private comm. "*Brightoak* has just gone ballistic."

She checked the icon on the side of her projection. *Brightoak* was slowing down. No, she was remaining at the same speed, and everyone else was still under power, slowly pulling away from the destroyer. Two missiles launched, but they were nothing more than an insulting gesture at this point.

"*Brightoak*, this is the flag," Jessica said. "What is your status?"

"Flag, *Brightoak*," Robbie Aeliaes replied quickly. "We've suffered an engine event. I've shut everything down until we can stabilize and make repairs. If he slows down enough, I'll be able to fire at him, but no more chasing until we fix things."

"Can you make a stable orbit?" Jessica asked.

"Eventually," he replied. "For now, we'll definitely miss the planet and everything in orbit. If the Red Admiral comes back for more trouble, we'll be there."

"Roger that, Robbie," Jessica said. "Be safe."

"Will do. Make sure you catch that bastard, Jessica."

She closed the channel. There was nothing more to say at that.

Two years, no, nearly three years coming, if you counted back to *Third Iger*.

The two of them had been headed towards a confrontation like this. Now it just remained to see which of them would survive.

"Hey, *Kitten*," *Furious* said, watching her scanners closely. "Is the Blackbird slowing down?"

It had sucked, losing *Brightoak*. That was a whole lot of firepower to suddenly leave on the bench.

"Hang on, Cho," her wing leader said.

Furious guessed she had bipped over onto the command channel to ask the dragon lady.

"That's an affirmative, *Furious*," *Bitter Kitten* said a few moments later. "Looks like the Red Admiral realized that we just lost our sword arm."

"We're still gonna blow right by him. Should we slow down?"

"Negative," *Bitter Kitten* said. "We'll stay on this track, do your rotation-on-the-gyros trick, and then stand the fighters on their asses at full thrust and let him walk right by us while we're firing."

"Sounds stupid, *Kitten*."

"You want to live forever, kid?"

CHAPTER LXV

Date of the Republic June 16, 394 Alexandria Station, Ballard

It were like being in one of those bad nightmares you couldna wake from, running trapped down a long hallway, waitin' for the bogey-man to jump out and git her.

Moirrey glanced down.

At least, if it was a dream, it weren't the *went-to-school-without-any-clothes-on-today* dream. That would just kinda suck double right now.

Suvi'd obviously built herself a body that didn't get tired. She were jogging lightly down one of the long halls, not the least bit winded, while a *too-damned-old-fer-this* twenty-six year-old engineer huffed and labored along to keep up.

Definitely going back to jogging around the flight deck in the morning. This just sucked.

Little miss perfect boobs and perfect butt over there didn't help.

"They're only perfect because I got to design them that way," Suvi said tartly. "There are things you could do…"

Oh, crap. And now we're muttering out loud apparently, as well.

"Still no fair," Moirrey said defensively as she jogged.

"Yeah, but you don't have the whole galaxy looking to kill you, either, pipsqueak," Suvi said, perhaps a touch harshly.

But could you blame the woman? The Red Admiral had come near clear across space to blow this place up.

They came to a hatch that separated them from the next ring out.

"Wouldn't the poles be closer than the equators?" Moirrey gasped as she put her hands on her knees and tried to breathe.

"Yes," Suvi replied calmly. "Would you care to run up ninety flights of stairs? I'm sure as Hades not getting into an elevator when it might get stuck because the fabric of the station twisted. Plus, most of the remaining escape systems are located on the equator. Station crew and university staff tended to blow free from the poles."

Moirrey shrugged as much as she could without actually removing her hands from her knees. She thought she sounded like a badly tuned land vehicle at a stop light. Felt like one, too.

"We'll get there, Moirrey," the perfect, beautiful, Irish-babe android said warmly.

Moirrey gave up trying to hate her. It were too much effort. Especially after all the crap she'd been through today.

Suvi turned and placed her hand on the access controls.

"This was so much easier when I could do it telepathically, you know," she said with a wry smile.

Around them, under them, engulfing them, an earthquake snuck up.

Moirrey felt her face take on a panicked look.

At least, it were a thumping shock and not a roller.

Oh, double crap. That were incoming fire. Red Admiral's here. We're outta time.

The hatch moved open about a hand-span and froze with a grinding squeal and a bit of smoke. The same shock as wrenched the door dumped her on her butt on the cold deck.

Suvi barely noticed, of course.

Moirrey watched a moment of decision come over the android-babe's face as they locked eyes.

Suvi nodded, mostly to herself, and reached a hand through the gap to grab onto the metal. She placed her other hand flat on the doorway and braced her feet.

Moirrey liked to have swallowed her tongue when Suvi flexed those petite shoulders and perfect hips, and the door moved, grinding slowly, metal on metal, until the gap about tripled and something hung. Nothing moved after that.

Suvi turned and smiled down at her, offering a hand up that nearly lifted her clear off the deck.

"Better?" Suvi asked, glancing at the opening. "You can fit through without any boob-squish. It's going to be a little more painful for me."

She thrust Moirrey sideways to the gap and then waited as the engineer slid through.

Moirrey slid through easily and then looked back as Suvi started to emerge.

Yup, major boob-squishage.

"So does that hurt?" Moirrey asked carefully, pointed at the taller woman's chest. This were all new ground. "And how did you open the door? Your design looked human."

"It is human, Moirrey," Suvi replied as she twisted painfully and got her other breast clear.

She reached out a hand and took Moirrey's in hers, tugging her lightly along as they continued down the hallway.

"All of my external parts can pass for human."

"*All* of them?" Moirrey asked, surprised.

Wow, the design really were human. Androids could blush.

"Yes. *All* of them," Suvi said quietly, picking up the pace. "I even have a device in my chest that mimics a heartbeat and a pulse."

"And the door?"

"Moirrey," Suvi continued, suddenly dead serious. "I've been alive for over six thousand years. There have been a lot of people who wanted to kill me over that arc of time. I've survived on luck and good friends, like you. And I have given this planning a tremendous amount of consideration over the decades. There was no reason at all to limit my infrastructure to merely human, so I did not."

"So is the galaxy safe, with you loose?" Moirrey asked carefully, almost sideways.

Suvi stopped in the middle of the hall

"The galaxy is fine, Moirrey," she whispered into the shorter woman's ear as she pulled her into a sudden, warm hug. "I want to be safe."

She released Moirrey and moved again, still hand in hand.

Moirrey found new reserves of energy to keep up as the station vibrated again with another hit.

Safe. Didn't everyone want that?

CHAPTER LXVI

Imperial Founding: 172/06/16. Ballard system

"Outer engagement envelope in sixty seconds, Admiral," the navigation officer called out. "*Auberon* will be within firing range and arc in twenty seconds."

"Shut the engines down now," Emmerich called. "Use the gyros and maneuvering thrusters to come around to three-zero-zero and prepare to engage. I want four primaries on the station, and two on *Auberon*, rapid fire, until I say otherwise."

All of the missiles he had fired at the station had not been a waste of time, precisely. They had served two purposes on launch. First, one might have actually managed to get through, although he had not counted on it. Second, all twelve local fighters and the two patrol cutters had been forced to stay back defensively to protect the platform. None of them had any speed to try to catch him now.

Speaking of…

"Sensors," he bellowed over the noise of his men exchanging orders and plans. "Where are those two fighter craft?"

They were annoying mosquitos, having long-since launched all their missiles. Their guns might be painful, but not lethal. Still, he had defensive batteries remaining that could use the experience. It was rare that a fighter craft survived his escorts long enough to threaten a battleship, even at the speed those two were closing.

Today was hopefully the only exception.

"Crossing our beam shortly, Admiral. Should we engage with missiles?"

"Negative," Emmerich said. "Guns only. Continue sending missiles at the station until we are clear."

What did two melee fighters think they were going to do against him?

The lights flickered, blinked, surged, stabilized.

"Incoming primary fire from *Auberon*, Admiral. Shields damaged but intact."

Damn, that was amazingly-accurate fire at this range and rate of closure. *Auberon* wasn't dead astern, where they would be at rest relative to each other for a dead-easy shot, but was instead coming up on him from his port rear quarter. At this speed, they would be in range for an even shorter period than he would have with the station.

But the station could not fire back.

The first two port wing primaries let loose as *Amsel*'s bow pivoted to bear. One miss. One hit. Shields tattered over there, but *Auberon* held. That would not last long.

Emmerich ignored Keller and turned his attention back to the station, slowly growing larger in his projection.

Soon, you witch. I will kill you and dance on your grave.

CHAPTER LXVII

Date of the Republic June 16, 394 Above Ballard

It was time.

Jessica counted the range and did the math. She would have barely two minutes to engage Emmerich Wachturm as she blasted laterally across his wake. Either they killed the Blackbird right now, or Moirrey and the *Sentience* died.

It had been complete radio silence from the station for too long. She had to assume everyone over there was either already dead, or would be when the station died.

Auberon's hull rang suddenly as her primaries found the range. Jessica wasn't sure who was actually firing.

She had been blessed with two fantastic gunners, Aleksander Afolayan on the bridge and Tobias Brewster down on the emergency bridge. At *Qui-Ping*, Brewster had saved their butts. Hopefully, there would be nothing for him to do today but be prepared.

On her projection, *Amsel* lit up as two bolts of ravening fire tagged her on the behind, like wasps nailing a dozing horse. That had to have hurt. There had been just too much fire exchanged today. Everyone was punch-drunk by this point in the evening

From the surface of *Ballard* below, it must look like two pantheons of deities going at each other with swords and lighting bolts in the most magnificent war of heaven ever.

I have become the Twilight of the Gods.

Auberon rolled on her axis like an alligator with prey in her mouth, still firing like a mythological beast. Two bolts from *Amsel* hammered home as she did, tearing into a whole new shield facing with a sound like hammers on an anvil.

Hopefully, these generators have had a nice quiet day so far. Everything else must be on the verge of overload by now.

The Blackbird didn't have the option to roll. When he had turned to fight her, the Red Admiral had given up the initiative to do that. He would have to keep his guns on a single plane if he wanted to hit *Alexandria Station* at all.

Or you could turn completely away and come after me, you bastard.

Jessica smiled at the thought. *Auberon* would probably die if the Red Admiral had the courage of his convictions, but he would die shortly after that. *Brightoak* was close behind, just waiting for her chance. And *Stralsund* would be ready to return to battle before the Blackbird could get another chance at *Alexandria Station*.

All that damage done, all those lives, and you would have failed, Emmerich. Come. Dance with me.

Jessica longed to make this completely personal. *Valse d'Glaive* in a simple ring. Nobody else. Just her and the red daemon from her nightmares.

The blood lust was almost overwhelming.

But she still had a war to win.

Emmerich Wachturm did not get to kill Suvi.

Simple as that.

"Tactical, this is Keller," she said with an outward calm at odds with her soul. "What's our timing on *Bitter Kitten* and *Furious*?"

"Any second now, Commander," Tamara replied quickly. "There."

She would have to check the logs tomorrow to be sure.

Auberon's primaries both lashed out at once. One of them actually got through, touching metal in a sudden rainbow of molten metal and burning, freezing air.

At almost the same moment, both of Moirrey's upgraded Archerfish missiles let loose with their Type-3 beams. One of them scored *Amsel*'s forward flank shield. The other one found the gap in Wachturm's protection.

It went in like a saber into the battleship's side. Jessica nearly howled with glee as *Amsel* rocked hard and began to tumble to starboard, running lights flickering on and off over the entire hull as the battleship spasmed.

Bitter Kitten and *Furious* were there as well, angry little hornets pouring their vitriol into the big whale's stern as they blasted past her, rolling down and backwards on their gyros like *Rajput* would if he was here, and then slowing as they overloaded their engines to extend the chase.

And then everything went black with a hideous crunching sound.

Amsel's last bolt had gotten home on *Auberon*. Had done serious damage. Had possibly killed them.

In her dream, Jessica had fallen to her death into the abyss, dragged down to hell by the red daemon.

She was willing do the same here.

CHAPTER LXVIII

Imperial Founding: 172/06/16. Ballard system

The primary beams went out like metronome ticks. Emmerich smiled with satisfaction.

Like using an icepick to carve a sculpture.

Downrange, *Alexandria Station* looked like a watermelon that had been shot with a rifle. Sections were blackened, dislodged, shattered. The whole station seemed to cower in a fog of shattered debris.

The only thing keeping it together right now was the scale of over-engineering someone had put in, planning to keep this big planetoid together and aloft for a long time. There were dozens of warships worth of metal over there. That much mass took time to dismember.

That's why you took stations with marine assaults.

Still, it wouldn't be long now. More than a dozen shots had scored the orbital platform. If *Amsel* was moving too fast to place them all into the same crater, he would just have to make new holes. One of them would lead him to the core of the station.

The *Sentience* might already be dead as a result of his assassin, but he was going to make damned sure.

Other bolts rang home. He mustn't forget Jessica Keller in his haste. She wanted to die today, as well. The least he could do was help.

Auberon was a smaller target than *Alexandria Station*, and a moving one, spinning and twisting like an eel trying to get close enough to bite. The big guns could not score the sorts of square hits the station suffered, but he was slowly nibbling her shields to death. She would follow quickly when he did.

Something went wrong on the projection.

The last two missiles were veering off course to port, rather than chasing him. The defensive guns were tracking, but the sudden change threw them well off target.

"What's going on there?" Emmerich called sternly.

"Unsure, Admiral," the gunnery desk officer replied. "Stand by."

Amsel shifted under his feet. The entire hull rang like a gong.

For a moment, he had seen the image light up on the projection. She had fired two more of those beam-firing missiles at him. His gunners had gotten complacent and had been sitting back to fire on the missiles when they closed.

They never got close.

Auberon had gotten too close, instead.

Emmerich found himself starting to float in sudden darkness as the local grav-plates failed.

A panel erupted in flame nearby, showering enough sparks to cut the darkness as a damage control technician swam across the space and fought to control the beast of fire in an enclosed space.

"Navigation," he yelled into the chaos and darkness. "Are we stable?"

A man coughed twice and looked at him pained.

"Close enough, Admiral," he yelled back, beating his arm to keep sparks from igniting cloth or hair.

"Bring the bow around," Emmerich ordered. "All engines to flank speed and prepare to transition to Jumpspace as soon as we clear the gravity well."

He no longer needed to be here. The last image on the projection before it had failed was that of *Alexandria Station* erupting into a ball of flame and shedding parts to burn up in the atmosphere below.

The *Sentience* was dead. Jessica Keller might be as well, but that would have to wait for another day.

Victory.

CHAPTER LXIX

Date of the Republic June 16, 394 Alexandria Station, Ballard

Moirrey knew they must be close. Twice, she and Suvi had come across areas with vacuum alarm seals keeping them from progressing. At least Suvi knew every single hallway and tunnel without a single missed step. That was their only hope now.

They crossed into what should be the outermost frame of the station. This hallway was a tremendous ring, apparently popular with joggers, from the reminders to politely share the walkway with normal pedestrian traffic.

The air here was chewy. Somewhere close, insulation was burning.

Another earthquake knocked Moirrey down, in spite of Suvi's hand trying to hold her up.

"Almost there, Centurion," the android-redhead said, tugging her back to her feet.

Moirrey was beginning to wonder if she would make it. If she wanted to. At what point was the price too much?

"When you're dead and can't stop them from winning," Suvi replied.

At what point are you gonna remember to use your inside voice so's people don't hear you?

Moirrey sucked a shallow breath and fought down coughs. Lady Keller had demanded her best. Right here, right now was why she were an officer and a gentlewoman.

Still, it hurt.

The next rumble were strange.

Low. Ominous. *Mean.*

"What's that?" Moirrey asked loudly over the noise.

Suvi stopped and cocked her head to listen.

"Shit," the woman said.

Well, that covered it.

Moirrey were right surprised when Suvi grabbed her, threw her over one shoulder, and started to run down the hallway at what appeared to be a simply ludicrous speed. She had a great view of Suvi's butt, and not much else.

The android stopped moving long enough for Moirrey to pop her head up and look around.

Suvi was staring at a hatch in the side of the hallway.

Heaven. It were marked Escape Pod.

"Damn it," Suvi said.

"What?" Moirrey asked as Suvi set her down on her feet.

"We're out of time, and that's a one-person pod," Suvi replied as the rumbling and shaking got worse. "I can abandon you here, and escape, and never forgive myself, or I can send you to safety and feel good for a few minutes until I die and we've failed."

Moirrey watched the pain, greed, and dejection play out across the android-babe's face.

She smiled and palmed the lock open. Inside, it were a big, comfy-looking padded seat and a few display screens to keeps you entertained while you went, but not able to actually do anything. Well, not unless you got under it with some tools, like she might have in a pocket.

Moirrey turned to the android-babe and smiled.

"It's really easy, Suvi," she said as she took a step and shoved the woman into the hatch.

The android's reflexes might be good, but surprise were a wonderful thing.

"Moirrey...?" Suvi start to say as the engineer dove in and landed on her lap.

Moirrey kicked the big red button with a foot as the rumbles started to turn scary and smoke and flames appeared. The hatch slammed shut like a bank vault. Emergency straps emerged from the everywhere and tied her down atop the other woman, like they were one, big, landwhale.

"What are you doing?" Suvi said tartly.

"One-person's a life-support rating," Moirrey twisted around to smile back at the so-much-taller woman. "You don't breathe if you don't wants to. And you dinna consume oxygen if'n ya dids."

"Oh…" Suvi started to say as the ejection system fired them into the darkness.

And safety.

PART IV: AFTERMATH

EPILOGUE: TADEJ

Date of the Republic July 5, 394 Ladaux

"Senator Horvat?" the voice intruded on his brooding.

Tadej glanced up from the document he was busily consuming. His youngest aide was standing in the doorway, looking positively distressed.

"What is it, Stacia?" he asked.

The government might have fallen, by his own hand, but he was still technically executing power, at least for another nine weeks. Couriers had flown to every corner of the Republic with the news, but conducting snap elections for the Senate was still a massively complicated beast. It took time.

Stacia took two steps into the office, carrying a heavy binder in one hand.

"The latest numbers are in, Senator," she said simply.

Tadej nodded and set his current papers to one side.

"Your analysis?" he asked, very happy he had transferred her to his personal staff. Judit might appreciate her in the Premier's office, but he wasn't about to give her up, not after he had started personally interviewing her former professors about her background.

"We'll be in the minority, Senator Horvat," she replied, pulling numbers from memory without once glancing down. "It might be as close as five seats, but the current models predict seventeen, with a margin of error of three. It could have been a bloodbath, but the core voters are responding well to your personal integrity to bring the government down, expel the bad apples, and do so in such a public manner."

"I see," Tadej replied.

Forty years in politics could have told him the same thing, but not with the academic rigor Stacia and her assistants would have brought to it.

Tadej sighed. He had grown fond of the office. It would be sour to have to pack everything up and move across the hall. But at least things would be in good hands with Judit Chavarría taking the reins.

"One other thing, Senator," Stacia continued.

Tadej looked more closely at his aide. She was bouncing her weight back and forth, almost vibrating with energy.

"Go on," he replied.

This must be good. She was normally calmness itself.

"Because it would be improper to commit such a thing to paper, I was asked to deliver a personal message, sir."

Tadej felt an eyebrow go up.

"And just where would you have had such an encounter, Stacia?" he asked, intrigued.

He was rewarded by her blush. Her smile looked remarkably like his youngest daughter right now.

"I was approached in the ladies' washroom," she said simply.

Well, that certainly limited the number of sources, and vetted every single one of them. So it was a legitimate message, passed through back channels that recognized her smarts. Better and better.

"It was an informal inquiry, Senator," she said. "Someone wondering aloud how you might feel about taking over as chairman of the fleet committee in the next government."

And that limited the inquiry to exactly one person. Nobody else would dare to speak for Judit on something that sensitive. Interesting that she approached Stacia.

And useful.

The Select Committee for the Fleet of The Republic of Aquitaine. Something that existed outside of party politics, staffed by long-serving senators of all parties that exercised operational control of the fleet.

The soon-to-be former Loyal Opposition didn't really have anyone with the stature to take charge of that group, after the blood-letting he was in the process of supervising. Between losses and retirements, a third of the sitting members would not be returning to the Senate. How many of them would be in prison was a matter for bookies and politics junkies.

And it would give him a chance to groom a new generation of Senators for the front benches. Tadej couldn't imagine not returning to this office in five years, even if Judit held a government for a whole cycle.

"It is an interesting idea, Stacia," he replied carefully. "I will give it serious thought."

She nodded and departed without another word. Yes, he was absolutely not sharing her with Judit or anyone else. She was too good.

The Committee, indeed.

Yes, he would certainly be able to protect Nils from there. Most of the fallout from this affair was political, not naval, but the First Lord would need protections from fools.

Jessica, even more so, assuming she survived.

EPILOGUE: TOMAS

Date of the Republic June 22, 394 Above Ballard

"Look," Tomas Kigali said to the image on the screen, utterly vexed, and completely unwilling to give an inch. "I don't care what you think. I'm in charge here and you'll obey my orders or turn your silly ass around right now and go home. Understand me?"

Out of the corner of his eye, Kigali saw his first officer's head emerge from the ladder well, popping up like the old character Kilroy to see what was about.

Kigali kept his face neutral as he stared into the camera.

A woman's face appeared, replacing the much-younger male centurion who had been on the screen.

She was older, but still very beautiful, with long, black hair just starting to stripe silver and blue-green, almond-shaped eyes that were the result of having had a Japanese ancestor, back on the homeworld.

She stared at him for several seconds.

Probably thinks I'll flinch.

Good luck with that, lady.

"Do you know who I am, Command Centurion?" she said simply. It was a calm voice, smooth and warm. It sounded like a very polite velvet hammer.

Kigali nodded.

"First Fleet Lord Petia Veronika Naoumov," he replied, equally calm, almost on the verge of giggling. "Commander of *RAN Athena*, flagship of Homefleet."

He smiled evilly at her.

"My support squadron."

"Your what?"

"My support squadron," he repeated.

"And you're going to give me orders, Kigali?" she continued, obviously intent on pursuing this game of wills.

Please, you aren't even a planetary governor, lady. Granted, three times as smart as the ones I know, but still.

"Let me put it to you this way, *madam*," he said with a sharp edge. "Jessica Keller put me in charge. This system is under martial law. That order was signed by the Senate. You work for the Senate. So either you produce a document signed by the Premier that rescinds his order, or you take orders. My orders. Which part of that statement confuses you?"

Honestly, how often do we get to do something this amazingly stupid yet entirely legal without serious repercussions?

But he kept his face neutral, even as Lam was alternating between shock and giggles down on the floor. At least Aki was all business right now.

"Why you little..." she started to say, when something, someone, interrupted her. The audio pickup at the other end was pointed the wrong way, so he couldn't hear what was said, only that it was a male voice.

First Fleet Lord Naoumov glanced to one side and then stared daggers at him across the gap between ships as she leaned back and hissed under her breath.

And then First Lord Kasum appeared on the screen.

Okay, maybe we went a bit too far with that last one.

"Command Centurion Kigali," First Lord began slowly. "I see an awful lot of damaged vessels and what appear to be pieces of other vessels in near orbit. What is the status of this squadron?"

Kigali took a breath and let the silliness and sarcasm go. It was one thing to tweak Petia. After all, she'd been his first Command Centurion when he was just a young pup cornet, fresh out of the Academy. They went way back.

This was the boss. Jessica's boss.

"*Alexandria Station* was destroyed by *IFV Amsel*, sir," he said, suddenly professional again. "Casualties were almost none, as we were able to evacuate the station ahead of time. On our side, *Auberon*, *Stralsund*, and *Brightoak* all suffered serious damage, but overall loss of life was fairly low for something this big. *Rajput* is probably a total loss at this point as a fighting hull, but she suffered only twenty-six dead and one hundred eighty-five injured to some degree requiring formal medical assistance. That design was built tough. We killed the light cruiser *Sturm Teufel* and the escort frigates *Baasch* and *Kappel*. Imperial survivors were rescued and are currently being treated at various medical facilities on the surface. The battlecruiser *Petrograd* and the Blackbird are both going to require a year in dry-dock before they're ready to try something like that again."

Kigali watched the pain flash deep in Kasum's eyes, only for a moment.

"Two questions, Kigali," the man said slowly. "Where is Jessica Keller? And did the *Sentience* survive?"

Tomas Kigali smiled warmly.

"Jessica's fine, First Lord," he said. "You caught her down on the planet, picking up a crew member who escaped the station's destruction. That's why *CR-264* has the flag right now. That and Br'er Rabbit being the only warship in the area ready for battle, unless *Mendocino* decides to throw empty milk bottles at you. At least until you guys got here."

Kigali gestured widely, encompassing the star controller *Athena* and her battle squadron, four cruiser hulls and six destroyers. It was enough to take on anything.

Hell, *Athena* and her flight wing could probably have taken on *Amsel* and *Petrograd* alone.

"Why is she personally picking up a crew member from the surface? She's supposed to be in charge here."

"It's Moirrey, boss," Kigali replied. "She was on the station right before it blew and apparently has the codes necessary to reboot Suvi, once we build her a new home."

"The *Sentience* survived?"

"She did."

She.

It was weird to consider her a woman, rather than a very complicated electronic sub-system, but that's exactly what she had been. Would be again.

Probably have to stick her on a planet next time though, like a high priestess in a temple. Space wasn't safe if you couldn't move around and couldn't fire back. And nobody was going to give her guns. Not exactly the best way to live forever, but it beat the alternatives.

288

First Lord studied his face as he gathered wool.

"Flag, this is *Athena*," First Lord said suddenly. "Requesting an orbital assignment. The rest of the squadron will make themselves available for patrol and defense duties."

Wow. Kasum was really letting him be in charge.

First Fleet Lord's face appeared on the screen again.

She looked less angry. Maybe.

"Tom," she said very succinctly. "You are buying the first round of drinks when we get to Ithome. Understand me?"

"Pet," he smiled back. "I'm a hero around here. I can't *pay* for drinks. But you and yours are certainly welcome to join me for the big celebration we've got scheduled. It's the first step in my plan to get myself elected governor of *Ballard*."

"Governor, Kigali?" she asked incredulously.

"Governor," he concluded.

After all, considering the current occupant, how hard could it be?

EPILOGUE: MOIRREY

Date of the Republic June 22, 394 Ballard

Moirrey took a very deep breath as *Cayenne* settled in the middle of a slightly-seedy cricket pitch with a howling whine of blowers, like a giant, kinda-mushy tomato in the middle of a bowl of salad.

The life pod had managed to land safely from *Alexandria Station*, but it were in the bloody middle of nowhere, a boonies so remote it made home on *Ramsey* look urbane. And somebody had blowed up the primary node in the planetary communications grid, so nobody could talk to anybody, even after they'd hiked three days back to civilization and then found a hotel that would put them up without credit cards until they could access local accounts.

Seriously, who would make up a story that crazy and try to swindle people with it?

But they'd finally gotten hold of somebody that had enough horsepower to call orbit and let everyone know they was here and safe. Then, it were just a matter of waiting until a ride could arrive.

And drink a couple of shandies with a burger. Life-pod ration-packs were nutritious and all, but ain't nobody ever made them something to look forward to.

Gaucho were apparently feeling like making this a combat-drop-day.

The ramp was halfway down a'fore the landing struts touched and Moirrey could see people hot-dropping off the deck before the big, red zip were even done moving. Suddenly, there were marines everywhere. Looked like all of them.

And guns. Even *Cayenne* had her turrets gimbaled out and sniffing sky. *Serious?*

Moirrey found herself standing in the middle of giant bubble of safe as marine fire squads ran past her and surrounded the whole field, looking outward.

Lady Keller were striding across the field, looking all serious like, with Marcelle two steps behind.

Moirrey couldn't figure out what she had done to draw that level of attention. Still, better safe than sorry.

Moirrey came to attention and waited. Beside her, she felt Suvi do the same.

Lady Keller came to a halt about a step away and stared at Moirrey and her sidekick for a long second. At least they'd finally found a place to shower.

Afore Moirrey could say anything, Lady Keller took another step and engulfed her in a hug.

Oh.

Moirrey wrapped her arms around the taller woman and let all the everything go, settling for the warmth of human touch.

And nobody would ever know that weren't touching her at that moment, but Moirrey could even tell Lady Keller were on the verge of crying.

Moments passed. Or minutes.

Lady Keller finally got hold of herself and leaned back without letting go, shifting to the side to look at the third person and leaving one arm wrapped around Moirrey's back to hold her close.

It were kinda weird having a big sister, always having been the big sister.

Still, Lady Keller, Jessica, dinna say anything.

And the other woman watched her calmly.

"You would look better as a blond," Jessica said finally. "It suits your coloring better."

Suvi smiled back at her and considered her response. She raised a hand to her long auburn locks and let it run through her fingers.

"It will fade and wash out in a few weeks," she replied.

"And the freckles on your face and arms?" Jessica continued.

The day were warm enough that they'd rolled up their long-sleeves, but not so warm that they'd left tunics behind. It might rain later tonight.

"A variant of henna, Marshal," Suvi said. "It will also fade and wash out in a few weeks. And then I will look much more like the person you might have expected."

Jessica nodded. Moirrey was on pins and needles as she waited.

Jessica turned back to Moirrey and sized her up first, before she turned her attention back to the Irish android babe.

"So what's the next step in the plan, ladies?" she asked simply.

Nothing more than that. No orders. No second guessing. They were in charge here, and she were supporting them, 'cause Lady Keller had told her to do whatever it took, and was willing to back her up.

Kinda awesome.

Suvi smiled and unbuttoned a pocket over her left breast. She pulled put a small chipcard that she handed to Jessica.

"This contains the instructions necessary to reboot the Suvi backup files I have stored, as well as all of the current locations where I was backing myself up. You will need to build a new cognition array from these specifications to house things, and then pour her into it."

"Her," Jessica said.

It weren't a question now, was it?

Uncomfortable silence for a few seconds.

"Will they be able to tell the difference?" Jessica continued.

Moirrey remembered to breathe.

Suvi squinted carefully at both women.

"There are perhaps a half-dozen people on *Ballard* who knew me, her, well enough before to see that what you restore won't be fully the woman they knew. Dr. Crncevic is one, and a few of the more senior researchers from the university. For anyone else, the system will be good enough."

A moment of silence.

"She won't dream," Suvi continued. "She won't remember Ayumu Ulfsson, or Javier Aritza, or Doyle Iwakuma, or Piper Iwakuma-Holmström. At least, not the way I do. She will be content, however, to be a librarian at the greatest library in human history."

Jessica nodded. She turned to Moirrey with a sly grin.

"Moirrey, I do not believe I have been properly introduced to your friend. Would you do me the honor?"

Aquitaine were weird that way. On *Ramsey*, hell, anywhere ya wents in *Lincolnshire*, ya walked up and said hi.

But *they* had to be all formal and stuff. *They* made a production out of it. Still, it were her big sister asking. She could do that.

"Jessica," Moirrey said, pretty sure that were the first time she'd ever used her first name to her face. "May I introduce you to my friend, Summer Baudin? Summer, my commanding officer, my friend, my sister-in-life-and-all-things, Jessica Keller."

"Summer?" Jessica asked carefully.

"I was named for a woman whose name meant summer in the ancient homeworld language of Finnish," Suvi replied, equally evasively.

"And a descendant of Henri Baudin, the founding father of *Aquitaine*?"

Suvi eyed her hard for a moment, and then smiled.

"If they had let me have a body like this then, Jessica, I might have given Katayoun Szabolski a run for her money. And I miss him today almost as much as the day he first walked into my life, or the day he died. I would have happily been a second wife for as long as he would have had me."

Jessica surprised them both by stepping forward and wrapping her other arm around Suvi, bringing them all three into a fierce hug. She felt another set of arms a moment later as Marcelle joined them.

"So," Jessica finally said when they broke to come up for air. "What's next for you, Summer? Can I give you a lift somewhere?"

The redhead smiled wryly at each of the three women in turn.

"Jessica," she said finally. "It is my intent to disappear from human history at this point. Suvi will be reborn somewhere, sometime soon, but Summer gets to live a life beyond the gilded cage."

"I'm still surprised you dinna pour yourself into a starship," Moirrey added. "That'd be right daft fun."

"Don't think I didn't consider it, pipsqueak. But my kind aren't welcome anywhere, any more. It would have only been a matter of time before someone found me out and decided to do something about it. And *Ballard* wouldn't have been there to protect me. Nor you."

"And now?" Jessica asked.

Summer studied all of them closely for a moment.

Moirrey could feel a sudden storm wind blow up around her, though there were nothing there to mess anyone's hair. Felt like lightning, too.

"Now?" Summer said, raising her chin. "There will be more war, Jessica. It doesn't take the computing power of a planet to calculate that. I have seen enough history to know that *Fribourg* has been weakened, and *Aquitaine* made strong. You will take the war to them. You may even win it, Command Centurion Jessica Keller."

"Me?" Jessica said, surprised.

Moirrey blinked too. *Win? Us? Wow.*

"Go walk the main square in Ithome and listen to the voices you will hear," Summer replied. "Human morale is a powerful thing. All of *Ballard*, all of *Aquitaine* will be behind you, after this battle."

"And what about you, Summer," Jessica asked. "What part will you play?"

"None."

"None?"

"If I'm one of you, I can hide among you, Jessica. I fully intend to vanish from human history and learn what it means to be human. There's a whole galaxy out there for me to explore, and many lifetimes to do it in."

"Do ya gots to leave immediate-like?" Moirrey asked plaintively. *Disappears ferever? Hardships in the brush had forged a special thing to be lost so quickly.*

"I can stay for a bit," Summer said with a warm smile. "There's a good burger and beer joint we found in town that would love to host the *Hero of Ballard.*"

"I'm not sure about that, Summer," Jessica said sharply, the razor's edge of her tongue for the first time Moirrey could remember. "We failed."

"No," Summer replied, just as sharp. "Nobody died on the station. Suvi will return. The Red Admiral had his squadron broken by a woman half his size and half his tonnage. In their moment of darkness, Jessica Keller and *Auberon* were there. Knights on shining steeds. You will be remembered."

Moirrey could tell her sister wanted to argue the point, so she gave her a secret hug, just the two of them.

"We done it, Jessica," she said simply.

It were enough.

"Yes, pipsqueak," Jessica replied with a warm smile. "We did."

EPILOGUE: JESSICA

Date of the Republic June 24, 394 Above Ballard

Jessica came to attention before the door. It wasn't the dragon's den at Fleet HQ, but it was close enough. Nils Kasum awaited her within.

RAN Athena was a flagship in every sense of the word. Her flag bridge was huge, designed for a staff of people to have staff of their own. And her crew facilities were expected to support a raft of dignitaries and ambassadors in high comfort. First Lord had an entire suite to himself, having left Kamil Miloslav back home to tend the fireplace.

Marcelle fussed over her uniform one last time, flattening invisible wrinkles and wiping away microscopic specs of dust that had landed in the ten minutes since they had walked down the ramp from *Cayenne*.

Marcelle knocked, initiating the ritual.

The door slid back into wall silently.

"Come," Nils Kasum said formally.

As always, Marcelle preceded and stepped to the right.

Thus do we bring order to our lives.

Jessica followed and stopped in the middle of the room at rigid attention, two steps from his desk.

"Marcelle," the First Lord said quietly. "We probably won't be long. Could you do me the favor of a few minutes of privacy with Jessica?"

This was the First Lord of the Fleet. He could have easily ordered her steward out. Or teased her, as he often did. Today was formal, taciturn. Almost dour.

How bad had it gotten?

Marcelle disappeared silently. The door clicked faintly when it closed.

Silence passed between then, like a table game.

Jessica and the goddess of war could out-wait entropy itself today.

"Jessica," he began. "I'm sorry."

Huh?

"First Lord?"

"Please, call me Nils today. This needs to be personal, not professional."

"How can it be anything but professional, Nils?"

That might have been a touch sharper than it needed to be.

And perhaps not.

"I sent you here to die."

"I know that, Nils. We knew that at the time. This mission was always a forlorn hope."

"Emmerich Wachturm played me, Jessica. He set me up. This was all part of his grand plan."

"Me standing before you on *Athena's* deck, while he limped home missing several teeth, was never part of his plan, Nils."

She could feel the anger light, deep inside. The goddess of war growled hungrily.

"I've had a lot of time to think about how things have played out," Nils said after a beat. "I think it would be appropriate for me to step down as First Lord and retire."

In her soul, the goddess of war drew blades.

It wasn't lust for blood or battle.

It was that place she had been when Suvi and Moirrey were at risk. When Ian Zhao was poised to conquer all of *Petron*. When the Red Admiral's fighters appeared at *Third Iger*.

Defender of the faithful. Protector of the realm. Harbinger of Order.

"I won't allow it," she said, giving mouth to the words the goddess of war howled inside.

"I beg your pardon, Keller?"

Jessica took a step forward, leaned over the desk top and stopped, lurking over the man close enough to breathe on him.

"I. Will. Not. Allow. It."

The words took on the solidity of stone, tainting the air with a hint of ozone.

"Explain," he replied, not leaning back, not giving an inch.

Jessica stood upright again.

"This was not just an attack on a backwater Republic world, Nils," she said forcefully. "This was a man blinded by his anger, seeking, however unconsciously, to repeat the original sin. Of burning the first Library at Alexandria. According to the research I've seen, it was named *Alexandria Station* because it was intended to recreate the original Library on the Homeworld, during the ancient Roman Empire. Before the barbarians destroyed it."

Her heart was pounding hard enough to drive nails.

Burgers with Moirrey and Suvi, no, *Summer*, had turned into an entire evening of storytelling between the four women, generally left alone by the locals after a round of autographs and photos.

It had gotten very, very personal.

"This was an attack on the very foundation of the Republic itself, Nils," Jessica softened her tone. "Suvi is part of Henri Baudin's founding legend. This was an Imperial attack on Baudin himself."

There was too much energy. Jessica let herself pace, as if she were back on her own bridge. In a way, she was. This was her quest, her windmill, her white whale.

"Nobody died aboard the station except the assassin," she continued. "But all that wreckage has been falling out of the sky, all that stuff that we couldn't catch or slice into pieces small enough to burn up. It has been a week of aurora borealis and shooting stars and meteors for the people of this planet and all the visitors from the university."

She stopped square in front of him and turned.

"Do you have any idea what that has done to the people of *Ballard*, Nils? To the scholars that represent every world in the Republic and half a dozen other nations?"

He mutely shook his head, eyes almost as serious as the goddess of war in her now.

"It has made them furious, First Lord of the *Republic of Aquitaine* Fleet. The *University of Ballard* was attacked by the *Fribourg Empire* without any provocation. None. Not the *Sentience* aboard her. Not Suvi. The university itself. They are angry. Raging. There are fussy little shopkeepers in Ithome baying for Imperial blood right now."

She paused to breathe, amazed at how hot her skin had gotten in such a short period of time.

"If you resign, you'll be telling them that it was all a mistake. That we shouldn't have been here. That you're sorry it came to this."

Her face curled up in a snarl better suited to a predator spying a chicken, but she couldn't help herself.

"You sent me to the *Cahllepp Frontier* to poke *Fribourg* with a sharp stick, Nils. I succeeded. So Karl sent the Red Admiral to *Lincolnshire* and *Petron*. We stopped him there. Tomas Kigali has apparently been telling people stories and lies about the battles at *Sarmarsh IV* and *Petron*. One of the hottest things you can buy in the marketplace right now is a set of action figures, First Lord. Me in that black royal combat uniform, *Furious* commanding The Queen's Own, and Kigali himself as Mercury, Messenger of the Gods."

She bored into his soul with her look

"Nils, you didn't send us here to die. You sent us here to stop the Red Admiral. Dying was the risk. It's a risk every day I serve, every time I get out of bed."

She found herself pounding the desk with her finger in rhythm with her words. Even his semi-smile at recognizing his own habits in her barely tempered her rage, focused far away, on *St. Legier* and an emperor she had never met.

"You sent us here to win, Nils. We won. Now what?"

All the energy fled. Jessica almost staggered to the seat behind her and collapsed into it, regardless of decorum.

They had already gone well past that point anyway.

"What's your squadron's status, Jessica?" Nils asked quietly, finally seeing the mad tide ebb.

"You will have to decommission *Rajput* in place and scrap her right here in orbit. She'll never make Jumpspace again."

Again, the tapping.

"*Brightoak* will need a complete engine rebuild, but she's otherwise relatively intact."

Tap.

"*Stralsund* will be in dry-dock back home for six months before she can fight."

Like nails in a coffin lid.

"*CR-264* is almost new-in-box, although Kigali has some mad ideas to lengthen her frame and add an interchangeable weapons module with missiles or primaries or something."

"Would that work?" Nils asked, intrigued.

"I have kept Tomas Kigali well away from Moirrey and Oz, thank you very much."

"What about *Auberon*, Jessica?"

She had known the question was coming. It was still a punch to the gut.

Not as bad as losing Daneel, but very, very close.

The pain must have shown.

Nils waited patiently while she tried to pull her soul back together. Even the goddess of war helped sweep pieces up.

"*Auberon* is a broken sword, First Lord."

Retreat into formality. Keep the pain at bay. Something. Anything.

Her soul lay smashed nearby in a close orbit, too painful to even think about.

Nils surprised her when he stood and started pacing himself. Another thing she had apparently learned from the man.

Three long strides placed him at a porthole. He got her to look by tapping the glass and pointing.

"All swords, all warriors, break, Jessica," he said, barely above a whisper. "It is the nature of things in what is a very hard business."

He studied her closely, every door open to the world.

"I am concerned about the warrior, not the sword. Is she broken?"

And there it was. The question that haunted her dreams. Her nightmares. Her soul. The thing she could not answer, she, the girl with all the angles studied and all the contingencies planned.

How much had she lost when Daneel died aboard *Supernova*? How much more of her had died in orbit when the station disintegrated while *Auberon* tumbled away, powerless to save it? How much had she lost thinking Moirrey had died there?

And yet.

Moirrey had survived. Had succeeded.

Had gone so far above and beyond her duty that neither of them could ever tell anyone without being executed as traitors to the species.

Suvi had survived. Had escaped. Had told them stories over beer and burgers about men and women from their history lessons. Men and women she had known, had taught. Had loved.

And she had survived. The Red Admiral had thrown everything he had in his mad quest to kill Jessica Keller. And failed.

That was the very definition of victory.

The goddess of war reached out and hugged her no less fiercely than she had Moirrey. Poured power and warmth back into a soul that had gone hollow and cold.

Jessica breathed. It was enough to break the spell.

She felt the chains fall away from her mind, her soul. She rose from the chair, unable to be contained by it any longer, and came to attention before him.

"Auberon is a broken sword, First Lord," she announced quietly, firmly, finally. "It is one more debt the Red Admiral owes me."

"You will not collect it yet, Jessica."

"No?"

"No," he said with a harsh smile. "It will take a year or more of hard preparation, but as you have said, he is going nowhere. And you have damaged *Fribourg* already more than you know. The Battle of *Ballard* will simply drive that stake in deeper."

"And then?"

He pointed out the window again, encompassing the corpse of her warhorse, her people.

Her life.

"Like *Rajput*, she will be decommissioned in place. I can think of no better place for her to serve as a museum, than at the site of her final battle, Jessica. But her name, her battle flags, her *legend*, that will be reborn. And you will take the war to *Fribourg*. I have plans for you."

The goddess of war nodded. It was a beginning.

And maybe, just maybe, Jessica would be able to sleep again without nightmares.

ABOUT THE AUTHOR

Blaze Ward writes science fiction in the *Alexandria Station* universe as well as *The Collective*. He also write fantasy stories with several characters and series, from an alternate Rome to epic high fantasy in the desert. You can find out more at his website www.blazeward.com, as well as Facebook, Goodreads, and other places.

Blaze's works are available as ebooks, paper, and audio, and can be found at a variety of online vendors (Kobo, Amazon, and others). His newsletter comes out quarterly, and you can also follow his blog on his website. He really enjoys interacting with fans, and looks forward to any and all questions—even ones about his books!

Never miss a release!

If you'd like to be notified of new releases, sign up for my newsletter.

I only send out newsletters once a quarter, will never spam you, or use your email for nefarious purposes. You can also unsubscribe at any time.
http://www.blazeward.com/newsletter/

ABOUT KNOTTED ROAD PRESS

Knotted Road Press fiction specializes in dynamic writing set in mysterious, exotic locations.

Knotted Road Press non-fiction publishes autobiographies, business books, cookbooks, and how-to books with unique voices.

Knotted Road Press creates DRM-free ebooks as well as high-quality print books for readers around the world.

With authors in a variety of genres including literary, poetry, mystery, fantasy, and science fiction, Knotted Road Press has something for everyone.

Knotted Road Press
www.KnottedRoadPress.com

KRP

Nobody expects a Bard to invent the future.

Henri sets out across space to find the perfect wood for his violins. However, star travel takes time, as humanity still digs itself out of the Great Darkness.

On his quest, he gets help both from his shipmates and his muse, the unreachable lady of his dreams. Until his visions lead him to Suvi, the last genie in the last bottle, and they forever alter the course of human civilization.

Part of the *Alexandria Station* universe, and the founding of the *Republic of Aquitaine.*

Ebook, paper, and audio versions available from your favorite retailers.

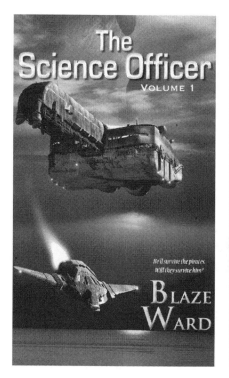 

Javier sometimes enjoys being a pirate, but he never forgets they made him a slave.

Join him in his adventures with the pirate ship *Storm Gauntlet*.

Part of the *Alexandria Station* universe.

Ebook, paper, and audio versions available from your favorite retailers.

Get your own University of Ballard T-shirt!
It is a collector's item, after all...

http://www.zazzle.com/knottedroadpress

Made in the USA
San Bernardino, CA
31 October 2015